chemical
palace

chemical palace

fiona mcgregor

ALLEN&UNWIN

First published in 2002

Allen & Unwin
83 Alexander Street
Crows Nest NSW 2065
Australia
Phone: (61 2) 8425 0100
Fax: (61 2) 9906 2218
Email: info@allenandunwin.com
Web: www.allenandunwin.com

National Library of Australia
Cataloguing-in-Publication entry:

McGregor, Fiona, 1965– .
Chemical palace.
ISBN 1 86508 764 5.
1. Dance parties – New South Wales – Sydney – Fiction.
2. Gays - Fiction. 3. Sydney (N.S.W.) - Fiction. I. Title.
A823.3

Design & typesetting by Ruth Grüner
Printed by Griffin Press, South Australia

1 3 5 7 9 10 8 6 4 2

The author would like to acknowledge the Literature Board of the Australia Council
for the granting of a Category B fellowship during the writing of this book.

For the Sodom Circus
and their co-whores

In song and dance man expresses himself as a member of
a higher community, he has forgotten how to walk and speak
and is on the way toward flying into the air, dancing. His very
gestures express enchantment. Just as the animals now talk,
and the earth yields milk and honey, supernatural sounds
emanate from him, too: he feels himself a god, he himself
now walks about enchanted, in ecstasy, like the gods he saw
walking in his dreams. He is no longer an artist, he has become
a work of art: in these paroxysms of intoxication the artistic
power of all nature reveals itself to the highest gratification
of the primordial unity.

Nietzsche, THE BIRTH OF TRAGEDY

It is interesting to find that Sydney is a corruption of St Denis
... St Denis was that saint who converted the pagan Gauls
to Christianity . . . However, the name Denis is yet another
corruption of the martyr's original Athenian name, Dionysius.

Thus we may say that Sydney's patron is Dionysius which,
in view of the blithe and irrepressible character of the city as
it has developed, is gratifyingly suitable.

Ruth Park, A COMPANION GUIDE TO SYDNEY

The music was new, black, polished chrome and came over the summer like liquid night . . .

Panic got started by a bunch of people sick of sitting around whingeing about the lack of places to go. They couldn't find music they liked in clubs on the strip let alone performers so they decided to put on a party of their own. If what you want doesn't exist already you create it yourself.

Up till now the parties had been mainly private affairs. James who DJ'd as Mr Hyde set up his decks and played, Stash helped Billy with the invitations, Fred installed rudimentary lighting as well as a slide carousel with Bee. Bee also offered a show with Bella or another mistress from Utopia. Turkish Jim Billy the Professor and James paraded in costume amongst the guests, absolutely everybody dressed up and danced. The thing about these parties was that although they were invite-only family affairs the numbers grew each time.

The ethos was simple. Open the living room doors and share the magic.

Living quarters.

Turn off Oxford Street head away from the harbour, bus station, police station then the maze of laneways. A crumbling brick facade, rusty mesh over the lower windows, immense in the narrow street and increasingly worn as the terraces surrounding were one by one renovated. Across the third storey cement signage corroded by decades of western sun, dissolved lettering once black pink and white of something no longer legible then PTY LTD. Another old warehouse on the west side of Surry Hills where the tilt down to Chinatown was so steep you were better off running. The area was changing. From the roof unpeeled a skyline sprouting cranes in every direction. Demolition reconstruction, a city centuries old not yet built.

Two years they had lived there, Billy about three. Bee was the first, arriving with her brother Stash and a crowd from the Gunnery in the early 90s. Over the years tenants came and went while Bee stayed, then Billy, friends from the days of Slut City. Shifty, Bee's girlfriend, moved in after Billy. For a while Stash used the third room as an office for his graphics business. When he was thrown out for not paying the rent, traffic and Billy had been seeing each other a few months and traffic's house was breaking up. Stash's vacated room was the obvious place for Billy's materials machines and tools, by now overflowing from her room across the warehouse. If a lover moved in the rent would be shared and a workroom still available. traffic was there within a week. She ended up outstaying Billy who was replaced by Holmes.

Eventually the warehouse was sold to a developer.

traffic and Holmes were the biggest pushers of the party idea. They saw the city through fresher eyes, what they had missed was that much more precious. Of the homegrown affairs their first had been Baroque. They hadn't seen dress-ups like that for years, they hadn't heard music like that before. That was the main thing that was the axis, the music of Mr Hyde.

He was their deepest and darkest and most loved DJ yet unwilling to transact when it came to his music and so remained cloistered inside his queer family. Oblivious to the familiar he charged out sets that smouldered and menaced rising from the dancefloor like a fire. A quiet man in life, in music he was abrasive, joyous and free, painting views you had to fall into head heart and body all at once. Any noise that could be reignited came into his music, revving motors crazed laughter political rhetoric and animal sounds.

Otherwise a computer programmer James reserved deals for his straight job. Here he was lucky and ruthless, earning enough to live on as well as feed his music with the latest releases and equipment. Dancing all night at parties that would become legends, the Professor and Billy and the girls would exchange guilty smiles through the crowds. These DJs were good, they got you dancing, they kept you on the floor but for no more than fifteen or twenty minutes at a time. They played straightforward journeys with blue skies and smiles, but poisoned by something stronger Mr Hyde's friends were less easily sated. Always they longed for his drama and mystery, his expletives and bliss.

Holmes:

When I moved back to Sydney from the south coast, I stayed in a crummy hotel on Bourke Street, just back from Taylor Square. It wasn't that I was rich, far from it, and I still knew people in town like Billy I could've stayed with. But traffic had just moved in, I didn't want to interrupt their honeymoon. There were others too, but I wasn't strong enough to set sail anywhere that drugs were likely to be floating around. And I was with Jimi.

This hotel was alright. A converted terrace with big windows in big rooms though all you saw from the street was a little doorway. There was a small courtyard and a bolt of fake Persian carpet down the hall like a try-out someone had unrolled years before then forgotten. It wasn't that noisy, in the courtyard of potted ferns the street was just a muffle. But there were no phones in the rooms so Jimi got a bit anxious because he had to make calls and he didn't have a mobile. I gotta do phone, I'm in *Sydney*, I gotta do phone Holmes! Jimi was from the 'gong, a hairdresser with a gothic bent who'd been positive about the same amount of time as me but was on combos already. He used to give me house haircuts down the coast and complain to Slip at how staid I was getting. He had big plans for the sort of work he'd get in Sydney. So yair, the day we arrived we started looking for permanent accommodation.

It was strange being back here, the familiarity, the changes. It was still a partytown of course, even more than ever. But my god all the changes, nearly every building on every street. Now I was straight the city looked like it was tripping. Drugfucked more like it, just one big building site. The years I spent walking these streets really out of it. It was like they were in another world, all the people, it was like being in a sphere. I used to think I was in a sphere and the people walked through me, it was like I wasn't really there. Eventually I never went out in the day, only at night, so I talked to hardly anybody for *months* on end. Just taking heaps of drugs, not eating, not sleeping, doing jobs. Eddy.

Funny how these are the memories closest to the surface. The screeching laughter of queens at the corner cafe reminds me of all the other times I had around here as well, the sceney ones, nice ones, nice upwardly mobile escort ones. The first memories are the brightest, like they're highlighted. Sixteen years old, fresh out of home and hanging around with Billy. It didn't all feel idyllic at the time or anything, it was pretty tough but it was new and full of possibilities. Then everything gradually sort of clouded over. And I'm talking prediagnosis. Before during and after Eddy was the worst. If the earlier times were happier why are the worst the first to resurface? Is it sadness that dominates our past or just my interpretation? I keep walking past the cafe, I don't like drinking coffee in a display cabinet, I keep moving.

Billy met traffic at Homoside. Lured out by Bee and Shifty and the flyer of a gun barrel poking through a button fly, Billy dressed up as Calamity Stain. In the downstairs bar were the venue's yob staff and some early arrivals. Billy had a toy gun from K-Mart with fluoro lights that flashed down the barrel when the trigger was pulled, so naturally she trained it on the barman for a vodka and lime. Within minutes he had fetched management to have her thrown out. Billy argued there was a gun on the flyer and that she was just following the theme *He's the lunatic!* The promoters came over and Billy was allowed to stay though the barman still refused to serve her. A guy further along the bar took pity and offered to buy Billy a drink but the barman wouldn't hear of it. Billy thinking What the fuck? Was there a shopping mall shootout this weekend or something?

She went upstairs. The music slightly better and a gorgeous girl in latex behind the bar. Billy had never seen her before. This was what saved her each time she went out, the sight of new faces new people proof of change. She went over to order a drink, gun idle before her on the bar. The girl refused to serve her unless Billy shot her. Come on, her arms raised offering black glistening torso, Shoot me shoot me! That's more like it thought Billy and pulled the trigger. The gun trilled its fluorescence and the bargirl staggered forward, her eyes on Billy. Billy shot her again. And again. The girl convulsed gripping the counter with one hand while the other squashed strawberry wounds over her latex heart. Then she fell onto the schooner tray and was still.

Billy left a couple of hours later when the music didn't pick up. Home with her the image of the latex barmaid sprawled elegantly on the schooner tray, tendrils of a tattoo running out from the shoulder. A face full of laughter and fury.

Billy wasn't the first customer traffic played with like this. Or the last. When Billy went back to find her two weeks later she was told traffic had been sacked and was working in a bar up the road.

The storms! Breaking over the city like collapsing buildings, moving from the horizon faster than you could walk to cover. The buildup all through the night and into day, thick air white-blue sky damp heat, sudden darkness of low cloud. Then rain, release, fat tropical drops crescendoing to deluge. The entire city could be stopped by weather.

The night sky from the airport, rich, endless, you could even see the stars. Bugs on her clothes every time she took in the washing, grasshoppers huntsmen little green gnats all through the house. Skinks slithering in every footpath crevice, the buzzing enamel of Christmas beetles, giant flying cockroaches. The bogong-laden westerlies, pulling out clothes months later powdered with moth remnants. After more than a year of northern hemisphere pallor traffic returned to the soft riot of late summer Sydney. These were the days of magic and wonder. Cockatoos drowning out Darlinghurst conversations, Redfern paperbarks shrill with lorikeets, the dawn and dusk skies with their black paths of fruit bats. The softness of the air the tap water the sea, the harshness of colour everywhere. The city was alive, it was seething.

On her third day back in Sydney traffic found a caterpillar. Just inside the door, long like her middle finger and even fatter, iridescent green with triangular ridges of white and ochre. She held a leaf to the carpet-bound creature whose feet slid along the edge like a zipper. Carried it outside to the ferns beneath the she-oak. She felt like she was living inside a giant cartoon.

She loved her bluff she loved her bravado. She loved traffic's legs the curve of calf muscle, she loved her front her face her back. She loved her body, compact, a coiled spring, tricking you with that energy she was taller than short. The way traffic knew she was still looking as she walked away, one hand lifted in nonchalant farewell. She loved traffic's greed, face between her legs within minutes of the first time sliding from cunt to arse then back up to her mouth. The way she strapped on dragging the connie down with hammed up horniness, she loved the way she fucked her the way she held her afterwards.

She watched traffic try on the doubletted shorts. They were more than ten years old and still intact.

You can have them if you like. I don't wear them anymore. I'm too fat.

Tell me about art school.

I loved it in the beginning, I wanted to do *everything*. I learnt lots of technical stuff. Printmaking, drawing, sculpture, sculpture was my favourite. I did a lot of stuff with perspex.

Perspex!

But I threw it all out. It wasn't very good. When it comes to sculpture, Turkish Jim's the man.

Have you still got anything you made back then?

Oh heaps, in that trunk over there. I'll have to show you some time. But at home I was still mostly making clothes and costumes. The sculpture helped with that a-bit but I switched to design full-time in the last year.

Bee said you came top of the class.

I was going to do my Masters but they told me I should remove all these things from my CV. Gigs like Slut City weren't considered legitimate. I'd done twice as many parades as anyone else but because theirs were in Australian Fashion Week or whatever and mine were these obscure things, I got lower on the list. And I thought about that and I thought Fuck you, I'm not going to disregard what I think are really *good* things that I've done just to please your academic record. She was playing with traffic, twirling, stroking, traffic moving to accommodate her hand.

So that's why you quit.

Yeh I was pretty pissed off. Billy's fingers entered.

What philistines, traffic moaned.

They're all cunts, Billy slid right on in. Arseholes, she whispered, sliding two fingers in there. The membrane between her fingers and hand felt taut and glowing, like a skin of cream. traffic's eyes rolling back, her body arching. Oh baby, you look so beautiful.

Kiss me kiss me.

They were falling asleep. Raindrops began on the tin roof of the workshop that shelved beneath Billy's window. Louder, more of them, building to a cacophony and they lay there blinking in the roar. Billy said something, traffic couldn't hear her above the rain.

I said it sounds like the country! I actually miss it sometimes.

What?

The country!! Rain on a tin roof, the BUSH!!

traffic sat up, put her hand on her heart, blew Billy a kiss.

It was spring when Holmes moved to the South Coast. Jacaranda flowers coated the porch, the path and street, melting cool between his toes as he loaded up Lizzy's car. And so it was lilac that Holmes left behind, colouring forever the usual waking view from his sister's Redfern window of a stark street in shadow by midday.

He took off his cap at Kogarah. Lizzy's eyes jerked from the road.
Christ Peter! When did you do that?
Down at the shops before we left. Stopped in at the barber.
You look like a leukemia patient.
I feel like one.
Christ! Why? I don't understand why, you had such beautiful hair . . . Who's this girl with the house? An old friend?
Nah, I've only met her a couple of times. We don't know really each other.
Lizzy looking at him, the highway, back at his baldness. To Holmes it was no more surprising than his flaws, his weaknesses and secrets, his whole character stripped bare. In his crisis he had let his family approach again, he had no more defences. He disagreed with their view of him as a newborn angel leaving behind the devil he had been and their sympathy was inseparable from an intransigent hatred of Eddy, but Holmes had hurt too much to pick and choose. So he left out the relation of his future housemate to Eddy. Lizzy was so fierce she would probably turn the car around and drive him straight back to Sydney.
So you think you'll stay three years?
I have to, that's how long the course takes.
You're such a city boy though Peter.
Well I'll just have to stick it out, won't I. And it's not that far.
That hair . . . Fuck you gave me a fright.

She looked so different, she looked even taller, he should have known a journey forwards would include backwards. He was still seeking the person he had met at the funeral and before by Eddy's sickbed but this Jo was clearer, more serene. The same pale skin as Eddy, same fine dark freckles but her eyes a darker brown. Eddy's yellow like a tiger's when he was stoned.

She left him alone in the house that afternoon and after Lizzy had gone Holmes wandered through the kitchen, surprisingly sparse for a commercial cook, into the bathroom big and blue to a sunroom of books records a stereo and pictures. And a low makeshift couch on which two cats, part black part Burmese, slept in a monkey grip.

It was a two bedroom miner's cottage with a backyard bordered by vegetable plots and a shed that Jo had been cleaning out for years. Down by the compost heap through the neighbour's foliage you could glimpse the ocean. The rooms were small but the landscape was big. He went back inside, stopped by her bedroom, pushed the door wider. Bed desk wardrobe. Basket of dirty clothes. He looked around the doorframe and saw turntables in the corner. Tiptoed in as though Jo, two towns away working, would hear him. Later Holmes would discover that Jo had already begun to buy records but that night his probing yielded little.

I can't believe you've got those turntables. Eddy said he sold them.
What are they, hot?
Yep.
Oh well, what can you do.
Do they still work?
I haven't touched them. There was nobody else to give them to when he died. I'm the closest thing to a musician in the family.
You don't play bass anymore?
Haven't for years.
That's a shame.
I guess so. Do you like cats?
Well . . . I don't *dislike* them.
Cos if I go up to Sydney or something could you feed them? Would that be OK? I don't go up much.

She walked over with one of the cats and poured it into his lap like mercury. The cat became an animal and jumped off immediately. Holmes was lying. He hated cats. But these would seduce him within a week with their grace and vanity. Within two he would be in competition with Jo for their company at night. 3 am, insomniac, moving down to the foot of the bed to place his cheek against their velvet. Pussycats how do you sleep all the time? Please tell me how to sleep beautiful pussycats.

The cats said nothing.

Holmes twenty-five and Eddy twenty-seven when they met in a bar. Holmes had been stood up, a spare pill and ticket to Multifunk burning his pocket. Then Eddy came in. Skinny punky wogboy, Holmes's dream come true. Walking into Multifunk walking into Sounds of Darkness, he remembered that moment lucid as a discovery all those blissed-out faces. Thousands of men in the one room all dancing, he stopped on the edge of the floor and turned to Eddy jubilant. We're gonna take over the *world*! Eddy standing back glowering, arms folded against the atmosphere. It was everything Holmes feared. He fell in love instantly. They hadn't even kissed.

Holmes was at tech doing his HSC and working in one of the best agencies in town. Had a dozen or so good clients, was using but stable. Eddy was the wrong boy from the right side of town. He was living back home with his parents on the North Shore, said he was a year clean but was tracked up. Later Holmes learnt he'd been diagnosed two weeks before they met and had been caning it ever since, speed this time as well. They didn't stop for days.

Eddy had everything bigger but height. Bigger dick bigger appetite bigger habit bigger temper, louder voice doped hoarse. Urging adventures then shooting them in the foot, they never got much further than a room with a spoon. A total lack of clarity in Holmes's memories as though they lived those two years on a long piece of elastic, bouncing out into the stratosphere on smack pills and speed, whacking back in. Holmes's organisation crumbled. Up until Eddy he had made his own rules and kept them. No stealing, no scamming from friends. No nodding off or vomiting in public. Always together for his clients, minimum study to pass exams. He tried to feed his health alongside his habit, turning the sugar cravings to fruit and honey, favouring the veins on the underside of his arm, people usually so obvious checking inside the elbow. Drinking spirulina on old advice from Billy with whom he lost touch throughout the whole Eddy period. He lost touch with almost everything.

Eddy was a violent fuck though his seductions sometimes began with a tenderness that made Holmes swoon. Laying Holmes flat on his back, kissing him long and deep while hands undid the fly pulled out Holmes's cock, always hard always bursting. He'd move down Holmes's body rub his cheeks across Holmes's chest with animal affection, hands clasping Holmes's pinning them to the bed. Just the scoring of Eddy's stubble would make Holmes want to come. But Eddy wouldn't let him, he'd suck him to the brink then pull away suddenly. Fuck his face his arse his face again, Holmes laughing and crying all at once. And never was Eddy better than in his parents' bed.

    Got a light?
    I'm using it.
Holmes follows the voice indoors to the parents' ensuite bathroom where Eddy's cooking brown scag. They had a taste not two hours ago but Eddy always does more here. Even a cigarette is blasphemy in this hallowed house.
    You've gotta move out of here Eddy.
    Why? It's comfortable.
    Don't you think you're too old?
    Don't you think you're a fucken nag? Here.
    No.
    Oh don't be a girl.
Holmes took the fit.
    I've got a client at nine.
    As if those fuckwits notice.
    He's actually a nice guy. And my cock will notice is the problem.
Eddy's mouth on it again soon. Hot skin slow sex another appointment missed. Two weeks later Holmes is sacked.

South where the horizon spread out his mind Holmes watched it all again. Watched Eddy move into his flat and gradually embed himself into every aspect of his life. They were fighting about the housework pretty much straightaway. Holmes had sought another establishment to work from while Eddy preferred the independence of the Wall. Holmes did everything he could to provide Eddy with a better environment, made up an ad for him to work privately, introduced him to his own boss, still Eddy always ended up on the street. Holmes resigned himself. He liked to pick him up in the early hours, get a taste of the camaraderie Eddy had there. He was wild and funny and fiercely supportive of the other workers, an elder to the other boys some of whom were beginning to challenge his authority. But Eddy looked younger than his age, he followed the etiquette, respected their territory, though never the clients never the mugs. Sometimes Holmes and Eddy did doubles though Eddy was unreliable so Holmes began to sneak to jobs with another worker called Gareth. Gareth thought Eddy was a loser. He's like twice the age of most of those guys. If he just looked after his body a bit more you know, put on a bit of weight, he could earn more and be safer. Eddy and Holmes fought about this, Holmes still had the scar on his chin, they fought about everything. Holmes began to hate working, the men who came to him for an hour of intimacy fell lower and lower in his eyes. Eddy did that, he poisoned it made it negative. And Holmes let him. After a year together Eddy got sick. He aged ten years in one. He refused treatment. They fought about that as well.

Holmes wanted Jo's opinion.

D'you think he would've survived if he'd got treatment earlier? D'you think it was his fault? Is that unfair?

I'm not very good at what ifs. I tried to persuade his mother not to bring the priest in. I took him dope cakes to get him eating. That was my contribution.

He went down screaming. God it was so horrible.

He kept asking me to score but I'd lost my contacts. And I didn't really want to.

D'you think he was at peace? D'you think I'm wrong to blame him? I blame myself a bit too you know. Anyway he was a liar. Maybe he *was* at peace, and the drama was all put on just to make us feel bad. What do you think?

I'll tell you what I've got Eddy to thank for. The first bass I ever played was one pinched by him. He'd lift all this stuff then realise afterwards it was useless to him. So I started playing it just for the sake of it. I joined a band, then I left it, then I joined another that was better. The thing is Eddy always thought it was a joke but I ended up taking it seriously. The bass, that is. I must admit I felt bad for the person who'd lost their bass. That was the difference between Eddy and me. Cos once you start getting into music your instrument becomes really important. It becomes like your lover. I invested in a bass of my own eventually. It was beautiful, I loved it. Then it got stolen too. There's karma for you.

There was so much untold. There was always more left out than put in. Eddy was screaming tore off his oxygen mask, lips cobbled with blisters mouth full of thrush, for weeks Holmes had been scraping it out by the spoonful. All that frustration and the white fungal foam like fuel to his fire. Holmes going over to hold him, thick white spit of invective on his face his shirt. Don't let him in Holmes if that priest comes in here I'll fucken kill him don't let him in.

The dark cat came into the living room while Holmes was folding his clothes. He sat on his haunches ignoring Holmes's greetings. This was not the usual behaviour of the friendly cat, the hug slut, the one that would push against your body without invitation. Disturbed, Holmes turned to hang a shirt and when he looked back at the cat again his eyes were glazed, his tongue protruding, his stomach his whole body was convulsing. Holmes didn't know what to do he thought the cat might be dying, petrified by the wardrobe he watched the cat spasm. The cat vomited a clump of grass onto the rug then sauntered out tail in the air.

Sunrise and Holmes is awake in the floodlight of cicadas sweating old fear, the wave about to pound him. He recedes from his dream as a viewer from a Hokusai tsunami fragmenting a figure against a monolithic rock face. Finds himself in his new bedroom his new house, surrounded by unpacked cartons.

He was an *evil* little shit! Hot rod of anger piercing his entire day, Holmes goes to enrol in university but sees nothing hears nothing. Comes to gazing at the floor of the cafeteria an hour after setting out to explore the grounds. He should find the library he should start buying books but all he wants to do is score. He walks back to the station, it's hopeless, how would he know where to get drugs down here and even that escape route would lead back to Eddy. Eddy's exclusive use of the neutral pronoun for everybody, neutralising their importance and their pain as though he were the only subject and everybody else an object. Hey Homo check it out, that guy at the bar? It's a cunt believe me! It's the mug that asked for french then drove down behind William and held me down and fucked me without of course a connie. Chucked me out of the fucken car without paying too. Let's get it, c'mon there's two of us. Easy peasy, I know it's got money. C'mon Holmes, let's get it.

Oh Eddy though I know that I can't blame you the forgiving isn't easy. Lured him out of the Goldfish Bowl, stank of beer fat gut, he was an accountant from Ryde with three kids told you all this the night he ripped you off. Why they always think they can get therapy as well blab every petty detail. Waiting in the lane behind the vacant lot watching you through the cyclone fence all angles and lanky grace there's moonlight on your cheekbones. The guy is huge I can see how he overpowered you stoned and unsuspecting. It's a cunt a fucking cunt. Strung out in love, I'm willing I'm ready. Let's just get it over with.

Step aside to let you pass you floor him with a kick behind the knees then we're both in there. Can't bring my boot any higher than the ribs yours hacking straight into the face I can't tell it's all blood shitting myself my dick's hard can't help it, sick sick I feel so sick. Watching us pulp him from higher and higher like I'm flying away sometimes I hate being a man. You unrepentant, long legs tenting now over the body laughing unbuttoning, let's *go* for chrissake! Then a figure in the laneway you stoop for the wallet and we're running up Victoria into Hughes, press me against the wall. Your fly's still undone oh I want you inside me you're evil and I love you hate you love you.

The body so still. Scanning the papers every day afterwards for news of the death. Sometimes I hate being a man.

Summer came late that first year down the coast. It was November before Holmes was first aware of crickets at sunset. With a beer out the back he would watch the light change as they shrilled with coming darkness, burning the air like a midnight sun. And when he first heard the sea again from his bedroom he felt he'd come a full circle. The sound of his childhood joining the dots. He thought he could never live again without that sound to sleep by.

He built the fire as high as possible then lit the paper beneath the kindling. Fed back in the fallen sticks and wood ends left out of the main burn. In sunlight the flames disappeared, it was perilously easy to underestimate them. The barbecue was built on an old grate propped up and surrounded by bricks in a sheltered corner of the garden. Holmes watched the fire burn down, so much reducing to so little. Tomorrow three piles of wood would be half a bucket of warm ash for the compost. So the urn really had contained all of Eddy's ashes, his entire body along with the coffin really was represented by such a small volume. He didn't want to go so quickly, he wanted to be buried. To linger in the earth a little longer.

Still sleeping badly. Shock of sun across his bed through the uncurtained window, hot thick air. He took a towel from the bathroom and went down to the beach to watch the waves. A wild disorganised surf of kelp and foam, rips running into one another dragging around the sandbank. No one else down here yet. He thought of the Bondi Bay cannulae promising long smooth rides and the choice of icecream shops along Campbell Parade. Sat beneath his straw hat hiding from the sun which lifted the sand and sea to whiteness all around him, watched the tide turn. A quick swim then back over the grassy verge to the shop across the road where he bought ginger beer and chips, smoking rollies now no filters. Fifty dollars left in his bank account to be stretched across the rest of summer before the dripfeed of a government studying allowance. He sat watching the water, ignoring the holiday families beginning to cover the beach. Louis! Just be careful! At midday he tried to sleep in the shade of the Norfolk Island pines. A wide dark green room. He came down to the beach the next day again, sunburnt now staying in the pine shade behind his glasses. Ants crawling through the hairs on his legs into his shorts biting him, cushion of fat pine needles beneath his towel sandy already. Shutting his eyes and drifting over the talk around the barbecue. The cricket, the kids, the best mechanic around here . . .

For a week he went down to the sea every day, walking in either direction when the tide was low, around the headlands along rock shelves and coves and beaches. Stopping to piss between the shale strata letting the sun burn him, unpeeling his skin and shedding it into the tides his life behind him like a wake to the horizon. The metres of hair and nails, shit piss blood gas, fibres of wornout clothes, rubber and leather from the soles of a hundred pairs of shoes left in footpath cracks, fruit peels bones of animals he had consumed, used fits cigarette butts food wrapping crushed beer cans, essays burnt or decomposed. He peeled the skin off his shoulders and chest as he walked along the coastline, desiccated coconut floating out across a rockpool, peeled his nose his back, till the burning sliced across his skin like a knife. Spit in the ocean, sweat on a bus seat, his dream of the wave thundering over him, hot breath locked in a winter room, grime from his hand to the next on the phone, snot of withdrawal into tissues into bins, his cum in arses in mouths in condoms. Turning back finally at the third headland feeling fatigue grip his thighs as he trudged home.

And then sank through the pillows down into fever, his body aflame with all his life's summers. Burning in the bedroom of cartons still unpacked, a pyre, a fug, till his mind warped with heat floated through the house and into the speakers just rigged up in Jo's bedroom. The perfect surfer gliding to shore.

I ain't got nothin' to lose.
I'm full of leprosy
Any day I may die
I'm in quarantine
I'm away from my family
I'm I'm I'm I'm isolated
I'm depredated
I ain't got nothin' to lose.
The worst thing that can happen to me is I can believe what you're saying
and I'll get healed
The worst thing that can happen to me is I can get delivered
The worst thing that can happen to me is I can get free!
That's what you've got to tell yourself tonight.
You ain't got nothin' to lose in Luther Unit
But everything to gain.
There is a **healer** *in the* **house** *tonight*
And you gotta work it out and get it!

Fashion attack!!!

Holmes arrived at the warehouse while the girls were still getting ready. Door ajar, music on, he slipped in unnoticed and watched them from the couch feeling underdressed. Moved to an armchair to better view Billy's transformation, the way her true character emerged through party artifice. Everything she wore covered her entirely, he stared at her seeking her girlishness of before. Arcs of lilac appearing over her eyes long silver eyelashes and frosted lips, Billy was laughing and directing the others she was in control. These were the times Holmes associated with her years ago, before his time at the coast before Eddy. Backstage at Slut City, Holmes one of the only poofs among all these camp dykes undergoing makeovers for Billy's fashion parades. Warehouses usually, licensed venues for the last two, backstage any corner where costumes could be hung any surface on which makeup could be laid, mirrors often compacts tilted to the light of one naked globe. Now Billy was by his side with spirit gum and half a long drooping moustache. Holmes leant back obediently trying not to smile. Billy gave him a pair of sunglasses with a lens missing to match his mouth. There, you're dressed. She brought the mull bowl over. So you can go on joint duty . . . You've got nothing to worry about y'know Holmes, we won't be getting totally drugfucked. Then she went back to help traffic with her false eyelashes.

Back all those years ago when Slut City was dying and Heresy hadn't begun, Billy and Holmes would sometimes go out with Stash to have a break from the gay scene. They hadn't met James yet, raves were the only place they heard techno music. Stash had a set of pens in the dashboard including fluoro ink, potatoes and a sharp cutter. They'd pool their money and one person would go in get a stamp then come back out to the car. Billy usually the fraud artist, the stamps were the hardest. Her speed shaky hands cutting away under the leaky yellow car light, Holmes poring over her shoulder all of them pissing themselves. But Billy would pull it off. Once with the fluoro ink Holmes went in first flashed his wrist at the door and fluoro appeared the length of his arm. Billy pushed him through and rushed in straight after before the bouncers could do anything. He didn't remember from which party it was they had ended up going home together.

Why he had been attracted to Billy. She was so feminine, so soft and curvaceous, she was his image of the ideal woman. Big breasted white skinned, her porn star mouth. The sculpted hair, thin eyebrows or none at all, she was a picture of femininity that had been tampered with just enough. But once in bed with her he had felt overwhelmed. The impossibility of focusing on the invisible, he didn't know where to go. Holmes saw for the first time it was really her mind that turned him on, her aura, her otherness. The sex was good fast and funny and neither of them ever wanted to do it again. It receded as another nook along the path of their friendship. But he remembered the taste of her, the sudden amazing delicate surprise. They lied about women, their taste, their smell. Nobody had ever described it to him justly. It haunted him as something he would never know again. He supposed it was his own decision.

They went down to Heresy in the CBD. Cruising tunnels erected with black plastic, chillout space two bars large stage. Fred was there and the Professor in a long black dress, wire-framed glasses with amyl bottles suspended from the bridge to below each nostril. Turkish Jim in a pork-pie hat, fake shaving cuts and flies clustered across his face, a narrow beige suit onto which were laminated religious and porn cards. They pouted and posed and introduced their personae. The Professor named Billy in her ankle-length CD dress Jackie Onassid. And traffic looking vampiric with a lurid spill of fake blood from her mouth was named Jackie No.

It was a sexy party. The music got good around 4 am. Holmes took half an e, his first in years. An hour later still feeling nothing he took the other half. Sought out Billy as it came on to alleviate the panic, told himself over and over that his was her body or one of those millions that rode on chemicals out of choice not necessity, coming down staying down for weeks at a time without grief or temptation. So with the drug in his nervous system pure and hot he moved after traffic deeper into the centre of the dancefloor, into the snakepit among the smiles and blowjobs and dirty dancing. He began to smell his sweat, then the skin beneath it. He began to smell everyone in the room, their sweat their skin their bodies. traffic in a grind between Bella and Stash, she loved the fun and flirting but loathed the anticipation of Billy's accusing eyes, Holmes dancing next to her as reassurer not spy till the music took him away from other people's problems and his own. But Billy was holding court by the bar with a fresh bottle of cold water that she slid down traffic's back when she came off the floor. After the show they smoked a joint on the edge of the dancefloor with the Professor and Jim then Holmes felt himself drawn back into the slipstream. He closed his eyes and entered the Gaudi architecture, all around the whirling percussion and streaking of whistles, bass like a staircase, and it built and built and built and built then exploded at last and the dancefloor was on fire, everybody going crazy. He was dancing inside a chemical factory, saw giant pistons blue red and orange, a whole vast ceiling of bright machinery pumping and shaking, melting down over his entire being.

They put on their sunglasses and walked back through the city just before nine o'clock. The sun was brutal. Out of office tower wilderness and into the oasis of Hyde Park verdancy, stopping by the Archibald fountain. Jackie Onassid took off her platforms and danced barefoot across the grass while Jackie No with fallen branches from the kentia palms fanned the men in their hot outfits. Stash to one side in his high heels combing his long dark hair with fingers, Bee and Bella on all fours playing cows in the clover, their corset squeezed bums white as statues. It was Sunday morning and there was almost no one around, just a small group approaching to attend mass at St Mary's. Jackie No and Shifty set upon Bee and Bella with the palm frond floggers.

Summer, party season. They worked and played their various ways through the long hot months. The orgy of New Year's Eve fireworks hanging in the sky like giant chandeliers over the dark stage of city-fringed harbour, a small gathering at the warehouse where everybody dressed up for a strut. A cabaret season where they found another performer for their germinating party. A dance party at the Rooftop, a girls' play party off Cleveland the following week. There were cocktails on the roof of Holmes's Bondi building for his birthday in late February, hot pink moonrise out of the sea and later a party at the surf lifesaving club. Dawn by the ocean, bodies aching and loose from dancing. One by one they stripped off their outfits and ran down the sand into the surf.

Gay was getting groovy, people had started to take notice. Amateur photographers exhibited and sold pictures of their friends, sundry small self-affirmations passed down the years into publication. People from photo shops and journalists and tourists came in party season to capture the dressups, anyone on the street was public property. Bee brought home a postcard from a place on Darlinghurst Road of Billy in full kit watching the Mardi Gras Parade. Billy went back and shoplifted the remaining ones, the next year they were printed again. Caught unawares trashed or glamorous you didn't have time to say yes or no before the shutter clicked. Across Osaka fridges, through Parisian dining rooms, inside a lawyer's holiday album in Rio, Sydney queers partied into posterity. Dressed up pumped up messed up jumped up, over the limit and out of this world. Somewhere far away somebody was gazing at a piercing that had long grown over, shredded costumes were still being admired, a dead friend's makeover was discussed in the future in an incomprehensible language. Years later while you were sleeping a copy of your look was stepping out to party in a northern hemisphere winter.

Party animals could be careless about recording themselves. What really counted was the moment being lived, cameras were awkward the occasions private follies. If you saw yourself in the files of a social photographer you could ask to buy a print. You might see yourself in a book never having met the photographer. When sponsors came in and global corporations with products to sell there were those that were happy to pose for nothing or next to it. They didn't care what their looks were selling, they were unaware of the huge sums models usually earned, they were hungry for the smallest acknowledgement having strutted so long before silence or jeers. The giving had no limits because performance was a habit a custom a way of life. Performance was life itself. There were bills to pay. People wanted to get famous.

The parties got bigger the tickets more expensive, strangers outnumbered friends the community grew. Splintered multiplied mutated atrophied, sprang up elsewhere. The random march of queer seeding the world. People were always looking for something new, so much good partying led to high standards. There were never enough places to go for afficionados. Rebel parties became institutions.

And He will even preach that God is dead
and some of y'all will believe what the Devil has said,
and He will then act as the world's police
and the sun will rise up in the west
and set down in the east.
And when it came time for the end
and when it came time for the end
and when it came time for the end
the men will look like the women
and the women like the men,
and some will dance in a hypnotic trance
like as if they have no care,
but these are the signs
of the changing times
that the end is drawing near.
For it was prophesized many centuries past
that the end would come in a fiery holocaust,
and only the righteous people would survive the blast
and the Devil's machine will bring about His own end
and peace love and joy will reign once again.
And man will
                    understand man
and man will
                    understand man
and man will
                    understand man
and man will
                    understand man
and man will
                    understand man
and man will
                    understand.
And live in harmony and peace
and the sun will once again rise up in the east.

Cool nights and mornings, sunlight finally through the windows when afternoon swung around. An inefficient Dimplex followed the girls across the vast warehouse floor, they ate dinner at the long work table in their fake furs directing each other's sleeves out of the food. Quickly inured to this domestic cold their high-elbowed postures were a source of puzzlement on the rare occasions they ate out. During their first year together traffic and Billy hardly went anywhere except work, traffic in bars Billy at the leather shop or home in her workroom.

traffic was a talker but a learner first and foremost. Wise in externals of other countries books and history, what was freeform and innate eluded her articulation though it governed her utterly. With the utmost faith and curiosity she studied Billy, questioning her endlessly about her past and aspirations. Reading an order into every habit and gesture that collapsed beneath any extrapolation. The way Billy swanned through parties in the most outrageous outfits, imperious, untouchable, slouching taciturn in group conversation. Her refusal to even go to the corner shop unless dressed properly, her refusal to ever dress down. Answering the phone with a pick in her arm, talking on to Bee's mother through the rush and syringe disposal, saying no with stoic severity to scoring the next day. Obsessive with vitamins minerals and herbs every morning, constantly catching colds and the flu. Calmly squashing cockroaches inside her own fist, refusing to eat with crockery dropped on a clean floor. The fantastical objects that materialised from no prior discussion, her everchanging aesthetic. Billy was a series of pictures that traffic could not order. No sooner had she fixed one than another would appear.

traffic came to Billy like a flower just opening. Up till now too itinerant to own a large wardrobe, too impatient to spend much time getting dressed up, she fell on Billy's repertoire like a starveling on a banquet. Watched her skills learnt her advice and practised on her own. traffic was a renovation waiting to happen.

traffic questioned everything, her lover her friends the thoughts of strangers and the most familiar actions. The past the present and the future of all things. She questioned the deeds she questioned their motives, she questioned what it was that held them together, what the initial attraction had been. traffic was a thinker but the bond wasn't intellectual. She was a show pony but it wasn't demonstrative. She was an aesthete but so much of Billy fell outside her ideal vision. A big-boned girl whose only exercise was walking dancing and fucking, and Billy hadn't had much of that for a while before traffic. Pheromonal, unspoken, their first teeth-clashing kiss back at Billy's warehouse. Pulling each other's clothes off while the kettle screeched behind them. The miracle of Billy's cunt, so neat and demure to the eye, open and moist around traffic's hand.

They fucked each other deep and hard for never less than an hour. Their hands emerged wrinkled after so much soaking, crushed, aching, they held each other into sleep. On her knees on a roll, Billy over traffic, one hand on the bedpost the other on her clit while traffic's fist slowly turned inside, her face widening in wonder when Billy started to come, down her arm over her chest and face. And on through orgasm through Billy's clamped cunt, traffic's hand still moving till Billy receded behind her blood-filled eyelids, body in meltdown fluids pissing on her lover.

traffic got lost in their sex, had or anticipated. To and from work it dripfed her system. Loose knees hot skin distant eyes. Buying groceries, paying bills, starting her weekend bar shift. These were the moments that marked her daydreams, and the endless endless changing of sheets.

traffic cleaning up shuts her eyes sees Billy, straddling her stomach moving up to her face. Saliva rushes into her mouth.

It wasn't just Billy that traffic had fallen for. She fell for an ethos she initially thought they shared. A life that was lived and not saved up for, a daily creation. And Billy all the while was wanting something elsewhere, and commitment, stability. traffic threw away all of her plans while Billy was just getting around to making them.

31

Once a week traffic took an outfit from Billy's wardrobe and joined her for the Lesbian Doubles shift in the peepshow of the strip club they called the Tunnel of Love. Coins poured in as soon as the punters thought they were seeing lesbian sex. They recounted their day's stories doing het porn oral, flicking their wigs back and spreading each other's labia, smooth as little girls', waggling their tongues facetiously. Pretend fucks became real when their excitement mounted with the coin volume down the chutes.

Billy lay back on the bed, traffic standing over her a hand on the ceiling for balance.

Like my new shoes?

Oh you didn't.

Well they were only a hundred. I can't keep wearing all your stuff.

We're supposed to be saving.

traffic lowered herself over Billy, sat on her mound.

You're squashing me, I need to do this traffic. I'm over thirty and I've never been out of this fucken country . . . Have you saved anything?

I really *really* don't want to go back to Europe.

OK, I've been thinking. We can still meet in the States . . . You haven't changed your mind have you?

I want to be with you, I've always said that. Hey look, full house!

Billy:

I sometimes got the impression that Holmes still thought I was this megaexperienced amazon or something. Darling Homie, I think he may be one of our first great Dyke Hags. I was talking to him the other day then forgot what I was saying midsentence because I suddenly had this image of us in bed together. I nearly burst out laughing right in his face. Funny that, how you can be friends with someone for years then suddenly remember you once fucked them. You hardly even recall the details of their body. God, I hardly *ever* did boys. My twenty-first birthday, him still a teenager, fumbling, drunk, we spent most of the night just laughing. So we got the hots for each other just that once, just that night.

Yair, I don't know, I knew plenty about some things but nothing about others. When Holmes came back from the coast having made so many changes it made me feel even more like I was in a rut, like nothing much had moved for me since the last time we'd seen each other. I was sick of the grind, I don't know, I felt kind of trapped. I was sick of Sydney, it was getting so pretentious. I wanted a bit more acknowledgement for my work and the boys'. Or should I say our *play*. They said they didn't care, but I reckon James did. I wanted to do something bigger, like get into theatre or film design or something, but you have to know all the right types and go to school to do that.

I get all these big plans. Plans for outfits, plans for party designs. I'd like to make something totally over the top for traffic where I can really use my creativity. There's nothing better than when I can actually make something I'm passionate about, there's no better feeling. I think what I'd really like to do is create big theatre sets but how can I? Who'll hire me? So going overseas seems the best option. I've got nothing to lose.

traffic doesn't want to go though. Sometimes I think I'm scared of her or maybe it's just that I'm scared of losing her. She herself saying the other night I love you so much it scares me. I think she's the one, though I never thought I'd say that about anyone. Sure we've got our problems but we'll work through it. A relationship's hard work, isn't that what they say?

Who left the lid off the toothpaste again?

Probably Shifty.

What traffic? What've I done now?

I can't even get it out of the tube. It's *really* annoying.

Christ Bee, you sound like I feel. Are you about to bleed?

Don't trivialise what I'm saying Shifty!

I'm not, you self-righteous harridan, you're not the only one!

The phone's ringing.

Put some clothes on will you traffic.

Why? It's hot.

Don't interrupt her, she's picking her pubes.

For *you*, my darling lover, I'm preening myself for *you*.

Yeh well two other people live here y'know.

The light's better here.

Save it for your girlfriend.

Can somebody get the fucking phone?

Can you all shut up?

You're the closest.

Yeh but her head's up her arse getting the ingrowns.

Oh get a grip. Bee?

If it's that fucking journalist I am *not* home!

It's Holmes.

Hallo!

About fucken time traffic. What's going on there? Catfight?

Oh look Holmes, we're premenstrual! What's your excuse?

Oh . . . I'm just a faggot.

traffic Holmes and Billy began their venue search towards the end of winter. They followed up any and every suggestion, hard selling Mr Hyde to venue managers who had never heard of him. Few remembered Slut City either so Billy began to feel her experience stood for nothing. A basement on William Street no longer operable since a bust by the licensing cops the night they stayed open half an hour too long, a new venue in the city doing retro nights only, another in the Cross only available for regular club nights organised by select and established promoters. Another who said yes then no then yes then no again. So they came back to Oxford Street knowing at least that most of their crowd was likely to be near the area. Treading the grimy stairs up and down to every venue they often wondered if it wouldn't be easier finding a warehouse and setting up their own BYO bar. But the money that would be needed to bring in a sound system, the alacrity of cops to close down this sort of party now. They barely had enough for advertising.

They asked Skunk to play as well in the hope that a better known DJ would give them a foot in the door. It didn't seem to help. The managers listened more closely when Holmes came with them. If Holmes went alone it was assumed he wanted to put on a gay party, gay assumed to include women and heterosexuals. If the girls went alone a manager who thought he was hip would get excited at the prospect of a night for lesbians or refuse them if there were lesbian promoters already working in the venue. So it was that even here they were relegated to the periphery. They joked about getting in drag to approach the venues but of course that would frighten them off even more. Billy suggested it might be easier to wait until their dick was available before approaching venues. traffic said fuck it and pushed on, visiting places alone when Billy was sick or Holmes was working.

They made their own fun in the absence of parties, Shifty arriving from retail therapy one Thursday evening in a brand new second-hand pinstripe suit with presents for everybody. Lilies for Bee in one hand, from the other a cascade of neck ties from St Vincent de Paul. Blue silk paisley, a wide brown printed with beige vintage cars, a Felix the Cat tie. Dinner was finished the music turned up, they fell into dressups. Boy drag all round.

Billy slicked her bob back from a centre part, its faded orange a perfect foil for the vintage car tie and a dark brown suit. Bee went for the paisley with flares and wide lapels, pushing her long amber hair into a black mop wig. Shifty applied unctuous moustache and goatie, emulating the look of a gangster from old Shanghai. Billy was finicky with her moustaches, always using her own hair, cutting gluing and trimming it to perfection. traffic went tieless in a safari suit and long white socks, hiding her grown-out mohawk beneath a pith helmet. Billy found a fake fur guinea pig and stuck it in traffic's top pocket then handed her the clothes brush. Here, can you do me? Drugs, I want drugs, traffic dragged the brush down Billy's body. No time no need, Billy shrugged. We'll just club hop till the energy wears out.

They reconvened in the living area to admire and criticise one another. Moustaches wigs and ties were adjusted and Bee went back into her room to get a butterfly net for traffic. OK, shall we do it?

They went up to Lip Service at Shifty's request for a blast of lesbianism, Billy drawing one of the promoters aside to talk about their plans.
    You haven't done anything since Slut City have you.
    No. Just private stuff.
    Have you got a venue?
    We're still looking.
    Just don't do it on the first weekend of the month cos it'll clash with us. And you know how it is, we've gotta support each other in this community.
    Sure. Don't worry.
    And we've got plans for the third Saturday in November too.

OK, I'll make a note. Can we flyer up here?

No.

Why not?

That's just how it is. If we let you in everybody'll want to leave their flyers here.

Can't we just leave a little pile at the desk?

The other promoter came over then. You're early, she said to Billy. Drag Kings are next week.

Billy went inside. The venue had changed but nothing else over the three years since they had been here. Same music same graphics same type of dyke. People loved tradition. The King is dead, long live the King.

traffic and Shifty went to the bar, Shifty turning slyly after ordering. Hey traffic, I thought of a new drag name, Mal Practice. Mal! My long-lost cousin! Back at their table they realised pretty soon that due to lesbian incest they had all been named after the same grandfather, traffic a Function and Billy an Adjusted. Bee's mother had married twice, first a Treat then an Icious. The four Mals scanned the room for other cousins. Billy came across Mal Nutrition throwing up in the toilets, Mal Adroit was spilling his drink on the dancefloor. Formation walked past in really badly cut leathers. Retro disco through the sound system, Mal Efic on the decks. Administer Faesant Odorous and Ediction all looked like they'd been drinking since the office closed. Mal Aise at the next table the only man in the place. There were Contents and Ignants everywhere.

Christ, said Mal Icious. I feel like I've taken really bad acid.

Half your luck, said Mal Function.

Whose idea was this anyway? said Mal Adjusted.

Alright, said Mal Practice. Let's go to Pawn.

Mal Conduct was outside pissed as usual abusing doorbitch Evolent for not letting him in.

Pawn was going off. They danced themselves to exhaustion, arriving home at dawn.

The Professor:

It wasn't true there was nothing happening. There always was and always will be something happening. Heidi was becoming critical in her old age, of all including herself. God forbid we had become two fussy old queens. You didn't put my whites in with the colours did you, and Daryl remember to strain the olives before you put them in the martinis, and Everything's so safe now, and on and on and on. By the time James went to Adelaide, I couldn't *wait* for him to leave. I began to relax, to become once again the tenant of my house, leave the washingup. Then I began to miss him again. I remembered the fun-loving gay boy I'd met ten years before and missed his weird ideas, his hairy chest and short thick cock. Not that it was offered to me on his return. Never mind, there was always gorillas in the mist, and for a while there a very persistent PhD student. I tutored his girlfriend as well, but that didn't stop him. I am not averse to acolytes, I am hoar, I take what I can get. Oh, how I relished the sight of my genius-filled sperm bursting forth like a hot geyser behind my desk in the office!

I went out more without James. Not so much parties as clubs or just the local for a drink. Pawn was on every Thursday and Sunday and sometimes it was great. Skunk played Pawn, mostly dirty house with the obligatory porn movie soundbites, and I danced in a fantasy I was that hot black mama. Hot, black, strong female vocals . . . I allowed myself a little more credulity in my husband's absence, maybe I even had a crush on Skunk for a while. He was so tall and short-sighted he had to bend double to find the groove, biomechanics tattoo glistening on his forearm, a displaced Quasimodo necromancing the turntables.

Billy began to come down occasionally once she'd started going out with traffic. It was nice to see her in love and out of the house, to see her with somebody who actually had a brain and the gift of the gab to go with it. traffic lived on the dancefloor while Billy was more inclined to stand on the side and watch. The venue was small and nearly always overcrowded, it was the best club on a recovery Sunday. Best music, free entry, friendly crowd. Sometimes it got so hot down there the walls would drip. Billy remained immaculate, wig or no wig, cool, unflustered while her kitten worked up a sweat. That's what traffic was. A kitten. Kitten of wickedness at the bottom of the basket where the gingham met velvet. Miiaaaooooowww . . . !

The parties of the past were idiosyncratic in their inception. Clone was Turkish Jim's birthday, his head superimposed on a sheep's body for the invitation. Once the RSVPs were secured, all names were put into a hat then one by one drawn out and placed next to the guest list. Each person had to dress up as the designated friend or one of their incarnations. A strict code of secrecy was observed ensuring no one knew who would arrive as their clone till the night itself.

Shifty got Fred and dressed as him ten years previously, an old style leatherman in chaps and handlebar moustache. Fred couldn't take his eyes off himself. Fred got James, James got Billy, Turkish Jim got Bee and did a bad pastiche in flairs, stuffed bra and frosted lipstick. Bee got the Professor, the Professor got Shifty and over leather redid her cyberheart outfit with a powerboard. Unhappy with the job he made of emulating Asian eyes, he improvised a helmet with a red light that pinged from side to side above the visor, leaving him with tinnitus and a headache for the next few days. But the best was Billy who got Turkish Jim and for the six weeks leading up to the party every night after work concocted not an outfit he had created already but one that he might have. She began with inner tyre tubes found in a skip outside the auto repair then accessorised with a bag of empty plastic thread spools Jim had given her a year before. She cut riveted glued and stitched an ankle-length dress of black rubber patchwork. Made a long headdress with the scraps, noded the cape with the plastic spools and wired the remainder end to end then attached them like snakes to the headdress. She called the costume Rubbishman and cued by Professor Bee made her entrance two blocks before the party venue, rising up out of a skip bobbing and quivering when Turkish arrived. It was Saturday afternoon, the streets full of people who stopped in wonder. So that even when the parties were small and private at some stage some part of them was shared with the public. The street was their stage.

Then there was Baroque, Bee's celebration at the warehouse for acquisition of film funds. Embossed invitations, a show, Mr Hyde DJing, two of Bella's slaves as sentinels at the entrance. With brocade battery-lit lampshades over their heads and naked bodies sewn by Bee and Bella with beads and crystals they were living chandeliers. Inside was festooned by Billy with lanterns and silk fabric, a feast laid out on the long table around the body of a reclining girl. Three weeks after Baroque Bee learnt her funding had fallen through and stored photographs and memories of the party in compensation.

On the night of her birthday, traffic came home to a room lit by a scorpion of twenty-nine candles on the cement floor. A pencil stroke of incense rose from a spiral on the bedside table, the bed strewn with red roses dozens unopened on thorn-spoked stems. She threw herself among them realising the cirrus of shells and chocolates above. The click of a button somewhere then Third Eye came through the boom box hidden in the distant corner. traffic waited. From between the clothes racks a creature appeared in a long black garment with upraised talons throwing shadows against the back wall like Murnau's Nosferatu. It moved towards the bed with Billy's gait and a mask of horror with a long pointed ivory snout, ridges of yellow teeth along each side. Netted sachets depended from the talons of one hand. Adrift in music, incense and airborne shells and chocolates, traffic fell again into her lover's nightmares. Watched awestruck as the creature deposited packages alongside her body and stood over her talons raised as traffic unwrapped everything. Chocolate sovereigns, chocolate cigarettes, a tape from James, new willy.

But the best is yet to come. I want to make you an outfit, and I want you to help design it.

Come here baby. I want to kiss you.

Aren't those thorns sticking into you?

It's quite nice actually. Do the eyes fog up when you laugh?

Let go.

You made my bed, now you're gonna lie in it.

Yow!

With *me*.

You bitch!

traffic cleared a space for her, helped her take off the mask. Billy's face hot and damp. They stayed in the bedroom through the sounds of Bee and Shifty cooking watching television showering going to bed.

How did you attach the shells and chocolates?

Fishing line. The shells all had holes in them and I threaded it through the chocolate foils.

They cross the whole room! It must've taken you ages. We could do something like that at our party.

What party?

The moons of Saturn have a direct influence on Saturn's rings. A natural tendency of ring materials is to spread both toward and away from the planet, but the moons and a complex interplay of gravitational forces shape the rings and define their structure. Mimas . . . Tethys . . . Dione . . . Rhea . . . Enceladus . . . Iapetus . . . And Hyperion . . .

The most intriguing of Saturn's moons is Titan, larger than the planet Mercury. It is the only moon known to have an atmosphere. Nitrogen and methane gasses shroud Titan with dense clouds which our cameras cannot penetrate. The chemistry of this atmosphere is unlike that of any other. If we could descend to the surface of Titan, we might see ice mountains softly eroded by a persistent rain of complex chemicals, and a deep chemical ocean, a strange parody of the oceans of earth. Titan's atmosphere, like the ancient atmosphere of earth, contains prelife chemicals, but is too cold for life to evolve.

The moons of Saturn have a direct influence on Saturn's rings. A natural tendency of ring materials is to spread both toward and away from the planet, but the moons and a complex interplay of gravitational forces shape the rings and define their structure.

Her greatest strengths were her greatest weaknesses. It was her energy that got her hired and her energy that got her fired. Energy that came off her like sunlight on water, her loud rasping voice, heavy tread, her indiscretions. traffic had worked in nearly every place on the strip and beyond over the last decade. Losing a job when the novelty wore off, propelled by her attitude to dismissal, always saying she was quitting.

Her timing was perfect when she applied for a job at the Royal, the management looking to employ more women. She chose the weekend and late shifts because they were more entertaining and paid better. Hard enough to spend decent time with Billy but traffic was a night owl. She would climb into bed wanting love with her two weeks later, Billy shifting irritably at her touch and turning away.

She loved the late mornings when everybody was at work. Even with the sounds of industry the warehouse was serene, alternations of direct and pebbled afternoon sunlight widening across the floor, blue cloths rippling in the breeze. An old Chinese family spent most days on their verandah across the road, next door to them was a brothel. Sometimes if she'd had a shot of speed before work the night before and had smoked and worked her way through comedown at the bar, she would fall into bed exhausted and sleep heavily hanging onto Billy's body till it left her in the morning, then sleep through to the afternoon. Waking to people and activity, missing the solitude.

traffic came home to a dark quiet warehouse. Put away the shopping, went into the bedroom. The window was ajar, curtain ballooning and sucking, Billy lying on her side in a cradle of rippling light. traffic eased herself onto the bed and hugged her from behind.

How's my baby?

Ratshit.

D'you want a massage?

Billy rolled onto her stomach and traffic slid her hands beneath her jumper, pulled it over her head and covered Billy's body with her own till the shivering left it. Turned on the bedside lamp and reached for the bottle of oil. In the cone of electric light a scattering of grey hair glinted amongst the pale regrowth close to Billy's scalp. The freckles of a country childhood sank beneath the pallor of clothed city life. traffic began to work her shoulders and neck.

I think I might have found a venue today. Six hundred capacity, new management. We get the door, they get the bar. They're straight but they say they want the gay community to do stuff there.

That sounds familiar. The lure of the pink dollar.

Well the gay places don't want to know us anyway, what difference does it make? Straight gays or straight straights, that's all you're going to see in the upper echelons of clubs. Besides, the manager's a woman and doesn't seem so hung up on the notion that dykes are only capable of producing women-only events.

What's her name?

Anna.

Do they have a licence?

A cabaret licence.

Oh yair. Are you intending to dine? We'll take your money then throw you out at three.

They reckon they can go till six.

So the cops are paid up.

Look, Billy, there's just no other way. How many clubs d'you reckon have proper licences in this town anyway? Do they even exist? Can anyone afford them? You may as well blame the government. I know they're shits but me and Holmes'll liaise with the management. You're the main props and graphics person so that's heaps of work already. You don't have to worry about them.

Mmm.

And the dancefloor takes up most of the space, it's got like a main section and a dark and sleazy section. There's a whole corner of couches and tables and chairs for chillout. And an area near the bar perfect for a stage. Come on Billy, we've been trying for so long!

I'm not gonna go through all the headache and heartache and backache of getting a party up only to have it closed down.

They *won't* close us down.

Who says?

Me.

Billy turned onto her back and laughed. She laughed at traffic, slapped her. traffic kissed her on the lips.

Now get dressed so we can go and have dinner with Holmes.

What's this place called anyway?

The Cool Room.

Oh traffic!

The Cool Room. A dingy space down the bottom of Oxford near Whitlam Square above a Lebanese takeaway. Downstairs besides falafels and kebabs you could buy bags of hydro. The owner's other club in Bondi Junction briefly infamous when a teenager was shot dead by a rival dealer. The Cool Room closed for two weeks after police were caught selling drugs there, reopened with renovations incomplete. Perfect for the Panic! team because a pristine space would have been impossible to decorate. As long as the sound system and airconditioning were intact they had everything they needed, although they remained nervous about the place's reputation as a haven for cops and gangsters.

traffic woke up speaking. Pan had seven pipes symbolising the harmonies of the seven spheres. Like this, she made a crude sketch for Billy at breakfast. So Billy took her template of the Panic! stencil, block letters underlined like a tabloid headline, and redrew it in her lunchbreak. The ascending pipes were inserted on either side of and in between the letters. The name lost its exclamation mark and gained some ancient music.

Billy in her canny softly spoken way reduced Stash's fee for the flyers in a bid to recoup some of the rent he still owed them. She had Bee's support in this, and easygoing unreliable talented Stash let himself be taken along for the ride. Holmes was in Bondi without a car so the girls did most of the footpath stencilling, Billy meeting traffic when she finished work at the Royal. The city after midnight on a Monday so peaceful, stripped back hosed clean waiting to be marked again. They started down at Whitlam Square and worked their way up Oxford Street, taking turns to hold down the stencil. Up to the Albury across the road back down the other side, they worked fuelled by excitement stopping at Gilligan's Island for a quick cigarette. Falling into bed at dawn falling into sleep while others woke and walked the red stencilled trail of the woodland faun through the modern city.

Slippery Jo, it's your old mate Homo. Don't panic, just Panic! We got a venue! You are no longer starved of a dancefloor.

She went up to the city and bought a stack of new records, incense, bath salts, fresh meat for the cats. Found a bud forgotten weeks ago at the back of the candle drawer, smoked it and put on Krüder & Dorfmeister. She was in debt thousands, the laser hit the best track. She turned it up and cooked dinner dancing.

She didn't have a sampler but experimented with Holmes's message manually over her latest mix. Hit the button at the beginning at the bridge and again at the end. You are no longer starved of a dancefloor no longer starved   no longer starved   floordanceflawdanceflaw

By March when the storms from tropical cyclones came blowing down the coast Holmes had acquired the habit of walking the shoreline to the popular surfing spot four beaches south. One after another along the final promontory like chapters in a book the cenotaphs appeared. First the most recent, garlands and wreaths and bouquets of flowers battered by salt wind had been tied around the trig post for John 'Spit' Stegh, a twenty-four-year-old taken three weeks before Holmes's arrival. Further back on the grassy verge a seat with a plaque for another gone in the same month four years previous. Down on the rocks there were more plaques hammered into niches, palimpsest of corrosion eating the lifespan and name. The highest appeared at middle tide, then another. Then at low tide another. Only one older than twenty-eight, all boys. It was Jo who helped him find the last and when months later he arrived home claiming discovery of one more on the far edge of the rock shelf she stopped what she was doing to walk out and see it before the tide turned.

Still they came and surfed here. All year in all weather they came along the beach in wetsuits or down through the heath in the pencil line of track. Watched by their friends and Holmes and sometimes Jo they picked their way across the flat brown rocks then pitched themselves half body half board over the back of a wave. The long thick Malibus steered by slow stepping, the small boards of children fast like swallows, sometimes a boogie board. Holmes had let another summer slip by without keeping his promise of buying a surfboard but in his mind paddled out anyway to sit upright in the sea among the spirits of dead boys and all the other unnamed from shipwrecks, fishing accidents, swims gone wrong. Out there he watched his teenage years when surfing was his drug then again from the rocks with fear and envy the sharp black figures take off over the reef.

During his last week, with a degree in social work and a job in the city waiting, he photographed the plaques at the ebb of one of the last king tides. The kelp and brine entered his lungs like a solvent as he collected mementos from the rarely exposed shoreline. Pieces of wood and metal from the jetty that had once been here, old bolts kinked by rust, large, phallic, heavy in the hand. Stones with rings around them, sometimes shells. More ship debris in the form of a forty gallon drum and way out on the edge of the waves a long anchor chain welded to the rock with rust.

Then along four beaches and home to the wind-cracked house on the hill, setting out too late for the company of filtered sun. So much cloud and rain coming in now there was no division of sea and sky just a dark grey mass pushing the vivid peaks of waves against the beach. Nothing else visible along the brumal headland but the immediate sand and foam till the town lights came on drawing him forward.

His three years out of Sydney had grown to three and a half and now shrank again to what felt like a few months. A cool pale block of time, without thrill without pain. Two new friends, Jimi and Slip. He couldn't remember exactly when he nicknamed Jo. Maybe around the time she was starting to play records and in a jungle phase put together ninety minutes worth for Holmes who listened to it on his walkman during the train trip to and from university. But it left him dissatisfied, it felt too slippery. Like trying to run across a polished surface or negotiating the moving walkways at Coney Island, though even their wonky rhythm was easier to fall into. Until they played the mix one evening while smoking on the verandah, Jo telling Holmes what she liked about the music.

And he shut his eyes and found her moments, the top end drums, warping bassline, the whole length of his legs began to tremble. He saw the arabesque of cymbals and somewhere above his heartbeat a shimmering rapid and delicate as insect wings. Sounds carried by wind fading in fading out. So he listened to more jungle and drum 'n' bass after that, to radio programmes and compilations and an hour in the chill room of a university party. But since that dusk on the verandah with Jo he never penetrated it again which made him wonder how much of what he heard was music and how much the meanings found by others. And that was when he named her Slippery Jo, the girl who could find stepping stones blind running through slush.

Of course it didn't describe her playing style very well, especially not later when she got known and hired for hard deep rolling trance. But she didn't care about her nickname one way or the other. It seemed appropriate to be called one thing by your family, another by your friends and another by the public. One could never have too many aliases.

The other thing was this. A new name gave the lie or possibility of a new beginning. Because they had all most likely crossed paths many times over the years before formal acquaintance. James too would later remember with them the Darlinghurst dives of the 80s like French's, might have even seen Slip play though he couldn't recall it. Holmes with the connection to her cousin accorded himself the sharper image of her on stage, head hanging to one side over the bass the way it later would over turntables. Parties like Multifunk were thus reconstructed from a variety of memories. To think we passed each other on the street, on the dancefloor, never knowing we'd end up friends years later.

But Jimi was different to the Sydney people, Jimi came out of nowhere. A cleancut acne-scarred boy with a mohawk, pierced eyebrows and the barrel chest of a man ten years older drifting around the chillout of that same university party. Each could see the other wasn't having a great time, they left the party together and cruised through town looking for somewhere to go. It was about 2 am. Dense cloud cover as though rain were imminent. Holmes knew nothing about the place, he had lived down here less than a year, came into Wollongong for classes, never hung around. The town obviously boasted a handful of poofs while up on the coast Holmes was convinced he was the only one in a sea of heterosexuals, children and dykes. Meeting Jimi, he felt like a teenager again, mischievous, eager, he felt that old solidarity. The only club that stayed open late was closed for renovations and they stood together on the main street, at a loose end, the southern sky before them aflame and smoking. Another blue-orange jet shot into the clouds from one of the tall thin chimneys in the distance. Holmes was disoriented. You've never been to the steelworks?! Jimi exclaimed. Let's go.

They drove down through Coniston where Jimi grew up, past his childhood house, past the cemetery, closer and closer to the apocalyptic sky that smothered the whole landscape in a hot sultry glow. There were candles burning in the cemetery, little shrines carefully attended. Dad's buried there. He was a steelworks man. How old were you? Ten. I couldn't understand why they had to take the body away then bring it back when it was going to be buried across the road. I wanted the whole ceremony to take place in the cemetery, I loved the cemetery.

They turned onto the empty highway and drove alongside the steelworks, then turned again towards the harbour. I can't think of one single culture that thinks it's okay to live close to a burial ground, mused Holmes. The housing's cheaper dummy. And I wouldn't call my background a culture. They were inside the whole complex now, all orange and blue lights and silver grey buildings, smokestacks spewing forth plumes of dense white steam, the cumulus dissipating in the glowering sky. They drove inside the ever increasing hum of industry past yards crammed with cranes and earth-moving equipment, past small silver tanks emerging like bombs from vast corrugated iron warehouses, then stopped at the end of a little road in front of a row of massive gas tanks. Before them was the coke-making section.

Jimi turned off the ignition and lit a joint. They were completely alone. The stench was incredible. Doncha love the smell of fossil fuels? That's our planet, burning itself to death. Jimi put his hand on Holmes's crotch.

Holmes followed him through an old gateway down to the cyclone fence that separated them from the blast furnace. High above them rose the jumble of smokestacks all different heights belching steam in a random orchestration, then the crisscross of stairways and along the front two levels of railways carrying wagons of coke. They stood in the hot orange light with their fingers linked in the wires and watched a wagon fill with coal, red hot, spilling, then move along fifty metres to unload, returning wreathed in smoke. Jimi insinuated his shorter body in front of Holmes who pressed into Jimi's arse, one hand around the front stroking the bulge in Jimi's jeans, the other up through the coarse hair across his belly. A top wagon went in for another load, flames burst out and the thud came through the ground into their bodies. They went in further, past the Private Property Security Cameras In Use signs, across a set of railway tracks, closer to the blast furnace and its interconnecting labyrinth of walkways, tubular covered conveyor belts and railway tracks on three levels. Then Jimi dashed across a small open space and disappeared around the side of a small container. Holmes couldn't see him, he ran into darkness, ran straight into Jimi. Jimi had his cock out.

Now, closer, the noises came over them. The bleeps of turning vehicles clank of metal grind and sigh of wagons loading and unloading, the all-encompassing roar of enormous exhaust vents and way off in the distance snippets of a voice over a loudspeaker. Down in this crack of darkness between container and crane Holmes wondered briefly if anyone would see them, he whispered the thought to Jimi, got more excited. Kissing Jimi now their cocks slippery with precum and spit, tinkle of coins and keys as their jeans fell around their ankles, cold steel of the container against his arse fuck where's the connie I left the fucking condoms in the car. I don't *care* Holmes just fuck me, you can't seroconvert twice, fuck me, please fuck me. And in that place of constant activity, slow, ponderous, beastly, inflamed, Holmes who hadn't had sex for months and none unsafe since diagnosis, felt when Jimi's flesh enclosed his that he was being resurrected.

A month later amid talk of haircuts, music and this hick fucking town, Holmes and Jimi drifted into friendship. Three years later they drove up to Sydney with all their belongings packed into Jimi's car and booked into the little hotel on Bourke Street.

Anna told them there was a ghost in the venue. She had been there with the workmen installing more fixtures to the bar when all the lights had suddenly gone out. They stood there in darkness all four of them, somebody saying A fuse, it must be fuse. Silent, wary, eyes adjusting to move towards repair when a dull whirring began in the DJ booth. Anna was the first to move, the layout of the venue tracked in her mind by now, stepping around the bar down the two steps across the floor to the whirring sound. She stood on tiptoes and peered over to find the pencil light illuminating two spinning turntables. My blood ran cold, she said. She turned back to the benighted bar then the lights came on again and one of the workmen checked the fuse box. Nothing out of place. Okay, Anna walked back over to them, I give in. Addressing the spirit, not them. The workmen sniggered. The next week the fridge doors were all open when they arrived in the afternoon, a mysterious wet patch stained the middle of the dancefloor. I give in, said Anna to the spirit, what do you want us to do?

Don't worry! she said to the Panic promoters, we brought a team of spiritualists in to exorcise the spirit. Ten of them, no less. All of different religious persuasions or none at all, equally adept in their own ways of reaching the spirit world. Pacing around the venue, touching the walls pausing here turning there in search of the presence. A consensus was met along the wall around the DJ box. One of the spiritualists took Anna over, bade her hold her arms up and place her palms on the dark red concrete. I felt, I swear, a trembling, a charge, some kind of weird energy coming through the wall at me. I left the room for the exorcism.

traffic didn't agree with the exorcism, if a spirit was there how could any mortal drive it away. She thought the answer was coexistence and liked the idea of a spirit in the venue. If it was a happy spirit, it would bring them good luck. If it was unhappy, their party would console it. Billy wasn't fazed either, the Newtown venue where two Slut Cities had taken place had a ghost as well. The owners had shown them photographs of the walls stripped back for renovation. Here, down the brickwork stencilled by an old staircase, a falling figure clear as a

53

shadow, the figure of a woman. A ghostly imprint of the place's history, once an illegal gambling den whose cuckolded owner shot his wife as she fled down the stairs to her lover.

Everybody had a ghost story. Shifty's Malaysian grandmother communed regularly with hers, the ghost a part of the family. Jimi as a teenage goth had conducted rituals in the Coniston cemetery to lure out ghosts. Stash told them of a woman in a yellow dress who appeared in the kitchen of the Kings Cross venue where he'd run a techno night years ago. Stash was convinced it was the ghost of Juanita Nielsen and lit a stick of nag-champa each week, blessing her when he came in to set up. The week he forgot, one of the speakers blew and the door count didn't cover wages. But Holmes was sceptical. A spirit, he theorised, was a good scapegoat for the failure of a night. Mr Hyde agreed with him, the Professor disagreed. Everybody had a ghost.

traffic offered to do a glassie shift in the cellar bar in order to better flyer Panic. She liked the staff down there. Apart from Craig there was Jason a leatherboy, Gary a law student and Shane a designer with purple hair and a scar that ran the length of his entire arm from a childhood car accident. Out on the floor instead of on display behind the bar, she was the selector. She was inside the cinema of clientele or in the corner by the bar watching from afar. Round after round, quiet then busy then quiet again. If there was a cute girl on the other side of the room traffic had a good reason to keep walking past her. It was the best bar on a Saturday night. Street, diverse, warm. Always somebody with a good vibe. Even on alcohol a gay crowd was prone to conviviality. On recovery Sundays it got good and messy, all the staff in sunglasses jaws clenched, at least one pair of knickers on the floor by sunset. These were the shifts that yielded the best booty at cleanup, drugs sunglasses foreign cigarettes of tourists, once a red rubber jacket that nobody came to claim. traffic was short enough to move easily through the smoke and noise and bodies, glasses racked up against her torso. She had hardly trained her body in the decade since high-school diving yet through menial work and congenital hyperactivity had retained muscularity, so in the darkness the men often thought she was a boy. Their eyes lusting over, approaching retreating approaching again when she smiled, never was she treated with such deference and affection. The night she packed, in chaps and her Tom of Finland T-shirt, some of the men cruised her heavily while others were disturbed to anger. traffic glided away. The boy glassies, especially Gary who was black, got sick of the nonstop sleaze factor but traffic was not so much object as subject in this homo universe, neither man nor woman enough to threaten them though some feared both in her. traffic played up to it. She flirted all night if she felt like it. Otherwise she switched off the clientele as you do a light and communicated only with the towering glasses full ashtrays dirty tables. The faces for the seconds it took to request passage. If the bar DJ was good not even the crowd had to be good for the shifts to pass in pleasure, but if the music was bad she was trapped inside of the worst job in the world.

The smallest events took so long to prepare. Everybody lent a hand. Bee and Bella offered to dress up and hand out lollies, the boys offered to do a show and Shifty in her green Mazda Esmerelda drove Billy out to Rosebery where an old cable place threw away their rubbish already sorted. From the piles Billy selected five sheets of fine tin and secured them to the roofrack for the ride home.

Following Billy's directions earlier in the week, traffic and Holmes had cut out, painted, then riddled with bullet holes four human targets to be placed around the dancefloor. A fan of Mexican folk art, Billy added to the props a plan to cut skeletons from the tin. After dinner when the dance music programmes came on air, she began to draw shapes onto the metal, starting with homo sapiens, morphing into mermaids, centaurs, satyrs and other mythical creatures. traffic and Holmes followed her with the tinsnips, cutting the skeletons into sections, giving them mobility when they were later joined with rivets. Holmes whose work day began the earliest crashed on the couch at 3 am.

4 am, halfway through, traffic cutting in gloves now over bandaids over cuts. She stopped for a cigarette, leant on Billy's shoulder and watched her working. Oh wow, that one's wearing a skirt. It's a party frock!
      Apparently they sell for about one cent in Mexico. Maybe they use machines.
      Meanwhile, back in Australia, slave labour continues . . . Couldn't we just wriggle our noses and they'd be magically all done?
      No traffic. The magic happens after. Witches *work*, y'know.

5.30 am, exhausted, in bed.
      Guess what?
      What?
      I love you.
      How weird! I was just thinking the same thing.

She yelled it next time, right out across the venue on Saturday as they hung the skeletons over the dancefloor. I love you! Billy up the top of the ladder bright red, delirious, everybody laughing. They draped the bar with police ticker tape and toxic waste warnings. Begged cajoled and pleaded with management to let them draw on the parquet body shapes with fluorescent chalk that would be danced away by morning if they got enough through to cover costs. Fit bins in every toilet along with the safe sex packs Holmes had brought from work by the carton, taped on the walls in the shape of winking eyes. Leaving a few hours to take home food and have a disco nap, traffic the heliotrope asleep in the sun patch, Billy behind her, face pressed between her shoulderblades. Then they got up got dressed and waited for Jimi who came over to trade haircuts given earlier in the week for two grams of speed. At night the temperature didn't fall.

Good evening parents. Tonight I'm gonna take you on a tour of Club
Bad, where all the bad little kiddies go   and try   to leave   their
bodies by various means and methods – anything necessary! – some things
that you quite won't be accustomed to. So I recruit each and every one of
you, with your own individual camera, so that you can take pictures of
these bad little kiddies doing these baaad little things, for tomorrow's papers.
So whip out your fifteen dollars and prepare to enter . . . **Club Bad.**

Three body bags were carried onto the dancefloor, little circles of dancers forming around them. Soon the shapes inside began to move, the zippers open. First out was a catlike person, all in white, white mask and two pointed ears. Tall and gangly, probably the Professor, unfolding his stiff limbs, ghoulish black circles for eyes little gaps of nose and mouth. Next to him something mechanical, metallic, bristling close-fitting headdress, spine of spikes and stumps for hands. That would have been Turkish Jim. The third creature, the smallest, resembled a headless chicken with skinny red legs and masses of dirty white moth-eaten plumage. James. With difficulty they climbed out of their bags and staggered among the partygoers. Then the white cat lurched back to his bag rummaged for a while till he found a collection of large red spots which he began to stick to his body. The mechanical creature found two tiny fans in his bag and attached them to his stumps, the chicken found his head. Complete and coordinated they moved through the entire venue, the mechanical creature with fan hands held forward to all the hot faces.

Holmes was at the cash register, traffic was stamping. Frocked up painted up they rocked up in droves, by 1 am there were hundreds, by 3 the doors were closed. Friends full of congratulation, acquaintances trying to get in cheap or free trying to push past traffic in the entrance, couldn't even see through them to the stairs. Extended family who'd happened on one of their small parties, people who'd heard Mr Hyde or just heard of him, Skunk's fans the Heresy crowd, Stash and his raver friends and later the mistresses from Utopia in full kit. Holmes was happy to work the desk in the busiest hour. That way the crowd filed past one by one in close up. Gary in a harness dancing fast and perfect, a sprinkling of other leatherfolk, the girl with red glitter eyebrows extending the length of her shaved temples, the classic butch femme couple, the sequinned fat drag shimmying determinedly inside the remainders of a chalk outline, the boy in lime green mini and wig, bodies undressing kissing sweating. The party was full and the music peaking, there was too much distraction, too much to look at. So when Holmes came off the door at three to see the fandancer he found himself unable to go any further than the dancefloor.

Eventually he went to the women's toilets for a solitary piss but every cubicle was full of people doing drugs and sex, there must have been at least three of them in the disableds. So he checked the safe sex packs, went back into the men's to do the same, had a piss whilst checking himself in the mirror seeing a cute boy checking him as well. Waiting for a cubicle kissing the boy stroking him, then inside shut the door. He could hear Skunk in the cubicle adjacent cutting up lines with a friend. Sorry 'bout that. Didn't they give you a free list? Yeh but only one. The boy was a good sucker, strong deep mouth, Holmes all the while hearing Skunk's complaints at not having four freebies. I'm fucken over the alternative scene, especially those smartarse lesbians like traffic. *Who?* Snorting. I prefer trains. Holmes unable to shut his ears, bent down and kissed the boy. Sorry, gotta go. On his way out of the toilets he was ambushed by Anna. He didn't know what to do. He went to get Billy.

Anna wants to close.

What! Billy was into the office before he could say anything. Are you *serious*? Have you seen the crowd out there? So much for your late licence.

You should know the laws regarding performance. I didn't find the last show very funny.

What?

Those two girls. Julie and whatshername.

Look, I don't know what you're talking about. I've been on the door. And we don't dictate to our performers what they can and can't do.

I'm sorry, we have to close.

You close us and you're name is *dirt*. You'll never put on anything in this community again.

Billy went and emptied the cash register. She paid Skunk then Bliss and Genie who had just come off stage. Put Mr Hyde's money in an envelope which she gave to the Professor on his way out from the kitchen they had hijacked for a dressing-room, put the rest into a cash box and locked it. The party stayed open and Mr Hyde continued.

traffic was dancing near the DJ box with the Professor and a man in a green latex shirt. When the Professor moved back a step traffic saw a phone on the floor. The Professor said It's a toy, I've seen them in the kiddies' section at K-Mart. traffic bent over and picked it up. Suddenly the phone started to ring. Hillooooo! traffic fluted. What? I can't hear you! Oh. Just a minute. She passed it to the Professor. Phone for you Daryl, it's the babysitter. Professor Daryl listened for a minute then spoke wearily. Just give them some heroin. It's in the bottom drawer. Then dropped the phone back onto the floor. The man in the latex shirt danced over, Can I make a quick call?

The long deep late set when the crowd thinned to family, Fred brought the lights down and pumped out more smoke till the dancefloor thickened into disappearance. Mr Hyde saw the whiteness closing in as if the bottle had been polished and he was issuing forth now playing like a demon. Torch over the turntables the last light remaining, fingers from the dials to the rim of vinyl lifting and replacing. He was playing outside of himself and everything he'd known, all the sex horror and ecstasy flowed together in a sea of celebration, the charge you could get when your playing peaked exactly like lust. Sirens distorted, babies crying, fog horns on a harbour, a woman's sob cut midinhalation, sundry trippy sci-fi space sounds. Kookaburras slotted perfectly on the beats as they whooped in unison, then fell out of time with the last carolling laugh. And traffic and Holmes and even Billy on the floor below him, raising their faces in thanks and triumph. It was dawn and light pressed against the badly blocked windows, the party still full, people dancing everywhere. He put on the last track and when the lights came up traffic called to him through the cheers. The new voodoo dancemaster of Sydney has been *launched*!

traffic went down to the Tunnel of Love, through the long airless shop to the peepshow up the back. A flickering of beads where the corridor turned. She moved between the violet painted rooms, looking for a space. The other girls' things everywhere. Sushi, tin of guava juice covered in Thai writing, a book about serial murderers, Issey Miyake and ashtray scent in the air. traffic had a sip of the guava juice and took out her bra to sew on the last of the sequins.

Don't finish my juice.

Sorry, I was just having a sip.

Genie took it, finished it and threw it in the bin. Packed her things in her Astro Boy satchel and took it into the room adjacent, then finished her sushi out in the corridor, thighs swinging to the beat from the peepshow room. Tall, shapely, draped in beads and feathers like a girl from Crazy Horse or the Moulin Rouge, blue glass dangling from the encrusted bra and looped around her head beneath the cone-shaped hair, Genie was a vaudeville bombshell. A different person today to the polite if distant performer at Panic ten days before. traffic had been seated on the floor at the front for their show when they came out wrapped in bandages head to foot then tantalisingly unravelled one another naked, Genie climbing onto Bliss's shoulders for the climax and releasing a high stream of piss like a red silk ribbon that most spectators ran from though a couple ran towards it mouths open. traffic sewed and talked to Genie as she unpacked her bag. Did you like the party? Which one? Panic. Oh, we didn't stay long. We're not doing drugs. It wasn't *that* druggy a party. A beep from one of the booths and Genie was gone.

traffic cut the thread, knotted it, then tried on the bra and g string. The latter sequinned with an eye after Man Ray, the former with kissing lips. She admired her intricate needlework and design, all Billy had done this time was show her some tips in the beginning. It was the time needed that had most thrown her, a stillness and meditation she was unaccustomed to, hours of sitting, squinting, pricking her fingers. But now it was finished, and finished well, she felt vindicated. When Genie returned traffic was dressed and fiddling with the green television. traffic suspected the ice had set long before over a grudge Billy bore against Bliss and Genie from an incident at Slut City, something catty Genie had said about Billy's designs. traffic wanted to smash it, she wanted new beginnings. And I loved your show Genie. Oh cool. The carmine shower, it was hilarious. The what? Someone was freaking out saying fuck is that *blood*. Genie put her mouth over the straw and drank, Genie la Wee-weenie, she held the backstage hilarity to herself like a secret, couldn't they tell it was just red lighting? That television's fucked, y'know, you can fiddle with it all day 'n' you won't get a better picture, reaching past traffic to retrieve her sunglasses. I'm outta here.

So when Billy arrived four hours later after the first slow shift traffic had ever had, traffic was no longer cheerful.

Genie was here before.

That must've been good for you.

It wasn't actually. Watching her lover dress, talking to the legs which Billy hated for being too fat, wanting to run her hands down them. I complimented her outfit and she ignored me, I complimented her Panic show and she glowered at the mention of the piss, I was going to compliment her dancing but by then it was too late. traffic snorted.

That's a lot of compliments.

She couldn't take them.

She doesn't need them.

Anyone needs feedback. I haven't got any qualms about telling someone I like their work. I don't care what she's like, the Panic show was up there with the best. I like her as a promoter, Heresy's a really good party most of the time,

She can't take all the credit for that.

and she is a spunk.

Why defend her when she's such a bitch? D'you wanna fuck her or something? Somebody oughta put her back in the bottle.

I'm not de*fend*ing her for chrissake! but traffic couldn't help laughing.

Their poison stayed shut in. traffic had been playing something German from Mr Hyde. Hollow, metallic, funky. Billy wanted to put on Sasha and Digweed. An argument reignited by the time she was dressed, they spent the entire shift dancing and shouting at one another. It was Billy who had brought traffic to work down here a year ago, wide-eyed, trepidatious, somewhat giggly. traffic had soon taken on two shifts of her own, throwing herself into it as fulsomely as any other venture, seeing more extracting more than had ever occurred to Billy. Earning more within one month than Billy and most of the other girls and doing two strips a week in the cinema whereas the peepshow room alone was more than enough exposure for Billy. Billy had always thought it was she who patronised traffic, now she saw it was the other way around. They didn't touch each other once. They made heaps of money.

They walked back up to Surry Hills a metre apart, traffic stopping at a shop for juice. Coming back out to see Billy, still outrageously made-up surrounded by men from the corner pub. They were following her in a pack, yelling, Scum, ya fucken scum. traffic caught up and they extricated themselves to walk the rest of the way home holding hands.

What a perfect ending to a really excellent day. I haven't been hassled for over a year now.

Makes you feel like you're alive, hey?

Keeps up my immunity.

What about my sequinning, by the way.

What about it? It's great.

Thank you Billy.

I'm sorry baby, honestly. Honestly, you did great . . . We've got some leather in you know. Colours. They're fantastic. I want you to come and have a look, I have to get started on your birthday outfit.

I've been thinking red and green.

If we do another party, I'll use it as my deadline.

She wanted for herself all the ideals she saw in others. A lover like Bee or Shifty with whom to enjoy the sex appeal of strangers, the single status of Holmes and the freedom it gave him. The fresh excitement of Jimi who was just discovering the pleasures of perversity. traffic wanted the bulwark of James and the Professor's domestic history alongside their agreement of sexual independence. She wanted somebody like Stash as a brother, a kinky straight boy whose world enmeshed happily with her own, that tacit support might replace fear and explanation. A mother like Mrs Stanislawski who cheered on Stash and Bee as they went against the grain. She wanted Turkish Jim's artless detachment, from his calm disinterest in sex to the removal from his birthplace across the Tasman Sea. She wanted to be to have and to feel everything and everyone beyond herself.

Billy had never had much money so when her earnings rose saving was easy. Five days at the shop, one or two peepshow shifts, almost a thousand a week if she made someone an outfit or if traffic and she got a bulk order of speed on a party weekend from Neil at the leather shop. Panic had been successful in every way but financial though in inspired moments they dreamt of making more the next time. Billy didn't want much. Money was necessary only for the basics. Bills, food, art materials. Everything else came from friends or the streets.

She walked the city at night thinking of others she had never seen. Towards the lights of Chinatown imagining Kowloon across Pitt Street, the Ramblas behind Taylor Square, San Francisco Bay from Jim's Beare Park window or the Statue of Liberty, but there was only fog rolling in from the Heads and the same endless deep sky, the same equivocal attitude in everybody's expression, the same declivity back down to the warehouse opening like files the different vistas of each laneway.

She imagined it all. Her lover performing behind the bar, the girl clientele minimal but most likely. She imagined her handing over their phone number, quick words and flirting the meeting of mouths. traffic in the toilets crouched before a stranger, traffic bending over, traffic's hand disappearing. At her work table cutting the trousers, finishing the applique on the jerkin, stitching the diamond onto the codpiece, obsessing about the body which would fill this outfit and all of its hypothetical betrayals. Out again past midnight, senses in every direction, every street transformed by nocturnal shadows. Moonlight, streetlights, footsteps behind, another pile of rubbish set aside the loot. Old clothes, a wok, a lamp in need of wiring, a set of tiny wooden drawers begging for a paint job. Buttons, bags of them, hundreds and thousands of plastic buttons, huge, all colours! She could make an entire outfit from those buttons, buttoned up, she imagined traffic's wry comment. Down a laneway through the corridor of scents from small lush gardens like jewels behind the paling. Frangipani jasmine belladonna honeysuckle, collecting flowers between her fingers. To a pub for cigarettes, the R'n'B crowd smiling through smoke and the band's drunken number following her back outside. You're sixteen, you're pregnant, it ain't mine.

Dawn, autumn, rain lashing iron. traffic returns from the bathroom and burrows under the covers, moves up Billy's thighs, puts her mouth over Billy's clit, slowly, slowly. Billy wakes up coming.

Billy went into a Claude Cahun phase. Got a book from traffic for her thirty-third birthday, got lost in the world hidden between its covers, and so began to emulate the 1920s artist. She coloured in nipples on a long-sleeved white top, between them wrote I'm In Training Don't Kiss Me around a pair of giant puckered lips. Slicked kiss curls down her forehead, applied layer after layer of carmine lipstick and gunmetal eyeshadow to the heights of her thin painted brows, sealed blood red lovehearts on either cheek. Then improvising further turning the reds to blues, the lovehearts to spirals, washing wetting and restyling her hair. Inverting the kiss curls, pulling them up and out, spiking and sculpting, she turned heads in the streets. Billy turned heads wherever she went. People looked at her in wonder in fear and often in contempt. And traffic fell in love with her bravery all over again.

In a side street cafe they meet to discuss the next party, Billy and traffic holding hands under the table like new lovers. A lunchtime meeting for Holmes and Billy, breakfast for traffic.

Three shows again. Stash and Bella, Bee and Ben, and the fan dancer.

DJs the same.

Holmes is cautious.

I don't know about Skunk.

Well if he doesn't want to play, we'll just get someone else. There're heaps of people starting to get into this music.

What's the problem anyway?

I heard a rumour.

Oh, here we go.

Hear the one about the blind skunk?

You told me at the party traffic, when we were doing the door?

So now I'm telling Billy.

What about it?

Honestly, we don't need Skunk.

Tell me would you traffic!

Fell in love with a fart.

The meeting erupts.

Holmes can keep a secret but not tell a lie. They badger and beg him to reveal the toilet gossip. When he finally cracks, traffic says she'd catch trains *everywhere* if only the tracks were laid, and Billy is silent. A week later she snaps, I don't align myself with *any* scene, thank you very much.

They had wanted originally to have music beyond the usual house but Chrissy is too busy running Playschool and there is still no queer club or party that features harder, deeper, progressive music. Holmes thinking of Slip all this time but she is invisible to Sydney, the little doofs and private raves she has begun to play on the coast too far removed. Placing too much importance on his unimportance Holmes is disinclined to promote his own taste in music and for two weeks after Panic where Slip handed him a tape he agonises over whether or not to mention her. Then he takes the tape, still warm from playing, out of the niche it has occupied in his walkman all this time and brings it over to a meeting at the warehouse. While traffic and Billy serve dinner and draw up party plans he slides it into the second pocket of traffic's twin cassette sound system. The stereo on auto reverse, by the time it shifts over to Slip's tape Bee is home with flowers and chocolates from a client, commanding their full attention. But the box is *huge*, what did you do to him? Shat on him. Mmm, lucky guy. traffic chooses a chocolate. At the end of the table a groan from Holmes. Bee speaks up. He earned it, I respect poo men. Urk, they're soft-centres, I think he should be punished for that. One by one, Billy's half bitten rejects refill the box. Is there a fudge? I'll have a fudge. Gareth had done some B&D on the side but Holmes had been amazed when he first met Bee and Bella at how much more the women got paid. Debriefing workers, the endless vista of the hidden side of human nature. Arriving one evening at an apartment for an appointment, booked for a routine fuck with Clive a regular who surprised Holmes by suggesting a scat session. So for a hundred dollar tip Holmes sat him in the shower cubicle and forced out pellets. It was humiliating. Holmes by then was permanently constipated by his habit. Clive began to favour Gareth. An intelligent conversationalist, a good tipper and fun when he wanted to be slapped around, Clive was the first big loss for Holmes. Visiting Billy the next night with Eddy, drunk and stoned, overloud, Eddy stole some jewellery when Billy was in the kitchen and Holmes didn't see her for almost two years after that. Billy with her face buried in traffic's neck, traffic moving to the beat all of them talking over the top of it. Holmes leans towards the music.

Peter speaking, can I help you?
Holmes, you're a dark horse.
What?
It's fucking great! Who is it what is it where does it come from?
Slip, the girl I lived with down the coast. She was at the party. I tried to introduce you.

70

Well what are we waiting for? Let's get her!

What about Billy?

She nicked it to play at work today. And nooo, we won't let it out of our clutches. You thought we weren't listening, eh?

It was a wet winter. Slip was loath to go up for more than a few days, just cruise some record shops and maybe catch a film. She got soaked on the run from Darlinghurst to Central, flat plastic bag of vinyl shoved under her jacket. Got lucky and happened on an overheated train, thick with drying clothes. Fell asleep in the outer suburbs, woke in a landscape she couldn't see, her fingerprints running cold moisture down red roofs crouched in rainfall. Subdued streets, industry, waterways, bridges, lobes of sparsely housed bush through the port, then jagged escarpment falling to the ocean, all along the horizon fogbound ocean. She ran hunched through empty streets to a garden almost knee deep in rainwater. And inside the letterbox, nearly soaked through, another tape from Holmes. Mr Hyde's Spells for Bad Kiddies.

Listening to Mr Hyde was like travelling in darkness. An acid techno darkness etherised with trance and random samples. Rippling pulsating, black water surrendering fluoro motifs like first life or aliens. Sudden shapes of sound loomed then disappeared, you were moving so fast you hardly had time to see them before they'd gone. In a moonscape a tree, skeletal dying gone, and there a horned animal, leaping to coverage. Flashing, teasing, so you chased the music as it chased you.

Holmes had been sending her tapes regularly since moving back up to Sydney. They arrived with no notes, just one or several words. She sometimes didn't know if he had written the title or the artist or the label. Autechre, Illuminate the Planet, System 7. ReactTest Art of Trance Techno Slut Audio Psy Harmonics. Some of it she knew already. Others more clues to the racks in city record shops. Little by little the staff got to know her and a stack of new releases was set aside each time she went in.

But best of all the tapes by Mr Hyde which she neither copied nor loaned. At the kitchen table with Rhada who had moved in with her soon after Holmes's departure, Rhada stopping midsentence, What is this? It's so good! Slip knew some of Mr Hyde's material but what she mixed smoothly he temperamentally threw together. It was angular, his music, it had no prediction. It took her from what she knew towards what she didn't. He was coaxing out anomaly while Slip honed it down leaning towards simplicity. She tried to imagine the mind behind this music, anguished passionate bizarre, and unlike everybody else when she finally met James wasn't surprised to see it living in the body of a small, quiet, bearded man approaching forty. His style ranging everywhere. He didn't play genres. He played music.

But by the time the night of Panic had finally come Slip had dissuaded all expectation and her body unprepared for so much movement ached for days afterward. It was the first time she had fully entrusted herself to a live DJ in years, for the entire set he had had her in his thrall. She remembered the salient moments of beauty and absurdity. The Indonesian waiter in schoolgirl drag at her first Sydney dance party, awestruck, in heaven. The beautiful couple in corsets who shared a joint with her, all the friendly poofters. At 5 am when cigarettes were scarce, the compulsory drag in the toilets with a queue of dykes to her forty pack of Horizon. A room full of misfits who all seemed to be in love, the props the lights the shows, what shows. And most of all the music.

A gale could blow for a week on and off, wind shearing the beach to a tabula rasa, lifting the sand like a desert storm. It silted up the car park fifty metres from the water's edge. The sea so churned up it couldn't organise waves. High up the beach debris accumulated. The bloated, spiked corpses of stone fish heavy as melons, driftwood, coal. Spume that wobbled like blubber on the edge of receding waves, breaking into chunks of flying polystyrene, vanishing on contact into grit on wet skin. One approaching figure, hunched and hooded, trying not to run in front of the weather. Slip leant into the headwind, sideways for forwards.

She woke from a dream where there was no music, just water, water everywhere. A wave loomed out of the sea, silently rushing her. It was Holmes's dream, left behind with the faded textbooks, tapes, T-shirts, broken coffee plunger. Two more weeks to get a set together, already sleepless nights of anxious dreams. She woke to the blue of dawn in a sweat beneath the wave. Couldn't get back to sleep again. She got up carefully so as not to disturb the cats and stepped into yesterday's jeans. Walked out into stillness, no birds, no sun, no movement on the sea. It was about six o'clock. She turned south and walked along the rocks above an incoming tide, around to the pebbled inlet. Sat facing the horizon. Blur of cloud, waves lunging then raking back across the pebbles. A crackling sound, like fire, she always thought. Her landlocked sister said it sounded like wind through dry undergrowth. Holmes used the word blistering, like tyres on a wet road. Like fire, like water. The hot, dry sound of water, altering in every ear. To make one sound, one word, that took in its opposite and the spectrum between. To play.

Train full of football fans. The fulsome jargon of amateurs rising and falling like the graphs of an esoteric science. After a while, she can see patterns. He's fast but turns to jelly in a scrum, he's not built to be a forward. Otherwise it's a good side. St George's problem is that they don't have a big enough oval. Ex-actly. You reckon they'll merge? Will you still follow League? Norths've got problems, d'you see the game last week? They were eight nil at half time, they shoulda lost but not that badly. I follow the Saints. I'll stick my neck out and say we'll have sixteen teams next year. Hey, it's all money 'n' politics these days.

People needed something to follow, rules, a game, a language to call their own. The air loud with opinion. Everybody was an expert.

I follow the Saints.

Roger had tickets to the theatre. He arrived dressed in black to take traffic and Billy down to the harbour. It was a treat for them and they had been preening for over an hour. Since leaving home ten years before, Roger had married, had a child and made his way up the ladder of one of the city's most important conveyancing firms. And since leaving home at the same time, three years younger, traffic had worked in bars, travelled and slipped further and further away from her family. Roger had seen her with a succession of lovers but now she had lived with Billy for over a year the veil of wariness had begun to lift from his eyes. He sat at the long table telling Billy about Clive Spencer the director and the play's rave reviews while she listened studiously examining Roger for clues of his sister's idiosyncrasies.

Going into the theatre now, overdressed, too many eyes on them. The hallowed silence like a funeral or a lecture. Like waiting for an oracle. The centuries old play had been fiddled with for its contemporary audience, words like fuck and cock sending a thrill through the stalls. Blue sky behind the backdrop and brassy accents denoted a Sydney setting. By the time the young male protagonist was pretending to shoot up drugs on stage, traffic and Billy were up in the rafters whispering party arrangements.

They sat by the harbour drinking coffee afterwards.
So Roger, will you make it to this one?
You know Katherine, she's not a party girl.
You can come alone. I'll look after you.
I'm sure you will. But it's not really fair if I go out and leave her home to babysit alone.
Well you did tonight.
Come on Rodge, support your little sister!
I am, I'm taking her to the theatre with her girlfriend.
Well come to *our* theatre.
. . . What are you doing traffic?
She's flirting with the waitress.
Give me a break Billy, she's about twelve. I'm leaving her a tip.
I already gave her one.
Fifty cents isn't enough Roger.

Look at this place. They'd get paid a *fortune* here. And she wasn't that good. We had to wait for ages.

It's a shitty job and she was trying. And nobody in hospitality gets paid a fortune.

Fair enough, you'd know. I don't know how you do it actually.

He's frustrated, said Billy as they entered the warehouse. I don't mean that in a bad way, I really like Roger. I mean like, does he do anything creative? What's his wife like?

Smart. Pretty . . . And pretty dull.

Shifty and Bee were home. traffic and Billy tiptoed into the bedroom, undressed in silence. Billy lifting her top naked now but for black stockings to her thighs. Lifting so her ribs showed through the soft white stomach, then her breasts moving slowly. traffic pushed her face in there, into the hills of yielding flesh kissing sucking, slid her hands around and down, over the globes of arse up the spine. They walked to the bed like that laughing, blind and crippled. Kissing shoulder neck mouth, till Billy impatient took traffic by the wrist and pushed her hand in. Billy's mouth still now, moaning into traffic's. Afterwards traffic lit a cigarette and started to speak about her brother. Don't. Billy put a finger in her mouth. Then another, then another. Don't speak. Twirling her fingers across traffic's tongue, traffic opening and taking her thumb in as well, drinking her to the knuckles. Gagging on her hand.

No sleep, no rest, no time out in the buildup to the party. Press release, ad placement, the endless phone calls confirming these, fending off frustration when they were erroneously published or not published at all, the endless phone calls confirming performers, negotiations with other promoters over dates, searching for a projector to replace Fred's broken one, the journeys through bars clubs and parties to hand out flyers. But the excitement of strangers when handed a flyer, their raves about the first party. Out after dark spraypainting footpaths, traffic in hysterics fleeing at the sight of a cop car, stencil flapping in the wind splattering paint down her jeans.

*** STOP PRESS ***

Get off ya bum and get down to

SCUM

Hardcore camp for freaks and fetishists

of all persuasions

Saturday 21st April, 11 pm – 8am, $15

@ The Cool Room, Oxford St, Darlinghurst

DJs Mr Hyde & Slip
3 surprise shows

and remember . . .

SCUM rises to the top.

brought to you by Panic Prod.

James took the tape nervously, standing back at first, running a sceptical commentary over the top to the Professor. He listened like a predator, hunting out the tricks and weaknesses, she was too sparse too reticent, the tracks not closely enough knitted. You have to admit she's good though. I know Daryl I'm just saying. He waited to lose his balance as the beats spread wider but there was nothing out of sync. When the next track swung in fully he realised she'd been perfectly in time all along. He stepped into the music the second time loose, stayed the full revolution with his guard down. They listened to the tape for days on end, the end meshing with the beginning so you could enter her story at any point and still travel its entire length. This house was never silent in James's presence, the small crowded rooms echoing day and night, sounds from the stereo filtering and cueing all communication. He wondered how it would be living without Daryl, he tried to imagine solitude, coming home to an empty house. His mind burrowed back inside the music. Adrift in new sounds that bled across the house like a digital image, him at the controls like a muezzin. Light stands became minarets, doors were archways the walls a dusk horizon till halfway through side 2 James realised he was in a city at night, skyscrapers looming over him. The invisible landscapes of music. There were things it took him several hearings to perceive. He appreciated this, something that grabbed his attention while eluding him, demanding more scrutiny. He played the tape again.

Slip started out playing bass in a band. She was fifteen when she first decided that this was what she wanted, a Canberra girl visiting her cousin Eddy. Down the dark end of Riley Street near William, Darlinghurst quiet like a village asleep, Eddy finished his long neck and threw the bottle into the car park of a modern apartment block. Jo followed his tall skeletal figure up some stairs into a room full of people drinking and yelling and jumping around to the XL Capris' thrashing version of My City of Sydney. It was her first trip to Sydney alone.

Years later when full of wine at a family Christmas and playing in a semi-successful band, Jo cornered Eddy to reminisce. He was a month clean and embarrassed. That song, that night, he'd relegated to the scrapheap of teenage rage. More years down the track, Eddy dead and her a year diagnosed, Jo was cornered in a cafe by an old band acquaintance who wanted to reminisce about the same Darlinghurst past. Some guy now in television with a wife and kid, talking about the good old days, saying did she still play? Jo was obsessed with healing and embarrassed. Those times were over and she had moved on. Yep, said the television man. You can't do it forever. Work, kids, you know what I mean. But those were the days. And Jo looked at him with his brand new trainers, his pot belly and air of regret and nostalgia, and knew it was wrong. Wrong to enter a no fun zone, wrong to equate maturity with domesticity, sensibility with staidness. She looked at him and saw it all then went back home to her quiet life, re-emerging years later as Slip the DJ.

She was out of home, out of Canberra and on a Greyhound to Sydney as soon as she was out of school. When the bus pulled into Kings Cross the streets were steaming in a sudden horizontal sun. Jo waited on the footpath amongst her bags and the smells of rancid food, alcohol vomit and cheap perfume. Eddy wasn't there. Jo waited anyway, for someone or something she didn't know. Dusk turned to night and Jo wanted to walk but with two bags and a nervous heart, she caught a cab instead to Eddy's house down near the hospital. From the overpass the city dipped suddenly under a red western sky. New city, new weather, a climate that entered your skin like a transfusion, a virus. She surrendered.

Sometimes she went with Eddy to gay clubs. To Patches where she felt intimidated as one of the only women. Or else they went to the Berlin Club or Stranded where there were kids with coloured hair and piercings, the sex in the air going in any direction, the music more experimental. Here they felt more at home. Three more months before she would be legal, Eddy older but not solicitous. I don't know what I'm doing after, if you lose me just get a cab home. OK?

Once they went to an impromptu Dead Kennedys concert in a burnt-out terrace in Redfern. She watched fascinated as Eddy got ready, gelling his hair, looping the shoulder straps of his leather jacket through the Mercedes hood ornaments he had prised off cars in his parents' street, sticking a nappy pin through his septum. She watched the wince in his long-lashed eyes as the metal entered his face. Obsessed for weeks then one day when he was out sterilised Eddy's nappy pin with the flame of a bic, pulled out her septum and drove the pin through. Held onto the bathroom sink and looked at herself through the hot bolt of pain. Fuck it, it was crooked. She wore it around the house anyway, giggling privately for over an hour. The rush longer and deeper than any chemical's. When Eddy came home the nappy pin was back in the bathroom cupboard and Jo had two new earrings in her left earlobe.

It took forever to restore to the past its several colours. Only distance afforded a view of more variety. All across her history in deeds or the subsequent flight from them, Slip saw so many mistakes and so much misfortune that nothing seemed worth keeping, everything was tainted by death and failure. She saw this in Holmes, she saw it the first night he was at the house when they sat on the verandah in shy conversation. But couldn't explain the increasing suspicion that in health and stability it was just as easy to be stuck in a cycle of escape and obliteration.

She was always at her stereo, cruising the dial for the best programmes. Fiddling through static for community radio that played music not words. She struck a late show of electronica and edited out the announcements, pushing pause with the remote while writing down track names. What for she didn't know, she had no money to buy music. Lost the paper on which she wrote the tracks, but years later was still listening to this entire broadcast. A piece that put her on a coast road every time she heard it, waves of chords flowing deep into the track, streaked with high notes like sunlight on water, the ghostly entrances and exits of a huge soprano choir. She listened over and over asking is it real or is it synthetic? It was coming at her through the speakers, it was sound, it was real.

She fell upon Holmes's early house compilations, he only had a handful, and listened over and over, turning the knob full volume while he was out of the house. A visceral seduction, she cleaned the house dreaming in rhythm till her ears could lift the trails of one track from the next and omit those that grew thin with constant listening. Sometimes she thought she knew which she would have bought and played if she ever got around to trying those old turntables of Eddy's.

Space Time Continuum was the sound of summer nights. Crickets and trickling water, waves on a distant beach. Swimming through darkness along the liquid organ line shifting then down a plucked bass octave. She wanted to get inside this music, travel its underlay of eery breathing and freaked-out voices. All sounds were part of the one timeless world, there was no such thing as beauty or ugliness, every sound told a story.

Her father dead a year and Eddy half as much again, Slip was coming out of sickness when Holmes moved into the house. She'd lived here already for six months alone. Went to work, watched the weather, the sun moving across the sky. Watched her small wage and inheritance trickle along the arteries of food and rent. She needed spare dollars, she needed a housemate. She wanted to be inside music again.

She sets up the turntables, stacks the records along the carpet below. Skirts around them apprehensive, leaves the room and shuts the door. For three days she speaks to no one, enough food to avoid the shop. She walks along the beach, watches the tides come and go, looks into her memory for riffs she once played or knew by heart from other bands' favourite songs. But there is nothing.

The moon wakes her the third night and she lies there listening. Silence, absence, the beginning and the end. She throws off the doona and pushes the pillows away from her head. Lies back in darkness, ears beaming outwards through the cold blue air. Somewhere on the edge sounds are moving. Sea zippering wind through eucalypt canopy, leaves scattering along the narrow side path, the high groan of a truck taking a dogleg beneath the escarpment, endless clatter of a long slow coal train. And close like a skin the creaking house around her. Inside it all her blood pulsing through her body, liver, brain, heart. She's breathing, she's awake, she can hear, she's alive.

She went up to Sydney to attend a basic workshop then started to play with her small record collection, to slot the tracks into one long movement. It was a different way to make music. The ears got tired. You could complain of a sore back as with the long cafe hours, but Slip was accustomed to working standing up. There weren't however the excuses of unfamiliar fingering or slack embouchure, the music didn't rely on the pulley system of tendons or depth of lungs. Sleight of hand, yes, and memory infinite memory, the minute quantities of each notch on each dial for each nuance in each track storing slowly inside her fingertips. But the demands of DJing were placed first and last on the ears, and the imagination between them.

house
house music
garage deep house
tribal dirty latin progressive
hardhouse happy house hiphouse
acid house tech house vocal jazz house
Stockhausen handbag cheese anthems gay
house full house haunted house techno acid techno
trancetechno tinny techno goa rave industrial techno
electro techno chipmunk techno trance deep trance hard
trance ambient trance psychedelic trance acid trance spooky
kooky sick trance smacked-out trance technotrance dark abstract
filtered minimal metabass trance funky trippy twisted high ground
underground electronic dance music dance music electric eclectic
electro electronica fucked up fully worked punked up beats breakbeat
bigbeat fuck beats jungle drum'n'bass hip-hop trip-hop strip-hop clip-clop
non-stop rap NRG high NRG sydney detroit chicago melbourne adelaide german
israeli english belgian dutch japanese swedish funk phat funk metal funk chunky
funk junglefunk jazz free jazz experimental jazz fusion acid jazz afro jazz
swing dixieland bigband ragtime honkytonk bebop blues r'n'b soul
black hole rock'n'roll rock folk rock clit rock cock rock hard rock
glam rock metal heavy metal grunge powergroove dub neo
-dub electro dub dancehall roots ska reggae ragga rai
gabba socca bangra samba rumba calypso tango
flamenco disco retro disco tuff disco psycho
audio disco à go-go vamos amigos juju
boogaloo voodoo who do senVoodoo
full-bore hardcore slamming
pumping
dance music
dance music
dance music

Freakie Plastiquie

I think therefore I ambient.

84

James:

When I first came to Sydney I worked at a place called Flo's. It was 1979, I was seventeen. Moving wasn't such a big deal to me, it seemed inevitable. My mother from Chile, my father an Australian, we'd packed our bags and got on a plane the hell out of Santiago when I was too young to know the details but not the feeling of real political fear. Queensland wasn't the best place for dissent either, I got poofter-bashed twice by yobs and once by the police. Soon after that I got a bus down from Brisvegas, been in Sydney ever since. Oh yeah, I can tell you some stories.

In those days you had to eat to get a drink because of the licensing laws. (Some things never change, eh?) Flo's was this tiny place on the south side of Oxford Street. It was near . . . let me see . . . a block up from the Cool Room? It was tiny but the crowd was quite diverse. All the drag queens used to come there. This was in the days when all the venue operators were dealers. Some of them still are, how old-fashioned. But maybe that's just my age, and Sydney. Anything that lasts seems old-fashioned.

So, Flo's. You'd come in and order your hamburger or whatever from the food counter, and the different sorts of food available were code for whatever drugs you wanted. You'd see these people coming in and ordering hamburgers with the lot, or hot chips or a sambo, then throwing the food into the bin and walking straight out again. Or straight into the toilets to do their drugs, then straight out again. (More like crooked out again.)

I worked at Saddletramps too, that was the new Exchange bar. I was still underage and lied to get the job. It took me till I was eighteen to realise the place was full of teenagers and most of the staff didn't really give a shit. They had those saddle things as bar stools, you can imagine people trying to sit on them when they were out of it. And the big deer horn candelabra. Very nice.

I liked French's and the Oxford when it was still a rough punk place. Full of sweet young androgynous boys, a few hardcore fags. Till one night me and Fred went down to French's and the whole vibe had changed, it was really hostile or something. We didn't stop to ask questions, just got out of there quick smart and never went back.

The staff from Saddletramps'd usually end up at Patch's for a drink

85

after work. DJing wasn't taken so seriously then. Half the music was golden oldies but we had a lot of fun. Oh, but I loved the uplit chequerboard floor. It wasn't that there was no good music being made, just that you wouldn't hear much of it in gay clubs, (like I said, some things never . . .) apart from maybe Kraftwerk down at Stranded or something like that.

Still, there was something about the street back then . . . There was something more special about being gay when it was illegal, though it's probably very politically incorrect to say so.

You know, I've realised I'm not really gay. I just like fucking men.

Oh, young man!

This is the last time I'm doing this, Billy mixing up breakfast the day of the party.

What, no more parties?

I mean better organisation so we don't have to speed for a bloody week to get everything done.

It was the outfit that did it, I'm so sorry about that.

That was my fault, Christ I've had months.

I hate how we have to hide in here when we're doing drugs.

It's just easier traffic. You know what Bee's like.

Sharp clean rise through her nasal passages, sweat trickling from armpits. She placed her fingers on the glistening path down traffic's spine, traffic's skin varnished with months of it, back tightening as she bent to the bottom drawer. Almost two weeks since their last fuck and Billy felt the old lust rising. But there was too much to do.

They had dreamt up this outfit together. Not black, something different, can you do applique? Gee you've got expensive taste. Is it too much of a hassle then? No traffic, but it's the *feel* of it I need to know, the shape. I mean what do you want to look like? I don't know. Well, what do you feel like? Like an idiot, a fool. I feel like the court jester. And Billy looked through books studied films and ruminated endlessly to finalise a design. Came back from the video shop one night with a medieval drama, she and traffic both leaping up at the entrance of the coxcomb.

So that night after bump-in, dinner and half an hour horizontal with closed eyes, Billy dressed traffic head to toe in red and green leather. Tight green trousers that laced up the sides trimmed with red, a jerkin of red and green diamonds that laced up the sides as well, green skullcap with an open zig-zag down the centre for the red crest of hair, red cod piece with a green diamond in the middle. A pair of flat pointy shoes found in the street, sprayed red with car duco, completed the attire. While Billy laced her up, traffic leant over to kiss her on the back of the neck. I honestly think this is the best thing you've ever made. You're not going to have time to do that makeup you were talking about. I'll take the bag and do it at the venue. But you look pretty fucken hot without it I must say.

Come with us

Leave your wheat fields

Leave your back street shops

Your fishing boats

Leave your offices in the tall skyscrapers

Leave all that is routine and commonplace

And come with us to the wilds

Come with us to where man has never been

But where he will go

As certain as the passage of time

Come with us to the **moon**

The rocket

is waiting . . .

Slip started her set with sounds. CB radio helicopters screeching cars, and as traffic deposited the makeup bag beneath the cash desk the rhythm slid under her, like walking blind onto a moving footway. That blessed first hour when things were calm enough to take in the crowd passed in seconds. The people were slightly different to the last party, more men, more fetishists, a group of bears who laid claim to two of the couches and lolled there for the next four hours like a flokati rug. The music was too good to greet friends properly, to remember her face was naked, the party full and getting hotter, Slip's music burning. Eventually traffic would know to listen for each set's motif, like a key Slip cut out one sound and locked it into the music hour after hour, filtered, reverbed, delayed, transformed. Tonight a pounding drum break so subtle by the time the next track came on it was a whole new sound, so powerful the entire dancefloor changed direction. And Bella out here now putting the final touches to a web of red rope linking two columns, inside which Stash, his entire face and body powdered white, was cocooned like an insect. traffic watched him squirm and glower as she danced by the door, watched her own ideas until in the music and energy of hundreds dancing she saw a mask emerge. Holmes came on shift and she went into the kitchen dressing room.

Her cosmetic adventures had always been minimal, there was nobody here to help, she would have to fumble through. She began with whiteface, blotted it with white powder, applied dark green around her eyes inside a crude black outline. Quickly quickly she had to get back out there. The line was crooked, too bad. Bee and Ben arrived to prepare for their show. Hey showgirls. Hey Scumbag, it's going off out there! I know and I'm not even dressed yet. D'you guys need the mirror? No, we're wearing hoods. So traffic continued to follow the images that had surfaced by the dancefloor. Drew two high eyebrows in black, the centre of the left one veering to mimic the edge of the skullcap. A wide, full Leigh Bowery black mouth, a narrow green stroke down her chin, a small black tripod on her right cheek. There, that was it, she had arrived at a new persona. The stranger in the mirror tried a few faces, a grimace, a smile, a frown, delight, then turned with a flourish to greet Bee and Ben who were too busy stuffing their orifices to notice. I'll come back and give you a ten minute call OK? and dressed, armoured, never so well prepared, traffic went back out to the party.

Like everybody else she had performed before. She had pulled looks and moved through dancefloors enhanced and altered. But nothing this developed, nothing this refined, nothing that went so far from herself that the circle kept turning till it rejoined her core. Viewed by all as the court jester not traffic, she had been liberated, as inside a wig and scant costumes when stripping. The whole party was now her stage and she moved through the dancers free from the flaws and history and responsibilities of traffic, accountable to no one, amusing to everyone. She went to the cash desk, put Slip's pay into an envelope, took it to her with water, took water to Bella and Stash, cued Fred and Slip and Mr Hyde, then went back into the kitchen to fetch Bee and Ben.

In clear latex catsuits and hoods they stalked on stage and faced off. Drew closer then jutted their heads forward and sprayed each other with a thick white spit rich as cream or a young man's cum. Each spread the silicon lube across their bodies with vigorous rubbing then Ben stood over Bee hand on crotch while Bee squatted and unzipped, thrusting and pulling something from her cunt. Stood with the gossamer square held before her like a weapon and slapped it onto Ben's shoulder. SCUM, it was the word, written in black on a dental dam, the crowd roared. And so the battle went, the aggressive circling, the squatting and spreading and working of holes, the words appearing then slapped randomly all over each other's bodies. CUNT FILTH WEIRDO LEZZO PERVERT SISSY POOF SLUT FAGGOT TRUCKER WHORE SICKO DYKE. Bee's cunt empty they advanced retreated advanced again, elegant sexy and menacing in their platform patent leather boots and catsuits, taunting each other's noses with their hands, moving their hips to the nasty techno soundtrack. Then back to back, bent over, they began to work their arseholes in tandem and one by one more words appeared. BITCH PRICK FREAK, turning now so their greasy holes faced the cheering audience, the longer words like COCKSUCKER POOJABBER

ARSEHOLE AIDS-CARRIER written on two dams glued together. Till finally finished, the sleek invective-plastered figures strutted around one another once more then turned disdainfully and exited either side of the stage.

Billy was at the bar looking for traffic when a girl in a gingham frock wielding a gingham broom stopped before her. Billy offered her some water. Just fly in did you? The girl fixed her with a glare. I've been cleaning this place all night and it's *still* filthy. She pointed to the crowd. Look at it, trash everywhere! then swept away. Billy wished the good witch would cast a spell for them. She had caught Anna's look of horror at Bee and Ben and knew now their days were numbered, maybe even their hours. But 3 am had come and gone without threat of closure and everybody was having such a good time. The bad news could wait. Bella appeared with a tray of Minties and Fantales.

traffic got a water and sat on the couch near the flokati rug, stretched her legs, arms, torso, curled her spine forward down between her knees. Now the shows were over and everybody was paid the strain of a week on her feet splintered her entire body. Then a hand was on the small of her back massaging the vertebrae one by one then her sacrum and neck. She surrendered her flesh and went into the pain. Two hands now, she whimpered against her legs, watched the feet passing, lights behind merging to sea blues and greens, and as the music darkened she came through the other side and sat up to thank the masseur. It was the man in the green latex shirt from Panic. He turned her face to the light. The coxcomb, I knew it!

He had a blue and red rooster tattooed on his left shoulder. He was the same sign as traffic, looked a dozen years older. Sinewy body, black moustache, laugh lines, naked but for an industrial light cage over his crotch. He told traffic his name and she immediately forgot it. He was a fan of Mr Hyde's from the earliest parties, he told her things about those events she had heard from the other side only. traffic enrapt leant through the lights and music to his stories, the conversation changing channels from parties to books and myths and fairytales via his tattoo of Chantecler. Then two hands on her knees. Billy. *There* you are. Your face, it's brilliant! You like it? Except I can't kiss you. traffic took Billy's hand and sucked her fingers one by one. Took the other half of Billy's ecstasy and pulled her down onto the couch.

The man with the rooster tattoo left the couch for the dancefloor and Billy and traffic stretched out in each other's arms to watch the party at groin level. The long late trashy hours, everybody in a trance, drifting dancing cuddling smiling. Boots platforms stilettos trainers wading the sea of water bottles, the flokati rug at last upright and dancing two of them naked, hands to amyl bottles in pockets up to noses back to pockets, hands on arses, swaying hips, Jimi pinned to a column by a boy in chaps eating his nipples, Holmes shirtless dancing and smiling, Slip dancing beside him, Stash crawling over from the couch adjacent grinning slyly. Crap party girls. Yeh sorry about that. It's just not good enough, you'll have to put on another one. Fair enough. But I rolled you a joint anyway. You reckon we deserve it? Think of it as a consolation prize.

They consulted a calendar and other promoters and decided on a date four months away in spring. traffic rang Anna to book the Cool Room. Phone muffled then the man's voice returned. She's just stepped out, I'll leave her a message. She rang two days later then two days later again. Anna was never there. Holmes rang a week later, Billy followed his call with one of her own. All three waited by their home and work phones but no return call came. The next week they opened the papers to see an advertisement for events at the Cool Room. A retro night on Thursdays, a lesbian night called Pandora's Box on Fridays, a gay night on Saturdays.

They had lost their venue.

UNKIND CUTS

Censors in Ohio tried to ban Treasure Island for fear it may lead children to piracy. The Marx Bros' Monkey Business was banned in Ireland in case it provoked anarchy. Bing Crosby's Going My Way was banned in some countries because it was 'unseemly' for a priest to wear a baseball cap. The Muppet Movie was cut by New Zealand censors on grounds of violence.

First birds, first light. The alarm clock bleeped. Holmes knocked over a glass reaching for it, cold chamomile tea splashed the bed. He was up and in the shower.

He caught a bus and ferry and another bus to his mother's. This little semi where he grew up had increased in value and now she could no longer afford the rates, Mrs Holmes was moving to a one bedroom flat in Manly. Half the house had been packed up, there were just the small things left. The pile of sentimental paraphernalia she didn't know whether to keep or jettison, the clothes of two decades, knickknacks, appliances. Beneath the bed in the spare room Holmes found a carton of old photographs, letters and clippings. It was the family archives. Holmes considered this, his family's entire history a warped shoe carton full of dusty yellowing paper. There were some old letters, his parents' marriage licence and Lizzy's and his birth certificates. Further into the box past 1970s vouchers for a free Whale car wash, Holmes found photographs of his great-grandfather into which his eye sank. He asked his mother if he could keep the one taken on one of the northern beaches. A tall man with a sepia tan beside an even taller board, the weight of the board holding the flat image.

He was one of the first men to surf, you know. Holmes's mother peering over his shoulder then leaving the room. She re-entered and passed him, gin wafting around her. In those days it was illegal, you know.

What, surfing?

Well yes. At the turn of the century when your grandfather was a boy, swimming in Sydney was illegal before sunset. And even men had to cover up. You couldn't go around in shorts and no top like that on a beach. So when you think about it, you're looking at a photograph of a criminal.

Laws for everything, laws against nature, laws from another country. Holmes wondered how his great-grandfather had come to surf. Whether he was a conscious outlaw or just a man whose passion happened to be illicit. Where had the passion come from, the great-grandfather a son of poor Welsh farmers who came to Australia in the 1850s. Where did he get the idea to surf, who had taught him. Deeper in the box Holmes found another photo of a man holding a board on the beach. Aboriginal or Islander. Written on the other side beneath the local newspaper's stamp, Jim O'Toole – Awabakal.

He never found out who Jim O'Toole was but heard many stories of the big wave. A tsunami some believed would one day rise from the South Pacific Ocean gathering the Tasman Sea to swamp this stretch of coast all the way to the Great Dividing Range. Holmes imagined his great-grandfather and Jim O'Toole riding out from the shadow of the wave over the mountains towards the red centre.

Warren the Rat had left his mother and though living would be difficult without his money, Holmes was glad. She was drinking too much but happy and purposeful for the first time in years. Even while they were still together she had begun to speak of Warren with contempt, whispering things to Holmes when Warren left the room. Years before, light-headed and reckless after a boozy lunch, his mother's eyes red from crying again, Holmes told her the nicknames he had always used for her second husband and she accepted the information with barely concealed delight. Ratso must have always disgusted her even if she had never had the courage to break it off. She used to put him down with the fervency of desire, he made her burn with lust which she interpreted with disgust. Just like a little girl, like a little teenage girl embarrassed by sex. Holmes had been shocked at the likelihood that at the age of twenty-three he was more sexually experienced than his own mother. Now the three of them, Holmes, Lizzy and their mother, sat around reminiscing about Ratface and other past adventures in the packed-up house. They snickered together uncontrollably. Not since Holmes had dried out had the family been so united.

Business at the shop increased tenfold during Leather Pride week. On the day of the party nobody got a lunch break and there was a permanent queue to the one cash register. Neil complained about all the yuppies wanting to look leathery but having no idea of the culture. The majority of customers had never been to a leather party and wanted only a simple accoutrement like an armband, most automatically applying it to the right. Billy would explain leather S/M protocol to them partly out of salesperson duty and mostly to amuse herself in the hectic exhausting afternoon hours. Now you know if you go to a leather party wanting to score, lots of people will read you according to dress codes. So if your armband's on the right it means you're a bottom, and if it's on the left it means you're a top. Oh really? Almost all armbands swiftly moved to the left. Of course if you switch you can wear one on each arm. Oh right. That was always a good way to sell two instead of one. The shop sold out of armbands and thousands of dollars of old stock passed over by afficionados. Oh and by way, Billy would say as they chose a bandana, there's a hanky code too . . .

So Billy, sore all over from standing for eight hours and full of contempt for the customers that would later be on the dancefloor, took to her bed on arriving home and swore that she wouldn't go to the party. It was traffic who urged her up with a massage and dinner and the offer to help finish her outfit. It had always been Billy who would help dress traffic, now traffic, having invested in her own colours and perfected the makeup for the coxcomb outfit, was the one who was ahead. Throughout her years in the shop Billy had accumulated a whole bag of damaged stock. Bandanas, for instance, that arrived badly seamed, an oversized stained skirt, chaps cut against the grain. She had consulted the most outlandish and comprehensive lists of hanky codes and bought or fabricated all those she didn't already have. Constructed a bustle with a recycled piece of costume from years ago and stitched the bandanas in cascading layers along each ridge. A small unattached pile remained on her work table and while Billy showered, traffic stitched the last of them into place. The result was magnificent, billowing behind her like a nineteenth century ballgown. Billy paraded around for traffic and Bee, who had fetched her camera.

Fur! Bee exclaimed. And on the *right*! Better watch those dogs sniffin' down the alley.

That's alright, I already got me a bitch.

traffic got down on her knees and howled.

Often the best moments were found beside the main events. The incidental, unexpected, like the comic foil bearing the truth in disguise. So that while this year's Inquisition was unremarkable its aftermath endured. Coming out of the showgrounds drugfucked in full kit to find the city that Sunday morning overrun by an international marathon now halfway down Flinders Street. They stood there stunned as thousands of fit sweating bodies pounded past them, the street thick with athletes all the way to Taylor Square. Shifty in her cop uniform scored a wink from a bemused official. Been out to a party? God no, officer. We're just normal people trying to go to work. Jimi as Brave Tart blue-streaked in a leather kilt with a blue dildo attached to his sporran approached the official who tried not to look. Where can we cross? You'll have to wait for a break, there's one coming up. They gathered on the sidelines. OK . . . now! So in uniform, kilt, bad drag, a bandana bustle, a red and green coxcomb, a welding mask corrupted into something far more fear-inspiring, and the ankle-length CD dress that Bee had borrowed from Billy, they bolted across the street before the next onslaught of runners.

Cleveland Street, 5 pm, traffic and Billy emerge from a recovery party. traffic's due at work so they wait for a cab. There are two bears across the road in matching leather shirts and jeans, long grey square-cut beards like bushrangers. They smile at traffic and Billy through the four lanes of vehicles, the girls wondering if the bears know the recovery is over. After five luckless minutes traffic and Billy run through a break in the cars to a spot further up the road and look out for a cab. The bears seem to be waiting for a cab too. There are none. They all wait, checking each other out. After a while the bears cross the road to stand where traffic and Billy were before. All four now laughing at each other through the trucks and cars and buses. Billy waving her bustle, traffic opening her coat and lying back seductively on the nearest car bonnet, the bears responding with crotch-grabbing and lewd grins. Cars keep driving by. There are no cabs. They keep themselves amused.

Hanky Codes

Worn on LEFT		Worn on RIGHT
Wants Head	Light Blue	Expert Cocksucker
Sixty-Niner	Robin's Egg Blue	Sixty-Niner
Cop	Medium Blue	Cop-Sucker
Pilot	Airforce Blue	Wants a pilot
Fucker	Navy Blue	Fuckee
Genital Torturer	Teal Blue	Genital Torturee
Catheterizer	Turquoise	Catheterisee
Fist Fucker	Red	Fist Fuckee
Dildo Fucker	Light Pink	Dildo Fuckee
Tit Torturer	Dark Pink	Tit Torturee
Double-Handed Fister	Dark Red	Double-Handed Fistee
Likes Menstruating Women	Maroon	Is Menstruating
Into Navel Worshippers	Mauve	Has Navel Fetish
Pit Lickee	Magenta	Armpit Freak
Piercer	Purple	Piercee
Rubber/Mud Top	Wine	Rubber/Mud Bottom
Likes Drag	Lavender	Drag
Pisser	Yellow	Pissee
Spits	Pale Yellow	Drool Crazy
Has 8" or more	Mustard	Wants a BIG One
2 looking for 1	Gold	1 looking for 2
Anything, Anywhere, Anytime	Orange	Not Now, Thanks
Two Tons o' Fun	Apricot	Chubby Chaser
Foot Fetish, Top	Coral	Toesucker
Cowboy	Rust	Horse
Spanker	Fuchsia	Spankee
Rent boy	Kelly Green	Looking to hire
Military Top	Olive Green	Military Bottom
Daddy	Hunter Green	Boy
Dines off Tricks	Lime Green	Dinner Plate
Humiliator	Light Green	Likes being humiliated
Mummy	Green Lace	Girl
Scat Top	Brown	Scat Bottom
Has Uncut Cock	Brown Lace	Likes Uncut Cock
Circumsized	Brown Satin	Likes Circumsized Cocks

Headmaster	Brown Corduroy	Student
Smokes Cigars	Tan	Likes Cigar smokers
HEAVY S/M Top	Black	HEAVY S/M Bottom
Brander	Black Lace	Brandee
Takes videos	Black velvet	Will perform
Bondage Top	Grey	Bondage Bottom
Latex Top	Charcoal	Latex Bottom
Actually Owns a Suit	Gray Flannel	Likes Men in Suits
Electrician	Silver	Shock Absorber
Rimmer	Beige	Rimmee
Victorian Scenes, Top	Beige Lace	Victorian Scenes, Bottom
Voyeur	White velvet	Exhibitionist
Cums in Scum Bags	Cream	Sucks it out
Beat My Meat	White	I'll do us both
Likes White Bottoms	White Lace	Likes White Tops
Likes Black Bottoms	Black/White Stripes	Likes Black Tops
Likes Latino Bottoms	Brown/White Stripes	Likes Latino Tops
Likes Asian Bottoms	Yellow/White Stripes	Likes Asian Tops
Bear	Black/Red Stripes	Cub
Vampire	Red/Black Stripes	Bloodgiver
Rapist	Orange/Black Stripes	Rape Victim
Shaver	Red/White Stripes	Shavee
Sailor	Blue/White Stripes	Looking for salt
Safe Sex Top	Black/White Checks	Safe Sex Bottom
Park Sex Top	Gingham	Park Sex Bottom
Likes White Suckers	Blue/White Dots	Likes to Suck Whites
Likes Black Suckers	Blue/Black Dots	Likes to Suck Blacks
Likes Latino Suckers	Blue/Brown Dots	Likes to Suck Latinos
Likes Asian Suckers	Blue/Yellow Dots	Likes to Suck Asians
Involved but available Top	Gold Lace	Involved but available Bottom
Group Sex	Red Lace	Group Sex Bottom
Wears Boxer Shorts	Paisley	Likes Boxer Shorts
Bestialitist, Top	Fur	Bestialitist, Bottom
Star Fucker	Silver Lame	Star
Likes Bottom Musclemen	Gold Lame	Likes Top Musclemen
Has Tattoos	Leopard	Likes Tattoos
Nibbler	Houndstooth	Will be bitten

New in Town	Calico	Tourists Welcome
Sauna Top	Terrytowelling	Sauna Bottom
Dish Pig, Top	Teatowel	Dish Pig, Bottom
Cuddler	Teddy Bear	Cuddlee
Kicker	Kangaroo	Likes being Kicked
Chicken	Kewpie Doll	Chicken Hawk
Wears a Dirty Jock	Dirty Jockstrap	Sucks 'em Clean
Has Drugs	Zip-lock Bag	Looking for Drugs
Stinks	Tissue	Sniffs (or has a cold)
Gives HOT Motor Oil Massages	Handywipe	Wears it well
Biker	Chamois	Likes Bikers
Bartender	Cocktail Napkin	Bar Groupie
Tearoom Top (Pours)	Doily	Tearoom Bottom (Drinks)
Outdoor Sex – Top	Mosquito Netting	Outdoor Sex – Bottom
Lover's Out – My Place OK	Toothbrush	Lover's Home – Your Place Only
Coach	Baseball Cap	Jock
Fights To Be Top	Rebel Flag	Fights to be Bottom
Worker, Top	Eureka Flag	Worker, Bottom
Skinhead Top	Union Jack	Skinhead Bottom
Pirate	Skull and Crossbones	Treasure Chest
Mummifier	Gladwrap	Mummy
Likes Giving Enemas	Enema Nozzle	Needs cleaning out
Ritual Scenes, Top	Rosary Beads	Ritual Scenes, Bottom

traffic went to Turkish Jim's to return a gas mask borrowed months ago for a party. His apartment a tiny box afloat in a view that stretched from Bradleys Head to the Bridge. In one corner stood a kinetic sculpture done by Jim in the 80s of fists on an old bicycle wheel, every other spare inch decorated with old sculptures, outfits and props. Jim had some amino acids that Fred had left there and traffic suggested they try some in a smoothie. Jim padding around quietly, white surprised face poking back through the kitchen doorway. I haven't got a food processor, I forgot about that.

So he let traffic the cocktail expert loose in his kitchen where she whipped the smoothies by hand at the small laminex counter, eyes travelling across photographs stuck to the fridge and cupboards. The gym period, wide shoulders, full chest, neck in an unbroken line through the jaw to his small, white blonde head. Then the time of drag, bad sad and twisted drag. A little girl like the Bad Seed. A proud fifties housewife, prototype of the Green Woman. A whole series of her doing a Mardi Gras parade and Party with ex-boyfriend Harry all in orange. Jim in heels suddenly enormous as the first grand Green Woman, her wide green skirt hooped with wire over scratchy pastel green tulle petticoats, green bouffant wig and green lycra mask that stretched down over face and neck to a full green bustier, the neck bejewelled with a choker of fake emeralds, long green eyelashes and green lipsticked lips peeping through, green stockings painted with blue-green varicose veins, long green satin gloves weighted with more emeralds in many rings, and an oversized lime-green leather handbag. Best of all were the peep-toe green shoes on a clear plastic wedge heel which gave the impression she was walking on air though by the end of the Parade the Green Woman in fact was walking on blisters. The Professor would later claim they had exuded green fluid when burst back at the house. traffic brought the smoothies out asking to see more pictures. Jim documented his dressups from the moment of their completion inside his own living room. The initial startled expressions as he tucked the last edges of himself into a new persona, the blossoming as friends arrived and stepped inside the frame with him. traffic peered into one after another of Turkish Jim's lives, remembering her attendance at some of the same parties but rarely what she'd worn. She had never owned a camera. She kept no records, she threw things away.

And how's that talented girlfriend of yours?
She's thinking of going to visit her family.
Where are they?
Somewhere northwest, near the Hunter.
Really? I always thought she was a Sydney girl.
You've known her for years, haven't you?
We never talk about our families.
Billy doesn't give much away it's true. She's not the easiest person beneath that calm exterior.
I love that foreshore, how I can sit here in the city and see acres of bushland opposite. I love that about Sydney.
D'you reckon this stuff works?
What, the amino acids? I don't know, I don't *feel* any different.
We could always pretend.
Yes. We're good at that.

Even before he moved here, years before when he had just moved in with Harry in Darlinghurst, when all of them but Harry were still going to the big parties, Jim used to go down to Beare Park and spend dusk by the water emptying the day from his head. A further distance from the fabric shop but it was summer and there was more time between work and nightfall. Almost every night he caught a bus from the city and walked down to his favourite bench. He thought about his situation, the two-headed monster, he had never lived with a lover before. Three more months till Mardi Gras, Jim sat there thinking about his outfit. When the sun dropped behind the Bridge, if the harbour was still all the water transformed to burnished metal. The fetters of party shibboleths. The two-headed monster. From the dense canopy of fig trees came the squealing of fruitbats then a stream burst forth, like ash chips, little devils, and flew across the darkening sky.

He carved from polystyrene a tapered torso that fitted against his back, the shoulders enormous looming over his own. Made a series of belts to secure it. From foam rubber he fashioned arms that locked across his chest pinning his own arms to his sides. Pulled apart his military jacket and using the pattern as a template cut another to fit both himself and the clone. The head and face took a week to carve, its features modelled on his own. Each day thereafter Jim applied a layer of liquid latex, carefully dyed, building the skin to a fleshy sheen, the scattering of pockmarks on the polystyrene disappearing to just a few acne scars. Fitting the head into the clone's torso at just the right angle, so that it looked over Jim's shoulder, took another week again. Then Jim dyed his hair black, cutting it afterwards and gluing the clone's and his own moustache with the spare hair in a style identical to Harry's. Harry wasn't happy but had already refused to go to the party. Jim loved Harry and everything he was trying to do with his art but loathed his need for public approval, Harry in turn never forgave Jim for giving up a potentially successful career as a sculptor. Jim like James was too sceptical and insecure to cope with the vicissitudes of the art industry, trained in self-effacement he could not admit to ambition of any form though one look at his costumes as one listen to James's mixing told you they were the most ambitious people in the world. Jim's creations nevertheless blossomed inside these self-imposed

limitations and the freedom of not pleasing galleries nor compromising tenders was often just compensation for wider success. At
night while Harry drew up designs for corporate gigs by his stereo
blaring Latin music, Jim worked on alone in the dining room. By the
time the clone's face was completed it had become its own personality.
It resembled Jim vaguely but not Harry at all, Harry's moustache
being generic, like Fred's, almost Prussian, old-world militaristic in
this context. With its chiselled jaw, mean hooded eyes and grim
mouth, Jim saw the clone was now a General, his own dark shadow,
the forces that oppressed him. He sorted his collection of military
decorations, the medals and stripes and epaulettes would be
transferred to the clone and Jim beneath it would become a cadet. He
took his US ARMY patch down to the old Chinese embroidery place
near the newspaper offices at the bottom of Surry Hills and ordered
two the same with a W in front. He got out his Captain's cap, beefed
up the trim with red braid and fitted it onto the clone's head.
Experimented with foundations till he found the hue that would
match the glossy skin of the chiselled General's face. When Harry
yelped in fright at its final unveiling, Jim knew that he was onto
something. Last of all, on the night of the party, at James and the
Professor's place beforehand, Jim was locked into his costume with
handcuffs between his and the General's wrists. They stood back and
marvelled. Oh fan-tastico! crowed the Professor, In-cred-ibilo! It's the
Two-Headed Monster! The General of the WUS Army with his
hapless cadet! Out on the dancefloor his friends lifted bottled water to
handless Jim's lips, amyl to his nose. Many of the partygoers moved
away disconcerted, sometimes even disgusted. The notion that it
would be easy to get someone to help him piss was fine in theory, but
in practice Jim and the General frightened the fuckers in the toilets
until the appearance of an enthusiastic cowboy whose day job was
special effects. The General chafed a line across Jim's shoulder and left
sweat rash for days down his entire back. No grand costume could be
worn without discomfort but he regretted the lack of a mechanism
that would enable the head to turn its cold clone lips to his own for a
kiss. He could have created this, he had the expertise and the materials
but never, with full-time work, the hours in which to do it. As it was
he and his General brought quite a few people's acid on. An Elephant

Man tried to pick him up, and a girl called Billy with her friends Bee and Shifty appeared out of nowhere and prostrated themselves on the dancefloor before him. And all night they danced with him, James, Fred and the Professor, feeding them gum and water, rolling them joints.

Turkish Jim:

I was a small-town boy from Palmerston North, New Zealand, and Bondi seemed the epitome of Sydney when I first moved here. I lived for a while in a house by the water. Oh, we had wild parties there in the 70s. People fell in love and fell off cliffs, New York Dolls on the stereo.

Later I moved to a warehouse space near the corner of Crown and Oxford. This was before the Boulevard was built and the first thing I saw when I woke up was the Opera House and Harbour Bridge between my toes. When the warehouse was redeveloped I moved up the road to Little Oxford Street just near that fuck club the Professor loved so much. He left one night literally an hour before the police raided. One of his teaching colleagues had been there and subsequently got the sack. I wasn't very good at fuck clubs, I just got bored.

But I used to go down to that little toilet at Taylor Square before it was shut. I used to run my hand over the tiling beneath the peeling graffitied paint, try to imagine the colours. I had a wild fuck in there once, this big Lebo guy pounding into me in one of the cubicles with no door so everyone could see. Beers with the Professor across the road, him musing that our civilisation of shame has relegated most of its erotic art to the walls of public toilets. He was probably right but apart from that one amazing afternoon, I was more turned on by the fluidity of the design. The queens thought I was dodgy because I was ogling the architecture instead of their crotches. Simply divine, darling! It's still there, that toilet, all closed up for decades now. There's always talk of doing stuff with the space but hardly anything happens. They'll probably do it up and sell it to some rich queen to run as a gay tourist site. I can see it now – rainbow flags, la-di-dah para-phernalia, opera houses, harbour bridges and a million and one dicks or dick-related items.

The best year for me was when Miss New Zealand won best parade entry. Not a minute too soon – what a trooper. Nothing to do with patriotism. On the contrary, I am a citizen of the universe. Prim, provincial, and proud, Miss New Zealand we need more like you.

In winter they hibernated. Billy kept saving to go overseas and entreating traffic to join her, Holmes got a job in housing for positive people and began to grow his hair, Jimi frustrated by the lack of freedom at his salon began to glassy at the Royal. Turkish Jim went to New Zealand for a holiday, Bee tried working in a photo shop but the money was lousy so she went back to mistressing. Shifty began nursing at Sydney Hospital, Slip began looking for gigs in Sydney bars and clubs, James and the Professor bought a new car. Then in spring a new party started with Mr Hyde and Slip heading the roster.

Fag Rag

HOT SPOTS COMING UP

SICK of the dearth of happening dancefloors? Tired of too cute handbag and cheese? Rise from your torpor fans of hardcore beats, a new party is coming your way. And it promises to blow your heads off!

Sam, Mark and Aaron took time off from the exhausting task of party preparations to come into our office and give us the hot wax on **Chronic**.

Just back from Europe where he took in the latest cutting edge clubs of London, Amsterdam and beyond, Sam is promising *the* party that Sydneysiders with a taste for difference have been waiting for.

'We've got world class DJs here and we want to showcase them. It's criminal that nobody else is giving them work.'

Chronic will be bringing you the latest and best in thumping, pumping, techno, trance, hard house and nu-energy. Heading the roster will be our very own home-grown Mr Hyde, Slip and Mandrake. Future line-ups will hopefully include other spin doctors of fast and furious beats Chrissy and D Coy.

'I guess it's a bit of a risk promising a series of parties,' says Sam. 'But we're pretty confident that Sydney's ready to support the sort of thing we're offering. You look at the line-up for this year's Mardi Gras and Sleaze Ball and you wouldn't even know that harder styles of music are actually becoming really popular. They're about ten years behind. There's a demand in the queer community for more progressive music. We're just aiming to give the people what they want.'

Chronic will be taking over IN on Saturday fortnight. IN of course is the new club at Taylor Square with latest high-tech sound and lighting, as well as state of the art security. As Aaron is keen to point out, 'The metal detectors might be a bit off-putting at first but we've had a word to security and they've promised us a friendly approach. The metal detectors are there to keep the wrong people out.'

Changes to this state's licensing laws now require venues, especially those in areas like Taylor Square and the Cross, to be more vigilant about asking patrons to show ID. 'Most of us aren't used to having to show ID at gay and lesbian venues, so it's a bit of a culture shock for us,' says Mark. 'But management have assured us it's nothing personal. Just an unfortunate but necessary licensing requirement.'

So polish those dancing boots boys and girls and get ready for **Chronic**. Tix $20 pre-sale and $25 on the door.

She followed him tentatively at first, what's that track? Often an unknown artist on a one-off label, the brains behind the music a producer who could be traced back to a fringe band in the 80s. On an expedition through the record shops she found a 12 inch she had heard him play the month before. Waited for a free booth tripping with excitement only to discover how much of the beauty she remembered was his own arrangement. His the extra snare, filtered bass and barely decipherable entreaty of a woman on the verge. All of these were colours applied by Mr Hyde. Without them the track was a mere outline.

The Professor once told her that when James first started DJing it was all screechy girlie house. Since the late 70s he'd amassed a library of all the more obscure stuff but he couldn't seem to strike middle ground for ages. She had been up to that attic and seen everything by the Plastic Ono Band through to Primal Scream, and British and Northern European labels she'd never even heard of. He had a shelf of African music, two of South American, he even had a recording of throat singers from Tuva. In a way anyone with an ear could anticipate a lot of what evolved. Acid techno, trip-hop, big beat, grungey house, anyone could predict those fusions would occur. But James melded things into forms you never would have dreamt possible.

He saw the trees, she saw the forest. He heard the detail of every section immediately, collaging nuance, suggesting never telling. She compressed everything into the rhythm, a coiled spring a turban, combing and twisting every strand into one solid shape. He taught her to decorate. To see the possibility for new beginnings at any point, dare to highlight the bizarre at random make nonsense right like a dream. She taught him to strip back. To hold the continuum like a path an elastic looping through the entire set, to appreciate simplicity always keep moving forward, to welcome silence as a part of sound.

Each never left the floor, never held a conversation while the other was playing, a buoy a hook, floating below the booth. They played back to back traded private jokes, reaching through the stroboscopic air dropping quotes into one another's pockets.

Listening to them all night was sheer joy. Together they could take you anywhere.

You fucked her didn't you.

We were in there for all of five minutes Billy. And for the third time I'm sorry.

But you did didn't you.

We just mucked around, like I said.

I don't believe you.

Billy I'm not a poof. I can't get off in five minutes in a toilet.

It amounts to the same thing though.

Look, I was ambushed.

Yeh right.

And yes I went along with it. For *five* minutes. And I've said all of this already.

God you're a bitch. You really don't give a shit do you.

Look Billy, did I ever say I wanted a monogamous relationship?

No but I did.

And I have no say?

So don't go on at me to come to the next Chronic. Why would I wanna go to a party where my girlfriend fucks whatever she finds in the toilets.

Jesus Billy, you're blowing this out of proportion.

Besides which they charge too much. No shows, no props. Fuck that for a joke.

Billy, I love you and I want to be with you. And I want to have fun with you.

I told you we should have kept the same name for our party. Heresy, Chronic, they all rake it in and there's not half the imagination and work we put into ours.

I think Chronic's a stupid name.

Don't change the subject.

She was grim and strained when they went to bed.

What do you most dislike about me?

What?

You know. What irritates you, what would you change?

Nothing.

Oh come on, traffic. There must be something.

Why are you asking me this?

I'm just curious.

Why can't you just accept I love you for who you are? Nobody's perfect.

That's exactly what I mean.

She got up later to empty the ashtray. Breasts swinging as she bent to pick it up, outlined now as she paused in the doorway. traffic turned away from what she had begun to dislike. Suffocating, like jealousy. Sometimes when lying beneath Billy, traffic felt possessed and yearned for escape. To be as alone in body as she felt in her mind. When Billy came back into the room traffic pretended she was asleep.

What do you most dislike about me?

What?

You asked me the same last night. You must have your own answers.

I don't want to talk about this.

You can dish it out, can't you. But you sure can't take it.

Getting up from her half-finished breakfast, going into the bedroom, putting on a jacket.

traffic, do we have to ruin our one morning together this week?

I think it was ruined already Billy.

Oh don't do this, don't storm out.

She walked down the stairs hearing Billy's tears fade, watching their descent. The standoff, the unsheathing, all the petty irritations, the wounding at will. She stiffened against grief against remorse out in the street, stiffened against emotion. Went to buy the papers and couldn't stay away longer. Bought pastries and flowers and took them home with the embrocation of silence. They met with their bodies leaving breakfast untouched till evening.

Chronic, 5 am. They waited patiently by the two big bouncers though there was no queue then once inside forgot the midnight argument that had robbed them of Mr Hyde. They left all the ordinary pain of living on the threshold and went down the stairs into a dark smoke-filled room.

Billy was right. Like the first Chronic there wasn't much colour. Apart from a banner proclaiming the name of the party there wasn't much to look at at all. But the music was fantastic, it was hard dirty and mean. Faster than usual, relentless, hair-raising. That continuous chugging, the way Slip could make even 160 bpm funky. Her music was busier but still not crowded, it hit them in the hips never leaving the head alone. Nagging. As if she was running really fast nearly tripping then just in time regained her footing. It was a solid macho beat with whirling percussion and fever-pitch harmonics, they couldn't get off the floor not even for a minute. Check their coats have a smoke get a drink forget it. So they danced on hot coals, skating the undergrowth of acid-laced percussion, dense, breathless, flying over bridges that thinned leaving them hanging till the pounding bass drum shelved beneath them again.

Later back at the warehouse everybody pooled their resources on the coffee table. Cigarettes, joints, tea, coffee, enough speed for a bump each. Mr Hyde and the Professor brought croissants and cut up their last three microdots, Jimi had some valium, Holmes and Slip arrived with juice and chocolate biscuits. Billy ransacked drawers to find sunglasses for everybody, moving into the stash of shonky ones from traffic's bar-floor collection. Shifty got wraparounds, Bee heart-shaped ones, Mr Hyde paint-spattered welding glasses with little visibility. He seemed relieved. The Professor in little kiddies' from Coles, coin-sized, covered in dust, his one false eyelash peeping over the top. traffic got the reflective ones with the right lense missing that had last been worn by Holmes to Heresy eighteen months ago.

Jimi was beckoning traffic from the bathroom door. Can you do it for me? She mixed up while Jimi entertained the mirror. Since his arrival in Sydney traffic had watched him grow rougher, louder, funnier, less easy to please and more comfortable with his own reflection. No shooters on our mirror, Jimi, we just cleaned it you know. Don't be disgusting, I'm not squeezing pimples. Yeh right. Pump, will you? Jimi proffered his clenched forearm. No, *I've* moved onto bigger things, traffic, like herpes and HIV. She injected him swiftly, leaving no blood, then Jimi left for 32.

It was the Professor's idea to play scrabble, giggling with Mr Hyde as they cleared the table. The board an old one found in a skip by Billy, its missing letters painted in Gothic script on thick white cardboard. By the time the eight of them had taken out their first letters, the game was almost over. Scrabble on acid. The Professor went first.

Egads! It's the recovery party! T-O-N-I-C. Fourteen.

This is even better. C-H-T-H-O-N-I-C.

That's not a word, traffic. You need new glasses.

Yes it is! Twenty-three, but I put down all my letters. Which makes it about ninety-five.

Is that an ashtray?

No, it's a crab.

Slip, can you please pass Mr Hyde the ashtray?

Here. It's an ashtray in the shape of a crab. It's a crab ashtray.

Oh. How amazing.

Shifty fell asleep and Bee selected the best of their letters, throwing the rest back in. Q-U-I-M. A hundred and four.

What's that?

Don't know. But it looks alright.

The pubis.

Oh wow, really?

But it's not worth *a hundred and four*.

No, I've undercharged as usual. A hundred and fifty-three.

E-X.

Bil-ly.

Well I can't . . . ! OK. E-X-C-U-T-H.

What?

As in excuth me I'm intocthicated. Two hundred and ten. Professor, are you scoring?

What'd you get?

Three hundred and ten.

C-R-U-E-L-L-A. Four hundred.

Slip's in the lead.

Is this game multicultural?

But it looks a bit lonely all by itself in the top corner. Aren't you supposed to connect all the words?

I think it looks rather fetching, actually. Holmes, pay attention!

Yes Mistress. T-D-J-W-D-E-D. World weary in Welsh, in case anyone's still got a brain. Who's scoring? I just got a thousand.

Your go James.

James, knock-knock.

Hei-di, yoo-hoo!

I feel like I've been looking at that ashtray for about a thousand years.

Later when everyone had left or gone to bed and the sun had begun to swing down through the windows, traffic woke on Billy's lap, hand under her skirt. You're *wet*. It's the acid, I'm gonna crash out. traffic followed her into the bedroom, climbed on top of her. No you're not. You're not crashing out on me. She began to move her hips. I want to fuck you. Billy lifted her pelvis. I want to fuck you. First I'm gonna lick out your sweet little arsehole. Then sit on my face so I can suck your cunt. I want to put on my cock and fuck you. I want to feel your cock inside me. I want your whole hand . . .

Ricky Morrison is dead. Ricky was going to be a lawyer. He was twenty-one, captain of the university football team. He had a high IQ. The Dean said he was the most popular man in his year. Now Ricky is dead. He got into trouble with acid. Lysergic acid diethylamide, L-S-D. A friend offered Ricky some LSD at a party. He said it would make him feel euphoric, that he would sense all sorts of things he hadn't even known existed. So Ricky tried it, and his friend was right. At first the LSD made him nauseous   At first the LSD made him nauseous   At first the LSD made him nauseous, then Ricky began to hallucinate. His mind seemed to be expanding, he began to float through the atmosphere. He saw every individual particle of air, when he looked at his skin he saw every cell, every hair follicle. When he listened to the music coming from the stereo, he understood the features of the invisible musicians and every single note had a different shape and colour. They melted around him like a river of rainbows. It was amazing! Inside himself, Ricky felt sublime, at one with the world. Then he looked into the mirror, and something awful happened . . .

Couples. The completion. James and the Professor, Bee and Shifty, Billy and traffic. Holmes and Jimi coupling with nameless men in sex venues. A single man was a free agent, a single woman pitiable, threatening. Slip left the warehouse with James and the Professor, walked up to Oxford Street and caught a cab to Bondi. Left her records next to her bag in Holmes's flat and walked back out into the first hot day of spring. Lovers, partners, companions, spouses, arm in arm all along the esplanade, kissing on benches facing the ocean, oiling one another's backs on the beach. She walked amongst them down to the water, ran through the waves then dove under. Shock of cold. The surf boiling with people and surfcraft and clouds of brown kelp. She began to swim away, stopping only when there was nobody else alongside, turning to see the shoreline warped and distant and the place she had entered the water indistinguishable. Now she could feel the needles of salt and icy southern currents, sun closing over the land like a dome. She sat frozen in the surface of water. Help me. One after another the board riders receded. She watched the crowded beach and saw herself swimming east through the endless sea. She was scared of everybody. She didn't want to talk to, touch or know anybody ever again.

The sickness. Hard to say when it began, so much a part of her she felt she'd always had it. Lethargy, listlessness, gut aches, headaches, the stiffenening or liquid bowels. The chef's amusement at her sudden reverential bows, Jo holding the kick behind her ribs with a pretend search for dropped saffron. Night sweats, dry yellow eyes. Did I drink too much last night? But no, the night before? No. She was always depressed, thought she must have been born like this. Was she, as her sister suggested, a drama queen like her mother? Jo took no notice of herself, considered herself lazy. The endless catatonia and Carol's impatience. Come on Jo, get *up*. Sometimes she couldn't even get out of bed. Too much effort.

A slow world, blurred. Flaccid, long, tainted days. Work all week, spend the weekend in bed while time wasted away. No will no reason no desire, no energy no passion no point, no point in anything. Couldn't concentrate, couldn't focus, sometimes couldn't even read. Fogbound in the darkness of her polluted body. She ate meals full of tears.

Her bass was stolen and the band broke up, Jo soon stopped playing music altogether. The way Carol had laughed at the band, experimental, obscure, not easy on the ears, hurt although Jo's own burgeoning lack of belief soaked it up like a thirst. She went to sleep dreaming that the body she held was in fact the warm smooth wood of her fretless bass. Woke hungover though not a drop of alcohol had passed her lips in weeks. Fogged head though she hadn't been smoking. All that purity and still she felt polluted. All the lows of getting high but none of the highs to balance them, she was getting closer to the ground, going down, crawling.

Where did it come from? Through the eye of a long forgotten drug buddy's needle, a microbe releasing its tint slowly along her twenties, silting the years with melancholy and inertia. The sickness came on without her even knowing it.

She watched the red tinted foam swirl down the plughole. Rinsed and spat, rinsed and spat. Rinsed again and spat. Carol was waiting in bed for her. Jo climbed between the sheets with that taste still in her mouth, ancient, ferric. She wanted closure, of her veins her mouth her body, of obligations to a lover. When Carol began to move towards her, Jo felt frozen. She was poisoned, she was poisonous. She wrapped her arms around her knees and turned away.

You're pushing me away Jo.

I'm not, I'm just cold.

Well let me warm you up . . . please, let me fuck you.

I can't. I'm sorry.

You're using this as an excuse. It's not fair, it doesn't change anything!

It does.

It doesn't change the fact that I love you. Does it change the way you feel about me? Is that it? . . . This isn't new, you know. You're using the hep as an excuse. It's not fair.

Carol began to cry and Jo held her, saying nothing. She felt weightless, as though her spirit had flown away. They cried themselves to sleep, alone together. Jo woken in the dead of night by Carol's thighs, her arm shifting. Sound of tobacco burning close in the darkness, puck of lips releasing the cigarette.

She went to a doctor.

Have you made a decision about interferon?

What are my chances?

About twenty percent.

And massive side effects?

Well . . . that's usually the case but you might be lucky.

I think I'll leave it.

Very well. Now if you have a biopsy it will only be an academic thing. As I said before, it won't affect management.

What is management? Last time you had no advice about regimes or anything.

That's right. There is no management.

She went to a specialist.

What can I do?

Give up alcohol.

I gave it up over six months ago. You're a gastroenterologist, what about my diet?

A healthy diet is always good, but there's no guarantee it will get rid of your symptoms.

Look I'm a cook, I know food. I know what's good for the liver, I've already started eating more carefully and I'm actually feeling a bit better . . . You don't think it makes a difference?

There's no scientific evidence.

What about coffee? Sometimes it makes me feel sick. Should I give it up?

There's no scientific evidence.

So what you're saying is I could eat McDonalds every day and it wouldn't make a difference.

There's no scientific evidence.

She went to another doctor then another specialist.

How did you get it?

I've got a rash too, I was wondering if it was related. It's getting really bad.

The only symptom of hepatitis C is fatigue.

How do you know that if you know nothing about the virus? And I had B for a while too.

How did you get it?

Is that relevant?

I know you're thinking of consulting a Chinese herbalist but our methods are different. It is relevant to epidemiology. How did you get it?

Well I think we can rule out mother's breastmilk.

He got up and motioned her to the door.

I hope you're not still taking drugs. Absolute foolishness in your condition.

Her ailment had no language. Knowing nothing and clinging to the relief of her HIV negativity, Jo approached the matter with calm curiosity. The possibility of death drew closer like a stormcloud and she surrounded herself obsessively with information as if building a shelter. There was almost nothing about the virus itself, only the stories of its consequences. The woman whose husband insisted her eating utensils be separated from the family's, the man refused entry to his local swimming pool. The politician's suggestions of marking with wristbands all HCV-positive hospital patients and quarantining them in wards with HIV-positive patients, the letters of anger about those dead from liver failure. There was the friend of Eddy's reduced to an emaciated depressive after six months on interferon, there was her own dentist who refused to treat her. There was the support line but it was always unattended, she had no bolsters, she had no direction.

She fell into despair, she lost five kilos, she lost her libido. She wanted death, she wanted transport, to be taken, to be delivered. She wanted silence. She imagined all the possible departures. The quick violence beneath a train or moving vehicle but too many other lives would be involved. Exhaust, but she had no car, gas but her oven was electric. Hanging or wrist slashing but she didn't trust her ability with knots and although she loved blood she neither trusted her ability to find the right points. She imagined falling through blue from the Harbour Bridge, a beautiful vision but if the water were broken she would resurface. And once again there would be too many witnesses. In the end it always came back to an overdose, neat, discreet, private and alone. Easy enough now she had no tolerance. She could choose a place to do away with herself, she could even do it at a favourite spot on the harbour. Sunlit, airborne, flying free, not sinking into the darkness of her small bedroom. Two points or three just to be sure. Push of the barrel, tourniquet released, then soft white nothingness forever and ever.

The first thing Tina said to her was a comment about her hair.

Aren't you going to do anything about it?

Like what?

Well, look at this Giovanna. Reaching over and pulling at the fringe, touching her like that at their first meeting in two years with the presumption of intimacy only an older sister could have.

I don't have the money or time to redo it.

God, I didn't mean re*do* it.

But the blue's almost gone.

I don't know why you always have to make a statement, Jo. Tina irritably emptying the ashtrays of their mother, visible through the window overwatering the garden, pretending not to listen. I mean, there's a time and a place. This is Dad's funeral we're talking about. What about the Italian community?

Oh spare me the ethnic guilt trip.

She wasn't ready for this. She had been concentrating on the leaving of Carol and the leaving of Sydney, the leaving too she hoped of illness. She thought throughout the months she had known her father was sick that some sort of preparation had been taking place. But now the news had reached her and now she had reached the house she still wasn't ready. Eight hours since the phone call, four of them on the bus home to Canberra. A trip in limbo in a capsule of unreality. Woken at 9 am by her sister weeping Dad's dead, you have to come home. She had been put into a movie mouthing all the wrong unlearnt words, the usual nausea leaking from her liver swamped by another deeper. She drank and drank and drank at the wake but didn't feel drunk, didn't feel hungover. High tensile emotion keeping her upright, above, and far far away. She fell involuntarily from conversations like a person falling asleep at mass. She fell into blankness.

She lifted books down from her mother's bookshelf. The livingroom was now full of them, mostly history and theology. Her mother had lapsed but remained immersed in the religion of her upbringing, pursuing its mystery now with her intellect. She spoke in English almost always these days though her children finally wanted to speak Italian. She spoke to Jo about her father. I envied his faith. He didn't question anything, he didn't question all the persecution in the Church, he didn't question the subordinate role of women. He just wasn't interested. So you must understand his position on your . . . sexuality Giovanna, you musn't take it personally. Long into the night Jo and her mother talked about the Catholic Church and religion. Pope Joan, the Gnostic Gospels, Jesus the man, the Jewish prophets. The Israelites Canaanites St John Chrysostom and the desert fathers. The Book of Job and its purported female author, the apocryphal Gospel according to Mary Magdalene.

What did she know about him anyway. He was silent he was dutiful, he was a hard worker. The arguments about cigarettes and religion were always won by his wife. She smoked a packet of Winfield Red a day, cut down to Blue and then smoked thirty, they were part of the nicotine generation. Disappointed in Jo and disappointed in themselves as the source of her deviation. Leaning on her father's authority wasn't very useful. When Jo's school reports were declining he sat on the edge of her bed on her mother's orders as though the room were caving in on him. He would come back to her when she returned home two weeks later. In the correct placement of seedlings and the old silver cigarette box her mother gave her on the last day. In her dry eyes, in her handwriting, the tight even strokes of her father struggling to contain the florid loops of her mother. But Jo's signature resembled no one's and changed with every signing.

Three days after the funeral their mother caved in. Put the phone back sharply, missing the cradle. It dangled down the wall as she ranted.

God I'm sick of it! I'm sick of everybody saying At least he went peacefully. Oh yes Giulia, it was a good death though, and that's all you can hope for. A good death! What the hell does that mean? There's no such bloody thing.

Come on mamma, sediati, take it easy.

Smetti di fumare, *please*.

Why? Your father did ten years ago and that didn't save him.
She lit another cigarette

D'you want some coffee? I'll make some coffee.

Oh stop fussing over me like I'm a stupid old woman. If you want to do something for your mother then be nice to each other. This kitchen's like a bloody mausoleo every morning with you two sitting opposite each other glaring. Talk, will you! Parlatevi! You're sisters!

She left the room weeping. The daughters sat stricken. From the brown house of grief Jo could see snow clouds over the Brindabellas. Alone once again, the fetter of one parent cut, and pulling away from or pushed away by her sister. The stretched blue sky. The cold, dry Canberra air.

She heard her mother later, much later past midnight. She heard her go down the hall past her bedroom and into the kitchen. Flick of a switch and a cupboard creaking open, then the flow of water. The first smash contained liquid, the next two were hollow. Silence again. Jo got up and walked quietly to the kitchen where her mother beside a pool of shattered glass and water was smoking and drinking scotch from a tumbler. She looked at Jo sheepishly. It was an accident. She put down her scotch and began to sweep up the glass around her feet, both of them trying not to laugh. Here I'll do that if I can have a scotch too. Her mother's feet retreated then returned. Salute! Drinks in hand, they surveyed the far wall, one yellow shard stuck, the floor below littered with them. That's a pretty good accident, mamma. Her mother affected an arrogant pose. I hate these glasses anyway. She drained then raised it behind her head. Jo followed suit.

She can't feel, she can't mourn. Sydney's too loud, too messy and cheerful. She feels like a foreigner. She had always deprived herself in fantasy, invoked hypothetical catastrophes that demanded her family her lover or her music. She would hand them over to the grim reaper in that order, her music if nothing else she needed her music. Now her father had been taken, her lover given away, the bass stolen and the band broken up. Her mother and sister crying for the loss of her father, Carol crying for the loss of their love and Jo crying for the loss of her music. Her selfishness dismays her, she hates it she hates herself. She cannot climb back out to meet the world, to start again.

With a new blade she cuts a series of shallow incisions into her thigh, rubs alcohol into the wounds till the burning seizes her leg, her entire body in its hot fist. So the blood is pumping and she feels at last. The next day she goes to get her nipples pierced. The pain is fantastic.

She went to a herbalist in Chinatown. Middle-aged woman, plump, thick glasses, almost no English. The herbalist took Jo's wrist in her fingers and stared off into the distance. Hot. Very hot. Energy blocked. She moved her fingertips around, fell silent again, asked to see Jo's tongue. Periods? They're late. Yes, very hot. Slow liver. And I have this rash. The herbalist filled a page with Chinese letters, Jo took it into the next room then left the buildings carrying two bags of herbs. Two days later she began to bleed, three days later the rash disappeared. She went back to the herbalist twice. Three months later her ALTs fell.

She became aggressive about her health. She had never liked her body, it was too soft, too shapeless. It was irrelevant. But the pollution that clouded her viscera clouded also her brain. This body was her first and her last, her entrance and exit. She only had one. For months she maintained nutritional purity, food her only hedonism and her only medicine. The bitter herbal brews from the Chinese doctor, thick as bitumen with a hint of licorice. When she dipped her finger in to check the temperature a green film remained on her skin, drinking the liquid made her gag. She became intimate with all her body's workings, the links between each organ and emotion, the chemicals endemic. Fear charging through veins and tightening around the liver, flush of excitement from armpits, hardening of stress around viscera, melancholy weighting each and every step. But living like this became monotonous, there was no opposition, no struggle no pain. So every few months when going up to Sydney Jo changed at Central for a west line, another fifty minutes and she was in Cabramatta. A ridiculously long journey for a few rocks but she knew no dealers anymore and after the quiet life new scenery and passengers were an entertainment. She got off avoiding the white dealers waiting on the platform, walked a little way with a Vietnamese boy then walked back to the station, an office worker watching her with disgust. They were wise to the transaction but not to the usage. Well, you can have your drunken nights at the pub.

Then to be lifted, swaddled, cocooned. To be wrapped in white clouds and walk back out of Central station on another plane, drifting . . .

She accepted two kittens from Rhada at the cafe who bred burmese on the side. They were worthless to Rhada, being the progeny of an intrusive black tom and one of Rhada's older Burmese. Jo had never owned a pet before and these weren't the sort of animals appropriate for a garden full of native birds but Rhada was persuasive. The cats alleviated the solitude Jo had chosen and feared. She felt herself starting to mellow after a time, she felt herself emerging, like a flower from a cactus.

She could listen for hours but it filled her quickly, still people talked, saying what had already been said. In one ear and out the other, passing across her brain leaving their imprint. Down here the world was still too close. She imagined their pasts floating like cloud across the Tasman Sea, returning as rainfall. She forgot nothing.

First Holmes unburdened himself then mistaking her silence for boredom or disapproval shut himself up. He was empty, naked, felt owed something of her in exchange but she spoke so little he sought clues of her reckless dead cousin instead. When Eddy's eyes blazed with opiates there was judgement as well but in hers the light was muted. He was angry the day she returned from Sydney stoned, the truth was he missed it. He had been lively on smack in the first years, it helped him to work. A good mark, a fun client and maybe even a tip. For a while life for Holmes had been perfect. But Slip wasn't one of those loud rasping talkers, she retreated and Holmes grew to accept then forget it. She was so *quiet*. You never heard her enter a room. You were alone then from the kitchen behind you the chink of ice cracked by a measure of cordial. Hearing her out of the corner of your eye.

Sometimes Holmes would turn and notice an object missing or some rearrangement. Unnerved he would replay his memory of the past hour, listening for the cue of her ghostly entrance and exit. He grew careful with his gestures, his mind mimicking her discipline and self-containment. Grew accustomed to her eyes watching him from far away as if outside of her body, returning then to drop the gaze.

People died in winter. Her father had died in June, Eddy in July, Rhada's mother in August. Death, the ultimate silence. A silent, inward time of year. They thought about the people who had died. Sifted through the past. Searched for things lost forever, carried what could never be discarded.

How the moment of death returned, piercing her like a high note. Arriving at her parents' house twelve hours too late, farewelling her father's body on the bed, kissing his cold waxen forehead as evening approached. To have walked into the house at dusk and seen Holmes like that, bent over the couch cradling the cat. Arriving at the hospital five minutes too late, Holmes bent over the bed, Eddy just gone. So that was him, her cousin's lover. Living in her house now.

Spring is here. Time to sleep diagonally.

Sometimes she wished she were a cat. To sit like that, slant-eyes staring, thinking feline thoughts. To sleep half the day, be fed, be caressed, to make an art of idleness and vanity. Alert to the whole animal world, intimate with every scent and shadow along the house's underbelly. Through sunlight, chin to chest, dancing midair at an insect. They snuck in when she left the door open. Crossing the floor to answer the telephone, two dark cat's ears poking over the bed-clothes, glint of jade iris, settling out of sight once again.

Down through daylight to the Tunnel of Love. A fifteen minute strip to start in the tiny cinema, never more than a dozen spectators, she held them all in the palm of her hand. Then through the shop to the red round peepshow room, her three metre universe. Fairy lights running the edge of the floor on a delayed flash, the bed covered in her own indigo cloth or Billy's leopard skin fake fur, backed by mirrored panels and fronted by eight narrow booths of which two were usually broken. traffic as Amber with russet hair to her shoulders would sprinkle some bush buds into a racehorse at the beginning of a shift then follow her music into the peepshow room. So the girl the customers saw on their arrival was often dancing already. Then on through almost four hours of movement, running to the back room when all the coins finished and opening her throat to the bottle of cold water. Walking home through the dusk streets in the pleasant lull of physical exhaustion that had filled her wallet.

She glimpsed them all, watched some closely, watched herself most of all, toned and nubile in the warm flattering light. Gave her body in minutes to the sweet old men who couldn't get it up anymore just came in for a perv, to the sheepish cockies just off the train, to the shy, the ill-at-ease, the lonely, the po-faced, the churlish and arrogant who beckoned for her to look at *them* though the only person who could sustain her interest was Amber her reflection. Persuading their money from them coin by coin with the lie of her body. Later when the bed had been pushed to the middle of the room she used it as a podium delighting in the altitude of her cunt and arse, seeing from up here the customer who drew attention to his own performance with a cigarette lighter. Wow, thought traffic curious, I've never seen a man with a dick as big as mine. Placing then a highheel beside his window, levering closer so her cunt filled his vision entirely. She loved it. She loved herself.

Sometimes boys would bring in their girlfriends. Amber would go to the glass and say Come on guys, only one to a booth. So they'd reappear separated and Amber would put on her best show for the girls who stood back timidly grinning, barely visible.

After a while she started stripping down to a strap-on. The men went off.

Billy knew someone who worked at the boy peepshows on Oxford Street. traffic went there with her one afternoon but they were stopped at the counter. Sorry ladies, it's men only.

Amber's surname was Fluids.

What I like about women.

Their legs their arms their brains their headspace their bellies bums sphincters arseholes cunts clits labia cervixes their mystery their instinct creativity fire silence voices their lips mouths tongues teeth faces kisses their skin soft skin fine body hair saliva piss blood cunt juice their fingers hands fists their struggle their resistance patience persistence their wisdom their attitude their tits nipples tears laughter spirit their emotion intelligence fluidity their dildos strap-ons cocks their variety their necks throats skirts feet heels high heels their strut their hips their walk their dance their joy sorrow hope generosity their orgasms multiplicity infinity their strength.

What I like about men.
Cock.

traffic was a good nurse, seduced as anyone can so easily be by another person's need. She had her secrets now as well, a Dutch girl here one week before when the warehouse was empty, a customer with cocaine in the toilets at work. Although traffic found it virtually impossible to hide anything, by now the pain of disclosure had made it necessary. She was pleasantly surprised that guilt brought such tenderness. She thrived when Billy got the flu, she thrived on Billy's need for her strength and her help. She was strong, she was capable, she was a good person. But felt herself slipping away all the while, that part of herself that needed absence and challenge was being starved and fading. She longed for the sight of Billy at her workbench, intent, preoccupied, but there was no party for which to prepare props or costumes, there were no orders, and at the play party though Billy didn't want to play she hardly left traffic's side. Perhaps it was that traffic could only love someone when they were partly turned away, when their main focus was elsewhere, that she herself could roam around freely. That her object of desire remain complete and evolutionary all in itself, bringing new nourishment to her with each encounter. She was revolted by the float of Billy's breasts, her flu breath, the constant coughing hawking and sniffing. The love chemicals had worn off. So when Billy finally turned to her once again, pressed her bare body with desire against traffic's, offered her white face, her neck to be kissed, when she wept and thanked her and told her she loved her, this Billy so reduced and close, traffic could hardly hold her because it felt like she was holding herself, she sank further into a dark space of doubt. She doubted Billy, she doubted the two of them, most of all she doubted herself. As though her desire had waited so long that it had spent itself without her knowing it. She had to summons herself constantly to be present at all times. She was fucking other people in her head, she was making love to something dying. And when she realised this, she began to grieve, and when she began to grieve each fuck was a farewell. Bittersweet, agonising, utterly desperate. Billy still recovering, her hot feverish skin, shudder of coughing torso midfuck. traffic joined her in helplessness and need. She fell into drama, she lost herself all over again.

Royal Tunnel of Love, Tunnel of Love Royal. Upstairs making cocktails, downstairs pulling beers, in the kitchen in the cellar, she worked at one time or another in every part of the machine. The neverending demand of customers, the world was one big open mouth.

traffic's history of dismissals haunted her only in the initial weeks of a new job. Then she took it for granted, a wage and position were no longer important merely a means to an end, expendable like everything. So inside the Royal traffic unravelled all the extraneous parts of herself she had been taught to hide when working in public. From the aesthetic variety of all the other workers she saw she could come dressed in whatever mood she had woken in. Garish or dull, girl or boy, bald or bandanaed or sprouting the coloured spikes of Jimi's latest folly. Bone or ring through her septum or retainer pushed out of sight, the occasional outlandish cosmetic experiment by Billy on her afternoon off. The freer she felt, the harder she worked. Craig always friendly, Well, well, and who are we today?

She was good at her job. Didn't overdrink, had an eye for detail. Could assess the room in minutes to know what needed to be cleared away and what restocked. Was always on the move, had an answer for everybody and was cute enough to get away with the acerbic ones.

She was in her second decade of bar work now, she took it for granted. It was all she knew, all she thought she could do. She needed people, she needed money, she needed entertainment. The pattern had always been the same, when a job became routine traffic acted up and got the sack. From a cocktail bar on the edge of the CBD for flashing her arse at a flirtatious straight woman who turned out to be the wife of one of the partners. From a pub in Surry Hills for leaping over the bar when too many drunks were crowding its entrance. From an upmarket Kings Cross restaurant for turning up late twice in a row and plying a pickup with free cocktails till closing time. From a bar on Oxford Street for calling a table of eight who left no tip a bunch of fucken losers, from a straight pub for smoking a joint out the back, from another for spilling a Midori cocktail on the white linen trousers of a rude customer. For refusing to conform to dress codes, for being in general too smart with her mouth. All things permissable or at least forgivable at the Royal but she was older now and less inclined to take advantage. One day traffic woke up surprised to find herself heading to work in the same place as over a year ago.

It never occurred to her to climb the bar hierarchy. When Craig offered her a management position, traffic politely knocked it back. She didn't want the responsibility.

On a Sunday afternoon at the beginning of summer the Professor hired a little pub in Surry Hills for his fortieth birthday. He called the party CATaTONIC, the small a on the flyer a cat curled up with its tail twisted overhead. It was almost a year since Scum, and several since the boys had put on a public party of their own. They had hoped to be celebrating with a bigger event but a week before signing the contract with the venue, Fred and Turkish Jim were gazumped by a promoter who was bringing out a DJ from New York. So they put their ideas onto the backburner and threw instead a more modest affair. A small sound system was hired, Mr Hyde brought his decks down and he, Turkish Jim, Fred and Slip played. Friends and dancefloor buddies and other fans came down and danced through dusk into the night. The Professor in his cassock hid for most of the afternoon inside a confessional booth he had set up between the toilets. traffic was his first penitent.

Bless me Father, for I have sinned. It is about three thousand years since my last confession.

I can see that, my child. Tell me the details.

Father, I desire every woman that walks in the door. I *lust* them, father. Every time I go out I see someone I want to fuck. Father, I'm a slut.

That's not a sin my child. It's a natural healthy impulse called Libido.

I know Father, let me finish. My girlfriend disapproves, being a rampant monogamist. She doesn't trust me, she's hurting. This makes me feel ashamed, I'm hurting too. All this pain, Father, which I seem to be the cause of. That's my sin, I'm the catalyst of pain.

In that case I can't help you. Pain isn't a sin either.

Christ, Father! You're missing the point! Can't you at least give me penance?

Very well. Seven hairy eyeballs, six wet-at-the-sight-of-hers, five gropes-on-the-dancefloor, four I've-got-a-girlfriends, three toilet snogs, two I've-gotta-work-tomorrows, and one reasonable fuck.

That's a fuck of a lot of penance, Mother, I didn't know you were a lesbian priest.

We must move with the times.

Look, I only wanted a placebo.

Stop whingeing.

Forgive me, Father.

I now absolve you of your sins. Go in pearls with Dionysos.

Sometimes these were the parties she liked the best. The low-key afternoon to evening affairs, neither private nor public, no cover charge, a secret vat of acid punch for friends. Where the diversity of people was all the more obvious for the smallness of numbers. Where the decks were open to others like Jim and Fred with their eclectic old-time tunes by everyone from Popol Vu to Shirley Temple. Where Mr Hyde played Severed Heads and Slip James Blood Ulmer before warming down as night fell into hard driving beats. Bee mincing over to the turntables, Scuse me, have you got any Kylie Minogue? From the back a jeer, *Fucken poof-tas!* The Professor had handed out flyers to fetish family the night before and they trickled in from 2 pm onwards in all their party finery. Friends with gifts disappearing behind the narrow black curtain of the confessional booth, reappearing in laughter or with the smug wide eyes of a trader in secrets. When the Dutch girl came in, traffic went to the bar and stood with her back to the room, the pub so small the girl was by her side in minutes anyway, hand on the back of her neck. Hallo. traffic tried to slide away gracefully. Sorry, you gave me a fright. The girl stood back affronted. You don't need to pretend you don't know me, you know. What? Your girlfriend's here, is that it? Which one is she? I'm kind of trashed, that's all. Turkish Jim ordering drinks beside her now in a refurbished Green Woman, head sprouting a multitude of snakes. Hallo! the Green Woman fluttered her green eyelashes at the Dutch girl. Hallo, she replied, agog at the outfit and waiting for an introduction. traffic the meat in the sandwich looking from her to the Green Woman and back again picked up the delivered drink and handed it to the Dutch girl. Here, have this, I'm going to the toilet. The Dutch girl put the drink back on the bar. I don't drink lemonade. You don't even remember my name, do you? From the other side of the room, Billy saw everything.

Bless me Father for I have sinned.

Already! It's remarkable what naughty girls can get up to in the space of two hours.

Actually, this happened a while ago. So I guess I've committed perjury as well.

Confess, my child.

I fucked someone in the conjugal bed.

A long sigh through the hatch in the cardboard wall.

You have committed the mortal sins of Disrespect and Tackiness.

She didn't sleep there or anything, she was only there for a couple of hours, she got my number one night at work. I never thought she'd call but she did then came over straightaway. Billy was at work y'know and nobody was at home so . . . Father, she was pretty keen, I don't know, I wasn't even that into it . . . the thing is Father, I'm a *girl*. So a discreet quickie at a beat or sauna is impossible. And this was my first infidelity, well fully *fledged* one, though my girlfriend's been expecting it since day one, so

You're full of excuses, my child. But do you have remorse?

Yes, Father. In abundance.

I now absolve you of your sins.

Father, what's my penance? I'm serious this time.

Taking into account the extenuating circumstances, penance won't be necessary. Your punishment is your crime.

Later in the toilets traffic and the Professor decided it would be fun to turn all their clothes inside out. Her cheap leather jacket transforming into torn black polyester, his tall fur hat into buckled synthetic red and white stripes. They made their way down the items of clothing on their bodies one by one reversing, pockets revealed in all their crumpled ink-stained glory, covered then by old Y-fronts. But by the time they reached their shoes they were laughing too much to succeed. Out by the bar a queen she didn't know approached traffic and touched her jacket admiringly. Wow! Where did you get this? London. Oh typical! He swanned away. And the Professor after doing a strut around the room sponging attention and all the latest gossip and scandal, returned to her side and whispered in her ear.

Guess what I had for breakfast this morning.

What?

Poached eggs with sauce *hollandaise*.

traffic, Holmes and Billy would be approached by friends and strangers alike. When are you guys going to put on another party? Please, we're hanging out! Often by performers who had nowhere to perform. Acrobats and strippers with a well of personal and quirky ideas they were unable to air inside the conventions of their professions. Mistresses, dancers, anomalous drag artists, stilt-walkers, hula-hoopists, contortionists, others locked in day jobs. All famished in the months between marginal cabaret evenings or parties where their true passions could take flight.

Chronic settled into a bimonthly rhythm, Homoside returned after more than two years' absence. Mr Hyde and Slip played parties like these dedicated to progressive music, and other like-minded DJs came out of the woodwork. D Coy who for years had played commercial house to get club gigs, poured out her true passion for techno at Chronic. Mandrake who worked in a record shop and Chrissy from Playschool where the music never got hard played Homoside and Chronic as well. But neither of these events had openings for performance. And Billy didn't want to put on another party. The baton had in fact been passed to the boys who were still searching unsuccessfully for a venue.

So when Heresy announced a date in February, everybody was happy for a party to go to with props and shows. Bliss and Genie had gone away and Tony, promoting alone now, approached Bee and Bella to do a show. traffic would come home from work and pass them planning at the long work table, sit there with a nightcap bouncing back their ideas before going to the bedroom and climbing in beside Billy's sleeping body.

She had been ashamed when Billy confronted her, kept telling her to keep her voice down, didn't want Bee and Shifty to hear. How often do you bring people home? Never. It's the only time. Bullshit! The slap took her completely by surprise and in the red light of its sting she slapped Billy straight back. Then they were both in tears. The second slap traffic saw coming, turned away only slightly as though she had earned it, her ears ringing louder than any argument. Then Billy was kissing her, hauling her on top, traffic fumbling then inside and moving, Billy's short but sharp nails dragging down traffic's back again and again, till Billy who hadn't touched traffic's birthday gift of nipple clamps put her mouth around traffic's nipple, and without warning or request sank her teeth in hard, traffic bellowing into the pillow.

Coming down Oxford Street, lights melting in the downpour. She leans alongside the driver's cage to give directions over the drumming on the roof of the taxi. Outside on the footpath a man gesticulates violently. She searches for the combatant, another man standing five metres away. traffic watches them while the lights are red. A poetry of recrimination and entreaty flow down their arms through their fingertips. She wishes she could sign, to talk to friends with ease through loud weather or loud music, to intimate in solitude among people. To argue like that without need of cover or quiet. To be free of words.

She entrusted her with everything. Wrapped her flaws dreams memories up in anecdote embellishing the possibilities, and handed them over. It was a gift, an act of love. Later she found herself wanting them all back again. Desperately seeking her original meanings. When they were flung at her like missiles during the months of argument she swatted in vain, appalled by the shapes they had assumed inside a mind so intimate. A peripheral strand taking root, growing an entirely different version with her name still at its centre. She owned nothing. Not even her stories.

It's traffic's turn to do the shopping. She wakes with only two hours to spare before the start of work. Goes out to the kitchen where Bee is washingup.

If you hurry you'll make it traffic. The fridge is empty and I'm hanging out for some home-cooked food.

Coles is open twenty-four hours at Christmas. I thought I'd go after work. Be a bit more peaceful then, I won't get waylaid and have to gossip.

Yeh but all the warped people'll have the same idea. Four o'clock in the morning and you'll be chatting for hours.

traffic returns to her room for a quick hit, the task now appears easy. She takes the kitty and list from the table.

Down at the supermarket, filling the trolley. Nobody here she knows, she feels peaceful. Then suddenly from behind hands are placed over her eyes. Listen! traffic is still. Through the musak like ice cracking in sunlight comes a delicate crepitation. traffic begins to smile, the hands are removed. It's the man with the rooster tattoo holding up a Wonka bar. Isn't it fabulous? Here, have some. And traffic wheels the trolley over to confectionary with a mouth full of explosion. She runs into him again at checkout. Got any parties or shows coming up? traffic shakes her head laughing. They look at one another in confusion. They were just one-offs, I'm a barmaid you know. He shrugs, hefts his backpack around his shoulders. Well *I'm* one of your biggest fans!

traffic, come in here. I've got something for you.

Oh, she looks beautiful. Thank you!

Here. Put these on her.

traffic fits the clamps behind the rings in the girl's large pink nipples. The other girl tugs on them gently.

She's hanging out for a bit of torture. Aren't you baby. Come on, say thank you.

Thank you.

Nicely.

Thank you traffic.

traffic takes the clamps between thumb and finger, squeezes them. Tugs the chain again, the girl biting her lip.

Keep going traffic, harder. Is that enough? No it's not, is it. Say please.

Harder, *please*.

Harder, traffic.

It's Mickey Mouse bondage, the rope wound crookedly too loose too tight but she seems the kind of masochist who enjoys it like that. Her face stretched open by the girlfriend's grip in her hair like a gift handed over after the unwrapping, traffic swims into the eyes brimming with pain, pulls on the chain gently persistent till the clamps snap off and the girl yelps. traffic places her hands over the girl's breasts, kissing her mouth while the girlfriend feels traffic's arse. After almost two years living in this street traffic is visiting the house on the corner for the very first time. Bee has wagged Hanukkah, Shifty Christmas and Billy has postponed her trip home to all go camping on the Hawkesbury. traffic who has stayed behind for the lucrative public holiday shifts is alone in the warehouse and out more than ever. The Christmas Eve party beyond the closed bedroom door is emptying as people leave to avoid hangovers at family lunches or catch midnight mass at St Mary's on acid. The taller paler badly tied up girl has stalked past traffic with beseeching eyes since sighting her at Panic but until tonight the girlfriend that followed her didn't appeal and Billy was always too close behind. traffic has gone home twice for more wares, insisting on the strength of the e's and dissuading the shooters from doing a whole at a time. The dark girl lying back now on the bed, the other recovering to drag the clothes off her. traffic has promised Jimi she will come to the Royal Christmas party but now she has accepted the girls' invitation she takes the total offering. She takes control. Asks the pale girl to bend over the bed, asks the dark girl to bend over beside her and takes the rope and ties their hands together. Moves back around to admire their arses, with two girls surrendering the turn-on has doubled. Crotch twitching traffic begins to spank them. This is for having dirty thoughts, and this is for having the gall to act on them. Spank! Spank! The music next door loud enough to give her a rhythm to spank to, traffic spanks up and down the four buttocks harder, stops to rub and hug them, starts up again, both girls squealing squirming and laughing. Spankspankspankspank!! And this is for bringing *me* into your den of iniquity when for all you know I was due at mass tonight. She stops and feels their cunts. Wet, open. Feels them with her tongue, reams their sweet smooth arseholes. They fuck each other messily till the drugs wear off, falling together amongst the latex debris in fitful sleep.

Sunlight, movement, voices through the wall. traffic watches the dark girl dressing by the clothes rack at the foot of the bed, grey jacket over a full-length grey skirt.
    What's the time?
    About ten o'clock.
    What are you doing? Dressups already?
    I have to be in Chatswood by twelve for lunch with my family. Burning beneath traffic's smiling eyes, she hitches the skirt up to lace sensible black shoes like something a private schoolgirl might have worn decades ago. Look, I'm a Baptist, okay? Don't give me a hard time, coming over to kiss traffic then the girlfriend goodbye. Happy Christmas.

Sleeping again wrapped around the girlfriend whose pale face moves into her armpit away from the sun. Waking to an argument in the room next door, Are you sure you didn't use it all? Why don't you trust me? Well I can't fucken *find* it. Keep looking then. Dust drifting down the light, rack of black clothes harnesses and belts, a table in the corner covered in junk, old boom box, dead flowers in a Vegemite jar. This room would be directly opposite her own and Billy's and how much more light from the unimpeded view. To look with lust into a stranger's eyes, touch new skin, kiss alien lips, to arc even wider outside herself. Through the wall now she hears murmured endearments. The makeup fuck begins.

Turkish Jim and the Professor go to the sauna. For ten years through three renovations they have come here, trying once then ignoring each new establishment. This place with its faux rococo entrance endless maze and large plush porn room remains their favourite. The Professor disappears into the steam room and Jim stops in the showers near three young guys playing with each other. Their backs turn so he goes into the maze. Nice and busy, lots of tourists lots of diversity in age and size. Around the corner a bear who feels him up then keeps walking. A lanky boy who pauses to check him out then disappears. Wanking desultorily in the doorway of a cubicle an older guy, thin, not Jim's type. Further towards the end a group of muscle marys adoring one another. Jim arrives back at the showers then does the circuit again. He still can't resist muscles but now that his own have softened and spread he is refused entry to that charmed circle. The lanky boy was a second choice, Jim finds him now lying on the floor of the sling room having his huge cock worshipped by a circle of men, Jim doesn't want to deal with that many people he keeps on wandering. The crescent of brown microdot the Professor gave him on entry had dissolved by the time they were undressed, it's months since he took acid and a year since he last came to the sauna. Persuaded tonight to come out for sex because he supposes it's true that so long without it is bad for his health. So he moves into the maze one more time and lets his face be urged onto the crotch of a guy about his age, cleancut straight-looking. A married lawyer, the Professor would have said. Not Jim's first choice of man or activity but he might get something back. The man comes quickly, gagging him then walks away. Jim blows one more, half hard half-hearted and when he gets up feels his knees begin to swim so goes into a cubicle and pours himself along the bench. A small man with a pot belly stops in the doorway, Jim shakes his head then closes the door.

He lies on the bench, shuts his eyes. Feels the ebb and flow in the pipes beneath the floor, footsteps low murmurs a constant hum. He was beautiful in the 80s and known as a steam queen, travelled and earned his nickname for the descriptions of foreign bathouses he brought back to Sydney, his favourite an old Turkish one in the heart of Paris. He fucked a lot in those days especially in Paris, arriving one morning when the sauna was almost empty, luxuriating instead in the design of the place and leaving surprisingly fulfilled and serene. Harry was already positive when they met back in Sydney, Harry's ghost from all the times they had come here together for sex with strangers was a source of comfort though Jim visited the place less and less often. The tales of debauchery of friends like Fred and the Professor now left him unmoved, the Professor only escaping the virus with the grace of two years of monogamy then one of haemorrhoids when first with James at the peak of infection. Even then it was a miracle, himself James and the Professor were all walking miracles. Fred just kept on fucking and it got him too eventually. Fred had been brought back from death by combination therapies but Harry went quickly. Billy was the only one in years to have called Jim beautiful, his own appraisal of the mirror usually clouded by how he can warp it and a quiet cynicism grown over the years at the ways men love men. He needs to sit up the bricks are wobbling is that a wall opposite? The towel can't get the towel it's stuck oh, I'm sitting on it. He marvels at the simplicity of his situation, alone in this small room with nothing but a towel and a bottle of water which tastes like the sky. The towel is amazing, soft here scratchy there, shroud of a hundred arses and cocks before him and girls too girls' bits for a women's sauna night has been held here twice. What on earth would women do at a sauna? Jim's imagination slides over Renoiresque figures reclining seductively on the benches, doors ajar, can't open them. He considers getting up for an eternity then finally does, the air opening to let his body through as he brings the towel over to the one dim lamp to examine it closer. He would like to touch the light falling from the wall he would like to feel its edges. But the towel is more alluring.

Red dark red, faded to the colour of rock or burnt flesh. He parts the terry, each loop dredded, to see the web. Moving into the warp and weft of the weave following each strand, Jim is startled to see the flaws. How the loops don't emerge with complete consistency, some are broken their direction random. So his detergent advertisement of web loosening and billowing in the perfect wash comes undone. There's something sticking out of the wall to the left, Jim's hand brushes silk, he bends to examine the object thin and purple and attached to a body on the other side of the wall. My god it's a cock. Somebody is sticking their cock through this hole for . . . *him* it can only be for him. Jim looks down at his own, flaccid, inessential. They're absurd men are absurd. He stands back from the wall and watches it closely, other holes open across its expanse like so many bubbles rising to the surface, then the probing of cocks through each one. An army of men is on the other side of that wall, all wanting him his mouth his arse. Jim hugging the wall now rolling across the surface in search of that hard silken touch but the wall is flat and the giggling has come back, can't stand up any longer. His laughter bounces around the cubicle as he lies back on the bench and drapes the towel over his face, sheltering from the basketball of laughter.

The towel engulfs him, each strand like a finger on his skin, tickling tightening, moving around to encircle his whole body, he is inside the terry clutching a loop spiralling down around and down down to its base then onto the floor of the weave. He begins to walk through the forest of terry the loops curling anthropomorphic like a forest of angophoras, he walks and walks in a corridor of tall twisting red cotton angophoras till he finds the sweatshop where women are hemming towels and notices the subtle variations in method of the same simple task as he walks among them aware of their lives beyond the grimy interior, children famished war rape disease, and twelve hours of daylight pass while they work. He follows the thread back through the factory amongst the pump and grind of pistons weaving then the great vats of swirling dye and the cotton mills themselves, threshers, harvest from which the thread unravels further carrying him through shifting seas of white cloud, the great cotton fields of America rotating through centuries, black hands deft around the barbs picking fertilising the history of cotton with their blood. Into the soles of his travelling feet the thread presses its texture, Egyptian cotton brushed cotton flannel cotton plush, till it coarsens telling his journeyman's callouses they are now walking on linen, linen he loves linen, along the Prussian blue of his aunt's spring coat past the buttons like flying saucers in a night blue desert to the beaches of Aoteroa studded with New Zealand flax. Wide flat straw-like fibres weave into the mat beneath his feet, the thread from it leading him over the pale blue of flax fields in Poland, the plants brought in at harvest divested of linseed then soaked thrashed pounded then spun to linen, the linen of Australian tourist teatowels. He is laughing again at the Big Galah and Sturt's Desert Pea still the thread tugs onwards down through the tropics with their own indigenous fibres, floating on kapok soft relief then walking again on sisal tired now sore, on along hemp scoring his feet. Cracking open the soles growing up his legs as he trudges on stiffly through China to the birthplace of silk, the worm a soft cock spinning in the mulberry its cocoon unravelled by slim careful fingers and Jim comes to rest in the soft air of silk, drifting taut, a fibre himself in the shimmering sussuration, stretching straining for the path of the thread. Till he saw himself woven into the fabric of the world and the cinema subsided and he fell asleep alone in the cubicle, waking hours later dehydrated disoriented and unbelievably horny, opening the door to the morning shift of more men cruising searching endlessly searching.

She was careful with everything when first living at the warehouse. Every object contained the magic of her lover and was treated by traffic with due reverence. Hats on their hat stand in the corner of the bedroom, often rearranged though rarely worn, boas hung from the end of the wardrobe next to the row of ties, the precise placement of each cosmetic on the dressing table, outfits exhibited across the thin partitions for extra insulation. The Shiva in the bathroom who had accompanied them to each party and greeted the guests from the top of the cash register, whose base collected any bindhi that had survived a night out. Everything was arranged and cared for like a shrine.

She arrived like water into a course established eons before, a season bringing only the smallest substance of herself. It suited her, to be contained by a solidity that she herself neither had to construct nor dismantle.

Once they were eating dinner alone, the afternoon shopping still in bags on the floor. traffic cleared the table and went into the kitchen to make dessert. When she returned the bags of spices had been opened. In place of their dinner remains were two eyes, one open the other closed with a teardrop falling from its inner corner. traffic leant close to the precise configuration of baby chillies on the white tablecloth, the iris the freshest red, the lids those yellowing, the lashes broken stems. All arranged above a red wine stain which made a sad mouth.

Stricken. Can't eat. It's back again, the fear. Walking the streets in private obsessions oblivious to greetings and all the small daily changes. Guts churning can't eat, nicotine taste clinging. Waking in sunlight, traffic turned away. Kissed her back, licked it, insinuated a hand. And looking up saw traffic's face upturned, rising to the ceiling eyes closed mouth opening, tears pouring down each cheek. That yellow light and the darkness it lent her skin, like a twenties latin lover. She looked so wanton and desperate.

She liked to watch them. The fetishists always did good dressups and were experts at posing and Slip was on the decks at this play party so the music kept Billy going. She knew it was only Stash lying beneath traffic, Stash broke as usual and too sober was asking everybody who'd had chemicals to piss in his mouth and traffic of course was only too happy to oblige. Billy said nothing at the time and stayed away when traffic caned Shifty, coming over reluctantly to hold her hand when traffic was later pierced by Bee and Shifty. But she was quick to anger afterwards when home on a roll on a high on top of Billy, Billy's hand withdrawing, traffic with a groan pissed all over her. *You* can sleep in the wet patch! But traffic was laughing too much to care. Billy loved the feel of traffic's cunt around her hand, the walls ballooning and tightening like a drum, she loved to watch traffic go wild when she then slid one two or three fingers up her arse. But had closed her mind long ago to anything more, closed her own arse against traffic's fingers and cock, even when writhing in the heat of her probing tongue. The possibility of shit repulsed Billy. Her girlfriend before traffic had put it in too hard too quickly and made her bleed. It hurt, she didn't want it.

Always thinking about traffic with someone else. Even when fucking her, when her wail rose then stopped against her neck, when the hot moist cave around her hand spasmed, the ghosts of other people were sliding between them. Couldn't help it, couldn't stop it, couldn't keep them away.

Though most of Holmes's blonde when they first met had come from his youth of sun and beaches, the darkness of his facial hair and roots still surprised Billy. He looked older with long hair and a goatie, butch in a muted elegant way. They went back outside and sat on milk crates away from the crowd. Even small events like this exhibition opening in a cafe off King Street were poignant for Billy now that she was leaving. It was Mardi Gras Festival, people on the streets, a celebratory air, the rich dusk sky, even the art looked good. She was drinking champagne to celebrate the purchase of her plane ticket. Holmes had tried but failed to persuade her to have a party. He had been ready for some time now to move back into the inner city, his flat was crowded with Slip staying there. He was looking forward to living at the warehouse but not to Billy's absence.

You could have an exhibition here you know. Look at this crap. Naked Men With Big Dicks # 5004. Ho-hum.

I've had an exhibition. And it was a failure.

Just cos it didn't sell. Everybody loved it. And it was like four *years* ago Billy.

I quite like these pictures actually, he's a good draughtsman. But I can take a compliment Holmes, don't worry.

Early the next morning Billy tried to draw traffic. Woken by the garbage trucks and with time to kill after a shower and breakfast, she came back into the bedroom with a sketchbook and pen. Her lover's sleeping body unfolded now across the entire bed, face to the window.

The face of traffic trod a line between the exquisite and grotesque, could have come from anywhere was incongruous everywhere. She had a crooked mouth from a scar inside her top lip, a straight unremarkable nose that lent itself to decoration. Thin straight eyebrows, lines shaved through the middle of the visible one broken by the forehead then continuing across her black scalp. It wasn't exactly beauty, she charmed them with comedy, her face went in every direction when she spoke. Learning to read her looks was a lesson in the world's endless variations of beauty. She looked so different sleeping.

Billy traced the line of the temple, the cheekbone, the jaw. Shadow of nose. She began to draw the eyes. Looked at the drawing, looked back at traffic, looked at the drawing again. It had lost her. One small stroke of eyelash and the entire physiognomy had changed. My god, she thought, there are six billion faces on this planet, none of them the same. The endless permutations of colour, shape and texture, and what was a face but the life behind it.

The face of traffic in repose was the uninhabited suit, empty stage, unlit room. Billy tore out the page, crushed it between her palms and threw it into the bin.

Bee:

When I first started mistressing it was more lucrative. It was 1989, I was twenty-six, doing straight sex work to get through art school when a kinky boyfriend set me on the right track. I was getting enough work to live on within a few months. There was one boom period where on Friday nights it wasn't unusual to get sessions back to back. We used to sit around the girls' room and say to each other, okay, the first to hit a thousand buys the Veuve.

I did good things with my money, invested in clothes and equipment and put all the rest into cameras and film. My big dilemma of course has always been finding someone else behind the camera when I'm the one in front of it.

I wanted to make films about our scene and get some decent dyke porn out there. God knows we're starved of that. Those long-nailed vanilla hair bears that het men serve up look more like lesbian deterrents. But it was so hard. When we were all doing the Slut City gigs the lesbian press wouldn't even place our advertisements for the first six months, all this bullshit about aping male paradigms. One venue threw us out for putting fit bins in the toilets. In most Australian states my films were banned and though I got into a couple of festivals in the States and was cheered in New York, I was booed off the stage in Los Angeles. Now of course fetish dykes have been well and truly commodified by the mainstream. Everybody wants to be kinky.

I can understand why so many girls from back then burnt out, gave up, got lost up syringes or down the bottom of a bottle. You get trivialised and put down long enough, even by your own small tribe, you start to believe it, you lose your sanctuary of pride. Not every heretic has the makings of a martyr. But fucked if I was ever going to end up like that. Maybe I was just lucky that drugs and alcohol never did much for me.

Shifty came into my life at the last Slut City when she was just starting to nurse in Ward 17. She was a godsend. Smart butch and beautiful, a party girl who wasn't drugfucked, skin like satin. And she always handled my working.

Shifty in fact maybe likes my working too much. In the sense I sometimes feel she's like so many others who define me with mistressing before photography and performance. James said the other day he gets so embarrassed when people ask him what he does and he has to say I'm a computer programmer, what a cliche. I said Well call yourself a DJ and he shook his head. Later I thought it all just sounded like semantics. Who cares? I guess we all do. Maybe I'm being paranoid, maybe it's my fault, I've got so many rolls in the fridge that I still haven't even processed. It weighs on me sometimes.

I'm a bit over mistressing, the truth be known, I'm working now mostly just to pay for my celluloid habit. The arse has fallen out of the industry anyway. In hard times luxuries are the first to go. Funny how sex art and fantasy are the things most people consider luxuries, even if us true believers know the real ones are whitegoods and mortgages.

Bella got sick the day before Heresy and Bee went into a spin. Shifty would never be the focal point in a show and Stash was incapable of not giggling in performance, especially with his sister. Two other possibilities from Utopia were rostered on that night. She walked down to the Royal.

Friday night in the cellar, wall to wall poofters, Mandrake playing dirty house. traffic had already seen Bee before she reached the bar, she knew something was wrong. She asked Craig for a ten minute break and took drinks and cigarettes through the humidity over to the corner.

Are you coming to the party tomorrow night?

Thought I'd wait and see. I get off at eleven. What's up? Is it Billy?

I need a body.

Tell me about it.

Bella's sick traffic. You sort of know what we were going to do. You up for it? Can you get the night off?

Yes! Relieved only that Billy is safe. Nothing is impossible. Oh shit, I just remembered. My brother's coming over tomorrow. Will it take long to rehearse?

All afternoon, and we have to prepare the needles.

Billy can look after him.

One good thing though. Tony's got some hotshot photography student to record all the shows.

Who?

I don't know her. But I trust Tony. You know those fuckers on the door wouldn't let me in? Think I'm straight cos I've got long hair.

She saw the bedroom in every shade of night, waking often, fearful, excited, rising late. Bee was waiting for her when she came out of the shower and talked her through the show over breakfast. traffic had a cigarette then the walkthroughs began. She launched herself into the scenario, entering each move with her own language, spinning Bee's work to another dimension, Bee disarmed by the translation of her story yet she had come this far in the creation and needed traffic to ferry it through imagination to the solid land of an audience. Shouldn't the puppet cut the strings at the end and fully come alive?

Don't get ahead of yourself traffic, you've never done a piercing show. Have faith Bee. I do, that's why I asked you. I don't want to be inanimate. You're a puppet, I move you. OK Bee, OK listen. Why don't you have scissors in your pocket or somewhere so if I'm up for it at the end I reach for them and cut the strings and if I'm not you just dance me offstage like in the original. traffic's ambition outweighed her experience but Bee agreed in order to silence her. Billy and Roger watched from the couch, chatting inaudibly. Shifty arrived home exhausted and joined them, glad for the entertainment.

traffic had begun to focus the night before when Bee had wooed her at the Royal. All through the rest of her shift she watched her hands pull beers and mix drinks over the imagining of her skin's performance. She dreamt she was a doll of cloth and stuffing, flesh hooking upwards into a sun dance till she flew like an angel. Measuring the strings, tying them to needles, the fear of pain and performance became a craving and with the craving came a strength. In those two hours a silent bond settled around Bee and traffic working side by side at the long table. As night fell they finished the props, traffic turning to Bee with a grin. I like working with you. You know what? What? We should be using hooks, god I'm an idiot. Don't worry about it Bee, we'll use hooks next time.

Jimi rang in the middle of their last run through.
    Howdy cowdy, can you do a drop-off?
    I'm running ragged Jimi. Come over here.
    I'm covered in blue dye, I'm doing Gary's hair. And she wants you too.
    Look I've been lured into doing a show at Heresy so . . . it's a bit of a hass, Cass.
    A show! Go girl. So I'll probably see you there then. What time are you on? Are you nervous?
    And then some. It's a piercing show and I've just started bleeding.
    Oh really?! Jimi is stricken. Where?

An hour after the girls had departed, Billy made the trip to the university buildings across town with Holmes and Roger who had dressed in his little sister's leathers and a snakeskin print shirt. Katherine was away, this the only time he would come out with traffic. A handsome man, like traffic Roger looked young for his age, the same compact acrobat's physique though not so olive-skinned. The first time Billy had met him was at a cabaret evening where traffic had assumed the role of older sibling, protective and proud as she introduced him to everyone and fed him stories of all her friends. The second was at the theatre where he was slightly more relaxed. With traffic busy elsewhere Roger told Billy another side of his sister that mocked her with its incongruous familiarity like a word backwards in a mirror. His fondness for her surprised Billy, showing itself as it did only in traffic's absence.

They slid into the crowd milling in the courtyard between the two dance rooms and chillout space. Shifty was backstage helping Bee and traffic, and Billy steered Roger away from what she knew would be the usual small makeshift space in chaos. The music deepened and people grew silent, shifting and smiling as their drugs came on. Billy had tried to dissuade Holmes from flirting with Roger but when she saw Roger move away to dance, unbuttoning his shirt and opening his body to all those men's eyes, she saw also the indiscriminate vanity of his sister. Roger loved every second of attention no matter the source.

They were at the side when the show began. Moving to the centre then going no further. Two metres back, close enough to see the stage and the people who winced and backed away once the piercing began, others pushing forward with blood fascination. The puppeteer in huge goofy glasses, an oversized suit the sleeves rolled up, hair demented by pipe cleaners. She pierced swiftly and deftly, tugging into motion the puppet's legs, belly, arms then shoulders. Billy and Roger moved forward when the puppeteer attached the final strings to a dowel overhead, pulling traffic upright so they saw her face at last flooded with the bliss of pain. And the febrile soundtrack of Mr Hyde building to climax as traffic reached for the scissors and cut the strings one by one, Bee's surprise and wonder beating through the puppeteer like the heart revealed in surgery. Billy watching traffic now from behind her brother as traffic came to life cut herself adrift and spun across the stage to her freedom.

Heresy was Billy's last party in Sydney.

Needles, she loved needles, and blood, her own. To see it pooling down the barrel slow thick and dark was to know she was alive. The constant liver function tests staining the years, to and from the doctor she went like one giant vial. How much had they taken now, how many vials, how many litres? LFT PCR genotype viral load GGT ALT AST LFT, blood from her veins into vials into racks off to the laboratory lined up end to end her blood cells circling the planet like so much red string. All the viral blood of all the positive millions circling Earth . . . tighter and tighter till blue disappeared altogether and the planet became red.

Slip sits back on her bed in electric and candlelight, measuring out sites with her fingertips. Swabs her belly, places four needles between her teeth takes a breath and unsheaths the first. Breathing out, she drives it through the skin, then the next breath and the next needle. She continues in a half-moon below her navel. The warmth begins, soothing body and mind. Then opening more packets of needles, swabbing again she continues. The stinging rises to a burning circle, she finishes with 19s, driving them through a pinch over her solar plexus, the fatter gauge eliciting a groan. A flower of fire, thirty-five needles fanning like petals around the green head centre. She moves into serenity.

She goes to her new turntables and begins to play inside the clawed embrace. She never pierced herself without a purpose, these little rituals were important. The permanent body jewellery added piece by piece on death anniversaries, tonight's smaller celebration done for the new turntables, at last some equipment bought by herself for herself. An hour into the music a pattern is forming, she unwraps a new cassette and begins to record.

The configuration of needles greets her the next morning as she had placed them upright on the table when extracting them before going to bed. Plastic tips aglow like a halo, needles invisible, the circle continuing to a spiral. She sweeps them into a disposable safe and begins to pack.

Slip saw Bee while working for the Annual Gastronomic Convention held over a three day weekend in October the year before. As one of the cooking staff, Slip was paid. The wages for the performers were only food and wine but the event had such a reputation in epicurean circles that anybody asked was happy to be involved. Bee and Bella joked that if nothing else they could put the Opera House on their performance CVs. Bourgeois foodies from all over the planet flew into Sydney especially to attend. From waking till sleeping they were wined dined and entertained in locales around the city and national parks beyond, arriving on the third night at the Opera House for the final dinner.

The theme of the dinner was Excess and the organiser asked Bee and Bella to do a slave-training show. Bee and Bella wanted to go the whole hog. Can we wear dicks? Hmm . . . No, that might be a bit much. Well what about guns? Great idea! Guns are fine.

Food as theatre. The guests were met in the forecourt by paramilitary uniformed waiters and frogmarched into the dining hall. At the head of each table, in cross formation, stood sacerdotal waiters with platters of wafers. Waitresses in black knelt at their feet holding aloft giant silver bowls of caviar. For entree the guests had to file to them to receive a Communion wafer spread with caviar. Some of the more devout who objected missed out. For main course the waitering staff dressed in drag. Vera City transformed from priest to postwar femme fatale in long clinging black frock long dark hair and long red nails, a beauty spot on her pale cheek. Bliss transformed from acolyte to dashing bachelor in tuxedo, slicked-back hair and thin black moustache. To an electronica backing track, they sang with smoky sarcasm their own local version of Who Wants to Be a Billionaire?

Bee and Bella came on between main course and dessert. By then seduced, the diners had relinquished piety and were an eager and relaxed audience. A drag queen bound to a chair with riding crops between her teeth was carried on by policemen who then stood guard either side of the stage. Bee and Bella put the slaves through their paces, ordering them to their knees for a machine-gun fellatio climax.

From then on the event became more and more debauched. The trek from the dressingrooms to the kitchen took the performers past the souvenir shop, taxi rank and up the steps outside. Drag queen waitresses, their e's coming on, staggered across the paving through the crowd now leaving the opera theatre. Kitchen staff lavished the performers with food and champagne and joints beneath the grill fan. Bee and Bella shrewdly found other uses for cooking utensils and tried them out on staff then compliant guests waylaid in the corridor to the bathroom. In the bathroom itself two or more to a cubicle for alternative ablutions. Dessert was a mountain of macadamia nut icecream covered in gold-leafed cones and carried on a stretcher into the dining hall by four waiters in loincloths, each cone served to the guests by the drags. It was Vera City intoxicated with MDA and hubris who playfully pushed the open-mouthed face of a French society matron down onto the cone of gold-leafed icecream before her, the staff in the kitchen doorway buffetted by the organiser's horrified exit. But the diners were delighted and without further sybaritic instruction the whole second table abandoned their cutlery and went down on dessert with Roman abandon.

From the doorway Slip watched it all. Cooking only casually in Sydney, playing enough to make the journey to and from home inconvenient, her doubts about moving back vanished with dessert. She had sun on water then an ink harbour in moonlight, South Australian olive oil with the lingering taste of grass, red wine like velvet, and all the city's finest perverts and party people in the guise of servitude leading the upper echelons in the art of celebration.

Later she was able to put more names to faces. Jimi and Stash the two slave boys, Amfetta Mean the other head drag waitress, Bliss the drag king, Neil from the leather shop and his boyfriend the policeman. A discarded cassock from the entree wardrobe would reappear on traffic years later in a photo shoot of Bee's and finish with the Professor when his own had fallen apart. So that everything was somehow linked even if you didn't know it at the time. And the tables were always turning.

Who wants to be a billionaire?
I don't.
Who wants a fabulous career?
I don't.
Who wants to speculate on real estate?
Real estate?
How false!
I'd rather be straight.
Who wants to shop in Double Bay?
I don't.
Who wants to pay and pay and pay?
I don't.
Who wants a personal minder too?
I don't
And I don't
Cos all I want is you.

Who wants to be a trillionaire?
I don't.
Who wants to triple their fair share. . . ?

Slip:

You have to remember things were different back then. Sydney in the early 80s was so much smaller. Leichhardt was WoopWoop, Oxford Street was starting to take off but was still pretty grimy. It had good food shops, it felt like a real community. There were squats and warehouses and cheap rooms all over the place. I rented a bedsit in Paddington for $33 a week.

There was no Eastern Distributor, no car artery wounding the village of Darlinghurst, there was parkland in its place beyond. There was no Monorail, no Darling Harbour, no Harbour Tunnel. There was no M1 Freeway.

There were jobs. Kitchen wages were about the same then as they are now. You could scrape by on the dole or live on it quite well doing casual work on the side. It was the Great Unofficial Arts Subsidy. Education was free. There was no Needle Exchange. Syringes you paid for at selected pharmacies, muttering your order around any clean customers.

Nearly everybody yearned for London or New York, Berlin if you were more underground. Foreigners were quite exotic, tourists an oddity.

The live music scene was going off. There were discos, there were dance clubs, there were endless endless parties, but dance party culture as we know it was just a whisper.

There was no ecstasy, no MDA, no GHB, no Special K. There was no Viagra and there was no Prozac. Rohypnol was available. There were mandies and ludes and serepax galore and the smack and speed weren't as pure.

Hepatitis C was unrecognised. HIV had just begun, an obscure gay cancer.

You could wander up and watch the Mardi Gras parade at any point along Oxford Street. There were no barriers in most places because there weren't that many spectators, mostly locals who'd join in if they saw a friend in a passing float.

Homosexual acts between men were illegal.

There were no answer machines. There were no mobile phones. There were no CDs. Stereos cost a fortune. I lived without a telephone for almost a year and that wasn't unusual. I didn't have a television and knew nobody with a VCR.

There were no modems, no World Wide Web, the net was what kept sharks from harbour beaches. Fax machines and computers were part of the sophisticated technology that only the corporate world could afford, or seemed to need.

But these are mere details. Material things always change quickly. The basics were the same.

We fled suburban banality and places beyond for innercity chaos, saw our salvation in subterranean night-life. We turned away from our upbringings, demonstrated against the government, we looked for love and purpose, got lucky or died trying. We wore black, we wore leather, bright colours and freaky hairdos. We fucked around. We partied, we took drugs, we dressed up and danced.

That was the same as it is now and ever has been. Always the congregation around music and performance, always the need for transcendence and fantasy. You can change a law overnight but it takes lifetimes to change an attitude. We weren't waiting. Partying was our font, our touchstone, it was our main reality. It was the world in which we truly came alive.

From his window, the wide wet sunlit street. Burgundy brick facades, cracked by rain and salt winds from the sea, a run of smooth footpath burnt the day long by skateboards. The suburb changed on every corner. A street of Spanish mission leading to pale 1970s apartments, the steep laneways and cul-de-sacs of lush gardens in the south, the long flat boulevards and faded shops in the north.

She was at Bondi by midday, recording the light and dimensions of each room. Empty of Holmes's possessions the flat looked smaller. Stains visible on the bare expanse of carpet, down the off-white walls. In a day the place would fill again with her things, in a week she would know the daily patterns of the sun, the sounds of different neighbours as they too would come to know her music. Slip went for her last swim of summer in the vicious rips of a cold nor'easter.

At three o'clock in the afternoon of his day off the following week, Holmes came over and they went out for a walk. Holmes as she hadn't seen him for a year, a figure in the distance stretching full length, not the random face and body parts encountered at close range in city interiors. Body like a blade, stepping across the shallows like a wading bird. They went along the beach then up to the cliffs and he asked Slip if she was happy. Sydney made her nervous, the pace the expense the people, even on a weekday afternoon in Bondi there were people everywhere. And yet the sensual rewards that began outside her window every morning, continuing through to innercity dancefloors, soothed her, kept her level. She had moved up to play a weekly bar residency and as many other parties and slots as possible but suspected the cost of living was still too high and that her cooking job would remain necessary.

Sometimes I wish I was James you know. With a job that paid well so I could fully indulge in anything musical.

But it means he's unavailable half the time Slip, he practically never plays during the week or on a Sunday night. And look at how your career's taken off.

Stopping now at the crest, wondering whether to chase or flee the weather.

I wouldn't call it a career Holmes. It's more like a habit.

She still cooked for a living, four nights a week. So that was her job, cooking, not music. The music was a luxury which paid for itself now, for that she was grateful. But living here she could play those midweek bar gigs more easily, she could go record shopping and hear others play more often. And she could believe more easily in the dream that her luxury would one day become her living. She grew up landlocked and never wanted to go back to that again. Thought she could live in the city as long as she stayed on its edge with a horizon to slip into, best to consider this a move up the coast, no more no less. There was the seaside sky even bigger here with no escarpment just low hills of terracotta roofs, a sky big enough to contain the storm in the south and blue above, so they walked towards a headland bright against horizontal sun, beyond it a bank of rain. Aubergine clouds, dark green sea. At dusk the rain moved across to Bondi.

She was sorting through clothes for the bush. traffic stayed in the doorway, bag hanging from her shoulder. The wardrobe empty of Billy's clothes was reduced to a section of wall that traffic had never seen.

How come you've packed everything away? What'll you wear when you get back?

I've got a bag of stuff in the storage space.

You're not allowed to come out of the bedroom till I say, alright?

OK.

traffic went back out to the kitchen. Unpacked the oysters and prawns and arranged them on plates with lemon. Unpacked the Veuve Clicquot and roses, tore off the petals and pressed them to the cold wet bottle then wrapped it in red tissue paper. Selected the largest tray, placed the liturgical candle in the middle and lit it, then arranged the champagne and seafood around it. Then took off all her clothes, tied a blue ribbon around her waist and took the tray back into the bedroom.

The following morning Billy borrowed Esmerelda and drove northwest through dry brown land. She missed a travelling companion for wider eyes to see the rise and fall of mountains. Her own parched, drinking in Visine on the side of the road. She stopped at Maitland for a bad cappuccino in a Greek place behind the shopping mall.

School holidays, country lull. Teenage girls at the other two tables that looked down a verge onto the slow brown river. A group of boys with skateboards sauntered past, trading insults and endearments. Billy was one of those teenage girls, smoking Winfields, eyelashes clogged with cheap mascara, feet baking in Doc Martens. Hating school, a misfit, on the verge of leaving. Interested in other girls, too afraid to touch them. Except that now they had eyebrow rings and labrets, maybe even a little rose tattoo hidden beneath their T-shirts.

Three hours later she reached her home town and stopped at the railway station on top of the hill. Tin roofs silver in the last sunlight, bougainvillea, ironbarks, apart from scaffolding up one side of the Presbyterian church nothing looked different. She drove slowly down the road to Aunty Elvis's, got out and knocked. Nobody home but the door was open. Too habituated to city protocol, Billy went no further than the end of the hall from where she saw a new 50s chrome bar in the living room and the remainders of lunch in the kitchen. She got back in the car and drove around the corner to her parents'. Nobody home here either.

The red brick house was still unfamiliar so she took her bag into the kitchen, drank two glasses of lime cordial then went into the living room and lay on the couch where she fell asleep almost immediately.

Belinda! She didn't wake properly, she wasn't there that night eating dinner with her parents and brother in the pale blue kitchen, editing the answers to all of their questions. She had last visited three years ago just after they moved here from the other side of town, they had renovated the back since but Billy wasn't listening. She was back in Surry Hills, in the warehouse, in the bedroom with traffic. Wordless, hungry, all night fucking tinged with the desperation of departure.

traffic saying Don't give up on me baby, I still might come to the States. No traffic, no, I love you but it's over. Though this was the traffic she had fallen in love with, tender generous funny, giving herself to Billy like that, the braille of tiny perforations from the show at Heresy fading across her skin. Crying when they came, kissing tears that stayed in Billy's blood all through the long drive here today.

Her father wasn't that old, he was still this side of sixty but overweight and wheezing, moving more slowly. Billy followed him down the garden to the long chicken run he had erected by the fence. He had begun to breed silkies seriously now that he was retired. There must have been at least two dozen, theirs were the eggs in last night's custard.

You're staying till the end of the week I hope. Emily's going to want to see you.

I poked my head in on the way into town but the house was empty. How is she?

Mad as a cut snake still. She's doing something for the RSL in Newcastle. You know she got a prize?

Really?

Yes. A regional prize. Best rock'n'roll dancer. Half the other girls were half her age!

He was opening the gate.

This is one of Rex's grandsons, see? Remember Rex?

Rex used to bite me Dad.

Oh he was just protecting his brood. Come and say hallo to Belinda, Rex.

She followed her father amongst the fowl. Rex flew at her ankles and she made a quick exit.

I told you.

Must be those boots. Don't you get hot in that getup?

Maybe Rex just doesn't like women.

It came back to her, that one flippant remark, in various guises for the rest of her stay. What would I know, I'm just a man. D'you let men into those dances of yours? Take the garbage out for your mother will you Belinda, I know it's a man's job but your brother's working late.

She walked down into the centre of town on the third afternoon. Bought a milkshake and sat on a bench to ring traffic. It was about six o'clock. There was no one else on the street, just a dog tied to a

173

telegraph pole across the road, inching back from the late hot sun. traffic was about to walk out the door to a gallery opening then the Circus with the Professor, later maybe dancing at Playschool. She murmured condolences to Billy.

What about your aunt?

She's in Newcastle. Back later tonight apparently.

What about your mother?

Oh she's alright. Even Dad's alright. Look they're all alright. I'm just bored. What about you? How are you?

Great! Except we still haven't got the photos of the Heresy show, Queen Bee's pretty shitty about that. I had a sexy dream about you last night. Your hand was up me then I woke up and I was alone. I felt awful. I'd like to eat your cunt right *now*.

Oh traffic *don't* –

I'm wearing the skirt you made me.

So you're going out to cause a sensation in your new leather mini, eh?

Yep, traffic laughed.

Oh god, I'm so jealous, Billy began to cry. I can't help it, I'm jealous, I know it's stupid.

What about the silkie?

My god the silk*ies*, you mean. He's got a whole fucken colony now.

The dog across the road was beginning to whine, where was its owner? Probably in the pub. The conversation was a miracle, free of fights. Billy felt angelic, tragic, magnanimous, and had flown over to release the animal before saying goodbye to traffic.

She had met Stan once before, he was her aunt's new boyfriend last time Billy had visited. So you're still together. She moved along the mantelpiece of photos. Aunty Elvis called out from the kitchen. Four and a half years, four years six months and five days of fun! She came halfway down the corridor. Stan's very short you know, people make fun of short men. But he makes up for it elsewhere let me tell you! The photos were swallowed by gaudy frames, Billy picked them up one by one and examined each closely. Stan in his shiny jacket with sequinned lapels playing ukelele, Stan with his band the Good Rockin' Jivebombs doing shopping mall gigs with a rhythm box and another man in a matching outfit on bass, three jiving couples in front. Is that you?

I've gotten thinner haven't I?

You look great. Are you wearing a corset?

Don't be stupid Belinda!

I *like* corsets. I wear them sometimes.

They're quite trendy again aren't they? Well you couldn't jive in a corset. I had an eighteen inch waist when I was your age.

I'm thirty-*three* now you know.

It's filled out a bit of course. I know how old you are. If anyone asks by the way, I'm still forty-nine.

But where's Elvis?

There.

Oh cool! You're doing Jailhouse Rock now as well?

Everything. I do everything. She moved behind the bar. What'll you have Belinda? Not still on that health kick are you? Bugger that, we're celebrating. Now tell me about these parties, I love parties!

There was nothing she couldn't have told her parents, there wasn't actually that much to edit. There were the props and the costumes, the chalk outlines on the dancefloor that more than one keen partygoer had lain inside on arriving at Panic, the body bags containing their strange handicapped creatures. Billy poked her red cocktail umbrella into her hair as the tequila sunrise lowered in her glass, and talked on through ten o'clock and two refills. There were the skeletons revamped for Scum, brightened and dressed which pleased Elvis. Neither Bliss and Genie's show at Panic nor Bee and Ben's at Scum existed. traffic didn't exist at all.

What about your friend? Where's she? I thought you met someone.
I did.
Why didn't you bring her?
I'm going overseas.
I thought about it you know. Two women together? I must admit I was worried at first. There was a girl in my class at school who turned out to be a lesbian.
Billy had heard this story before. She used to hate it, now she liked it.
Really? Go on.
She's got a guesthouse and restaurant in the Hunter now, she runs it with her partner who's actually quite good-looking. The restaurant's not bad, bit pricey. But at school, Belinda, she was so *aggressive*. Really masculine? She used to scare everybody. Even the boys, she used to bash up the boys too. But she's happy now and I can see why she might have been unhappy before. I can understand how two women can be in love. In fact I reckon you'd have a lot less problems without a man. Women don't sleep around like men for a start! Elvis leant forward. I can say in all honesty that even physically, two women together, I'm sweet with that now. I mean it's not enough for me, I need that extra . . . you know . . . God Belinda, I'm probably stretched from all those babies! Don't you laugh.
I'm pissed Elvis. These are more like Tequila All Day Longs.
But two men together. I'm sorry but I still can't . . . Anal sex, she whispered in case the townsfolk were listening. It's so un*natural*.

By midnight when Stan arrived they were dancing to Little Richard. Elvis steering Billy through the steps, Billy adorned with cocktail umbrellas, clumsy and laughing. She flopped onto the couch. You two should give me a demo. And watched them twist and twirl through her tequila-soaked eyes till Elvis told Stan to get his guitar and changed into her Jailhouse Rock outfit. The costume looked homemade and the hair wasn't quite right but when Elvis strutted into the room with that sky-high attitude, Billy roared. He was the best Elvis she had ever seen. Stan sidestepping past her tight and perfect like Chuck Berry. She would have liked to have hired them for a party.

Swamp head, drought mouth. Elvis woke her with tea and toast. Billy traipsed out to the kitchen with her breakfast.

I still think you should've brung your girlfriend.

Look I've just woken up and I'm really hungover and you can take the credit for that.

Well why not? I'd like to meet her. What's she like? What's her name?

Give it a rest will you Elvis.

Now look Belinda, you have to stop going on about how you're different. We accept you for who you are these days, you know that.

I'm going overseas in a week. Remember?

Well isn't she going with you?

No.

Why not?

God Elvis, she's not my girlfriend anymore! So let's just drop it OK.

Oh Belinda, I'm sorry. Oh god, now I've made her cry. God I crap on. Don't cry love. Come here, don't cry. I'm sorry, I'm sorry.

How could she be like that, clear-eyed and sweet-smelling at nine o'clock in the morning after a night of tequila and rock'n'roll. Hotly and freshly in love at the age of fifty-four with a lifetime of fun and dancing before her. Billy asked to use the computer before she left. Saturday morning and they would be waking, getting their outfits together for the Mardi Gras party. Holmes and all the boys were going for the first time in years. What they derided one year and painted black they embraced the next with hope and nostalgia. Like past lovers, one's country, city and family. On Sunday evening while Billy helped her father build the barbecue, they would still be dancing. She opened up the email and typed in Holmes's address. Pressed caps lock.

ELVIS IS ALIVE, WELL, AND DOING THE THREE O'CLOCK SHOW

Sex. It was everywhere. In their work, their play, in the shadows and backrooms of their preferred bars and parties. Heterosex in every newspaper television show advertisement, homosex underfoot clamouring for equal attention. The pulse behind the black band of the censor, the subtext of so much leather shop talk. Sex was the first and last thing she had wanted from traffic, it was what pulled traffic away from her, what threatened and united them. Epsom-laced speed inflaming her throat and groin, ecstasy and acid turnon. Drug lust, party lust, blood lust, life lust, sex in the nights too hot to sleep close afterwards. All the flesh across Bondi Beach through the long summer months and the sweatbox parties she crammed in before leaving, like a blast of humid air, a hot poultice, a gag.

Sometimes Billy wanted to throw it all up, she felt like she couldn't breathe see or speak, ever again. Took off in an aeroplane through a storm, left it all behind. Looked around at the passengers and flight attendants. Sex was the cause of every life on the planet.

Just close your eyes

Forget your name

Forget the world

Forget the people

Just close your eyes

Just close your eyes

Just close your eyes

Just close your eyes

Bee came home to find traffic and Holmes watching a lesbian vampire movie in their boxer shorts. traffic with fluorescent fangs in her mouth, clacking away to the dialogue. Hey, I thought of another good use for these at work today. Whipping off her shorts and leaning back to insert the fangs between her legs. After some scissor action they popped out. What a great idea! Bee took the offered fangs, disappeared into her room, reappeared in thigh-highs. Wincing she strode over to the obvious victim and placed a vicious heel on his shoulder. Now slave, you may worship your mistress's cunt, but only from afar. Be*ware* the vagina dentata.

Bit rough on the old cunt though, said Bee flicking the fangs into the lap of traffic.

So Holmes moved into the warehouse and Slip moved into Bondi, the living spaces passed between friends like talismans. Holmes, Bee and Shifty tense at first in the aftermath of Billy but traffic kept her grief and remorse and exultation in solitude hidden from all of them. Working as she did when most people played, their paths crossed infrequently. To avoid nights home alone, she took on another bar shift. To take advantage of the continual requests for speed from her co-workers, she began to deal more regularly. And use more often. Bee Shifty and Holmes would come home to find meals cooked, clothes washed and hung out to dry and traffic charming, witty and affectionate.

The luxury of being single in a double bed. To stretch out and dream your own private dreams.

She works the double shift on Fridays in the cocktail bar. Full now of office workers, Aussie Boys catalogue men and their straight girlfriends drunk on daiquiris and sparkling wine, dancing to cheesy house music played by one of the most popular DJs on the strip. This is the shift traffic grits her teeth to get through, keeps her head down eyes on the orders and the distant closing hour. She takes a tray of dirty glasses through to the kitchen, catching the door with a foot and backing up against it so she is pushed into the room as it closes behind her, into another dimension. Small white room ablaze with fluoros and honky-tonk music from an old boombox turned up full volume. Jimi is in here on his break from the cellar bar, dancing the Charleston with the kitchenhand behind the aluminium shelving. traffic deposits the tray and ducks to see Jimi's partner. It's Bliss, coming towards her now like a long-lost friend, piercing traffic's chin with her labret spike as she kisses her hello.

So Bliss is back and working at the Royal. Neat, petite, sloe-eyed Bliss with the fastest pelvis this side of Gracelands, who dances with a joy as hot offstage as on, who converses rarely and then with the awkwardness of a mistrustful child. Seducing traffic now into bringing her and Jimi, and traffic *too* if she wants, tequila slammers. Top shelf darling, Monté Alban. Back out in the cocktail bar like a shopping mall at Christmas, traffic tells Craig she needs a break and twenty minutes later has spirited the tequila into the kitchen. They slam and drink in unison then traffic hoists herself up onto the counter beside Bliss, Jimi packing a bucket bong in the corner hidden by the icemachine. He pushes it over to traffic, strikes a match. I was surprised not to see you at that exhibition last week. Smoke enters her lungs like lava, traffic questions Jimi with her eyebrows. Some girl from art college. She had a whole series of the shows from the last Heresy party. traffic stares, upright like a hot-air balloon. Exhales slowly. Nobody told me about the exhibition. She pushes the bucket back over to Jimi. Sick, light-headed, staring at Bliss who jumps off the counter and begins unloading trays. Jimi shakes his head. Did you know about it Bliss? Did Genie?

We got back to Sydney the day before.

God Tony's a fuckwit, all he cares about is making money.

So the photos were actually for sale? Full fucken *on*.

I don't wanna get involved! Bliss waves her hands. We were away for the last party! Tony promotes solo now!

You shouldn't let him go ahead with the next party. You've got as much copyright over the name as he does. Most of the crowd follows you and Genie anyhow.

Let it go Jimi will you.

White lights, shining shelves and ragtime music shattering her marrow, the room seems to be consuming her. Way off in the distance a part of her brain thrilling to the arrogance of Jimi the arriviste lecturing Bliss the old hand about party ethics. traffic slides off the counter and hangs onto the shelving, everything slowed down and distorted. She talks to the back of Bliss opening the glass-washer. So you've quit the Heresy parties for good? Why?

We're going in different directions now. I don't know, I don't really like Tony's politics.

Fuck politics. What's that got to do with it.

traffic goes back out to the bar.

When she brings the next tray into the kitchen Bliss stops her. I honestly didn't know traffic. I mean I didn't know that you didn't know. Cos there were a couple of girls from Utopia at the exhibition so I just assumed Bee would've known about it.

She walks home flanked by Jimi and Bliss. Feels so far away. The foreigner accompanied by friends of a friend, the acquaintance taken care of. Jimi's hair bleached, traffic's red, Bliss's blue. Jimi jokes they are a walking tricolour. They stop at 32 around the corner.

I'd ask you up ladies, but you know how it is . . .

That's alright, sweetheart. We've got community service to do.

Bliss gets into a cab and traffic goes home.

Two days later traffic and Bee go to the exhibition. Five large prints along the walls of a cafe behind Taylor Square, four hundred dollars each. The images are beautiful, traffic scarcely recognises herself. Bee disparaging everything right down to the type of paper and printing process.

My god, they've nearly all sold.

Yes. We'll have to write Tony a thankyou note for that. Did you see this caption? *Thanks to Tony and his performers?*

We don't even have names.

I'm not one of Tony's fucking performers.

Nobody is.

She wants to be free, aloft, unobliged and unattached, she wants to belong to nobody. The bird that flies in and nests for a season then disappears again. The weed uprooted, thrown aside, burrowing slyly back into the earth. To lose and continue, the skink without its tail, to grow again each part of herself that is taken away. Yet even the dust mite floating invisible lives off particles so traffic returns to earth each time. Gives into raw hunger and strolls back into the cafe, demanding to speak to the manager, telling him why his walls are positively *radiating* bad karma. Bee whose purity is her greatest weapon waits quietly outside and traffic returns with the photographer's phone number. Okay then, over to you. She puts her arm around Bee and they head home. Tony, by the way, is visiting his family in the States. No doubt on party profits.

Bee rings the photographer. Nothing is gained, nothing learnt that relieves or even surprises them. Simply that Tony told the photographer the girls had given their permission for the work to be exhibited and that it's too late to withdraw the photographs from sale. Bee gets angry and the photographer hangs up on her. A woman at the Arts Law Centre tells Bee nothing can be done without proof of contract. I'm *really* sorry, it's really fucked I know. We deal with this sort of thing all the time but performers have virtually no rights. We do what we can.

Two months later Heresy would advertise another party. Tickets would be ten dollars more than previously. The presales would come to a halt at two hundred and Tony would be forced to cancel.

She was single and free and loving every minute of it. Gave each girl customer remotely interesting her undivided attention, stayed back after work for staffies with the boys, sometimes went clubbing afterwards. Down to the last night of Pawn with Jimi where she danced for the first time in months to house music like a tropical heatwave in the cool autumn night. Head to toe in leather, with his long curled goatie and new tribal tattoos, his round hairy belly always exposed, twenty-nine year old Jimi could have easily passed for ten years older till he smiled and the years fell away again. The Professor emerged from the throng of shirtless men in baby blue fake fur chaps and a baby blue fake fur tie. traffic could have predicted it, his amazement at Jimi's evolution. Sure enough the Professor fixated on Jimi who slid immediately into the crowd and later returned with a blonde who wanted drugs from traffic. By the time they were in the cubicle transacting traffic knew she wanted more than that. I've seen you around. Yeh I've seen you too. Leaning up against the door and taking in the shape of her. D'you have any works? It just so happens I do! Pulling fresh fit, vial, swab and spoon from her pencil case. Aren't you having any? Let *me* treat you to a taste, traffic. Is that your real name? It's as real as I get.

Back out by the dancefloor there was the Professor, tall and bizarre like a wildflower in the forest of flesh, sentimental about the demise of the club. After this there would be nothing small and underground except for Playschool which he often found too young. At Pawn as well, few men responded to his wandering eyes. traffic knew he would finish the night at the sauna, wake in time to deliver Friday afternoon lectures, remain at home for the rest of the weekend with James and his books before re-emerging for a Sunday afternoon drink. Unless bored tired or unhappy, the Professor would never dress down to just jeans and T-shirt nor hide his lust to compensate his lack of beauty. For that alone traffic loved him.

Have you heard from Billy?

No. And I don't expect to. Don't look at me like that.

I'm looking at the dreamboat behind you!

She was angry with me when she left. I'm sure she'll contact Holmes.

Then a hand on the back of traffic's neck and the blonde's mouth delivering fresh water in a kiss that tasted like moonlight.

traffic took her by the hand, led her back into the toilets. The disableds was free, perfect. This particular cubicle had a history. Shifty cuffing Bee to the railing opposite the door, remembering then the key was in her cloaked jacket, going back out through the packed club to retrieve it while Bee stretched her not so long body the length of the cubicle to put a foot against the door and the constant stream of impatient patrons banging on it. Billy and an ambitious ex who insisted Billy stand on the toilet seat to make her cunt more accesible, the door pushed open in the heat of their moment and Billy falling feet first into the toilet, the ex fleeing so Billy had to extricate herself alone. traffic also interrupted in there years ago, sundry fucks witnessed by heads over the partition or bodies pushing the door in. But tonight the lock was working so traffic shut it, turned and started to kiss the blonde. Hands up each other skirts, traffic's free hand pulling lube and glove from her pocket, turning around and leaning on the cistern, wanting the blonde's whole hand, mmm deeper slower deeper, people banging on the door traffic screaming back I'm changing a tampon! but the blonde was withdrawing, peeling off her glove, arms around traffic. I can't do it here. And by the time they got back to the blonde's place four hours later, though traffic had the energy to fuck the blonde to orgasm, the blonde gave her nothing in return. So there she was, crazy with horniness after hours with trade. She smoked and wanked quietly in the darkness.

Morning, side by side. traffic watches her breathing. Places her finger and thumb to the divets by the girl's sleeping eyes, then to her own. Touches the girl's hot temples, her own again. The Professor saying they could have been sisters if traffic bleached her hair, she wants now to measure this. But each time her hand travels from face to face, she loses the correct distance. She gets up and dresses quietly to avoid waking the girl and the possibility of breakfast together, pulls the doona back over her before leaving.

The boys finally got a venue for a party. James rang traffic and explained the concept to her.

Want to do a show?

I don't do shows.

Well who's the traffic I've seen on stage?

Once. And that was Bee's show.

So what?

Well I can't, you know, invent things.

Look it's no big deal. We're all doing something. The shows are informal, kind of like charades.

No honestly. I'd love to help though. D'you want me to do some footpath stencilling?

No, they're cracking down on that.

Oh come on James. They can't prove anything. You just tell them you've got some crazy fans.

We don't want to take the risk.

traffic told Holmes when they crossed paths between work.

I love the concept for the shows. Are you doing one?

Have you ever seen me put on a show, like off my own back?

Well you strip don't you?

That's different.

She was sitting by the windows in the afternoon sun, Holmes was in the kitchen. traffic looked onto the street, saw the Chinese family on their verandah smoking and drinking tea. Saw a man in a suit leave the brothel next door.

OK then, she called out to Holmes. I've got an idea. You're doing it with me of course.

No way.

Come on Holmes. I've seen those videos of you at Slut City. You were so *cute*.

That was like, eight years ago traffic. And I was very stoned. I'm not a performer.

Just listen.

By the time they saw each other the next day Holmes had a list of very good excuses.

Look I can't come at the drag, I'm so over drag. And if the Green Woman's on that night any other drag will pale in comparison. So to speak.

OK then, you can be the man. traffic warmed to this concept straightaway to the consternation of Holmes. In fact Homie, in view of your dark past, it'll be even better if you're the man. The tables will have turned, it'll be *vary therapudic*.

Gimmee a break traffic!

That's exactly what I'm doing! Footlights! Greasepaint!

Look I don't have the time. There's all the costumes 'n' stuff.

There's practically nothing to actually make Holmes, just the prosthetics. And I'll make that. I'm gonna ring the Turk. He'll know how to do it.

She rang James and the Professor to offer them the show, the latter picked up the phone.

Perfect darling, *perfect*. Hotel Quickie would be incomplete without it.

I can't believe nobody's else's suggested it.

I think we all thought in the back of our minds that you would come forward with something of that ilk . . .

Is that a compliment or an insult?

Well *I* know how *I'd* take it.

Stash rang the next week and asked her to be in his show. It sounded so good and so easy that traffic agreed straightaway. Time flew by in work and chores. Two weeks before the party traffic woke in the dead of night. Jesus Christ, what have I done!? There she was working thirty-five hours a week, dealing as well, and she had agreed to do two shows. It was too late to pull out now. She and Holmes hadn't had a second to go through their show or sort their costumes, Stash hadn't rung back with any details other than the instruction to make a cardboard guitar, traffic hadn't even bought the materials for the prosthetic. It wouldn't work, none of it. Stash wouldn't come good, Holmes would pull out. The prosthetic would rip on stage the guitar would look crappy she would look like an idiot everybody would see how nervous and unrehearsed she was she would trip over and get stuck to the stage like that with her arse in the air. The whole thing would be a total fucking disaster.

Hotel Quickie.

From 10 am they arrived at the venue to decorate. Downstairs large signs painted by James. PLEASE DO NOT DISTURB, PLEASE MAKE UP MY ROOM, GAMING ROOM, and CONFERENCE IN PROGRESS. Turkish Jim made a giant papier-mache toothbrush, moisturiser, condoms, lube, dildos and other bedroom necessities which were hung from the ceiling all across the dancefloor with the help of traffic and Shifty. Upstairs where the shows would take place cardboard poker machines made by Turkish Jim and the Professor lined the walls, the stage made up like a hotel room, #69. They dragged an old chest of drawers out from the tiny dressing room and created a bed from milk crates lashed together, a foam mattress and chenille bedspread. The Professor painted two trompe l'oeil doorways, one opening onto a bathroom, another through which the hotel's flashing neon was visible.

traffic the night before had come back late from Neil's, now between set-up and the party she was late weighing up. Late therefore in gluing the last stars and jewels to her fluorescent painted cardboard guitar, late in finishing the long pink satin prosthetic, realising as she did the last of the fine stitches that they were inside out, cursing as she undid and redid them. You always need to give yourself twice as much time as you think it will take, Turkish Jim's advice had fallen on deaf ears. Shifty and Bee and Holmes left the warehouse while traffic frantically pinned the last bit. She was too late to enjoy her handiwork which in spite of the rush had worked as was intended, and was late getting ready having spent so much time on show props that she had no time to prepare a party outfit. So she had another shot, put on the kitsch and glitzy minidress that she was wearing for her first show, packed her things, hailed a cab and arrived at the venue too late to be nervous about performing.

The first show was the Green Woman. She came into the hotel room carrying bags from Dior and Chanel and sat on the bed fanning herself. Shifty entered dressed as a porter, carrying more shopping bags, Gucci, Armani and Yves St Laurent, which she piled up around the figure of the Green Woman. The Green Woman sat there preening and ordering

Shifty to and from the stage to fetch more shopping bags. The labels began to lower, David Jones, Grace Bros, Aussie Boys, as did the Green Woman, reclining exhausted across the pink chenille bedspread. Until the entire stage around the bed was piled high with bags from Target, Franklins and Woolworths and the Green Woman shopper had herself disappeared.

Next was traffic as a hooker with Holmes as her client sitting on the edge of the bed. The hooker sauntered on stage and began to do a striptease. One by one she removed her items of clothing, lapdancing the client, shaking her booty at the crowd. Once she was down to a bra and panties, the client pointed to the ground and the hooker went down on hands and knees, crawled over to him, undid his zipper. Pulled out a cockhead the size of fist and began to lick it, took it in her mouth. Stood up then and walked across the stage away from the client, still holding in her mouth the pink satin penis which still emerged from his trousers to stretch the three metre length of the stage. The show ended with the hooker pulling it from the client's trousers altogether and arranging it around her shoulders like a feather boa. And as the client lay back on the bed in ecstatic agony, the decorated hooker sauntered offstage.

So every forty-five minutes from midnight onwards, a scene was played out in Room 69 of Hotel Quickie. There were the three suits, James, Fred and Bee, who arrived with briefcases and in perfect time undid them, emptied them of money and bags of white powder, and slowly in sync, counted it bill by bill, bag by bag, then refilled the briefcases. Shifty the perennial uniform queen entered as a policeman and the suits handed their briefcases over to him. There was the Professor alone dressed as a bride. Arriving in a flurry of excitement, putting down her bag and doing her toilette, one eye on her wristwatch, the other on the mirror. The bride's show was the longest, most simple and poignant. She finished her toilette and waited on the bed looking at her watch while the audience watched and waited with her. For ten more minutes she sat there waiting, an eternity in dance party showtime, finally leaving the stage in tears when the groom still hadn't shown. And in between each show, Bella in her French maid's outfit, came in and cleaned the room and set it up for the next show. Seventy-five kilogram Bella bending over to flash her frilly knickers and suspenders to the cheers and whistles of her friends and fans.

The last show was Jimi, Holmes, Stash and traffic who by 4 am had all changed into leathers and dropped their party drugs. They traipsed on in long messy wigs as a metal rock band. Passed around a bottle of Jim Beam and a joint, injected themselves with air from large 20ml barrels, jammed with each other on painted, bejewelled cardboard guitars. Took turns in defiling an inflatable doll then piece by piece, excepting the chest of drawers which belonged to the venue, they smashed up the entire hotel room.

G'day mate!
G'day's it goin'? traffic the heavy metal star sat down next to the man with the rooster tattoo.
Geez you blokes know how to party, totalled that hotel room.
You can talk you trashy slut. Every time I see you you're all-night partying.
But it's the exception! I lead such a sober life these days, I hardly ever do this anymore.
But it's the exceptions that count isn't it. Not the rules.

Can we make it back to earth?

　　　　　　　　The risk is great. The decision, of course, is yours.

Couldn't this couldn't this lengthy therapy be replaced by tranquilising drugs?

　　　　　　　　The risk is great. The decision, of course, is yours.

make it back to earth　make it back to earth　make it back to earth　make it back to earth

Down in the cellar, Saturday night, the slow-moving winter weeks, the highs of Hotel Quickie long gone. traffic works the bar with Gary, Craig and a new manager called Pete. Short broad suntanned Pete, face like Stallone, works with his shirt off. He's difficult to reach around, flirts ostentatiously, pours the staff shots as soon as Craig's away from the bar. traffic goes over to the corner on her ten minute break and waits for Jimi. Another pumping Saturday night hot as summer, backs of the benches thick with coats. traffic in a military mood when getting ready for work is now soaked in sweat and regretting it. Jimi disappears to deliver two towers of glasses then comes back for a break. He's in military garb too. They size each other up smirking. traffic offers him a cigarette. Who's the new muscle mary manager?

Some prettyboy hired by the invisible licensee. Apparently he hires according to fuckability.

He's really giving me the shits.

Well honey you'd be in his shoes if you'd taken Craig up on his offer.

He's ordering me around like I'm the new kid on the block. I think he's the kind of poof Craig warned me about.

Oh he's alright traffic, his body's gone to his head is all.

Do you guys really go for bodies like that? Is that fuckability? He looks like a bloody mushroom. Do you?

I'd do 'im. Jimi shrugs.

Oh Jimi!

Don't give me a hard time.

Would you do me if I was in his shoes? She grins and feels his arse.

Maybe I would. He feels hers back, pursing his lips. Maybe you'd even like it.

I reckon I would. Maybe you'd like it even better if I did you.

Maybe I would.

Holmes comes in with Jenny from work who gives traffic the once-over as usual. Built like Pete gone to seed with a face that'd seen a lifetime's more hardship, Jenny wouldn't normally even catch traffic's eye. But the night's only half over, she's in need of some sustenance and Jenny is easy. Jenny makes a move. So what rank are you?

She's a private, Jimi intervenes. Private Parts.

Better watch out for Corporal Punishment, Holmes weighs in. I saw him over there just before.

Oh I don't mind him, traffic replies. It's Major Depression I'm worried about.

Jenny is thrilled. traffic goes back to the bar and starts to serve customers. Another elbow from Pete right in the tits, another beer spill. Sorry luv! He's back by her side in the next lull between customers. You look really cute in that military getup y'know. If you were a boy I might even consider it. traffic presses a bar towel to her shirt and trousers. Jenny's waiting at her section.

What do you mean if.

Clean-up, 4 am. Pete goes over to Gary and tweaks his sarong.

What's with this? You don't have the physique to carry off a sarong.

Excuse me Pete, but you were saying last week that the cellar bar staff never make enough of an effort to dress up compared to the cocktail bar staff. So I'm making an effort.

Well you're banned from wearing it. And ditch the flowers behind the ears. What are you, a drag queen?

From Chronic traffic took home a girl who told her anecdotes of an Adelaide childhood with grimaces of apology for having been born in such an uncool city. You've got a Sydney accent, she informed traffic. Oh yair? What's that? It's clipped, sharp. Broader than a southern one but you finish all your words off. Adelaide's more Anglo. Said once again like an apology. Stop cultural cringing Violet, I've heard good things about Adelaide. Aren't the streets really wide there? Don't they have great food? And isn't the speed really cheap? And the pot? It's the speed and pot capital of Australia isn't it? traffic gave them both a shot and Violet, twenty-three years old, twice as charged on half traffic's amount, told her more stories while traffic rolled a joint.

Violet sold tickets at the Museum of Contemporary Art where the windows behind the cash desk looked onto lawns then the harbour. Each day a woman in a hat and veil would appear on the lawn before Violet and conduct conversations with the bust of Governor Phillip at its centre. Violet stood and acted out her story, removing the sequinned garter she wore on one thigh and dangling it over her wrist for a handbag, taking the joint from traffic and blowing plumes into the darkness. I didn't know what she was doing at first. I thought she was just admiring the statue, then I thought maybe she was a bit flamboyant or something, given to grand gestures, you know, a bit *gay*. But I realised it was more serious than that the day she kissed the statue. On the *lips*. Goodness, traffic gasped. That's a bit forward. I know! Governor Phillip was frozen! Violet by now crying with laughter. I love this space, I'm looking for a warehouse space, did you have trouble finding it? Um, not really, but it's a total fluke, there are hardly any left in Sydney . . . finish your story. Well one day she had a fight with him. She stomped straight up to the statue, had words with it, and stomped away again. When I went out to lunch I saw her in the shadows of the unloading bay further up, crying. That was when I realised how madly in love with him she really was and it didn't seem so funny. She didn't come back for ages after that, we started to forget her. Then she reappeared with something in her hand, she was doing something to Governor Phillip with it, touching him, we were *shocked*. Where? On the chest darling, you know he's just a bust. Touching his bust, hmmm . . . traffic's taking off her shirt. Yes, that's right. And I snuck out to have a cigarette and saw it was a letter. She had written him a letter and was trying to place it in the folds of his jacket. She looked really contrite, like she was apologising or something. Poor thing. Coming back over to the bed for a sip of tea, falling onto traffic, traffic taking off her skirt. Amour fou, she was doomed to heartbreak. Yes, Violet sat up. She got really jealous. She brought sandwiches to eat on the bench in front of the statue one day, and I went and sat out there with my lunch, and every time I so much as turned my head in the direction of Governor Phillip, she got *really* pissed off. But the letter, she tried that one for a few days running, Governor Phillip implacable. He wouldn't read it, wouldn't even hold it. The tourists loved it, they probably thought she was a performance artist. She was, traffic put the roach out and picked a piece of apple off the tray by the bed, put it into Violet's mouth. Sounds like art to me.

Later when it got light they began to fuck delicately. What do you want, what do you like? I don't know, anything, I've never been fisted before. Want to try? traffic kissed her, Violet's cunt hot and swollen in her hand. Violet went down onto her forearms and slowly surely gradually surrendered, her small white body breaking out in a sweat, traffic's hand still while Violet adjusted, moaning and whimpering. Embracing Violet from behind, cheek against her ribs, one hand inside her the other on her breast, traffic inhaled all the beer and chemicals and excitement of the night behind them and when Violet opened up and started to come traffic was so moved she thought she could love her.

They met again the following week and traffic told Violet she dreamt the woman in the hat and veil had kissed Governor Phillip back to life. What happened then? I don't know, I woke up. It soon emerged through party talk that Violet had been to Scum dressed as a cleaning lady in a gingham dress and matching broom. Fuck that was a good party! traffic wondered if she had seen Violet and then forgotten her, she wondered if she had already seen the next person for whom her love would last. She knew now she had nothing more to give Violet and Violet receded cheerfully into the throng of dancefloor buddies. Three months later Violet was in love with the dark girl from the house on the corner. Six months later they had moved in together.

Slip was booked to play a fetish party called MenAce with Skunk, Mandrake and Mr Hyde. It had been dry lately in the shops, hundreds of records and CDs later she had only a handful that moved her. She hit a wall, couldn't hear anymore couldn't tell if her thin wallet was the source of caution. She probably ended up loving long-term only a quarter of her purchases, exhausted she went through those records again in search of as little as a few good bars. She began to plan her set the week before, finalising it the day of the party, give or take the inevitable changes that would occur on the spot. She whiled away most of the morning on domestic tasks, stopping beneath the clothes-line to read in the sun and ignore her nerves and the bigger task of playing. Finally in the afternoon she dragged herself inside to the turntables. When she took off the headphones three hours later she heard rain on the roof and saw black sky through the windows. She walked out to darkness and the smell of wet earth, returning from her journey to find the world had changed. Like casting a spell and stepping into another dimension, just like magic. Watching the rain fall into the dark shapes of her clothes. Stars in a distant chink of sky.

Mr Hyde's finest acquistion that month was a record of prank calls. He had ceded some of it to Slip when she came over to his place the day before the party. He had the second bracket, she the third. They planned sets with no vocals, the phone calls to be traded across their collective four hours. Mr Hyde whose habit was to listen to everything for hours over and over, first of all straight, then with a smoke, then with amyl, then straight again, knew every sound of every track intimately before he gave them to an audience. He never played the same thing more than once, connecting it all with flashpoints of the music's peculiarities. And Slip who had only seven new purchases, and whose habit connected everything with rhythm, reinvented her entire collection. They envied one another.

Marsha's Rubber.

. . . Hello?

Yes can I help you?

Yes please . . . Do you, do you have rubber?

Say what?

Do you have rubber? Like, for floors?

Oh . . . Yeah, we got rubber flooring.

Can I get some rubber from you now?

No, we don't do phone orders, you have to come into the store.

Do you got octopus too?

Hold on one second.

H'lo!

Yes Sir . . . I'm, I'm looking for rubber.

Okay. What kind are you interested in?

I like that rubber, that black rubber that goes on the floor and smells good.

Sure.

I like to roll around on it and touch and **sniff** *it.*

Well come on down to Marsha's Rubber! We got hundreds of metres of rubber flooring here. Can't beat our prices.

How much could I . . . touch and sniff?

As much as you want. You can buy everything in the store 'n' touch 'n' sniff it all!

I like octopus too.

Oh yeah?

I like to get octopus 'n' shit, and I touch it 'n' **sniff** *it,*

Oh whatever you wanna do bro'.

I like to stretch it out, then I **lick** *that shit.*

You **lick** *it, eh? Wow.*

Then I **spank** *it real hard, right across the room! . . . That shit is* **nice.**

Yeah.

I **spank** *it, that shit!*

Okay man, have a nice day.

Fred was waiting for him with a joint near the backroom. James had a toke, handed it back. Where's Daryl?

In there.

Of course. What's it like?

Bit boring now actually. There were some sexy boys around before but I think they've gone. I'm heading off soon to 32.

I could see it from the decks. I love watching people fuck to my music.

Is *that* what was distracting you?

Hey?

So you coming down to 32?

What, now? No, I'm gonna stick around. Slip's on. Hey I got a box set of Sondheim the other day. Out of the Forest, fantastic new version of Sweeney Todd.

Show queen. Fred laughed. See ya.

James was feeling better now. You could never tell. One month you'd take an e it would hardly touch the sides, the next time it would leave you reeling. These were from traffic, capsules, pink ones. He could see her through the crowd working on one of the only women in the place. Weird those girls who so loved the dirty boy parties, he would never understand them. traffic had warned him about the ecstasy but James had thought she was just talking big as usual and took it so late it hit him right in the middle of the third track. Spinning on e, the record in his hands warping and melting, the lights the heat the sweat his pulse pumping louder through his body in his ears, louder than the bass, sweating shaking pear-shaped, missed his cue couldn't get the record out. Hotel Quickie had been a triumph, the most perfect set he had ever played. The crowd of freaks art sluts and outcasts had cheered him on through the entire two and a half hours. And here, at MenAce, a party that attracted every poof in town, every booker and manager and barman and party committee member, Mr Hyde had played abysmally.

But Slip was driving him onto the dancefloor, he was dancing resenting and admiring her all at once. He didn't know what she was using, sometimes it was just the cross-fader. His brain returning, hearing all those tracks he'd written off remixed into something amazing. She turned the darkness to light and back again till they were one, turned things he had taught her into moves of her own, elbow bending ahead every time she played. She came off the decks elated, ran straight into him. I love watching people fuck to my music. Don't you?

traffic picked up a woman called Donna at MenAce. With an aching knee traffic knew she couldn't dance all night, with a new tongue piercing and growing party fatigue didn't want to talk or even kiss. They drove over the Anzac Bridge at first light, the woman's tall thin transvestite housemate in the passenger seat unfurling her Barbie doll on a leash of orange marabou. When Clarissa got out in Rozelle and disappeared into a terrace for drugs, traffic leant forward between the seats. What's your name again? Does it matter? Just curious. Diana, she drawled. Lady Diana Spencer. Clarissa returned, racked up some coke on a filofax then they drove back over the bridge towards Redfern. traffic watched Clarissa's Barbie doll clattering against the window and the steel cables flying past, and all around her from the crest of the bridge the city resplendent. Industrial waterfront, old grimy buildings, parks and fine houses the harbour and freeway, all of it was beautiful in the pastel dawn.

Donna was a PR consultant who'd done time for ecstasy, house bought with drug money, the kitchen never eaten in, bedroom full of toys. traffic was unprepared for the body, thick soft and white, hairy, strong smelling. So much pubic hair that traffic took a while to find her cunt, leaning over Donna's body rank with chemicals moving her hand between Donna's thighs, the effusion of chemicals from Donna's armpits especially, even the cunt, strong enough to make her gag. My strap-on'll fit you. Yair, up the arse. And traffic came just at the feel of it against her clitoris, the sight of it moving in and out of Donna who came just as quickly. Then reached into the chest of drawers.

I've got some G.

Cool.

Have you been drinking?

A beer at the beginning of the night.

You sure that's all?

Yep.

Donna measured out the droplets and poured two orange juice chasers. traffic waited for the drug to take over then moved into gear, moved into water. Down down blurred slurred guiding Donna's hand, slower more lube yair oohhh put on another glove. Her arse was already open, she didn't douche and dinner was twelve hours ago. Heavy limbless oozing across the floor, she was a camembert left in the sun, sap from the scission, molasses welling over the lip of the plate. Was that her moaning over the other side of the room? Can't stop but can't get there, Donna over her the proverbial bull. Till cell by cell traffic's muscles began to reattach to bone and she stopped exhausted, I need to piss. Donna pulled out, traffic farting wetly. Down there, Donna pointed with a shit-smeared glove. traffic tried to stand, couldn't, started to crawl. Crawled giggling through eternity head lolling thighs wet, in the fog an upside-down Donna crawling down the hall behind her. She was laughing too hard to move at all now, on the threshold of the bathroom Donna gaining fast. Piss! Pushing through traffic's legs, Piss on me! And traffic strained and pushed and strained and finally released a schooner a cranberry juice and three bottles of water over Donna mouth and chest. She left via the living room where Clarissa's six foot long sleeping body was accordioned into the leather couch. Took a cigarette from the packet of B&H on the coffee table and Clarissa opened an eye. Want a line of harry? It's yummy to come down on. traffic rolled up her cab fare then bent to the line. Snorting drugs, what a novelty. Byebye darling, Clarissa called out as she left. Take care.

She loved them all. The girls the women the dark the light the slender and plump, the disgustful the lustful. Those so tall their barefoot embrace brought her mouth to the curve between neck and shoulder, the petite whose bodies could be wrapped in her own. A person was a world and traffic was on holidays. Cruising, looking, tasting, travelling.

Hi, my name's Kate. I'm a very feminine woman with short hair, blue/green eyes, fantastic tits that loved to be stroked and caressed. I've a fantastic waist, a great arse that loves to be stroked, and great legs. I'm looking for a feminine woman, experienced or inexperienced. If you're inexperienced, I'll lick you, and stroke you, and show you the way. And you can do the same to me. If you're experienced, I'm just the woman you're looking for. So come on girls, give me a call.

In the cold months business was slower and the pain of old fractures closer to the surface. When her knee began to complain again traffic asked Craig if she could go off the floor. He gave her two evenings a week in the kitchen upstairs with Bliss who between loads of washingup practised juggling. traffic watched her intrigued, in her memory the clown juggling at the circus. Clubs, balls, his own hat and shoes. The float of spheres in the air above his hands, the absolute defiance of gravity. Bliss was no such sophisticated juggler, her hands in a hurry the balls diverging. She gave the balls to traffic and on cue traffic tossed them to her one by one, Bliss keeping them aloft for barely a minute. traffic said Caniva go? and dropped them all immediately.

The kitchen was another world. You could choose your own music, smoke joints, wear absolute trash to work if you felt like it. At the back of the pub where the tilt of the laneway placed the window at knee-height of passersby, you were visible from the footpath opposite though few thought to look. In summer Jimi and traffic amused themselves by dropping their pants for the too-curious eyes of tourists. The rest of the staff came in for smokos or refuge when unhappy or drugfucked. Gary too shy to ask a particular boy out on a date, Sarah the new security complaining about her husband, and Pete in tears at the sight of his ex-boyfriend kissing another man. They were all romantics, even Jimi who after two weeks with the same boy would give him the title of husband. Bliss gave advice and consolation, rolling her eyes at traffic when they left the room. I didn't realise you had to be a therapist to work in here. Oh yes darling, yairs. It's mandatory. Jimi came in. Now don't you start young man. Too late baby, I started years ago. traffic you've got a visitor, I think it's your brother. Bit of a spunk I must say. In spite of the suit.

Slip was now playing the cellar bar on Fridays, insinuating Mr Hyde in her place whenever she got party gigs which was more and more often. traffic would work on the floor above, disconsolate at the thought of what she was missing, nicking down to the cellar in every break for a feed of good music. So as soon as traffic had made Roger a cocktail, she took him down to listen to Mr Hyde. The music was rabid. If playing was conversing he was trying to say everything at once, he was adolescent, a soloist. The room almost empty, traffic in the corner watched the clientele's faces, Friday evening drinkers worn with the working week wandering straight into Mr Hyde's nightmare. He frightened people, some left without even ordering a drink. Sometimes it was only halfway through a set that you began to understand his order so the ones who stayed, who were hearing him for the first time or had come especially spent the next two and a half hours with the dazed look of people bewitched by the ravings of a madman. But where was the seduction, the Mr Hyde of Hotel Quickie on the decks like a muezzin? She wanted to stay, Roger was standing, putting on his jacket. Is this one of the guys you use? Yes. And you're using him for your next party? If we can find a venue, yes. Roger said nothing, Roger had every Ibiza CD. Mr Hyde would leave the next day for a month in Europe and the pub wouldn't employ him on his return. He had the choice of pleasing employers like the Royal for a nominal fee and small step towards public success, or pleasing his IT company for thousands of dollars and job security. He chose the latter. The music darkening and the high female vocal floating through

IIIII'm so confuuused . . .

IIII'm so confuuused . . .

IIIII'm so confuuused . . .

SERIOUS MIND

FUCK

SERIOUS MIND FUCK

III'm so confuuused . . .

She goes to the back bathroom they hardly ever use where the washingmachine is crammed just inside the door. Along the narrow corridor past Holmes's room then the storage space, looking for somewhere to mix up in secret. Too much activity out there and Holmes will be home soon wanting to talk to her about the latest failed attempts to find a venue. Too paranoid to feel safe even in her own bedroom, traffic removes herself from Bee and Shifty for opposite reasons, the first to avoid judgement the second to avoid sharing and the burden of an accomplice. Half a gram from a friend of Gary's to tie her over until the next shop, it's been jumped on so severely she'll probably feel nothing. It mixes down badly, thick, cloudy, she hates powders now, she has to keep squeezing in fresh drops of water. The filter emerges in a milky crust. Nearly there she's shaking and now where's the tourniquet. Fuck the light's bad in here. But like an organism unfurling down the intestine of the warehouse she has come all this way and can't turn back now. Winter, a wet one, veins thin and deep beneath cold flesh. Clenched, pumping, probing, missing, blood trickling down her forearm. Then yes, ah yes, but after jacking back she feels resistance and plunges home anyway, crouched beneath her mind looking down on the whole blunder with cool disdain. A groove is worn in the door from the spin cycle. She knows it intimately, the shape her body must assume in order to pass through here, but the door catches and follows, bruising her ribs.

Billy. I can never pass the storage space without thinking of you. Your things dominate. Cartons of clothes and outfits I too wore, magazines some books all with pictures, your sewing machine and tools. Everything you touched you turned to art. The birds-in-cages series assembled with Turkish's old doll collection and cages from a pet shop skip, this your one attempt at a legitimate exhibition but none of them sold. Lampshades from X-rays of Bee's asthmatic lungs, piercing their blur the stark white silhouettes of ouroboros nipple rings just like the ones I gave you. Masks headdresses the endless revelation of construction and masquerade. Buried in there somewhere the speed-induced miniatures so that even then you managed to rescue from uselessness. You never had any doubt your purpose in life was to create. Me I'm just as driven by the urge to destroy.

Cold, shaking, waiting in the wind at Whitlam Square. Jimi is late. traffic's got a mobile now, she waits in vain for his call, circling a pylon in search of the sheltered side, sunglasses down against the grit that stings her face. Should have said to meet in a cafe, Jimi please don't fuck me over. She starts to jog on the spot through the stiffening in her knee, chin pulled inside her jacket, moving again as the building behind begins to release its workers into the evening not seeing Jimi till he is standing right before her. Not noticing till they begin to walk away that all along she was standing on one of the first Panic stencils painted by herself and Billy.

Bit late mate, I thought you were cooking it.

The price went up and I had to go to the bank.

You're kidding! How much?

Two hundred. And I had two hundred and five dollars in my account. Ha!

Is it the pink champagne?

Nah it's beige.

So they had no crystal or ice?

Nup.

Did you try it?

No time. But I've had his stuff before.

For fuck's sake Jimi.

Well what are you gonna do? Your guy's been done, who else can you go to? I'm not bullshitting you traffic. And no, I haven't taxed it.

Hey, I trust you, OK?

Around the corner they bump into Holmes groaning fatigue, on the run from work to his mother's via an art opening. So with Shifty and Holmes's absence accounted for, traffic and Jimi drink beer impatiently while Bee gets ready to leave for the night shift. Then the ounce is laid on the table. Christ, it stinks! Unbelievable! traffic gets her envelope, counts out the bills. Weighs Jimi up an eighth, takes from it the gram he owes her, gives him a taste from the main bag for his favor. She had wanted to abstain, she could do this at night, to weigh it all up and stash it then sleep till daytime chemical free, but Jimi has risen from his torpor and talks and paces around her like an obsession. Don't you think you better try it traffic, just to make sure?

I know it stinks but it's good it's clean it's steady. So she mixes herself up a taste and they talk at each other while the candles burn down, are replaced and relit.

traffic brings out tea and stories of Violet. Jimi is her confessor and she is Jimi's, they tell one another about their adventures down to the last detail. traffic envies the ease with which men cut to the chase, Jimi the ease with which girls talk to each other. He passes her a joint.

Men. As soon as you start talking they run a mile.

I always wondered what was in the letter she wrote.

What letter? Who?

The woman in the hat and veil.

Oh.

Don't be so hard on homosexuality, Governor Phillip. It's natural! Or maybe she was warning him not to go to the northern arm of the harbour. Watch out for that mob at Manly, they'll spear ya!

What are you talking about? You've got the speed babbles.

Governor Phillip. Homosexuality. You know it was rife here from the day the British landed –

Uh . . . no . . . I don't know anything about Australian history. I've gotta go.

Speaking of Australian history, you know that venue we thought we had? They're charging a hire fee now, I mean four figures. I don't know Jimi, I just don't know if we'll ever put on a party again.

You will babe, you will. And if you need a hand with anything, just give me a call.

We will, we'll need every one. Free ticket of course.

I'm there for you babe.

He kisses her goodbye then leaves.

She goes to her room for bags and returns to the long table, music pounding through the ceiling from the new people upstairs. Work tomorrow then every day for six days and tonight's sleep is disappearing. What the fuck are they playing? Mariah Carey or something just as bad, her brain too awake. She turns on the radio, finds Slip playing Transfix, turns it up till it drowns out upstairs. Sits down next to the ounce of speed the music rising and filling her mind with the rest of the joint left by Jimi. Ten whole grams, the rest in half weights, snip the corners of the bags to differentiate. But the music is too good, she has to get up and go over to the speakers, listen harder listen closer dance. Shirt off now, sweating, lost in music. What's that weird mix, the banging's out of time, then the banging in the background persists across a break and traffic turns the music down then turns to stone between the door and table covered in speed.

Police!

What?

Police! Open up!

Fuck-ing Jes-us. She goes to the door on weakening legs then backs away again. There are thousands of dollars folded into clean sheets at the back of her cupboard a sheet of trips at the back of the freezer eckies amongst Billy's stuff in the storage space along with her last three points of crystal an ounce of pot huddled inside the stuffing of a pillow, all hopeless hiding places when it comes down to it and even now when low on supplies there's enough here to indict her. Neil got done, so why not her and is that how they got here was it Neil would he *do* that? Is he doing deals with the cops now? Handing over her and others to them?

Police! We'd like to talk to you.

Why?

You're making too much noise.

Um . . . I'm really sorry. I've turned it down now.

But the *worst* you fucking idiot is all the shit out here, right here in the living room fully on display *move* it. traffic grabs a cushion from the couch and starts shovelling bags of speed inside the cover fuckfuckfuckfuck fuck! Speed on the table, scales and spoon sticky with it, speed absolutely everywhere.

Open the door!

Do I have to?

She's at the door.

Yes, now!

traffic drops her trousers, throws them into the corner, opens the door the gates of hell.

It's just that . . . I've got no clothes on, officer.

Silence. A young male and female constable blinking in the light of the stairwell, blinking at her nudity.

You'll get a fine if you do it again. No warnings next time, just a twenty thousand dollar fine.

Yes officer, sorry officer.

We'll be back if it happens again, and you'll get no second chances.

I'm really sorry officer, I promise it won't happen again.

Shutting the door gently, busting for a shit, realising then that two whole hours have passed since Jimi left and upstairs is silent. In the clang of her heartbeat traffic goes over to the stereo, sees how loud she had it and the main bag of speed she had forgotten to clear from the end of the table. They would have seen that had she opened the door just a little bit wider. She finishes weighing up in less than half an hour, stashes it all and sits on the couch to pack a cone. Smokes till the scorching fog smothers her fear. I've got no clothes on officer. On officer, it's hilarious. Shifty comes home and finds her like that, packing another cone, laughing alone on the couch in the darkness in the nude in the middle of winter, heater drawn up close.

Everybody loved you when you were a dealer. traffic such a good one that she was bad. Giving mates rates to nearly everyone, giving free tastes to friends and trade. Critical of quality and passing that information on to even the most casual indiscriminate user. And without the cautionary hand of Billy, expanding her trade, using too much, selling too little.

Another sleepless night, another list.

USEFUL ACTIVITIES FOR THE RESTLESS SPEED FREAK

* *Make a list.*
* *Squeeze that pimple that's been distracting your other hand as you write.*
* *While you're at it, squeeze every pimple, blackhead or whitehead you can find.*
* *Not just your face, your neck as well. Get those sneaky ones in the clefts behind your ears and beneath your jaw.*
* *Now for the ingrown hairs. Not just pubes, legs as well. Check armpits.*
* *Stop obsessing over your body! You are wasting time! Do the washingup!*
* *But first of all cleanse, rinse, tone and moisturise your poor inflamed face.*
* *Dab vitamin E oil on all the marks.*
* *Vitamin E your track marks as well.*
* *Do the fucken washingup. In fact, clean up the entire kitchen. Spray 'n' Wipe all surfaces, scrub the cupboards. Throw out all food past its useby date.*
* *CDs cassettes vinyl in alphabetical order. Maybe you could clean them as well.*
* *Clean your room, clean the whole house. Vacuum if you can make noise, mop and dust. Polish.*
* *If you're that wired then do some exercises. Abs, pushups, back exercises. You can use packets of rice as dumbbells. Or even better yoga, it'll relax you.*
* *Make all those phone calls you've been putting off for weeks. If it's still the early hours wait till 9 am then hit the phone for the official-type calls. Real Estate, bank, work re your roster. From 10 or so onwards you can start ringing venues. Charm, seduce, sell your idea.*
* *Make tea. Cone it. Come down. Try getting something down your gullet.*
* *Lie down. Try shutting your eyes for a while. At least ten minutes.*
* *Have a wank. If you've got lots of energy make it a luxurious one. You know, porn, music, toys, all your favourite fantasies. Go for one of those long, wild, mind-blowing speed pot orgasms. Then sink into sleep.*
* *No good, OK then. Do more exercises followed by stretches. Have a valium.*
* *Daylight, still no good. Make a shopping list. Get ready for the world again.*
* *Have another shot.*
* *Go crazy.*

Nature programmes were always a remedy. For lethargy, friction, for lack of inspiration. He liked to watch the sea creatures best, the blue whale whose tongue was the size of an elephant and contained blood vessels down which a grown man could swim. The dolphins he had seen with his own eyes, a dozen surfing in unison at Wattamolla Beach cheered on by a human audience lining the shore. Showoffs, fun junkies, party animals of the sea. But best of all, even further down, the bioluminescent deepsea creatures. The seven endless seas seemed to contain everything, microscopic to gargantuan, primitive to futuristic. This was not Planet Earth but Planet Ocean.

James hardly had time to make costumes anymore, this idea had germinated over twelve months ago. He watched and taped every relevant documentary, sketched, bought materials, then fell away from the project for months at a time. But in London, after work, on his way to buy records, he had found a book on deepsea creatures in the remainder bin of a bookshop. It contained few photos, some sketches, but hundreds of pages of information the television commentaries had barely touched on. So he flew back to Sydney obsessed once more and set to work immediately in his first holiday week since summer. He put on a video and got out his sketchbook. Down he went through his television set with the deepsea submersible, down into the abyss where fewer humans had travelled than into space. Past the euphotic zone to the cold dark depths where many animals became transparent. Squids, jellies, propelled by tiny cilia, siphonophores drifting incandescent wreathed in up to forty metres of tiny stinging cells, a bluish glow lighting up their glassy bells. The flat silvery hatchet fish, so slender front on as to be invisible. He would have to use them somehow, those huge lugubrious tubular eyes, and use as well the gaping jaws of another fish whose strong pointed teeth were permanently displayed. Down, deeper down, many creatures had a dark red pigment, the gulping jellies like Martian spaceships, the vampire squid with their sensory filaments. Almost all of them with light organs in ventral rows, clusters near the eyes and ears, flashing spikes that poked out of the head or long flexible lures that attracted prey.

There were novel partnerships down here too, novel monogamies.

The female angler releasing chemicals for the tiny male to find her, attach himself to her stomach with his teeth and stay like that for the rest of his life feeding off her bloodstream, feeding her in turn a constant supply of sperm. Down and down, deeper he went, sketching madly the mad forms of these creatures, morphing them into one that he himself would become when the dreams became material and the work was done and the gods permitting one of the family found a way to put on a party worthy of such a fantastic apparition. Down four thousand metres to the Abyssal Plain where it was four degrees and completely dark and the pressure four hundred times that at the surface, where the animals used chemical senses. Echinadorms, sea urchins, sleeper sharks, kilometres down now James saw rattails with a gland along the belly the source of their strip-lighting, millions of luminous bacteria providing the glow. Into the massive trenches over eleven kilometres wide, in the deep sea submersible in the television in his living room, James arrived at a deepsea oasis. There were vents down here that spewed hydrothermal plumes hot as molten lead and laden with sulphur, an atmosphere considered toxic to normal life processes. But what were normal life processes anyway? He had read somewhere that scientists had found life forms even in nuclear waste. One creature's poison was another creature's energy, and in the cold, deep, bottom waters complete ecosystems were based on bacteria and toxins.

He arrived at a basic shape that would cover him from above his head to above his knees, a basic fish shape, narrow front on, as tall as it was long. That could be done with some sort of light sheeny fabric, preferably red, stretched over a wire frame. He went down to Turkish Jim's shop and bought enough fabric to make ragged strips as well that would drift from the frame behind to cover his legs. His photophores would be fairy lights along the ridges of the frame, hanging in fronds from different points above, behind and either side around the openings for his arms. Beneath the whole contraption he would have to wear something as simple as possible, a body stocking, god! But he had gone overboard in the purchase of the stretchy fabric, so he ran one up with the remainder of that while butting his head against the problem of the facial features. The eyes, how would he create them, and the teeth? He wanted big translucent spikes through which he would peep as through a cage. There was always a point at which you got completely stuck.

He was wandering around the house in the body stocking when Daryl got home.

Don't say anything. This is like the underwear.

You're in the ball*et* now are you?

Gorgeous isn't it. James did a clumsy pirouette.

It fits well though, you did a good job. Turn around. Muy chic!

Very flattering isn't it. James pulled the fabric tight over his crotch.

Not bad for an aging queen.

Oh get fucked.

You're actually getting hard in there. Aren't you Heidi.

He sat there grinning.

No I'm not, I'm always like this. You just haven't been looking. Oh stop laughing will you. You know the first time I ever performed I wore a body stocking? I was a tree, it was a school production. This is in Santiago before all the shit went down right?

When you were still an innocent.

That's right. Anyway I wore a body stocking and all this paper vegetation around my shoulders and head. And it was *really* embarrassing because I got quite excited, it felt really nice and I kept getting a stiffy.

A *stiffy*.

I was eight years old and didn't even know what it was. I know I know, men in tights and all that.

Can I see the outfit? I mean what you've done so far?

No, it's a secret.

Oh come on, you've told me bits and pieces, I sort of know what you're making.

No. I want to surprise you. Anyway I'm stuck. It's a mess up there.

You should talk to Jim.

I would really really *really* like to make something from start to finish for once without his advice.

You know the sea rose here six thousand years ago? Sydney Harbour's an old riverbed. I wonder sometimes where the old coastline lay. What's out there now underneath all that water. Whether we'll end up there too one day if the sea rises again. Or if there's a big wave.

He began his journey in the crooks of the Professor's elbows, down with his tongue through the bush of armpits, over his chest tugging at the nipples, up the sides of his ribs feeling the Professor's cock bounce against his belly. He ignored it and continued across the soft stomach swirling around to the tops of his thighs. Then into the divet licking his balls, pushing his thighs apart to lick his arse. As though in the year or so since they had fucked his lover's body had become a foreign land again. And yet it was all still coded. The smooth interruption of appendix scar, his hypersensitive glans, the little moans as he pushed deeper into James's mouth. James stopped sucking and knelt between the Professor's legs, slowly moving the skin of his cock up and down, the Professor's eyes smiling in the dimness. Then James turned him over reached for the lube and slowly entered him. Deep, slow, long thrusts, holding his hips, waiting for his lover to cry out and spasm then slamming his own cum deep inside. You know, said the Professor afterwards, no matter what I do elsewhere, no matter what state I'm in, you're the only person I ever let fuck me. Well I guess not the absolute *only* one ever, but still . . . almost. Talking into his neck, curling around James who was swimming already into another biosphere where he became ancient and essential and removed the oxygen from his body, and in this biochemical adaptation all the bacteria across his skin clustered into pores and began to light up, he was buoyant, shimmering, glowing till daylight.

For the third week in a row traffic went down to the Tunnel of Love without a cover for the bed. New manager Dimitri, empty shop, Genie packing her things up early. traffic went down to do her strip. Four men in the cinema, one her most loyal fan, a huge beaming fat man that always came in with family size blocks of Cadbury in a crinkly plastic bag. Amber! Amber! he clapped enthusiastically but it wasn't enough, Amber felt cold, her knee was stiff. She went back up to the peepshow, leaning against the wall in the narrow corridor while Genie prepared to leave. No wankers today? Nah, it's been dead. That's right, there's a train strike. It's always dead in winter, Genie talking to the mirror. It's not really winter anymore. Well whatever, it's still cold, it's always raining. traffic slid to the floor, lit a cigarette, levered her leg. The pain was getting worse, she could hear the faulty mechanics creaking inside. Drifting up from the video booths women wailing and moaning, the occasional discreet male grunt. Listen, she mused. All you hear in pornos, made by and for men, is the woman getting off. Ironic, don't you reckon? Pulling her legs in as Genie stepped past and turned. Hey, um, me and a couple of the girls are getting jack of whoever's been using our covers. It's not a good look, y'know, someone else's lube 'n' stuff all over your brand-new fake leopard skin. traffic thought that maybe she was supposed to laugh. I'm not pointing the finger or anything, we're just putting the word out to everyone, y'know?

She was listless this afternoon, covering ennui with nakedness. Another meeting with a venue manager after her shift, Holmes still the fatalist expecting another knockback, traffic quixotic as ever in their party planning. Hope was an exhausting emotion. She sat uncomfortably beside it in the back room staring at the green television, reading cheap celebrity magazines. Snap, two page spread of Nicole Kidman picking her nose. Snap, Jack Nicholson brown-eyeing the papparazzi. Beep, last customer forty minutes before the end of shift, she couldn't keep him for more than three coins. What's wrong with me aren't I good enough? She remembered Billy in here dancing desultorily, sexy in the red light. Billy in long sleeves doing the lunchtime shift with the Financial Review open before her, hand worming up the corporate skirt for a wank. Billy poking out her tongue at the booths, grinning back at traffic. Billy the living picture of art nouveau erotica with her copper bob and winter skin and stockings. Billy's unadorned state she had eventually turned away from. traffic looked at Amber's eyes. Dead.

Billy sent me a postcard, traffic heard Holmes say to Bee in the kitchen. Hoarse stage whisper they used to communicate in private. I got a photo a week ago, hardly recognised her, how's she doing? traffic crept out of her body and over the partition to listen. They moved away.

Beneath each mask another, Billy never stopped unpeeling. While loving all strata traffic still sought final truth in the underneath, finding only once it was gone it had been there all along in constant translation. Three weeks without a fuck and no one so far she could fall asleep with afterwards, her longing for Billy grew. The venue manager was receptive, the meeting had been a success, yet in spite of or because of a party to look forward to Billy wouldn't leave traffic's mind. The slow drawl, white skin. Long hands waking her, feeding cloth to the needle. Ashamed now by how her love had slowed when Billy discarded artifice by the bedside. Her undone self her most fragile and least precious, in cultivation or denial Billy placed too much importance on the pristine body. traffic had absorbed this, Billy's disgust becoming her own by the end. Yet this was what traffic wanted, what she conjured for the solitary fantasies, closing her eyes to small talk, fucking herself to sleep, feeling Billy's lips and skin.

She spent an entire afternoon changing the bedroom furniture around. Yet even now standing in front of the chest of drawers she was horizontal, hip height, on the bed with Billy. Fighting, fucking, fighting and fucking.

Without warning, from the spiral of airborne balls came one towards her. She caught and placed it under her arm as she had seen Bliss do. Then another, caught that one too and placed it under the other arm. She caught the third ball and passed it to her left hand, the fourth, passed again, she caught the fifth. Bliss put her empty hands together in applause.

I've found her!

What?

A new owner for my juggling balls. I've got a new set. I said to myself whoever can catch the old ones can keep them. So you're it.

But what'll I do with them? I can't juggle.

You've been watching, you can catch. That's the first step.

Show me.

Home alone. Switch on the stereo in darkness, volume at zero. Press tuner, check the station, bring the sound up gradually. Lie back and listen to Mr Hyde playing Transfix.

Where did he get his music from and what did he do to it? He weirded out everything, clotted sounds floating free, like spume, driftwood, then the escarpment of guitar chords rising. When the beats began to surface, long and dark, Slip went into the bathroom filled the bath and kept her ears above water connected to Mr Hyde as the evening's cooking soaked from her skin. Waiting for the beats to quicken, to push her body forward and tell it what to do but they didn't. So she pulled a speaker through the doorway to face the futon and went to bed like that, yearning for knowledge for the why and how of his music. Sometimes it sounded like tracks she knew but they were being played at half their usual speed. A striptease never ending, the body naked turning its back on her, turning again still covered. Till his reticent voice saying thank you to the listeners signalled to her that two whole hours had passed. Time out of the country seemed to have refreshed him, this was not the Mr Hyde of the cellar bar or MenAce whose impatience chopped up his entire set. The leathermen liked their music familiar enough not to distract from their main sexual purpose and mindful of that Mr Hyde was neither comfortable in his own territory which he knew was too weird for them, nor happy in compromise. She had never seen him play that out of it before but in the cellar of the Royal he had no chemical excuses. Yet tonight Mr Hyde had seduced and lost her inside his world once more only she hadn't realised it as she was looking for what she knew and he had changed it all again. Not like a movie where everything you saw and heard was right there, but a book, a fairytale, where your own imagination coloured the bones of the story.

traffic rang a week later and said she had a venue. Two rooms this time. Hard-core furious upstairs, downstairs more weird and sleazy. I know you can play either Slip, so take your pick. Where's Mr Hyde playing? Downstairs. OK, put me there too.

I'm sceptical.

Well that's obvious.

There's the price hike,

But we've got two rooms. And it's still a cheap party.

exactly, it's bigger, then there's the name change,

But Pimp is absolutely perfect for the venue, and we're still Panic Prod.

and the venue's too close to the Cross. And there's another gig on that night.

Which one?

Some DJ from the States. The 'Godfather of House'.

But Holmes practically every DJ from the States that comes out here is billed as the godfather of somethingorother.

Yeh but the punters like that. They swallow it.

They're charging sixty bucks! No shows, no decor.

People will pay that. They nearly always think overseas DJs are better,

Look Holmes, spring is sprung, the perverts are crawling out from under their rocks. We'll kick off party season!

and I'm worried about decorating a whole venue on our own. Without Billy.

Tall ceilings Holmes. Imagine what we can do with such tall ceilings. It'll be like a real ballroom, imagine the shows we can have.

Without Billy the party wouldn't be the same. Everybody missed her, not just traffic. Without Billy, traffic might never have put on a party in the first place, she might never have started stripping. Without Billy she lacked a partner in dressups and half her looks might never have materialised. Without Billy traffic might never have embarked on any of these creative endeavours that so successfully alleviated the treadmill of years behind a bar. But without Billy traffic had found venues, performed, done her own make-up, created her own looks, designed and sewn intricate sequin work. Holmes liked to play dressups, he was a good sounding board, returning her ideas with ones of his own that were sometimes an improvement. Holmes was the perfect support system but would never take initiatives with graphics, decor or shows. Holmes had the technology at his fingertips for photocopying, emailing and faxing. He wrote good press releases, had PR skills, was an excellent administrator, Holmes was happiest organising the crew and liaising with the venue. Now, without Billy, and as usual without a decent budget, traffic would have to design the biggest party they had ever put on. Without Billy traffic was alone, she had no protection no alternative no guidance. Without Billy traffic had freedom.

If music was the soul of a party, concept and preparation the brain, performance the heart, sets the body, then the partygoers themselves were the lifeblood. A dance party was an organism, a planet, living fiction. It was interactive theatre. Prime the partygoers with gifts, entreat them to indulge, give them a stage, bar no holds, and into the party they would flow as blood into a body, water into a river system. Here is the entrance mysterious and alluring leading to a vantage point from where to refuel and take in the sights and plan the next move, here the main artery down which most people will be drawn, there a narrow passageway so we'll provide a fork to avoid a bottleneck and some scenery to entertain along the way, finally a small pool in which to cool off with resting places all around it. Here for the intrepid the furtive and weary we'll make a secret little cave full of stimulations, and down there at the end where everything converges is the largest pool, the dancefloor, right beside the lip of the stage on which people can sit and watch and dry off.

She became obsessed. On elbows and knees in the peepshow room writing and sketching ideas while her arse wiggled at the punters, taking long smokos in the kitchen at the Royal to do the same. Tossing the juggling balls into the air along with her ideas round and round hoping to catch them. Best of all on the dancefloor at Chronic or Playschool where with the help of various potions powders herbs and crystals the dilemmas traffic entered with had been dreamt into resolution by the end of the night. Tossing the concepts to Holmes for a final polish, catching his ideas at the same time. Going out to Reverse Garbage in Esmerelda with Shifty, coming away with only one thing after two hours searching, gold cardboard riddled with geometric cutouts. traffic collected the back pages of rent boy ads from the poof press and took home from the Tunnel of Love old copies of The Professional and Picture. Sabotaged the best copy from the advertisement pages, begged pleaded cajoled the Professor and kissed his feet to extract the loan of his vintage Tarzan books which contained both the comic strip and photos of old movie stars like Weissmuller, Frank Merril and P Dempsey Tabler. Did the same to extract from Bee her vintage girl porn and Bizarre and Betty Page books. Took it all down to Holmes's work when he clocked off and photocopied and

223

enlarged then returned them all intact to the anxious owners. All day and all night she worked, producing giant bannerols of the briefer text like CALL ME NOW, XXX ACTION, FRESH SEXY TEENS, ASIAN LADIES AVAILABLE, HOT LESBIAN DOUBLES. The saboteur ads she enlarged as well, sitting up late with Holmes to mount them on cardboard found in the street. From the street too, one by one over the years, had come the mannequins on which Billy had hung clothes and Bee and Bella practised ropework. All but two were forgotten these days, traffic rescued them from the sad neglected line they stood in along the back corridor. Two she dressed in garish lingerie, a third, a male mannequin, she put in an old stained pair of Jockeys packed to bursting and painted ACTUAL PHOTO like a stamp across his chest. A fourth was wrapped in gladwrap, a fifth given a simple red rope harness. In six weeks the Pimp props were ready.

Lastly there was the narrow dead space to one side of the dancefloor, perfect for a backroom, for this she needed fabric. She knew there were bolts among Billy's things and hesitated in the door of the storeroom then walked back into the lounge room. She rang Turkish Jim.

What did you have in mind?

Well anything really. Velvet would be nice, but it's probably too heavy to hang. And too expensive.

We've got some damaged stock here. From those storms? Whole bolts of the stuff. They're water stained but you wouldn't notice it in a dark club. There's a dark blue synthetic, sort of pseudo velvet. It's quite light, I'm sure you could hang it. *And* it's fireproof.

That's sounds good. How much a metre?

It's damaged. You can have it for free.

I love you Jimbo!

She was walking across a bridge over churning water, water red and thick as blood, step by shaky step on the rickety narrow bridge till she looked away for one second only and lost her footing and was falling. She woke up sweating. Eventually went back to sleep again. Dreamt another dream in which she lost her footing and was falling failing falling failing.

Max's Cinema. Pornos downstairs, striptease upstairs. This the larger room whose floor had been danced on from the 60s to the 70s before the sex merchants took over. Black and white checked like a Vermeer painting with a block of sunlight falling through one high window when they came in to decorate. Closed for up to two years at a time, open again under dubious circumstances, Max's flat tangerine facade had been admired by everyone but penetrated only by Turkish Jim and James back in the early 80s for a gay dance. So one by one they walked through the Darlinghurst Road entrance that afternoon, DJs, performers, crew and helpers, smiling and dazed. Turkish Jim and James running up and down the stairs, peering into every corner. My god, they haven't even renovated! Fan-tastic!

Downstairs the seating had been removed, upstairs they stacked half the chairs and tables in the kitchen and pushed the remainder to the back of the room. They hung the gold cardboard in front of the long wall of peeling red paint, creating a sort of 70s 3D flock wallpaper, a couple of bannerolas were placed over this again. They wrapped the columns near the bar upstairs and the dancefloor downstairs with all the accumulated pornographic imagery, the good vintage pictures placed at eye height, then covered the whole lot with gladwrap. Over the two dancefloors the mannequins were hung, along with the saboteur ads. Lastly they hung the fabric provided by Jim around the long narrow dead space to create a backroom, then decorated both it and the toilets with safe sex packs in the shapes of little stick figures animal and human. By 4 pm Jimi still hadn't showed. D'you know where he is? He said he was coming. He's notoriously unreliable traffic. But he wouldn't want to miss out on this would he? I don't know. traffic sadly put Jimi's free ticket away.

Fred was agog at the reels of possibilities locked in the back office. Will they let us screen films? Will they let us access their 70s porn? I'm afraid it's all heterosexual. The venue manager stopping and jangling his keys, wry, defensive. Perfect! Fred beaming. But the office stayed locked and the cinema screen obscured by red velvet drapes and Fred, accustomed to low budget improvisations, waited till all the props were installed then set up his lights, fiddling for hours with angles on the props and signage, staying on through three shows' tech check. Just before he left, James came over to traffic. The place looks sensational. You've done a great job. Which meant more to her than the opinions of a score of partygoers.

Fred approached while she was decorating the backroom to pick up his order. Ooh, it looks sexy in here, where's the boys' one? Here. Isn't this for girls? It's for anyone who wants it. Fred looked perplexed. You didn't know did you Fred, that every fuck you had in a backroom at a party was being perved at by dykes through the glory holes, and that some of those humping figures were actually girls. Oh traffic, don't *frighten* me. Fred pocketed his drugs and said goodbye. She loved Fred's lighting but she hardly knew him, she knew only too well backroom reality. That the boys always outnumbered girls at parties, that anybody's backroom inevitably became the mens', that the girls who ventured into them like Bee and Shifty were so rare as to make no difference and were often too anomalous to feel comfortable, and that she herself running the party wouldn't get a chance to indulge and even if she did, finding a partner wouldn't be easy.

Once more Holmes and traffic had taken a week's unpaid leave to work on the party. Slept little, worked to exhaustion and the party not even started. They dreamt of the compensations as they taxied home in the clear spring evening. You know I haven't been out of the city for over a *year*? traffic wanting a holiday, to hire a car and go camping. Holmes wanting regular acupuncture and a new pair of shoes. Bee and Shifty's argument could be heard on the stairs, traffic walking heavily to warn of their arrival. It was her and Billy arguing, everybody hearing them. Holmes and traffic tried to sleep, the warehouse like a church in the absence of industry, Shifty crying softly in the bathroom like a solitary mourner. traffic did another half weight before getting ready then at the mirror watched tremors move down her fingers and through the eyeliner ruining her make-up. Pounding head tight heart vice tightening around her kidneys and when Holmes came into her room he found her like that, flat on the bed half dressed and breathless. She could still gasp. I know, don't say anything. Holmes pulled off her socks and massaged her ankles, finding the pressure points, squeezing them till she howled, flicking the pain back out into the air. It seemed to work, the pain seemed to draw from her body into Holmes's fingers. Sitting up now, talking again. Thank you so much Homie. And they spent much of the party in the same way, Holmes on his feet, traffic often sinking exhausted into the nearest seat or onto the floor itself. Both of them dressed in shiny suits and moustaches.

It was easy to say no to drugs that night. To knock back offers from friends, to leave her own at the bottom of her bag. Needing lucidity, missing Jimi and fearing the worst, craving serenity and fuelled by fear of failure and the dirty hit's memory, traffic later drew energy from the joy of the partygoers, from their entertainers the stiltwalkers who floated across both dancefloors in shredded costumes like driftwood, from Vera City and Amfetta Mean's twisted cabaret done to a medley of glam rock, from the boys in costume frightening and delighting the dancers, from the live electronica act. From the dance music on both floors she could never stay and listen to for long because the entire night they seemed to be running. To pay people, help the next performer, cue the DJ changeover, keep everybody supplied with water and beer.

4 am, doors closed. Everybody was paid. Upstairs where Mandrake was playing the floor was full but still spacious. Holmes stayed for a dance with Bella and Stash and a friend of theirs, a tall thin boy in a perfectly pressed Nazi uniform and polished shoes. Holmes tapped him on the shoulder. Into the ovens with you you old fag, you're taking up my lebensraum! The Nazi danced away. Holmes went downstairs to hear Slip and found traffic sitting at a table on the edge of the dancefloor. She had a good position, a little niche where you were almost invisible and could see most of the room. People milled around the columns, trying to decipher the dirty pictures. Others sat at the tables or along the step, mostly they danced. The step that led down to the dancefloor was shallow and unmarked and something of a liability. traffic and Holmes called it Whiplash Corner and stayed there for almost two hours, sharing a joint and watching the party. A feral girl going down for a low swivel, not rising again but dancing like that in a squat, fascinated by the floor. Over by a column, almost invisible,

227

Donna fisting someone. Bella and Vera City coming down the step and tripping, Vera City redoing the move with dramatic heroine effect while Bella rolled an air camera. Turkish Jim in whiteface, a barbed-wire helmet and strait jacket, sheep's heart skewered across his chest, dancing to some imagined soundtrack which looked twice as slow as Slip's music. While traffic and Holmes sat there at least three people approached and touched the heart gingerly then quickly withdrew, wiping their hands. Jenny came down the stair and tripped, followed by Gary who tripped as well. Stash came over and offered them laughing gas, unbelievable how he carted those bulbs and siphon to every party. traffic had a bulb and thanked Stash in faerie language. Holmes asked him where Bee and Shifty were. Gone home. Already? Things ain't good in that department. The Nazi arrived and sat in the spare chair beside traffic. She leant over to him. Are you a spy? You must be. They always use poofs as spy fodder. The Nazi stood up. Just because *you* haven't got the guts to wear it. No, but I've got the guts to respond. The Nazi stalked off, tripping on the step. James who had finished his set reappeared in his deepsea creature costume, a magnificent menacing luminescent vision to all but himself, he saw a small square of the world directly in front, caged by his long lethal teeth, and nothing below his shoulders. He walked along the edge of the dancefloor, all along the feet of the people on the step. Crunch, sorry! Crunch, ohgod sorry! Somebody was leaning over traffic, holding her hands. *Thank* you. It was the venue manager. Oh, thank *you*. No, thank *you*, this crowd is fantastic. Honestly, it's an honour. traffic elated signalled to Gary, asked him where Jimi was. At that other party. Which one? Some American DJ. The news stuck in traffic's throat like an ice cube. Come and dance baby, the music's wicked. I'm actually too exhausted to move Gary, but thanks anyway. Bella reeled over to the seat next to Holmes. Whew . . . ! Picked an empty schooner glass off the table, bent forward and discreetly threw up in it. Jesus, sorry, haven't spewed on an e for about ten years. Don't worry 'bout it love, you're talking to an ex-junky. Holmes pulled his pink pimp handkerchief from his breast pocket and handed it to Bella. She dabbed her lips, *Most* undignified, then stood, glass in hand. Where're you going with that? To find Stash. A man in latex fully hooded approached traffic. Hallo favourite party girl. Hallo my darling. Thank you for another *incredible* night. traffic realised it was the man with the rooster tattoo. Sorry, I always forget your name. That's OK, I've forgotten yours as well. They exchanged names again and promptly forgot them. Turkish Jim sighted traffic and approached. You know, if I saw myself on the other side of the room, I wouldn't dare go and say hallo. No, me neither. We're all mad. I know. We're all mad I know We're all mad I know. The Professor tripped and wobbled over eyes wide. There's a seething *mass* in the backroom. And some of them are dykes! traffic too tired to move was filled with joy and envy. Later came Violet who tripped the most spectacularly, landing on her back in front of traffic and Holmes. She stood, dusted herself off, turned slowly, and traffic grinned at her. They yelled to one another through the music, traffic soon realising that Violet didn't recognise her. Sorry about the step. What? Sorry about the step! We didn't realise it would be that invisible, we should've marked it with fluoro tape or something. What? SORRY ABOUT THE STEP. Trip, what trip? I *never* take acid. traffic gave up talking and flapped her hands. Violet was intrigued. She came closer, her girlfriend behind watching traffic suspiciously. traffic dismissed an image of the girlfriend's mouth around her cock one year ago in the Christmas Eve party at the house on the corner and leant towards Violet whispering in her ear. Where am I? You're at the Brisbane World Trade Centre. Oh really? Violet looked around. Can I dance here? I think I need to dance. Sure, there's a dancefloor just there. Violet turned in the direction of traffic's pointing hand. Put one tentative foot on the parquet, paused, then moved out onto the floor.

Cooked feet aching thighs pinched stomach sore eyes. 9 pm bed-time, sleep again till midday. Out to buy the newspaper, collapsing on the couch from the effort of stairs. Eat some cereal, yawn, try to read, doze. Blocked ears, yawning, blocked nose, yawning can't get my breath. Out of creativity into the abyss. Exhausted, ruined, nothing left to show for it, nothing left at all. The party is over. Try not to cry, stare out the window at the clouds passing by . . .

l e t h a r g y

She did it without thinking, she sent tapes everywhere. From the first jubilant set at Scum any opportunity to play was worth pursuing. She wanted more than anything the transformation of faces and bodies before her, she wanted to illuminate, to feed and seduce, she wanted to take people on journeys. She wanted to work, to play any and everywhere, she wanted to be heard. And the gigs came in.

She listened to everyone. Always got there early. With several options of the direction she would take Slip moved through the crowd feeling it out. Waiting behind the decks for changeover or seeking the point in the room where the sound coalesced so she could stand inside the other DJs' heads and listen to them singing. She unravelled their tricks, stole their wisdom and made it her own.

It was like a power when the fear and elation moved behind her, the windsurfer parallel to the water skimming, pitching her weight against the force that moved her. Drawn to opposites, she leant in terror against everything inside herself. The child horrified by violence drawn to the war memorial, the hermit slowly entering the city gates. She wore like an apron a bandana when playing, printing it with the sweat of fear that poured from her hands as she turned her insides out with electricity and sleight of hand, her body in the booth a mere decoy a prop. Accepting anything from small bars through bad clubs to weekend festivals, waking one night halfway through her set to see thousands of ravers all dancing in her direction hands in the air like a political rally, she had nowhere to hide anymore. Knowing then she preferred the small queer parties like Pimp where the crowd danced with each other instead of at the DJ, where the music the entire vibe was the focus not the person on the turntables. She was no pop star but a conduit a welder, shaping and joining all that passed through her. She loved the people when they were dancing before her, returning her energy hitting the same pitch, but off the decks never knew what to say. She was unaccustomed to the attention, it was overdone and embarrassing. She stepped to one side watching her person become recognised, the way they talked to her like they were talking to a mirror. Stuck behind the glass of other peoples' imaginations, smaller than the virtue or cunning they saw. They were talking to her mask and she was a ventriloquist. She began to appreciate the necessity of disguise. She needed friends more than ever.

She lost her cooking job when for the third time in a month a gig was offered and she took the night off. Secretly pleased to have escaped the drudgery, dreaming still of a life in which she could earn a wage from doing what she loved. Then there was a month of disasters. The Royal cocktail lounge closed by licensing police because people were dancing, another party she played closed for licensing infringements as well and being halfway through her set at the time she received no wages, at a third the promoters reneged on payment when the numbers fell short. So in the fifth week Slip found herself catching a bus to the dole office at the junction.

Five years since she had collected the dole. The allowance had risen eight dollars. She scanned the fifty-odd professions listed on the application form, the government's notion of legitimate workers. Business legal medical. Administrative, social services, teaching, trades. There were no musicians no performers no artists no film-makers. There were no poets. She didn't expect to find DJs listed but would have liked to have been proven wrong. She was right. She ticked *other*.

5 am, coming home from a gig in a cab. Commercial radio playing Promised You A Miracle. They swing by the carnage of road works through parkland, the cab driver hard to hear in his brand-new cage. He projects. Yair well our Premier could've done a rap to that. His bottom lip so big it seems to be falling off his face. The song ends and the DJ throws in his quip. That was Simple Minds who of course broke up years ago, but there's a new local version made up of members of our government.

ha ha ha

Hallo?

Miaoow!

Hallo kitten!

Can I come and get my cream?

Your cream is here, kitten. Although instructions were issued by your fifth personality, Ms Jackie No, to ensure the duration of the diet was at least two weeks, I have never been one to stand in the face of regress.

But it's for someone at work! You know what they're like here. The Professor's falsetto came piping down the wire.

Ten thousand scream-ing fag-gots, ten thousand scream-ing fag-gots!

Get back into your closet.

It's not a closet, it's a *palace*. You better be here within half an hour, kitten. I have an appointment at the Gentlemen's Club.

Oh really? Who with?

A . . . *stranger* . . .

She was there within five minutes, had rung him when already halfway, so excited at the sight of her drugs she could have sped all night on that natural adrenalin. The Professor never one to say no to anything or anyone, accepted a small line and was relieved to see her disappear into the bathroom. He was uneasy with that. The needle thing, blood. Once he had gone home with a man who injected him with speed. Closing his eyes arm extended in trust. The rush was so fantastic he never did it again. Afterwards, hours and hours after-wards because the sex took so much longer, he turned on the light to find his clothes and saw the red lines down the man's forearms. Short and raw like cat scratches. He watched him hit up again before he left, it was one of the horniest and most repellant things he ever saw. traffic came out of the bathroom with the same face the same body the same personality. He walked her back to the Royal, came in for one drink then went on to 32.

traffic and the Professor go up to Playschool, a room on the third floor with blacked-out windows looking over an alley. Full now of fluoro kids and ferals dancing to Primal Scream and the Propellerheads. traffic does a circuit and returns to their spot to find the Professor gone. The place is too young for him, there's no one fuckable, he's probably left. But traffic has made eye contact with a girl so now strolls over.

The girl says her name's Sailor and has a tattoo of Sailor Jane on her right shoulder framed by the words

Loose Lips

Sink Ships

and this shoulder is sinewy and firm. traffic is in love. Tall topknot of dreds, shaved widow's peak swooping Frida Kahlo eyebrows, within minutes of traffic sitting down, Sailor tells her she's coming off smack. Hasn't had a hit for six or seven days though she did speed the night before and her e's just coming on. She starts to massage traffic.

What'd you do to your shoulders? They're really tight.

Not my shoulders, my knee, it's fucking up my posture. I broke it years ago and now the pain's coming back.

Yes. Pain does that.

Bar work doesn't help.

Bar work's so unhealthy. How'd you break your knee?

Playing sport.

Sport's so unhealthy.

Sailor's from Manila via Auckland and Perth. It's her twenty-fourth birthday, she looks ten years older, never stops talking. Wears umpteen chains collars bracelets leather and rubber thonging that never come off, that leave traffic's vulva sore long after they've finished fucking. Wakes traffic with her hand, waits for her after work, goes home with her again. And the second night together, sniffing sweating restless, Sailor eats the last of traffic's valium. Syphoning her calm into the ravaged body of Sailor, holding her to sleep, traffic knows seven days maybe eight now are nothing. Nothing at all.

234

Speed pot ecstasy and the rest don't count for Sailor, not even a past speed habit that she describes as raging. It was the hammer that really undid her. Had my first taste at sixteen, I'd finished school by then, I skipped grades. School was so boring. I put in an appearance but I was like Give me something to do! So they put me in a higher year, I skipped grades three times. Eyes hungry on traffic's breakfast taste. traffic only asks for money from Sailor sometimes. Sailor's quick. Never swabs before injecting, never rotates sites, Sailor's a black hole junkie. Sitting back complaining the rush has worn off when traffic is only just going in. traffic running to the phone and arranging dropoff, returns to the bedroom to see Sailor picking up her spoon. Mind if I rinse? No, go ahead. traffic's mobile rings and traffic ignores it. It's party season and the calls are coming thicker than ever, the warehouse phone rings again and traffic runs out to get it. Why don't you leave it? Cos if it's customers I'm in deep shit from my housemates. Why don't they ring your mobile? Cos they're stupid or else they do and I don't pick up. Sailor one-ups her. Selling heroin, she says, it's like selling air. The phone *never* stops.

Hey traffic, we wanna catch the fast train. Got 'ny timetables?
Is Elizabeth there? Goodie. What about Sally?
Hey baby, I was trying to track down Michael Douglas Anthony. Is he with you?
Listen I don't have any dosh but I've got some of those green T-shirts. Wanna do a swap?
Got any party tickets?
Darling I have an absolute infestation here. I need some of that cockroach dust pronto.
I went out with Crystal last night. Pheeuuuugh, she's a dirty bitch.
Hey I know your outlet doesn't deal in slow cars, but can you recommend me to someone?
We've been watching When Harry Met Sally all night.
You wouldn't believe it but I've been horseriding all night and I've gotta get to work. Can Gonzales give me a lift?
Have you got any cardboard? I'm doing a collage.
I'm going to Church and I need a copy of that hymn. You know the one. Christalmighty!!

traffic always says goodbye to them in the morning but Sailor's still there four days later. They stay inside traffic's unaired room, the tension around Bee and Shifty stretching through the warehouse like barbed wire. Sailor's complex sentences scarred satin skin and fluorescent life draw over traffic like a dome. Fatigue of and unsated lust for adventure incline her to taking refuge for a while. She gets out the juggling balls and listens to Sailor while practising. The constant rescue of dropped balls has given her a sore back, so she stays on her haunches facing the wall to discipline the throws, two balls only, trying to catch. Sailor stops talking. What are you *like?* What? I'm listening, go on. I can't, you look too stupid. Sailor laughing. Come on girlfriend! Can't you do more? It's not that easy y'know, I have to learn how to catch properly first. Discouraged traffic abandons the balls and gets out her two metres of red fake fur bought months ago from Jim's shop. She needs to be busy, she needs occupation, she measures and cuts hot pants and a bra while Sailor talks on. In love for two days now, three, four, traffic will be able to say to the ghost of Billy that somebody else has finally found her. The threatened couples and all those others wondering why a girl like her is still single will have their answer. She needs to kick back, she needs to take a break, she walks bow-legged away from reality, falls into Sailor's dreams of designing more clothes like the ones Sailor wears already, raver stuff, techno wear. Sailor's old designing partner in a Perth label had a whole warehouse of industrial sewing machines. Sailor the designer, Jay the cutter and sewer. Jay was such a talented boy, Sailor talking again when traffic is barely awake. The way he juxtaposed materials, the lines, the colours, I never knew a craftsman that could match him. Then piece by piece Jay hocked all of his machinery. Then died of a taste laced with ammonia sulphide by a vindictive dealer. The bitch got busted anyway, otherwise I would've done her over, that's for sure. Anyway, enough of me, babe. You were saying you knew someone . . . Sorry but I just need a little bit to take the edge off.

Scaggin' in Sydney, Sailor reminisces. She once worked William Street, now she's moved up in the world to the newest B&D establishment in town. She shows traffic her graffiti from three years ago on the side of an old terrace in Erskineville. DEAD-END

WHORES, the name of the thrash band she played with back then and has just reformed. Sailor's not without a sense of humour. traffic likes their comparable height in platforms, walking with her shoulder in Sailor's armpit, aware nonetheless of the awkward alternatives her body seeks to compensate the bad knee. Where do you practice? We *don't*, girlfriend, that'd ruin it. Sailor can't wait and they go into the toilets of the corner pub for a taste.

Back at the warehouse Sailor becomes cheerful. Backache, runny nose, sore knees and quivers gone, all gone. traffic too has walked all the way home pain free. She cooks a meal then tops up, follows Sailor into the shower to scrub her back, croaking she's just discovered a note from Holmes reminding her of a house meeting tonight. The steam is too strong and standing too fast, traffic sinks back down to the floor white. Can't keep her eyes open can't throw up then can't stop throwing up can't even hold a cigarette. Feels her breathing depress. Staggers back to her room for some saline solution. Hand shaking can barely get in the vein. Then finally. It does nothing. Sailor comes in to find her going blue. Breathe! she slaps her. traffic gasps. Half of what cures Sailor has brought traffic close to death. Sailor leaves the room for a vomit bowl, returns to find traffic blue again. Throws water in traffic's face, drags her up walks her round the room, sits her back on the bed with the bowl, follows traffic's retching requests to mix up some speed. It opens traffic's eyes but the nausea and panic only increase, she throws up. Fuck I'm so wasted, I've got a house meeting in an hour fuck it. Stop talking, just breathe. I'm not doing this again, sorry babe but you just lost your source. Sailor shrugs. traffic throws up again. Stay with me please, she holds onto Sailor. I need looking after.

Fifth day on the go and they do half weights in quick succession, never feeling enough.
    Hang on a sec, was that my fit or yours?
    I left mine there.
    But that was where I put mine!
    Cool it, will ya! Sailor gets up and goes to the door.
    Jesus Christ, you haven't got anything, have you?
    Yeh, stage 4.

Don't fuck with me, Sailor.

Grrrr!! Sailor comes back in, climbs on top of traffic and bucks.
I thought you *liked* me fucking with you. She throws in a parting shot.
Shoulda thought of that before you went down on my bleeding cunt
sweetheart.

While Sailor goes down to the corner shop, traffic turns on the stereo
and begins to wash up. Fila Brazilia rippling through the air and now
she starts to hallucinate extra sounds. A tinny voice sampled through the
music or is it someone speaking on the answer machine? But isn't the
phone turned up? Wouldn't she have heard it ring? Is it the door, who
would be knocking this time of night is it the cops? Oh christ no please
no, is it Sailor will Sailor come back why's she taking so long she didn't
see my hiding places did she? She fucken rips me off I'll kill her. Maybe
she's just killed me. traffic rakes back through those moments with
Sailor like a pauper who has lost her last coin. Tries to see which needle
went where. Tries to remember. For a split second manages a miracu-
lous three-ball juggle then they fall to the ground and she's sure she was
hallucinating. She runs to and from the risks continually over the next
weeks. Like a sly knife the panic enters her at the supermarket
checkout, awake at dawn fretful premenstrual, mixing a complex
cocktail for a flirtworthy girl, drifting naked in the falling feathers of
her old boa, juggling in her bedroom when she's too awake to sleep. But
even if she does have it, even if she has both, it's done now it's there. We
all die anyway.

Sixth day on the go, work in the cocktail bar, Bliss in the kitchen. Still
not used to this friendliness, Bliss talking about the puppet show at
Heresy again, would she and Bee consider redoing it for an event she's
organising? Bliss is so clear, Bliss is so inspired, Bliss is studying butoh.
Talk to Bee, it was Bee's show really. traffic stocks up, clears tables,
stacks up dirty glasses, always always the dirty glasses. She's coming
down already. Blurred vision, exhaustion, nasal passages filling.
Blocked ears, paranoid. Bliss didn't even see the show, just that
fuckwit's photos of it. And why is she so friendly after that coldness at
Panic when she was still with Genie. Is it because traffic did a piercing
show? It's all so fucking easy . . . traffic . . . traffic . . . Hey? Sorry,

I didn't hear you. I didn't say anything, Bliss laughing as she leaves the room with a crate full of beer.

traffic limps out to the toilet. Gets up too quickly and her vision whites out. Ears roaring, cold sweat, she hangs onto the cistern. When her balance returns she sees her face shocked with fatigue. Sees her body in profile, arms like claws holding up her leathers, sees her back reflected in the mirror before her, sees herself over the wash basin. Too many fucken mirrors. This is not a toilet, it's a palace of narcissism. *traffic ... traffic ... ?* Running out of the toilet towards the voice calling her, running out to an empty bar.

For seven days and nights the stories of Sailor Jane poured through traffic's bedroom, the smell of death and damp houses and high times in every city of Australia rankling her nostrils long after she had gone. For seven days it seemed she saw neither darkness nor daylight, time illuminated by the flashpoints of Sailor.

On the eighth night traffic goes to watch Dead-End Whores in a small Waterloo pub. Sailor bug-eyed and skinny in Cancer Council sunglasses, screaming *You're hideous! Hideous!* over the white noise. Crouching by the wedge trying to hack out chords without losing her balance. The drums hobble ahead like a cripple trying to escape a runaway truck. Dead-End Whores are so bad that they're good, traffic laughing so hard she almost falls off her stool. Sailor sneers when they come off stage. What's so funny? You! You're great! Don't patronise me. Twenty minutes later Sailor's in another girl's lap and traffic's in a taxi home. Two days later Sailor knocks on traffic's door. After three days traffic says she thinks Sailor had better go, that she's not really into a regular ongoing thing. Two weeks later, Sailor's moved in with some girl. Two months later they cross paths again briefly on Jimi's birthday. Three months after that, Sailor's left Sydney in disgrace owing money all over. Couldn't handle the pace, says Gary to traffic when he comes over to score.

Get real

Get off

Get away

Get out

Get fucked

Get nicked

Get stuffed

Get a grip

Get off the grass

Get out of here

Get out of town

Get out of my face

Get with the programme

Get it together

Get a handle on it

Get a life

Get over it

traffic goes to the TV room where Josh is watching a Busby Berkeley movie on cable. He gets up and dances along to the routines, throws himself back down onto traffic, grabs at her face and clothes. Show me show me! Later Josh. She holds him still. Gives him his dinner which he refuses until she bribes him with the promise of an unveiling. He settles and eats watching her. Each time traffic babysits this ritual is enacted after Roger and Katherine have left the house, she has perfected the art of speaking in such a way that her tongue jewellery is invisible. Easy enough with people like Josh who are that much shorter. When she has cleared the plates Josh waits by the couch, twitching, jigging. traffic lifts her shirt and bends over before him. The delicate tracing of the child's fingers on her scapula recall the abstract red swirls, then her piercings are unveiled. Josh touches nipples and navel shyly smiling.

They're pretty.

Thank you.

I want to see the others.

You can't see all of them Josh.

Why not?

Because some of them are hidden.

Why?

Because they're my secrets. I bet you've got secrets haven't you.

Yep.

What are they?

Not telling! Josh rolls around, grabs her neck. What about your nose, I want to see your nose one.

OK. If you're good and come to bed now, I'll read you a story and show you.

I want hair like her. He points to the leading lady in the movie.

You'd have to dye it. I have a friend who could do your hair for you.

But boys can't have long hair.

Yes they can.

There was a boy at my school with long hair and they made him cut it.

Well not everybody's like that. You'll be able to grow your hair one day if you want to.

241

She reads Josh Where the Wild Things Are, his eyes roaming from her face to the book and back again. He props himself up to investigate her face cavities. She sits up straight and closes the book, pokes out her tongue slowly and he throws off the covers in his excitement. Show me again! Back into bed Josh, or I won't show you anything. When he settles she draws her hands up over her face unveiling the mask of protruding pierced tongue, septum retainer and eyes wide like a tiki. Josh lies beneath her grinning. She draws her hands back over her face and the mask is wiped away. Josh wise now squirms for a position from where he can see the glint of metal even when pushed deep into her nostrils. You're cheating. No I'm not. traffic shifts to a different angle and wipes her face revealing, wipes it again concealing, revealing, concealing. Kisses him goodnight, leaves the room. His voice comes to her from the darkness. The Aztecs pierced their tongues. And their thighs. Not for decoration, just to draw blood. It was an offering to the gods. I've seen pictures.

She leaves the door ajar and the hall light on. Down the beige carpeted stairs, every muscle in her legs gripped by the iron fingers of fatigue, iron thumb prising the kneecap off. A robot she is a robot, creaking, disoriented, a piece of old machinery, cogs jamming, wheels rusty. Is that the door? No. traffic looks out on the quiet Waverley night, dramas locked far away from the street, parked cars gleaming, potted cumquat crouched in the shadows of the porch. She goes back inside. Hears the knock again but there is nobody there. So by the time Slip arrives traffic no longer believes her senses and Slip knocks for ten minutes before being let in.

She has two new cassettes for traffic, one her own mix the second a recording of Arvo Pärt. What's this? It's called Litany. Hmm, I like litanies. She moves into the kitchen to put the kettle on. Or there's beer, d'you want a beer? No, tea's fine. Slip sits on the couch at the edge of the living area watching the top half of traffic's body move behind the long wooden counter. Everything in the house shines and gleams, the white walls, pine finish, stainless steel kitchen utensils hanging over the stainless steel stove.

Salubrious house you have here.

Yes, isn't it. We're hoping to pay off the mortgage soon. We've invested in some tech stocks.

How much did you pay?

Oh, only about two million. But that's Australian.

Bargain!

Yes, it's a very good area to buy in at the moment. I can give you the number of my agent if you like.

That's kind of you, but I've actually got my eye on a property on the North Shore.

O rally?

You know you should see yourself from here. When you bend down you can just see tufts of hair like seaweed. It's like a puppet show, you could do a show in that kitchen.

traffic disappears then a fish oven glove rises at the end of the counter and swims towards the sink. A wave of blue tea towel billows then swamps it. The seaweed grows again, the fish hiding behind it as the blue tea towel rises and bears down. Everything disappears. Then traffic stands and takes a bow.

It would be a good house for a party.

You don't think it's too *nice*?

Nah, we'd soon fix that. Clear the living room, roll up the rugs, you've got your parquet dancefloor. Show me the sound system.

It's over there.

Where?

There.

I can't see anything . . . Oh fuuuuck, it's a Bang and Olufsson! Can I put my tape in?

They sit listening to the tape, traffic trying to juggle finds her efforts improve with certain rhythms and tempo. She has been bitten and the balls now travel with her nearly everywhere she goes. She sits on the edge of the couch watching the TV screen the balls and her visitor. Slip now has a strength to her unapparent three years ago when they first met, not that traffic paid much attention till she first heard her play at Scum and even then she always saw Slip's music before her person. Slip has a serenity, a confidence, all those things that traffic aspires to.

These meetings alone in quiet surroundings are rare and traffic is surprised to find herself feeling nervous all the while wanting Slip's company. When she leaves two hours later the wide white silence of the house opens around traffic like a vacuum.

Tired wired tired wired, it's almost midnight. Clock ticking on the oven, fridge purring, upstairs a tap dripping and something else something strange. traffic gets up and creeps along the corridor in her socks up the stairs to Josh's room, pausing feeling every cell in her body every nerve ending, the shriek of raw track marks with every folding and unfolding of her arms, the constant thudding ache in her knee. She stands inside the doorway of Josh's bedroom one ear calmed by the sound of the child's breathing, the other unnerved by a rattling on the roof. Moves to the landing looks into the dark of the attic then creeps up the stairs slowly, every hair on her body listening. There is definitely something out there. She takes off her socks. Goes to the cupboard and takes out the stepladder quietly unfolds it, climbs and levers the skylight open.

It's high and beautiful and peaceful up here, lights of the distant football stadium painting the night, warm summer breeze, swish of tree tops and peeping rustles of birds and bats in the fig next door. She walks around the tilt of the roof toes gripping tiles then sits back down inside the dome of indigo sky. She could live up here she thinks as she reclines back on the knobbly tiles and shuts her eyes. But she'd need some padding. And it might get lonely. What's she doing up here anyway? traffic revives and climbs back down through the skylight, down the stairs faster now to the phone ringing in the bedroom. Quickly quickly fuck that phone's loud.
    Hallo?
    Hallo, is that Katherine?
    No, it's traffic.
    Pardon?
    Roger's sister. I'm babysitting.
    Oh. I see. It's Claire Dryden here. I'm the next-door neighbour and I'm terribly sorry to ring so late but I just saw someone on your roof!
    I *thought* I heard something.

Yes, I can't think how they got up there. The drainpipes or something?

I better check.

Would you like me to ring the police?

No, it's OK, I'll just go and check.

Well listen do ring me if you need anything.

Sure, thank you.

What did you say your name was again?

traffic.

Oh . . . Is that Slavic?

So there *was* someone up there, must have hid from her the little fucker. Right! traffic reascends heart pumping. Nobody. Nobody but herself. Oh Jesus, how embarrassing. Yellow BMW pulling into the garage. Quiiiiiiiick . . . !

Mmmmm dreaming. Smoking dreaming remembering music. Jamming in Helen's bedsit to Defunkt, Helen's brand-new tenor spilling breath over the notes after an angry neighbour turned off the electricity, and the lights the stereo and Jo's amplifier disappeared. They played on anyway with the saxophone descended, scrawling the tune alone across the darkness. Helen lit a candle and they took it from the top, the bloat of her face and neck highlighted as she leant closer to the whack of Jo's strings. Leaning closer to remember their frantic jazz muted like music from another room.

Jo met Helen at a Great White Noise gig. They came from opposite ends of the scale, Helen classically trained at the Conservatorium, Jo playing bass in her first band, part punk part funk part everything else. Helen at twenty-two seemed so adult, only later did her naivety become clear to Jo. Helen was soon coming from Newtown to Darlinghurst to score from Eddy via Jo and Jo kept her there in the large cluttered house, picking her brains for the grammar of music. For two years they swapped stories and records using together sometimes though Jo pulled back from that, music was always her main addiction. For six months they were lovers, furtive in the rock'n'roll heterodoxy. It was Helen who taught Jo the pictographics of sheet music and Schönberg's twelve-tone system which Jo forgot soon enough. And Helen who lent her Ornette Coleman, Lester Bowie, Sun Ra, taking back the Stooges, Eno, the Saints. Every piece of music told its own tale then layers of other listeners' like hers and Helen's. There was Charlie Mingus working for over twenty years to reach the stage where he no longer had to think when playing and only then did he really start to make music. He was doing a small club gig and in the middle of a phrase suddenly realised he wasn't anticipating the notes anymore. They poured through his fingers like electricity like water, poured straight from his soul through the double bass to the hearts of his spectators. There was another bassist who sat in with Charlie Parker during the war years. Donna Lee, one of the only female musicians in the bop dens apart from the occasional pianist or vocalist. Ruthless music, fast, hair-raising. After a protracted absence from the instrument Donna Lee's finger had become soft again and blistered immediately. Bird told her that the best way to raise callouses was to break the blisters and drench them with whiskey. She did so and took a break while her fingers cooled off. Then in the middle of a set the bass player threw his bass at her saying Finish this. So she had to play. And as Bird and the bass player sat there smiling the band ran the tune ragged for over half an hour till Donna Lee's fingers began to bleed. Donna Lee made it that night but was remembered now only as the name of a tune written by Charlie Parker and loved by bass buffs for its degree of difficulty. Later when seeking the stories for herself, Jo read Miles Davis's claim in his autobiography that a tune called Donna Lee was his first composition ever recorded. Dizzy Gillespie also claimed authorship. A web site said it was named for Curly Russel's daughter.

And Helen, what was the next part of her story? There was always someone in the circle fucking up on drugs, then it was Helen now it was traffic followed closely behind by Jimi. Helen got back from heroin but did she get back to music? Shedded like other playmates from that time, and even if they saw her name on a poster they wouldn't know that Slip was Jo. Slip liked to think she was old enough now to hang onto her friendships, that her friends like traffic were old enough to know when to stop. Slip couldn't keep up with traffic in her current state. Back then Jo could barely keep up with the Defunkt bass lines let alone any bebop tune like Donna Lee. Helen could though, and Helen's instrument could be played without electricity. What would Slip do now if the lights went out. She walks amongst the records and CDs spread across the floor from the afternoon's listening. German, a white label, the latest Fluke and Sand. Unlike James who stacks everything neatly she needs this visual spread, she needs to see the pieces of aural jigsaw. She can hear the arrangement contrived earlier and goes through it again from memory. And yet, and yet, it's no good being too exact, hitting delay in the same place every time, bringing this track in on the sixteenth bar. Each set to live had to be a life itself, part planning and definite structure, part improvisation. A fusion of senses reason intuition, an order of chaos. Standing over the records with outstretched hands, aiming her soft fingers, conducting . . .

When the plug was pulled Helen played so soft the tock of keys overode the notes themselves, till the bridge of Joseph Bowie's trombone solo when she tightened her lip defiantly across the reed and filled the night again with her screaming saxophone. *Make them dance, make them dance!*

Total

total

total

        fucking

total

        fucking

total

total

fucking

           habit

fucking

           habit

total

           habit

total

           habit

fucking

           habit

fucking

           habit

Total

Fucking

Habit

Habit

Habit

Habit

Total

Fucking

Habit

She had become addicted to the rush of hedonism like a bored child to television, she had engorged herself to mute inertia. The full fat businessman at his umpteenth lunch, the journalist arrogant with a million trivial facts, the barrister clocking up his thirteenth hour, the marathon runner exhausted all her muscles torn. Her work was her play, her play was work, a night spent partying was a necessity but a day spent house-hunting was a robbery.

For two and a half weeks traffic scoured the papers and windows of real estate agents for an affordable place. But traffic was naive. Summer was the worst time to be looking for a place and having lived overseas then locally in two established share-accommodations, Sydney's rents had gone over her head unnoticed. Without full-time bar work her wage had gone down. There was the ground-floor bedsit in Woolloomooloo that needed electric light at midday, then a place on Darlinghurst Road resplendent with neons. There was the room in Paddington cheaper at one hundred and forty dollars, barely big enough for a bed and table. Sundry Kings Cross flatettes for almost two hundred dollars, damp noisy and dark. Turkish Jim in Elizabeth Bay paid two hundred and thirty a week for his floating box, a fee well and truly out of her reach. So in the third week when Slip knocked at the door of the warehouse, the traffic who let her in was unusually glum.

She called out to Holmes on her way past his room then went into her own and shut the door. Silence from the living room, traffic turned down her radio and listened intently, eased herself off the bed, crept to the door. Competition of silence. Inside her head a wild animal paced around the bemusement at her games. Just before she opened the door again she saw Slip standing out in the street almost two years ago, holding a crate of records.

What are you doing!

There's so much *room* in here.

Slip stayed on the floor, arms and legs outstretched while traffic stood over her.

Holmes must've stepped out. Want a cup of tea?

Holmes probably wouldn't find it strange, Holmes was intimate with Slip's habits and signals. Her eyes following traffic's return from the kitchen while her body continued stretching.

So have you found somewhere to live?

How did you know?

Holmes even asked me if I wanted the room.

Well it's a great space. You should consider it.

Jimi's birthday.

At the warehouse, making them tea. Jimi, his latest boy Luke who worked with Holmes, and a surprise guest Sailor. Crystal had gone up so they requested speed. It was Luke who paid for the eight ball and Jimi who was getting first shot to celebrate thirty years of life. traffic and Jimi's shifts at the Royal had rarely coincided since Pimp. The truth was also that they had been avoiding one another. She decided to treat him as she would any client, politely, honestly, coolly and quickly. It's really strong guys, and I'm not just saying that. We can do it here, can't we traff. I'd rather you came into my room. But they'd already settled in and nobody was home. Jimi lounging on the couch like a lord while Sailor and Luke cooked spoonfuls either side. Okay now? He gave an arm each to the administers. Why didn't you just put it all in one syringe? They ignored her dumb comment. traffic was suddenly scared, or maybe this was just a cute little ritual. She moved closer wanting to disappear altogether. Sailor who had been cold with her right from the start, nodded at Luke then they injected simultaneously. Pulling out she spoke to traffic for the first time. Cos it wouldn't fit, we're giving him two grams. Oh fuck you guys what the *fuck* are you doing! Ssshhh!

Adrenalin pumping through her own body now as she watched Jimi's jerk with a small high sigh. Absolutely still. Agitated eyelids flushed skin breathing arrested. Seconds became years. Sailor and Luke gazed rapt as acolytes, Luke's hand a centimetre from Jimi's waiting to touch him the amphetamine deity. The sound of a key broke the necrophile silence. Turning traffic saw Bee come in and turning back the pulse crazy as a trapped butterfly below Jimi's jaw. So he was alive. With a gasp his eyes flew open. Wooooowww! traffic spoke through her teeth. Listen you guys just clean all this shit up right now and come into my room alright? Sailor looked straight past her at Bee. Hey, how's tricks. Bee glared back wordless. She hated Sailor. Since meeting Sailor here two months ago, Bee's industry gossip of the house where Sailor worked and its junky staff doing full service as mistresses had dripped into the ears of traffic like a poison. traffic went to her room avoiding Bee's eyes.

I've just been to the most *amazing* place, god I love you guys! See, I told you! Their excited voices carrying this far, fuck fuck *fuck*, traffic sat on her bed waiting for a bomb to go off. I know I know but I still kind've wanted to do myself y'know. You can, you can do it with butterfly clips and a bigger syringe, takes a little longer for the gear to go in which kind of spreads out the rush, I know a guy who did a whole eight ball. Deadset. Yeh but crystal's better obviously cos you can get more in the fit without it going gluggy not to mention missing out on all the crappy additives. Oh well next time. Jimi coming in her door now.

Hey dude, thanks!

It wasn't exactly free.

I don't care, *I* wasn't paying.

You might have the constitution of an ox but you're on ritonavir Jimi, you freaked the shit out of me.

I've stopped all my HIV drugs, they were making me ill.

Now you tell me.

You're one of my best friends traffic, you know that don't you. traffic stayed on her bed, flat on her back hands over eyes. Jimi smothering her with a hug and chemical sweat. You coming for a drink?

No I'm too tired.

She turned and curled towards the window. Sailor came in followed by Luke with the used fits. Got a disposal box? Over there. She heard Sailor's voice as they drifted out of the warehouse. Had a tanty did she?

She went out to find Bee after they had gone.

Hey I'm really sorry. They kind of sprung that one on me.

What, buying your drugs? Twist my arm.

I mean doing it here in the living room.

What's the point.

What?

I'm totally over drugfucked people in my house. And don't pass the buck. How about you pinned and speeding at the house meeting the other month. And was anyone here *ever* cool about your dealing? D'you think I'm stupid or something? You've got a month.

She didn't speak to anyone about being thrown out. Not till Slip came over that evening to visit Holmes who ended up being an hour late. Slip asked traffic what he had said and traffic repeated it exactly, that he was obliged to go along with the decision, that Bee was the warehouse's original tenant after all. traffic was nevertheless unaware that Holmes had washed his hands of her too, Holmes who always positioned himself in a supporting role was resigning even from that. Watching Slip stretch like a cat beneath her, traffic saw her own imminent spatial deprivation and a heedlessness in Slip she hadn't ever noticed. Slip looked up.

But you don't look that sorry about moving out.

I guess I had it coming. She wasn't contradicted. I want to live on my own anyway, I feel like I'm in the way here. Slip sat up, traffic kept fishing. But it's not like I ever reneged on bills or ripped anyone off or any bullshit like that. Or kept people awake all night. And Christ I sure did my fair share of cleaning. You know how long it takes to vacuum and mop this place?

Yep, that's one thing that speed's good for.

Tell me what you think honestly. D'you think Bee's right? D'you think I'm that drugfucked I'm impossible to live with?

Well I don't know traffic. I like you.

Don't stop for a cigarette now, cleanup's not over. traffic can you take the rubbish out? Wipe the bar down again, you didn't do it properly. Don't forget to marry the bottles. Trawl the floor later traffic, we've got too much to do. Knee ache, backache, headache, heartache. She hated Pete, hated being a barmaid. Maybe the kitchen four shifts a week but Craig wouldn't allow that, Craig had had trouble finding barmaids since Pete began managing and traffic's skills in this area were more valuable than any of her others. Craig wasn't the bemused bear she had been employed by over two years ago, he was irritable, gaunt, easily goaded. He waited for them to finish and come over to the corner with their drinks, then made his way through the list of changes. As you all know, the Royal's been sold. The new owners are happy with current management but they want to renovate. We're not going to close, we're going to do one floor at a time, the cellar bar first. From next week the plans will be available for anyone to look at in my office, but I'll give you a brief outline. The cellar bar will have poker machines. Loud groans from all of the staff. Not another gaming room! Craig went on. Not exactly a gaming room, there'll only be eighteen machines. Eigh*teen*! The DJ box will be taken out and replaced with a screen where we'll be showing music videos. Fuck that! Craig looked up sharply. You can give me your opinions afterwards, I have a lot to get through and I'd appreciate some silence. During the renovations everyone will have to cut back on their shifts. Once they're completed, we'll be reinterviewing everybody. If you disapprove of what we're doing you might choose to leave anyway. For which we'll require the usual notice. The cocktail bar will be extended and you will all be responsible for keeping things chilled, I don't need to go over the dramas that happened when people were caught dancing, besides which we'll be going for a more laidback and exclusive vibe. I think we've been unusually tolerant up until now of what you all wear to work, but staff will henceforth be required to wear uniforms. Speaking of tolerance a no drugs rule will be strictly enforced, once again I don't need to remind any of you about police crackdowns and we're absolutely unwilling to risk our licence. A guffaw from most of the staff. So you won't be laying out lines for us in the office on recovery Sundays? Craig glared at them. I don't think any of you can say we ever made a *habit* of that. Here on the ground floor the DJ box will remain, we'll pipe the music from it up to the cocktail bar. It will still be a street bar but with an absolutely open door policy and the tinted windows will be replaced with clear glass. The days are long gone when we had to hide in dark rooms. Oxford Street, as you all know, has gone through many changes over the years . . .

Gary and Jimi went down to the cellar to fetch their bags, Pete in the office showing a new Canadian barman exercise tips for external obliques. Happy for an extra audience when Gary and Jimi passed him on their way out, Pete addressed all three.

You know what shits me the most about guys coming onto me? What they say when they're trying to pick me up that shits me the most? It happens a lot at the sauna. I get these little nip cunts, these skinny little nip cunts coming up to me and saying God you've got a great body, god I wish I had a body like yours. But you know what? They wouldn't know the first thing about bodybuilding!
Gary walked out. Jimi turned.

Look Pete, I don't wanna know about your personal life. I come here to work and I'd rather we just left it at that.

They caught up with traffic on the next block, Jimi took her hand and wouldn't let go. By the time they reached Taylor Square Gary and Jimi had decided to leave the Royal. traffic knew she wouldn't last much longer. Gary hailed a cab and left the door open for Jimi. Aren't you coming? No I'm walking traffic home. The cab departed. You're walking me home are you? Yes. Is that OK?

The morning taste was the best. Chip of diamond in the spoon, stream of cool light, leap out of bed. Holmes in the kitchen, Morning gorgeous! traffic rushed past to the shower, on her way back to her bedroom hugging him from behind. Holmes twisted away. Your hair's wet.

He was holding it up to her, the white shirt he had been wearing, when she re-emerged to make toast and coffee. Two pink pools on the yoke from her wet devil's horns.

Thanks for that traffic.

Oh shit sorry!

Why are you always in such a bloody rush anyway.

I've got the lunchtime shift and I'm trying to finish an outfit.

He hadn't spoken to her since the eviction, wanted to avoid confrontation and the possible obligation to support her point of view. But traffic had evaded the issue even more adroitly which to Holmes signified guilt of some sort. Not that traffic was apologising. Two weeks later he couldn't stand it anymore. Staining his shirt with her hair dye like that was enough, he was going to be late for work, he left her eating in the kitchen and went to get another shirt. Never knew anyone who could speed and eat simultaneously but then again traffic did everything simultaneously. He came back out at her.

What about the house-hunting?

What about it?

Well it must be hard when you're working day and night to get time off to look for somewhere to live.

I'm looking every Wednesday and Saturday Holmes, like most people do.

Must be a bit full-on working the double shift on Fridays and Saturdays and looking for a place to live all day in between. Not to mention the gammy knee.

Don't hassle me Holmes.

He turned and faced her.

Look at yourself traffic. You're always going on about your workaholic family and how fucked their values are and meanwhile you continue working seven days a week for no good reason. You're in that classic trap of working too hard and needing drugs to do it and needing to work harder to pay for them. Look at yourself traffic, look at what you're doing. *Look at yourself.*

It was Jimi who was the bringer of good news to traffic, he was vacating the Potts Point bedsit he rented privately from a friend of a friend. traffic had once visited the small sunlit room whose parquet from the beginning of Jimi's binge had bit by bit been concealed by junk. After his manic five day birthday Jimi had come down so hard he almost suicided. He had no excuses for his neglect of traffic but didn't try inventing them and so their friendship continued as though nothing had happened. Now he was upgrading to a shared flat in Edgecliff. Starting new combos, no longer seeing Luke. Jimi had just got work in a salon that would let him look how he wanted. Jimi was on the move.

He left traffic a mattress a table and chair and owning nothing but a stereo, clothes and some rudimentary kitchen utensils, traffic's move was completed in two trips in Shifty's car. Sitting in the foreign twilight while Jimi went to the bottle shop, traffic felt desolate. Tapping in now to the drugs on the other side of the profit margin, wiring up the stereo, juggling by the time he had returned. The balls refused to coordinate, she put them down despondently.

What are you doing later?

Going home and cooking dinner. Where should I put this?

I don't know, on the floor. I don't have any glasses.

You'll be right as soon as you get a few things.

You know how much it costs to move. And I haven't got a day off for two weeks to do any household shopping.

Fuck shopping, the street faeries'll provide. What's your wish list?

God I don't know. More chairs. Shelves. Kitchen stuff. A heater.

You better start praying.

A couch or cushions or something. A television? Please God?

God doesn't care traffic, it's the street faeries who provide. Pray to them girlfriend. *Pray.*

Down to the Tunnel of Love, another cloudy day. Stripping to T Rex, look at my fine new fake fur outfit, my new moves, listen to my sexy new soundtrack. Amber lowers herself and her knee locks, can't get back up. Swivels on her back pretending, slides off the edge of the

259

stage and limps amongst the spectators teasing. They sit there po-faced looking at her body looking uncomfortable. What do they want what do they come here for where's the enjoyment? The guy in the front row cock in fist as she goes back up to the stage, can't even clap or smile. See ya, she waltzes off angry, deflated. Wouldn't wanna be ya.

Into the peepshow her own private sanctuary, darkness coming early down the alley then the onset of rain. Twenty minutes between customers, none of them stay. What's wrong with me god not this again this stupid insecurity. She is winding down running out drawing away, all the while realising this is exactly what she needs now, an audience, affirmation, a space to perform in. She needs the exchange of energy and power, she needs the immediate release and fulfilment but with nobody there or at best low-grade men the equation keeps returning a negative. What she wants is some kind of emotion, a deeper connection. The rowdy return of a dance party crowd, the animated eyes of a listening lover, coming off stage at Heresy face to face with the man with the rooster tattoo, jubilant like all those other happy strangers, the feedback of friends. This is not the Tunnel of Love, this is more like the Tunnel of Lassitude. The fall of coins so sparse she can count them and calculate her paltry wage. Which on signing out proves even less than she thought. And even less than a weekend shift of bar work.

Dimitri swivels the pay sheet back and signs his name next to hers. traffic reads the other girls' earnings upside-down. Nobody's doing well except for the new girl. It's hard being constantly new. The new wigs and outfits aren't making a difference. It all seems like such a waste. She tells Dimitri she won't be back for her shift at the end of the week, she won't be back at all.

When James got a new sampler the possibilities of sound widened like a clearing sky. With all that extra memory, details he hadn't noticed suddenly belonged to him. He stuck his microphone out the window for the clipclop of Penfold's delivery cart, going out later to Darlinghurst then the Cross. The bleating walk signals of traffic lights, wheeze of bus brakes, strip club spruikers, the music of each business changing as he walked down the street the tuner on the dial. He rediscovered the harbour with its foghorns speedboats chime of halyards on masts, the crystal quality of sound over water. After dinner, on the way home from the beat in Centennial Park he lingered inside the symphony of frogs. All the late-night bad television advertisements in Strine, the hours of textures dialogue and effects in his cache of old movies and cartoons, a double CD of industrial sounds and further afield to other peoples' stories. The jackhammers in the building site next door to Fred's. Bee's moody Russians in the deli at Bondi, going in and out and back in again to capture the shift of languages. By evening the curd cheese had melted on the back seat of the car where he left it parked in Redfern. He hung around the end of Wilson Street near the railway lines for a good hour, sound bandit waiting for the confluence of train horns that Slip had described living with in the 80s. The flattened fourth, she said, then as they pull together you get a fifth. If the right third train, or even more, were passing at the same time you might get a whole chord. But James didn't wait for a pattern just stood there with his microphone recording any and every permutation.

Instead of hiding inside from storms the Professor found him on a tall stool, one hand out the skylight the other desperately adjusting levels as the thunder drew nearer. He stood beneath James shouting as the storm broke overhead, he could hardly hear himself. You'll get struck by lightning! Watching James's body tense and swivel as the rain began to pelt onto the roof around him. James for godsake we only just laid these carpets! James's head appeared wet and wild-eyed. Fuck the carpet, this is special. Then a lull in which the Professor thought he was finally going to come down. But when sky next cleaved open and lightning speared down illuminating every corner of the room, James stayed up there like a madman. Electricity! Electricityyyy!!!

There was the Professor talking to himself in the bath every night, livid at the discovery of the tape recorder spy. The rhythms of the washingmachine the fan next door's motorbike answer machine messages Slip's interview on the radio. He took it in and locked it. Listening, always listening, to the tongues and machinery and weather around him, pieces of a jigsaw that he unpacked and rearranged in the privacy of his mind where there were no borders.

Interviewer:	So you started your career at Chronic.
Slip:	I actually started playing at private parties and little doofs on the coast. Then Scum was my first big public party in Sydney.
Interviewer:	Well, biggish.
Slip:	Big enough.
Interviewer:	Scum was a girls' party. How do you go about getting gigs in more male-dominated arenas?
Slip:	Well Scum was actually very mixed, you know. Predominantly queer but pretty mixed up. Two of the promoters were girls but that was just circumstantial. The performance scene is probably female dominated but in the DJ scene it's still more boys than girls. Scum was a *great* party, did you go?
Interviewer:	No. But I heard all about it.
Slip:	The lighting designer and Mr Hyde are part of the crew who put on Hotel Quickie. So they're all connected really. Then there was Pimp –
Interviewer:	Getting back to the original question –
Slip:	Sorry?
Interviewer:	How do you go about getting gigs in more male-dominated arenas?
Slip:	Oh. Just ah keep sending out tapes, return calls, and turn up on time!
Interviewer:	Do you get hassled much?
Slip:	What?
Interviewer:	Are you the victim of much harassment? You play outside the gay scene too. What about homophobia?
Slip:	I don't like that word victim.
Interviewer:	But it's a pretty sexist industry isn't it. It's a bit of a boys' club.
Slip:	Well I guess so . . . probably, aren't most things? Look it's really no big deal. The dance party scene in Sydney's pretty cool relatively speaking. Anyhow, my music's more important than my gender or sexuality or anything like that.
Interviewer:	So you're not a feminist.

Slip:	I didn't say that. I'd just . . . rather not have to think about it all the time. It's not like my main *cause* or anything.
Interviewer:	So what it is your cause?
Slip:	I don't think I have one . . .
Interviewer:	No raison d'être? . . . Go on!
Slip:	God I don't know just . . . keep creating. Have fun, keep going.
Interviewer:	Thank you. You've been listening to lesbian DJ Slip live in the studio talking about her music. She'll be rippin' up the floor before Serge Vice from Belgium in the hardhouse room at Xenogenesis this Saturday. Free tickets for the first two callers!

traffic had gone home elated after quitting the Tunnel of Lassitude, had a shot and even more elated rung the Royal to say she was quitting. She was free now, completely, and the fear of it blew into the room from the moment she put the phone down.

She had paid the bond, paid the electricity gas and phone connections, she took the remainder of her cash over to Neil's place in Waterloo. Neil let her in. She walked down the hall into the skylit living area at the back where a restless Luke was circling the room talking to no one, thin unshaven and dishevelled as though he had just got out of bed, face to face now with traffic in the doorway. Hallo there! Hi, what's happening? We were just having a quiet conversation. I didn't think that was possible. At about a hundred miles an hour. traffic sat opposite Neil on the couch to do business. Okay then, there's this and this in the speed department, the beige is better. No, no powders today. I haven't got any crystal, that'll be here tomorrow if you can wait. I tell you it's hard waiting, Luke chipped in, and I'd know, I was having six shots a day. But it's worth it, you'll get some rest. I'm on prozac now, just had a nap, I'm down to three shots a day. I feel soooo much better. So Luke was living here now, jabbering away in the background while traffic spoke to Neil, cool Neil, who smiled at Luke smiled back at traffic. That's OK, I just want ice. Oooh ice, said Luke. Ice is *nice*. These are the e's I had last time, V8s, they're very strong, have you tried them? And these are some new ones, Big Reds, they're more dancey and I've got some coke, fantastic, really pure, best ever. He puts a rock the size of a fist on the table. traffic stares. I don't have much money today Neil, I just want ice, I might come and get some e's later. I've got hydro, bush buds, I've got some new trips called pythons, they're pretty wicked. Honestly Neil, just ice today. So you're coming down in the world eh traffic? Yeh that's it, I'm coming down in the world.

Fear, sweet fear, of the cane swishing down, lightning stroke still white flash, then the pause into which pain rushed like a belt of fire. Then the next stroke, the next the next the next till her entire arse and thighs were raised and smouldering. Lying there in the dark, running her hand over the welts on Bee's arse. How many strokes did Bee take in those lucrative sub jobs, fifty, sixty, how long was it since she had delivered that to Shifty or let Shifty deliver the same. Bee sighed and turned onto her back. I can take more in a job context Shifty, you know that. I'm fully armoured and I've got a thousand bucks waiting for me, it makes a helluva difference. Shifty turned away. Bee's arse was out of bounds now for at least a week, probably longer, Shifty would have liked to have offered her own. But the longer Bee eluded Shifty, the longer Shifty eluded Bee. Shifty slept on the edge of the bed, turned away when Bee was there, missed her when she was gone.

At the play party, being caned by traffic, the scene the entire night muggy with Billy's jealousy. traffic drawing Shifty aside the next day to debrief, Shifty as always keeping a lid on things. traffic back then was just as fooled as everyone, assumed if the doors were open by mutual consent then both parties were always satisfied. traffic often whispering God I envy you two, you have exactly what I've always wanted. Hearing Shifty crying in the bathroom during those last torturous weeks, coming in to give her a hug. Without words Shifty knew that two years later traffic finally understood. That changing the rules wouldn't have saved traffic and Billy just as keeping them open didn't save her and Bee. It wasn't the rules that made a relationship it was first and last the junction of personalities. At the play party Shifty had signalled she'd had enough after only twenty strokes. She wanted sometimes to be more like Bee, to be able to take the pain with money from a stranger, to be more willing to play with strangers just for fun, to find as much pleasure in the delivery of a friend like traffic. But the truth was she always wanted it from Bee more than anyone, the pain the pleasure and the love all at once. With Bee she had no armour nothing else existed, she could walk inside each stroke and feel it in its entirety, all the colours on the spectrum of pain. Shifty was shy, Shifty was extreme, Shifty was a perfectionist. It wasn't easy wanking in the bed you shared with your lover, she took those fantasies into the toilets at work, her arse exposed being caned and fucked. She wanted to be the landscape invaded, reborn from carnage.

She was scared to be single, it had been so many years. She couldn't handle answering the same questions over and over, the looks alone were bad enough. People set you up as the golden couple, Fred actually used those words, then when you broke up you broke their dream as well. traffic was the only person not surprised, it wasn't just her physical proximity, traffic embraced the unexpected. Holmes was there too, Holmes was there even longer than traffic but was too much of a romantic to see the good sometimes just wasn't good enough.

And so it was traffic that Shifty turned to the most, loud chaotic freewheeling traffic. They were old friends become new friends, driving over to Oxford Street on a Sunday night, nervous and excited like kids on a first date minus the sexual attraction. Previously remaining at arm's length around their respective lovers, traffic and Shifty were alone together for the first time. Shifty found a surprising wisdom beneath traffic's levity and traffic was always curious when a personality unpeeled before her so studied Shifty for lessons in self-containment. She spoke like a queen, crisp sardonic sibilant. Was always impeccably groomed though too locked in diffidence to notice the girls in awe of her. Everything about Shifty was so neat, her cropped hair clear skin white nails on the steering wheel, even Esmerelda although an old car smelt fresh and clean. They stopped at the lights beside a boy being questioned by police on the traffic island. While they waited, the boy following directives took his jacket off then shoes, socks, jeans, shirt.

What's going on?

Looks like he's being strip searched.

What's his crime, standing on a traffic island? I mean it's winter for fuck's sake.

I drive past here nearly every day. He's a windscreen washer. Shifty pointed out the pregnant woman sitting beneath a fig tree back from the road. That's his girlfriend. He's been here about two years.

I s'pose that kind of thing's quite normal in most parts of the world.

Since when did we want to be like most parts of the world?

There were poker machines everywhere now. In the first three pubs on Taylor Square, further down in the cellar of the Royal where they went to finish off traffic's drink tickets. The tickets were no longer valid, all the staff were new and the clean shiny bar fittings depressed them. traffic was desperate for Shifty to pick up, desperate as ever to pick up herself, but Shifty putting away a shot and chaser in each bar was on her way to maudlin reminiscence and a crooked walk. They passed the long queue to a new venue, two bouncers with metal detectors, Celine Dion audible on the street. Drunken straight boys everywhere, they walked close together avoiding eye contact. Let's go traffic, there's nowhere we'll feel comfortable, let's go back to my place, your limp's getting worse y'know. I want lights Shifty, music, movement, I wanna score! I hate this street now traffic, we can go back to my place, how about it? They continued down to Whitlam Square, turned around and started back up again, Shifty looking and smiling at traffic. traffic couldn't do it, Shifty was her sister. traffic wanted to lose herself in mindless sex not find herself in a best friend's bed. Heading for Shifty's car now and who should they see but Jenny. Jenny eyeing off traffic, Shifty leaning against a telegraph pole ignoring her, Jenny saying let's go for a drink and traffic saying they may as well just go back to Jenny's place straightaway. Shifty looked at traffic looked at Jenny looked at traffic. traffic went up to her and gave her a hug. You should get a cab. No I'm gonna drive. We'll walk you to a cab Shifty. No I'm going for another drink. You sure? Yeh I'm sure. OK then, I'll call you tomorrow.

Back out in the streets at sunrise, saddlesore, weary, there's Esmerelda still parked in Little Oxford Street. So Shifty had taken a cab in the end or else got lucky though this was unlikely. traffic knew it was only familiarity and loneliness ignited by alcohol that had inspired Shifty to suggest it in the first place. traffic thought of all the women across the world like Shifty accustomed to restraint or at best analysis. So they chose the fast bliss of one-handed love or friends or old lovers over carefree meetings with the unknown. She thought there was no difference between her and them, in their makeup and desires there was no difference at all but a willingness to act. Which ultimately made all the difference in the world.

There was also the account of Bliss's performance night the week before during which traffic had sat at home feeling sorry for herself. traffic envied the continuing friendship between Bee and Shifty, she suspected if Billy were still here it would have been too difficult, they most likely would have only been halfway through an arduous demise. During those hours before Jenny, Shifty's stories had sickened traffic with their richness so the offer of forgetfulness in flesh had been even more enticing and Shifty's heedlessness in giving every detail quashed traffic's remorse at leaving her to go home alone.

Bee had of course done the puppet show with Bella for Bliss's performance night. Bella was after all in the show's original inception. They had taken it one step further and Bella the puppet had torn out the strings with hooks attached. The sight of her spinning offstage bleeding was awesome, said Shifty. And the hooks. But you were better somehow traffic, you were more puppet-like. Maybe it's just your physique, Bella's such an odalisque no matter what she does. traffic had trouble swallowing that, it was her suggestion to pull out the strings with the needles attached but Bee at the time had been too cautious, it was her idea that the puppet gain its freedom.

She didn't want that anymore, to be someone else's prop, to contribute without control. She didn't want to be anybody's puppet anymore. She wanted to be her own creator.

Overcast morning, bite of cold. Her knee ached, her back ached. She worried about Shifty, wondered where she was, took out her phone to ring her as she neared home. No reception. She should have known this would happen, the bill hadn't been paid and her phone was now cut off. She went into the hock shop on the corner and sold the handset. Further down the street a block from her flat she found a small bar heater, took it home and plugged it in. It worked.

Alone.

What she had then.
A lover to wake up with, warm flesh, stories, a mind to talk to. A full heart.
Housemates, emphasis on mates.
A stereo.
Some books.
A television and VCR.
A mobile phone.
A kitchen equipped with the utensils of at least 3 people accumulated over 10 years.
Likewise the furniture of others to sit in lie in eat on write on store things in.
Access to a computer (Holmes's), a pushbike (Bee's), sometimes even a car (Shifty's).
Endless clothes and accessories of others available for dressups.
6 pairs of shoes, all in reasonably good nick. Platforms, bike boots, silly fur boots, trainers, sandals, high strappy strip shoes.
A healthy body.
Two jobs. Three if you counted dealing.
Drugs and money.

What she had now.
A stereo.
Some books.
One pot, one pan, 5 plates from the Australian Defence Force left by the street faeries at the bottom of Macleay Street. Some cutlery.
Some clothes.
Juggling balls.
4 pairs of shoes. Platforms, bike boots, trainers, high strappy strip shoes.
A limp.
Desire.

Welcome to the next phase

Everything is past

There'll be no more fooling around

It's not a joke anymore

This time it's for real

The next phase
                    has
                              begun.

In an A4 envelope from Holmes's work, in another half as big from the States, was a large postcard of an eighteenth century Indian watercolour. Rich red background, flowing robes of green and ochre, faces all colours. In the right margin musicians playing intently and all across the rest of the picture villagers dancing in ecstasy. traffic turned the card over. Billy's handwriting.

Fear   loving   travelling   still
buildings   beauty   ♥ NY   disco so-so
miss amigos   rushing   traffic
sorry, i was a coward, sorry sorry

She rang Holmes a few days later. Felt so estranged. Wanted to apologise, didn't know how. The postcard from Billy was like a deliverance and traffic was falling, released, she was falling.

Driving out to Xenogenesis, peak hour over but the streets still jammed. Slip picked up traffic then headed over to Surry Hills for Holmes. She wasn't a bad driver but the wet bitumen, new highway and redirected roads made progress haphazard. Can I go up here? No, yes, I don't know yes now! Slip cut across then turned into a laneway, car coming over the crest towards her. They braked hard, headlight to headlight, traffic on the periphery pitching to the windscreen. Slip reversed onto the main road, horns blaring behind, then sped to the next set of lights. Alright, left or right? Right. But if I go right I can't go round can I? Yes, they blocked it off at the other end, round's the only way you *can* go. The lights went green and Slip started to turn left, traffic wringing her hands. Right! Turn right! Well don't *say* right then I'm a Catholic! What?! Tell me to turn right and I'll turn left! Slip let the car run to the bottom of the hill then parked, traffic exhaled. What a great excuse, I'll have to remember that. Got a cigarette? I didn't think you smoked. I don't. traffic lit a cigarette, passed it over. Where are we anyway? Paddington I think. Slip sat there laughing, smoking. traffic wasn't in a hurry. Slip's blue breath all around her.

Holmes had news of the changes at the warehouse. Bee was paying most of the rent now, kitting out traffic's old bedroom as a dungeon to enable her to work privately, converting the back bathroom into a dark room. She was printing up old negs and ready to start photographing again in earnest. traffic still suffering the sight of Bee turning her back on her when she had gone up to fetch him, listened to Holmes in silence all the way over to the western side of the harbour.

Inside Xenogenesis she was able to escape. How long had it been since she had attended an event done by strangers full of props and decor and performance. The stiltwalkers they had used at Pimp moving across the courtyard on two metre stilts, gargantuan ballgowns birthing aliens in body paint, masks, lopsided limbs. In the big room a Japanese DJ playing nothing but bass that bypassed the ears vibrating every cell in your body, kites and weird creatures cascading from the vaulted nineteenth century ceiling. Bad for acoustics according to Slip but great for lighting. They followed the lasers down to individuals, here and there some of their crowd as well. The young queer ravers awkward in Oxford Street clubs like punks at a disco, all those fluoro kids born for blacklight, pansexual, tempting, though not so flirtatious in this environment. traffic moved through the party with Slip and Holmes, found Bella and Stash and lost them again, lost them all and danced on her own. Turning, looking, listening, always turning, dancing in all directions against the tide facing the DJ booth.

Holmes joined traffic on the edge of the stage and sat watching the crowd with his arm around her. She leant into his warm body. I know it might not look like I'm trying Holmes, but I am, I am. I know baby, you'll get there. They made their way to the smaller room upstairs and now in a more intimate environment traffic began to relax. She felt refreshed by a night bereft of queer cruising, had worn her op shop school uniform as a party outfit but the joke wasn't that popular in rave repertoire. Still it brought her age down to one more compatible with the young crowd and their benign distance suited her mood. She felt unwanted and unwanting, she felt removed she felt good.

Slip took off at 4, coasting clear out of the previous set like a hovercraft landing into a darker sound and the lighting designer turned everything red. It was hot. People came in and stayed. Even on the sidelines a part of every single body was moving. Dancing with a more evil joy now, more carnal like a queer crowd, turning away from the booth and dancing with each other so the source was no longer her but everywhere, inside them, they were losing control. Slip knew when the promoter came to her an hour later and said the last DJ was too drugfucked to play that she might not get paid for doing extra. But these one hour sets never fully sated her and now with dawn light coming through the windows she was happy and had enough music so when they shut down the sound system and moved to the third room downstairs Slip kept playing.

Half inside and half out in the courtyard they danced in their coats against the early morning cold, the sky thick, opaque and protective. When it lit up suddenly they saw their canopy of low cloud. A storm was moving in, lightning flashing closer as the first full sun bled behind dense coverage. Then thunder came in long slow rumbles beneath the music like a didgeridoo. Slip played on as the lightning dissolved into spreading sunlight, the city embraced by clouds holding their rain till her last twenty minutes when cold drops began to fall. traffic turned when the hand stroked her hair, an even length again, white with patches of ultramarine. Like oceans the boy said. traffic usually hated people touching her hair but this one was different, from him beamed the invisible magnet of lust. They circled one another till the music finished then outside waiting for Slip and Holmes his hand roamed the oceans in her hair again, the other arm tightening around her body.

So what school do you go to?

Fools' school, what about you?

Um . . . The Independent School. What are you doing now?

I have to go home and do my homework. Biology.

D'you need some help? I'm pretty good at biology.

Sure, it's always fun studying together.

Languid with heat, new flesh and ecstasy aftermath, they stayed in the bath till the water cooled to room temperature. traffic shutting his mouth with her own each time it issued guilty mentions of his girlfriend. It occurred to traffic as she journeyed across his body underwater and later on her bed that Matthias the rigger with his compact muscularity and dark clippered hair resembled her more than any girl she had gone home with recently. But his scapula tattoo was far superior. A clean solid abstract arrangement of mechanical paraphernalia. Rough cheeks, rough kiss, rough mouth on her cunt so she grew then flinched grew then flinched. Lying between his legs sucking his cock, pulling it flat against his stomach and watching with amazement the tight scrotum transform to large swollen labia. My god we are so similar. Sliding her wet finger into his arse, him saying oh oh, cock twitching. She insinuated a second finger and Matthias reached down, No. He dragged on a condom and felt for her cunt, moving together, traffic clenching couldn't reach her clit, then he was further, faster, traffic saying wait, slower, hang on but Matthias was already coming. So quick, so easy.

He picked up the juggling balls on his way to get a drink of water. How are you with these? I'm learning. Matthias did a few clumsy throws. I tried to learn years ago, it's fucken hard, you've gotta be dedicated. He climbed back beneath the doona, hugged her, kissed her, sighed despondently. I'd love to fuck you again but I've gotta go. traffic's horniness departed immediately. He got up and began to put his clothes on. Can I have your phone number? traffic lit a cigarette and lay in bed watching him. Is that a good idea? I mean you've mentioned your girlfriend about three times tonight. I know, I'm guilty. If you think so. Look, I can't believe we met for no reason. We didn't, we met for a fuck. No, I'd feel crass just leaving it like this. It happened for a reason, it was special! I'd really like to get to know you, you're a really unusual girl, and I can't give you my number obviously. traffic wrote her number on a piece of paper and passed it to him. I want the number of your tattoo artist. Sure. He folded the paper into a tight square and put it into the coin pocket, came over and kissed her again. I hope I was of some help with the biology. Yeh I'll pass with flying colours now. He looked sexy in those jeans, hips jutting over the waistband, tight round arse. traffic called out to him as he left. The tattoo artist's number, Matthias. If you forget, you'll get expelled, you'll end up with the Fools. He grinned and waved and then he was gone.

Independent school my arse. No such thing.

It was expensive being a junkie. Nothing else mattered. Clothes and taxi rides and meals at restaurants were forgone, appointments cancelled, journeys elsewhere were interrupted by detours when you passed a place that you knew might, just might, have something that would send you to heaven. All week every week she trawled the stores, spent every spare cent on vinyl and CDs. What was a DJ anyway? A person who bought billions of records. It was always a race to get a rare treasure first, to play it first, remix it first but most importantly best. Mandrake had the upper hand working in a shop. Slip knew now to go in when the owner was working as well, point to Mandrake's personal pile and say Can I listen to that? Daggers from Mandrake if she wanted to buy something from it. Mandrake and Mr Hyde were as bad as each other, buying all available copies of a track they liked so that no one else could get their hands on it.

This is from Italy.
You're kidding! It's great.
You'd be surprised. I haven't heard anyone else play it yet either. There's nothing from London at the moment, absolutely nothing.
What about this? Where's this from?
Germany. Über alles!
I like the beat . . . but not the lyrics.
There's a mix on the other side without vocals, but the guitar here's better. I must admit I never listen to lyrics.
But James listened to vocals. There was Slip's old record of Neapolitan songs from her mother's collection, introduced to him one night over a year ago. No instruments just vocals, lilting, desperate. Stiff old vinyl, heavy as bakelite, a brick between the fingers after the wobble of modern records. Impossible to play live because the levels were so low. James was entranced, thought it was something Arabic. Now, finally, he had put it on his sampler and over slow tripped-out trance sent the songs of love and death drifting across the airwaves the night before. And Slip at the warehouse for a quick nightcap, missed one then two then three buses home. She was aware she would probably never hear him use it again. Since playing Pimp six months previously James had virtually disappeared from the public ear and their musical afternoons become increasingly circumspect. He rarely asked her where she had

been playing. Slip usually listened to his discoveries keeping her own in her bag until he asked. Sometimes she caught sight of herself, quiet, reticent, biting her tongue. Life was too short.

I wish you'd play more James. You were fantastic last night. Best of anything lately.

What's lately. I haven't hardly been playing.

I guess including the last party you played.

What, better than Pimp? MenAce?

Well both. It's like when you're playing a commercial gig you're half holding back cos they've given you a brief or whatever, but the other half of you gets more and more frustrated and goes Fuck it and throws in all these wildcards anyway. So it's kind of . . . erratic. Long silence. She blundered on. Whereas in a radio studio you can feel like you're playing alone. You soared you know. You didn't stop to wonder why every single person in the room wasn't on the floor.

There's a listenership of thousands for Transfix, and I played to it.

But you can't *see* them. That's why you let yourself go more.

Look Slip you're good at that, you compromise! You're ambitious.

I beg your pardon?

I mean you know how to play what people want. It's a compliment!

I never play anything I don't like James, I play badly sometimes but I never put on a record that I don't actually like. I play what *I* like.

I mean your style's easier or more accessible or something and you're cuter than me and hey we all know what looks count for in this town oh god this is *not* what I mean.

He stopped in the middle of the floor, hands over his face. Slip withdrew.

I know what you mean James.

Hey y'know that white label I got in Holland last year? Turns out it comes from Enmore, can you believe it?

Yeh I've got some other local stuff here if you want a listen.

He turned up the music. She didn't know the half of it. Because Rik from Transfix had his brief too, just like they all did. Don't go too weird, we've got an experimental programme coming on straight after us. Telling *him*, always, what to play. So he spends half his life working to order in the corporate world then returns to his true self and finds it commandeered as well. Well fuck the fixed menu. By midnight when Slip had left and the boys had been there for hours, James would be flying. But now with the ears of Slip in the room he couldn't relax, he rifled through genre and tempo like an impatient child. He was relieved when she picked up her bag.

Want some of this joint?

I'll keel over. I've gotta go to work.

Where're you playing tonight? We were thinking of going out.

I'm not. I'm cooking again. Chicken not wax.

Since when? James looked appalled. Why?

Because I need the money.

But I thought –

Yeh well that little raver dude that booked me for the weekend festival last month? He never payed me. Third time that's happened to me since Pimp. Xenogenesis was good but the other gigs I did for a pittance and they kicked me off the dole for handing my form in late. My own work doesn't count.

That's fucked.

That's life.

Saturday night. Another new club on Oxford Street. Enormous bouncers metal detectors queue to the corner. Where did these people come from and what did they do in there to need so much security, should put IN before the word on their bomber jackets. James more than anyone was the person from whom she needed affirmation but James was the one now least willing to support her. So that's what he thought, that she was compromising herself. But even then it wasn't enough to support her habit of music and pay the bills. Things might have been easier if she didn't need to live alone. The most frightening thing was the very real possibility that opportunities for a free reign in gigs were lessening. It was winter but things seemed even slower than usual, the continuum was constantly being broken. The boys full of plans after Hotel Quickie, Turkish Jim had wanted to refine the poker machines with lights and extra fittings, bring them to life like monsters in a show that would travel across two dancefloors. But the venue was no longer available. Max's Cinema was pulled down, about to be redeveoped, Bliss's performance night was supposed to be the first of a series but Bliss earned nothing from it and had too much other work to persist. All you could do was hope that somewhere something was still germinating, that like mushrooms in the dark new events would pop up when you least expected them. The line-up for the next Chronic had already been booked and advertised and James wasn't in it. He would be hurt by that, thought Slip as she turned the corner and walked down to the restaurant. Hating in James what she most hated in herself. Insecurity, self-consciousness, fear of failure.

Now a whole lotta things been botherin me because a lotta people think that things is cool. People ridin round in those cars 'n' ridin them aeroplanes, pocket full o' money, 'n' everybody think that things is cool . . . But I'm here to tell all ya . . . that we got a cross that we must bear. And the cross gets awful heavy. Now there's the black cross, the green cross, the white cross, the double cross, the criss-cross. And the lost cross. And the cross gets awful heavy at different times, but one is s'posed to keep on goin on and carryin the cross on 'is shoulders. Because you ain't s'posed to let no cross cross you up. You s'posed to let a cross help you get across. And if you let a cross help you git across you won't get crossed up but you'll be on the cross cos you ain't got across on the cross. So if you can remember this you won't get lost on the cross while you tryna git across. So we just here to let you know about it. I tell ya I know that you knew already cos y'all the hippest people in the world. Hip black and white. But you still know that you got a cross you must deal with. So when it crosses you up go on and deal with it. And leave it alone.

EVERYone had a gripe. A customer complaining that his rare steak was raw and the customer was always right. The boss, a non-smoker, furious at the ban on smoking in restaurants, this actually a gripe with which Slip sympathised. The Royal wanting Something a bit more Up and her shifts reduced since the renovations, she foresaw the loss of gigs there altogether. The Xenogenesis guy yelling when she approached the Belgian DJ's equipment, wasn't even dreaming of touching it. She had gone straight to another gig that Sunday, jampacked, new venue, the cold water turned off. Somebody fainted below the booth. Slip played in a mist, condensation raining softly on her records her face her arms. A beautiful swimming feeling except she had to be the lighthouse so it became drowning. The cops raiding, packing her records in bright light and a furious crowd, running the gauntlet of sniffer dogs, coming out onto the street into the blare of spotlights and media and paddy wagons. Pulling records from sodden covers all afternoon exhausted, most of them were ruined. Her sister waking her with a phone call, Party party party, till the break of dawn. It's work Tina. Oh sure, but it must be fun. Then her mother ringing at just the right wrong time saying why did she never visit she neglected her family. So if Holmes's report of the gossip were true then she had no believers.

Did James defend her? Holmes was silent on that one, and did *he*? But Holmes would say yes to anyone Holmes ever the lubricant washing himself afterwards of all opinion. Slip trusted no one. And why should she need defending who was the enemy? Was it her, was it really, was that why there had been an absence of invitation to listen to records at James' house these last weeks? She knew those gatherings would alter completely in her absence didn't have to be there to imagine the talk. When the chips were down people fell back on those stupid old prejudices. The trouble was the men themselves hardly heard what they were saying like they missed the eyes of straight partygoers grilling the first dyke to dance with her top off. The entire atmosphere would have changed and the men would be oblivious.

Premenstrual, sore, zonked out on mersyndol. The evening's cooking accompanied her out of the restaurant through all the Saturday nighters smelling of aftershave and alcohol. Holmes was such a nice guy you had to believe him, he took no sides and probably would have said nothing if she and traffic hadn't dragged it out of him. Slip who liked to think of herself as floating free felt buried now beneath each of their duplicitous lives. They marched across her heart as she headed for the bustop. Her job was in her skin.

And her mother this morning! Why did her mother haunt her as she turned the corner jaywalking through car horns. Somebody beside her. traffic. Oh hi. *Oh hi*, yair it's a bit like that. Slip kept walking head down while traffic bounced around her. How was work, stupid question, wanna go for a drink, nah it's Saturday, run for cover. But they were near her new flat and she changed her offer adding something facetious about etchings as a car full of boys screeched around the corner. One got out to piss on the footpath ahead, Slip thinking I'm such a crabby bitch she's just trying to be friendly. The drunk boy saw them and jeered the usual epithets, turning his aim at them. Piss off! traffic snorted walking out of range but Slip was flying at him with her bag, pushing him hard against the wall.

What the hell am I doing. She ran after traffic past the back of the car. Four more faces in there drunk and surprised while the boy came up behind them, the last drops of piss hitting the back of traffic's leg. Slip turned around and kicked him but felt no proper contact or maybe just the shielding hand. So her anger grew hungrier, devouring his taunts while traffic moved between them and two of his friends got out of the car to haul him away. traffic so polite saying Please just go away while Slip's hand curled around the keys in the bottom of her bag, waiting for the next abuse then spitting in his face. He spat back in traffic's.

Everybody screaming then. His friends dragged him back to the car and Slip shook off traffic, him yelling I can piss anywhere I want ya fucken lezzos. She followed him down to the car with the keys in her hand. She was crazy she was burning, kicked him again and when he rose out of the pike hit him on the side of the head. Solid contact. Relief. She watched him through her orgasm get pulled into the car screaming struggling back out towards her but traffic was steering her up some stairs shutting and locking the door behind them. They had been at the entrance of traffic's place all along. On the third storey of the building as traffic unlocked the door, Slip plummeted. traffic took her in.

You a *hellcat* with those pisspots girl!

Look. I'm shaking.

You were a bit full on. They know where I live now and this building's full of tranys and workers.

Sorry I'm really sorry I just lost it.

The piss was quite novel but I guess it makes you angry when the script's the same old cliches.

She went into the bathroom to wash her face and remove her jeans. Slip aware of the one bare leg visible. How long had it been, too long too long, just two girls in more than a year, nice, forgettable. Still thinking of the pissing boy with a mind full of violence. Her knuckles were bruised. She moved to the sound system, traffic even had a turntable, nobody had a turntable these days unless they DJ'd. A tiny place, clean but messy, decorated with postcards and party props, one of the Professor's painted banners hung at CATaTONIC now used as a bedcover. Cartons along a wall, pebbled windows open onto an alley, black hole of a vacant lot opposite. It was raining now. Slip put her trembling arm out the window and left it there till the sleeve was soaked and traffic was nudging her with a glass of red wine.

D'you think I got him?

Yair and he got me, fuck knows why.

No but I mean properly.

I must admit I nearly laughed then. Him going Ya missed! and you going Cos it's so small! then it's *me* he spits at.

Probably because you look more butch.

Yair like real big and threatening.

I wasn't satisfied y'know. I wanted to see him bend double and fully retch. Like they do in the movies.

And he's going No it's not No it's not!

Hey've you seen those DJ profiles in the poof press lately?
Very page 3 Sun.
What are they naked?
Waist up.
Whatshisname was in there last week saying anthems are going to be the next big thing.
Oh *puh-leease*.
They rang me up actually.
I should think so.
I reckon you should do it James.
Get out.
You'll have to take your shirt off though.
Show us ya tits love.
I don't want to frighten you.
That's alright, we're all girls.
Speak for yourself Fred.
Heidi's are getting that floppy they may as well be.
Get fucked Daryl.
No honestly go on, do it! It'll be good for your career.
You're unbe*liev*able Fred.
Do it and take the piss.
Just say nothing about music and they'll love you.
Borrow the Green Woman's brassiere.
She burnt her bras years ago,
Throw in a bit of astrology and uplifting-moments-on-the-dancefloor . . .
and they wouldn't have fit you anyway.
That's right, Heidi's a bit small in that department.
They grow with pregnancy don't they?
Come on Daryl, do your duty.
Slip's done a few interviews lately. She's going strong.
She's riding on that token woman token lesbian thing.
Oh come on Fred. She's a fucken good DJ.
Holmes loves Slip.
Yeh I do actually. She's one of my best friends.
I only caught the radio one. I taped it, I want to use it actually.
Oh I *hated* that. All that stuff about male domination.

I know, they're always going on about that,
It was the interviewer actually.
but there's another line in there that's really good. One of Slip's.
I wonder if she'll do the shirts off profile.
Probably. She's ambitious enough.
I tried to go down on a woman once. I nearly threw up.

I want what men have, I want security, the superior physical security of a man. To walk night laneways feeling less vulnerable, to travel through exotic lands without need of an escort. I want to sit in bars alone, unquestioned, to be the watcher not the watched.

I want what men have, I want to forsake responsibility for my emotions, to make mistakes with a little less retribution. I want my aggressive urges taken for granted, I want to participate fully in any sport I choose.

I want what men have, I want sex on tap, to do beats and saunas when I get the yen. I want my diverse tastes catered for by the sex industry, to be the subject not just the object. I want to feel less shame about my libido, I want to blame it on biology. I want to sew my wild oats, to test my mettle, to let off steam.

I want the multiple job options that men have, I want equal pay. I want to be a president or Supreme Court judge or CEO without twice the usual sacrifice and privilege and sheer luck. I want to see myself mirrored in the corridors of power, to be considered driven and dedicated not unscrupulous and self-serving.

I want what men have, I want less domestic obligation. I want my spouse to be the homemaker, the principal carer of our children so I can concentrate on my career. I want to be defined as an individual before a parent, I want nevertheless to be the head of the family. I want my children to carry my name into the future, I want to be the first heir.

I want what men have, I want history told in terms of my gender. I want to be seen as active not just passive, I want validity. I want my experiences to be assumed universal and relevant to all.

I want what men have, I want less judgement placed on my body and more on my mind. I want full control over my reproductive system, I want my biology taken into account by the research and development of new medicine.

I want to be the one and not the other. I do not want to be a man, I want what men have. The list is long and I want it all.

I want full participation in the rites of my religion. I, too, want apotheosis. I want to be a bishop, an elder, an imam, a mufti, a mullah, a bonze, a dalai lama.

I want to reach the peak and I want to choose the mountain.

I want what men have, I want it all.

I want to be the fucking Pope.

I want
I want
I want

287

A three ball juggle! A kinetic red bridge floating over her hands. She cheered herself alone in the room, she was floating, flying, riding the wave of balls. They fell. She jumped up and down on one leg whooping with joy. Picked up the balls. They fell. She tried again. They fell. She tried again. They fell. She tried again.

James was quite old-fashioned in some ways. Had the unbelievable limp wrists of his fag forebears. Called dykes lesbians, treated women like ladies, at the age of twelve had seen his father beat his mother unconscious. Had a girlfriend briefly but avoided having sex with her. In Sydney even in the gay scene it wasn't easy avoiding women. He had gone to one of the last Slut City's. Didn't know who the DJ was. They were playing all that sassy black chick music like Salt'n'Pepa and The Wee Papa Girl Rappers, music that had never really touched him though in this context he finally appreciated it. The shows were the main thing, those girls were outrageous. He saw more pussy in one hour on that stage than he had in his entire life.

traffic when single came at everybody full force uncovered. He hadn't trusted her at first, she was too big in the air around them too loud, but since the second party he had grown towards her. She took his music into her body, took him into her confidence. Consulted him on which girl to pick up, emerging from the toilets and waving her hand under his nose, mouth wide with laughter at his discomfort. She reminded him of himself when he was younger, before the Professor, when he believed a gay man's lot was to have sex with anyone and everyone never a relationship. And now here he was, twelve years with the same man. Sex was still necessary but not necessarily with the same person, there were other things more important. He felt fattened with history, the years of bars and parties settled around his girth. He had come of age in the sectarian days but the nostalgia he felt was selective, there were certain things he never wanted to return to. Now the leather bar didn't let women in the girls would probably retaliate in kind. Difference, the new, he had always craved difference. All that leather radicalism of the 70s and 80s had seemed so limitless but no, no no, most of the people who kicked against the pricks just wanted to become one themselves. traffic Bee Shifty and all those other girls pulling the door right off its hinges saying here, this is your realm too and yours is mine. But still he couldn't cross. There were the men like Holmes and Jimi who found it easy, there were the men like Turkish Jim and the Professor who kept a respectful distance as women for them still embodied some sort of ideal, then there were the men like Fred who deprecated women yet couldn't resist these girls. The men like himself just stayed on the threshold. With a woman it was all on top every emotion surfacing, so much at once you never really knew what they were thinking. traffic was never not talking but it was all to deflect your attention from the details she was taking in. Not like men who displayed everything trying to hide so much. He must have told Bee five times now the story of going to the toilets at Heresy, a leatherdyke arriving and pissing into the urinal next to him. Just like a man, head bowed vaguely legs slightly apart, eyes sliding to the men either side. She had a perfect aim. Bee grinned through the story each time.

He felt bad about Slip, alcohol and weakness had loosened his discretion. Daryl always maintained Fred put him on a pedestal. It's guilt James, admit it, you go along with him out of guilt. Fred's attitudes struck a raw nerve, it was so easy to agree with at the time, so hard to wake up with the next day. Not without bitterness James watched those others like Mandrake and D Coy take his style and clean it up for presentation at the big parties. Slip had her own style, she was the one who had taught him rhythm, she gave as much as took. But James was too proud, too unbending to acknowledge this easily. The shock of admitting to himself he had been hurt she hadn't mentioned him on air. My best DJ partner is Mr Hyde. He too wanted to be loved but couldn't stand the thought of that relentless DJ life, the constant dependence on the immediate public, judgement in minutes the game of fame. Like living in a glass house. Mr Hyde was secretive, he liked to retreat. Slip's criticisms came as a shock not so much because she was wrong more because nobody ever gave you much feedback apart from the noncommittal Yair that was good. Brooding brooding, he was still brooding on what she had said at the beginning of winter and something else on the phone before she came over, I was thinking about how you can get so caught up in erasing your ego you spend just as much time paying it attention as you would if you were elevating it, I was thinking that about myself James. He missed those musical afternoons, Slip made him think. Not in the way of Daryl or traffic with direct confrontation, just the seduction of her sets and the subtle remarks she left behind like scents. He had fallen in love with Daryl's array of mirrors as much as with Daryl himself, he envied that immediacy the immediacy of people like Daryl and traffic, his own way was more roundabout. He would light the fuse then flee the explosion, he was perhaps the biggest escapist of them all, happier up here in his attic or a radio tower than behind the turntables in public. Daryl was no better but Daryl could remember his remarks without cringing, James needed privacy to remember. In private his excuses had no gainsayer.

He was thinking of Slip's description of playing the electric bass unplugged, of having the plug pulled without warning halfway through a phrase. How it was then that the music really entered her body and her imagination took the reins. There was nothing but the feel of the notes against her flesh and the singing inside her head. Like Glenn Gould's epiphany when practising next to the maid's vacuum cleaner whose noise drowned out his music, or Beethoven's deaf compositions. James had never known such a visceral relationship between his body and sound, he had never played an instrument. He selected a record, turned the volume down to nothing, placed the stylus on the vinyl circumference. With the windows closed and Daryl at work the house was that much closer to silence. James bent his head to the thin vibrations from the needle. You lost the bass, you lost almost all the bottom end but with the chink of high hats and long moody brass lines all those rich dark buildings rose in his interior till what he heard and what he imagined became one and the same. So the unplugged version entered his listening rituals, he played it to himself when he *thought* he knew the music because that was when the deepest colours formed, when he began to invent bass lines and sew his own threads. Surprised to find gaps in even the most perfect track, to hear the silent versions unfolding avenues of his own contribution.

Shifty rang when traffic was on her way out to meet the boys at the pub. Her mood ballooned from the small hallo in the handset to fill the entire room and traffic had to sit down. Why not come down to the pub as well, catch up with everyone. But Shifty was too depressed. Home from work on a Sunday and no lover to share it with. Yearning for nonverbal contact and the company of men, traffic didn't want to hear another person's loneliness. But Shifty needed a knowing ear so traffic took off her coat and settled into the hour of persuading her to happiness.

I miss the communal dressups, you know? Partying together?

The arse has fallen out of the party scene fullstop Shifty.

We coped with lulls before. We made our own fun.

OK then, look on the bright side. We wouldn't even be having this conversation if we were still with them.

But they introduced us.

But you and me never got to know each other. We never talked one on one then.

I remember when you first came along traffic, I thought Billy's got herself a nice little butch number.

She loved that side of me didn't she? Have you noticed how much more I've been femming it up in the last year or so? You should try it Shifty, it's so liberating.

She was always getting caught up with these poncey scene queens. All attitude and Gaultier, nothing below the surface.

Honestly, you forget. But boy it's incredible how differently people treat you. You get hit on by heaps more men plus all these diesels who the week before when you were in your leathers treated you like a rival. Or didn't even notice you. Like the amount of people who don't even recognise you, it's hysterical.

It wasn't that Billy didn't have a brain. She just got lazy about using it. Like we all do I s'pose. I must admit I was sceptical about you at first.

So the doctor reckons I've got cancer of the knee.

What?

You're not listening to me.

I am, you're discovering skirts again. Good for you.

I'd love to see you in a frock, Shifty. You've got great legs, you should show them off. Why were you sceptical about me?

A frock is not the fucking solution traffic.

Vera City would disagree. You know what they say, put a butch – or a man – in a frock and you get the biggest slut of all.

Speak for yourself. Vera City ain't no slut.

No but she oozes sex. And slut's not a pejorative.

You know whenever Bee and me ended up in a straight bar they'd treat her like a bimbette because of the hair and lippy and frock? Sometimes the blokes'd even get blokey with me, as though we were playing on the same team or something. And the whole time Bee was lording it over all of us. It was pathetic! They just didn't get it.

Is Bee still not speaking to me d'you reckon?

Not right this second, no, this is Shifty. D'you reckon Jesus was butch or femme?

Definitely femme. So was Buddha. Mohammed would've been butch.

I don't know about that. He wore frocks anyway.

Could've just been a butch in a frock.

D'you reckon Jesus was well hung?

Now Shifty I *know* there's a pure little Catholic girl still buried somewhere deep inside that sick mind of yours . . .

Yeh but she was corrupted before she was even born. There's quite a bit of Daoism on my mother's side.

Well you won't be getting first class accommodation in heaven will you.

No but I will in hell, and that's where it counts. Bee used to say Jesus was well hung.

She would, she's Jewish.

That's got nothing to do with it you idiot. In fact on the contrary.

Sorry, that's *my* little Catholic girl speaking. That's why I buried her.

Bee's a femme is the point. I reckon she was right.

I don't know . . . He was an outcast . . .

Yair maybe.

You know, small man big message. Probably a lesbian actually.

Probably. With that hairy face.

Jesus was a drag king.

What do you say to a lesbian with no arms and legs?

293

Nice tits.
No. Nice lunch.
Getting back to me –
Yes, speaking of deities.
Maybe I'm turning into a fetch.
Actually traffic, I think you're more of a bumme.
Shifty . . . Do they know about you at the hospital?

traffic and Jimi went shopping in Double Bay. There was a cleanup campaign and in Jimi's flatmate's ute they cruised the verdant hills of mansions by the harbour for discarded treasures. There was more much more than they had bargained for. The ute already full of clothes, books, light fittings, kitchenware for both of them, as well as an old television and chest of drawers for traffic when she finally found her prize. A technical book on juggling published in the 50s. Look! she showed Jimi. There are heaps of tricks too.

Play said Jimi, I mean get creative. Playwork, you know. In this new salon I'm rediscovering the sculpture of hair. There's a mask in the salon made by an African tribe called the Guro who consider hairdressers artists. And baby it's so good getting creative again, I feel so much more fulfilled.

Rest said the doctor, rest rest. And physiotherapy, good diet, water, exercises twice a day. The stiffness should be easing now it's spring. But even now, on a maintenance dose, the odd day where she had nothing at all, traffic could not stop moving. Rearranging furniture, fixing her flat, running errands, juggling more correctly with the help of her book. The doctor had offered her sickness benefits but they wouldn't cover rent and bills, she had to work. It was surely time to put on a party but traffic had neither the heart nor energy and Holmes had told her the boys were looking for a venue.

A three ball juggle again! That continuous looping smooth as a machine, eyes hands mind body all switched on. She was in sync. Like climbing through static and finding the frequency on the crest, wobbling towards the centrepoint of balance, like green lights all the way down Cleveland Street, the eye of the storm, like riding a wave, freedom, flying.

Alone after a night out or a night in, traffic on drugs was in every way inflated, always in need of an object of desire. The new girl at the leather shop where traffic saw Neil when not at Waterloo. Smaller amounts now, crystal and a dozen e's. From down in the cellar where she and Neil transacted traffic tried to watch the girl's legs cross the shop floor. Estelle. New in town. Or an old face reinvented according to Shifty, which amounted to the same thing. Slanting red bars tattooed across her forearm, neck like a wick, shaved head dark skin. traffic cruised Estelle at Playschool two weeks in a row. Followed her into the toilets but Estelle shut the door so not till home alone did traffic get to fuck her up against the wall. Estelle of the suggestive eyes who slid all over then inside her while traffic masturbated never even stopped to say hello. In traffic's mind they'd had wild sex many times already when on MDA Estelle finally came across during the last hour of D Coy. But home in traffic's bed Estelle lay rigid. Said she hated men but didn't think she was a dyke. Scratching traffic with her too long nails then pushing a closed fist ineptly between her legs. Estelle was twenty-eight and had never had an orgasm. traffic was shattered.

Then fixed for two weeks on Bliss after seeing her do a show up at Playschool, the best show traffic had seen in a long time, the sort of show that gave her a lust to perform again. Nothing else was good that night, not the music nor the crowd just the show and the moment Bliss gave traffic a perfunctory peck on the cheek then passed on through the crowd radiant in white patent thigh highs and a white corset. The scent of Bliss's musk-laden sweat obsessed traffic's dreams while adjacent in actuality the abstruse messages of Estelle began to haunt her voicemail.

Then there were the women from elsewhere. The tall European ladies like Dominique Sanda, mannish in grey flannels in The Conformist, or Charlotte Rampling whose sex appeal only widened with maturity. The occasional male like Johnny Depp or the Querelle Brad Davis with whom traffic would be a man. traffic without a video player would borrow old movies and take them around to Jimi's where from the couch both could dream of loving the lightborne characters of film.

Or else the Professor's or Bee's pornos that she could no longer indulge in alone in her bedroom or with a lover like Billy, that had nevertheless dyed indelibly her erotic possibilities. That rare real dyke porn of lust and perversion where the femme on the couch masturbated with a clear dildo, pulling it out to ejaculate on the stomach of the butch. The endless array of men sucking and fucking through cursory scripts and cheap plyboard sets. The effect of a cum shot on her cunt was immediate and efficient and had an afterlife of disembodied cocks she called upon to come alone. They were on her they were hers or else they were inside her alongside girlcocks, she was hermaphroditic. Yet even these had their limits which traffic as ever strained to overtake.

Most intense of all were the scenarios moulded from castoffs of her own experience. In the replay of the pissing boy saying Suck my dick lezzo bitch, Slip's fly was undone just as quickly No straightboy, *you* do me. Slip's cock a black one with a red head. Lurid alien thicker longer and kinkier than the hottest porn star's and the boy was on his knees terrified, mouth wet and desperate for Slip's appendage. There were cocks of flesh in there as well now, Jimi would appear with Luke and other leathermen. Slapping him shoving cocks in his face, piss flowing from sundry urethras all over the boy. All that hard core masculinity leavened with camp humour into which Slip and her merged like blood into water. Throwing the boy up against the car, making him beg for it, everyone fucking him now at either end. Was it rape or just a good hard fuck because with the domino mechanism of a well-edited porno everybody came in the end including the boy. Where was she in all of this? Floating directing watching getting off. Getting off with Slip, coming alone, coming to exhausted and bewildered. Wanting to escape but it was all in her head.

traffic went to work on the fifteenth floor of a steel and glass building in the CBD. It was Violet who had told her you could earn up to forty dollars an hour doing telephone marketing. traffic had approached Bella to do a doubles shift in the peepshow only to find that double shows were now banned and the new tax had been passed by management straight to the workers. Violet had a phone sex job for a while which traffic thought might have been fun, but when more censorship laws came in every phone sex company had been put out of business, thousands like Violet had lost jobs and few were lucky enough to find alternative employment so quickly. Maybe it was them who were jamming the queues to the telephone marketing companies. But with persistence and faith traffic kept ringing, kept putting her name on the list of every company, making follow-up phone calls, till eventually she was summonsed.

On the first day she wore the wrong clothes, on the second was still hovering at fifteen dollars an hour. On the third she kept falling asleep in the hot silver sunlight. Hum of airconditioning, tea urn gurgling, beige decor, the specious telephone voices all around her, the thought of sitting here day in day out was like a terminal illness.

On the fourth day traffic went down to the fabric shop after work. She loved the old-world entrance, the dim church interior of the stairwell, the padded silence of stockrooms. The windows coated with decades of grime and eclectic eccentric staff from four continents. She entered the first floor and snaked down the aisles of fabrics stacked like books on shelves. She had been seduced by a pink synthetic satin when still with Billy who turned up her nose. It's so crass. It's camp! I think it's crass. That pink satin was still packed away, unused. She never came here with a purpose more specific than breathing the air, looking at the stock, the purchases like the pink satin were follies of the monied days. She wandered through the library of fabric, touching, smelling, looking, returning to old favourites, examining the new. Leaving eventually to walk up to the next floor where Jim's white head stood like a signpost at the back in haberdashery. Hallo gorgeous. Hallo Turquoise. Can I get you anything? Um . . . no, I'm not really financial. Turkish Jim was leaving work early to meet with the manager of a venue. traffic waited for him to fetch his bag then they walked together up to Whitlam Square.

Hey you know that new fabric, that satiny stripey one?

The blue and yellow?

Well there're two. There's also a green and purple.

Oh yes.

Does anyone ever actually *buy* that stuff?

An upholsterer from Double Bay. And the occasional mad drag queen.

Is it cheap, how much is it?

It's real satin girl. You've got expensive taste.

Bummer.

But come to think of it, I'm due for something new. And *I* get a staff discount. He grinned at her, she looked sad, had a slight limp. She seemed to be shrinking. Are you having money problems? How's that exotic dancing going?

Exotic dancing. I like that. Feels like a posthumous promotion.

I think of you every time I pass the sex shops now.

I quit months ago.

That's a shame.

I wasn't feeling very exotic anymore. The money wasn't was the main problem.

You look pretty exotic to me today.

It's the only skirt I've got. Jeans are illegal at my new job.

He thinks you look exotic too. And him. traffic, you'll stop the traffic!

I must admit I still get strut lust. And I miss getting paid to be perved at. D'you get cruised by girls much Jim? . . . Seriously. Do you? What about when you were bulked up. I've seen the photos . . .

Jim's face a white wall behind the sunglasses.

You never even thought about it did you.

No. Why would I?

Bliss at Playschool, alone on a chair hands in her lap. No music, no soundtrack, no costume or props, nothing but her naked body and face powdered white, auburn hair shawling her breasts. A presence compelling enough to silence the entire room, she moved so slowly she seemed to be still. Watching the face for a flicker of feeling you realised too late one hand had drawn the end of a scarf from between her legs. It was then that expression began to fill her face, a silent trickling behind her features as the scarf kept coming. Never for a second did you see what contained the scarf, her body was a sculpture perfectly sealed, it was the mind in her face that told the story. The scarf a classic magician's, endless, kaleidoscopic, and as each different colour slowly emerged Bliss's face morphed across the entire spectrum of human emotion. Surprise horror mirth melancholy pain longing disgust joy. It must have taken almost ten minutes but seemed like only one. Like watching a painting or a bird on an air current, utterly still, moving across the sky. Clear as a photograph in traffic's mind for weeks afterwards.

How did she do it, what was the key? Stillness, simplicity, poise. Emotion.

In the humid heart of the Botanical Gardens tropical section traffic watched Shifty arrive with lunch. Even thinner today or else the anonymous hospital attire had a reductive effect. She stood over traffic a foot threatening her chest then littered her with wrapped packages. traffic who was still waiting for her first pay cheque accepted the presents of food and tobacco gratefully. The last one an envelope containing an acupuncturist's appointment card.

I can't afford it Shifty.

Shut up, it's a late birthday present. I'm sick of that limp and you know you're facing a full knee reconstuction if you do nothing about it. You can get physio on Medicare but this'll help even more. But you're not allowed to crack onto her.

Why don't you just ask her out.

I'm not like you traffic.

What's me?

You know. The way you walk into a place and go Right, you, let's go.

I've been single nearly two years now Shifty and the trade isn't exactly thick on the ground. In poofdom I'd be considered virginal.

But you're not in poofdom.

But I am! We *all* are.

Hot today, suffocating. Boots off then stockings, traffic lay back on the grass beneath the palm canopy watching a clan of ants move into Shifty's lunch. The S of an ibis bobbed on the distant lawn. The conversation moved inevitably to ex-lovers, Shifty now turning the corner from accusation to apology. Since first cracking open to traffic Shifty had become unstoppable while traffic was increasingly silent. Didn't know what to say. She watched the parade of stories disintegrate into embellishment and repetition. All those years with Billy seemed like another country and the others even more faded. traffic spiralled upwards to nest in the palm canopy. Shifty poked her in the ribs.

How's your new career dear?

I don't know Shifty. I dress wrong, I talk wrong, it seems pretty wrong all round really. In fact I think I'll quit this afternoon.

Oh traffic!

What?

Well can't you just stick at it till you find something better? You know, get a bit of money together?

Shifty I come into the CBD I feel like my blood's being drained from my body.

Put on another party.

The boys are looking. They're having a lot of trouble too.

They lay on their backs beneath the throb of cicadas. The beginning of summer yet everything still seemed at an end. Shifty regretted her advice, regretted too such an aimless traffic. She had all that energy and wisdom and she was wasting it away like a glass overflowing with champagne poured by a distracted hand. It wasn't the drugs, traffic was always hyperactive, she always talked too much thought too much, drugs weren't the cause only the catalyst. And what use was she, Shifty, when it came to helping traffic slow down? Her first phone call when binging had been to traffic. Thinking as they walked back through the gardens to city streets that traffic in all her mopishness might have really cut down as she claimed. traffic trying to persuade her to delay going back to work, Shifty hesitating on Elizabeth Street.

That's the head of Gastro.

Where?

Going into the toilets, I don't know traffic I'm late already.

Don't worry, you can blackmail him. That's one of the oldest outposts of poofdom in there.

They didn't know about Shifty at the hospital, her thoughts on the universe sex and religion or what she got up to after hours, just like they didn't know what the head of Gastroenterology did in city toilets. They didn't know about the Professor at university, his acid parties and husky school trade. At the office, interstate, they didn't know about James, his repertoire of outfits like a book of bad fairy tales cataloguing almost twenty years on the dancefloor and his true passion music. Slip's buried as well beneath kitchen chores four nights a week. They knew a little of Turkish Jim, Bee and Holmes in their more lateral work environments, just as they had glimpsed Billy's other lives at the leather shop. But traffic as open and aleatoric as a wilderness felt everywhere exposed.

The CBD at dusk, her brother moving somewhere in the flotsam of suits and nice jewellery. Waiting to cross the road by a wall of dark glass she saw how hunched she became in this environment. Followed or pushed down or cold or frightened. Staring staring everybody was staring. Friday night, Christmas lights, department store bells chiming, all around her the relief of homegoing and the city cooling to emptiness. Broke and desperate, traffic had hoped coming down here on Monday morning that finally she would discover her double. An identity in whom to move easily along these streets to and from a secure home and career and family. A mask, an anonym, a role to be lost in. She wished at least to be like her friends who managed to hold down jobs they considered boring and still find the time to be creative on the side. She longed to long for material stability but the only thing that held her with any consistency was the unknown. She couldn't stop her layers from fragmenting, a double wasn't enough nor even a triple. traffic was boiling over, she had no secrets no cover no repose.

One month before Chronic when Slip rang Sam to get more flyers he told her that her time slot had been changed and Slip who after all this time was finally getting to headline couldn't hide her disappointment at being placed last.

But you play a great last set, I didn't think you'd mind.

I just wanted to go really vicious, I've got some great new music and I don't think it'll work that late.

Yeh it will, wipe the floor with 'em, ex*haust* 'em!

I'm exhausted Sam, I'm working four nights again.

Do drugs! She'll be right mate!

Slip stood at her window watching rain pelt the street, this the only hour of Bondi sky she would see that day and already it was darkening. It was almost December but sudden southern gales had brought heaters back out of storage and killed two people on the North Shore. Records and CDs across the floor behind her, she would be going through them again in twelve hours with headphones when the city was sleeping.

Would you have told me if I hadn't rung you Sam?

Of course.

And can I get more flyers?

They'll be ready in a couple of days. Aaron'll have them at the shop. No time then to think about worst case scenarios. Maybe she could work at the restaurant the night of Chronic after all, earn an extra eighty dollars then go to the party from there or else stay home and prepare for longer with enough time left over to feel the dancefloor properly.

What's the story anyway, couldn't Mandrake do last set?

Nah, he's not playing actually.

Why not?

He pulled out.

Why?

Oh politics, personal reasons, you don't wanna know.

So who's in his place?

John Steele from London! We're rapt! It's a real coup!

Slip said nothing while her anger walked over to the box of party souvenirs and argued with her patience to tear up the flyers of all the Chronic parties she had played. Those Chronic boys must be doing alright to fly somebody from London, wonder what they're paying him.

C'mon Slip, you know he's good, I've heard you play some of his stuff.

Yeh I like him as a producer but I've never heard him DJ.

So what are you saying. You don't want to play? Is that it?

No. I want to play.

She stepped into the gale when the rain abated, pushed her way past the bus stop on the beachfront down towards the sand. A long wide glimmering sky held a belt of rain on the southern horizon, she walked squinting and hunched towards Ben Buckler. It was low tide but the waves were hurling to the top of the cliff. Sand everywhere. Horizontal through the air in drifts against the pavilion across the grass all the way up to Campbell Parade, sand whistling into her ears eyes down her neck inside her clothes. She reached the promontory and hung onto the railings alongside other storm tourists who came and watched and gasped and departed, leaving her the only person on the cliff before the white ocean coming straight for her spraying her head to foot, subsiding again. She stayed there before the charging waves till her nose and throat were scoured to pain by the briny air then walked home behind a tight mask of sand and salt, stepped into the shower, unpeeled her sandy clothes and stood beneath the hot water till it turned cold.

Three days later she picked up the flyers from Aaron at the record shop. Ran into Mandrake on her way out and showed them to him.

I know I know, I got an email.

Maybe you were right.

They just don't get it y'know. Mark accused me of being jingoistic but I'm all for DJs from anywhere and everywhere playing at our parties. It's just that when they get immediate headline status and interviews and special blurbs and you can hardly even see the names of the local artists on the flyer, then it starts to look pretty skanky.

I feel like a sucker now.

Nah, go and play. Tell 'em with your music.

I hope he's good y'know. I hope he makes it all worthwhile.

He's alright, heard him in London six months ago.

Really?

Don't get too excited. He's alright.

The Professor left a message on traffic's machine saying they had a present for her so the following evening she walked over to the house near Moore Park, stopping two streets away by a pile of rubbish that looked alluring. Clothes mostly, good, she needed some. From the pile of garbage bags she selected a giant pair of men's checked trousers.

James answered the door and traffic showed him her booty. Eeuugh, are they clean? Pretty much, have a smell. He waved her away laughing and traffic went upstairs to the bathroom to try on the trousers. Soon James was knocking gently and passing an old pair of braces through the door. The Professor was there when traffic descended the stairs and did a twirl in the living room.

How do I look?

Suitably ridiculous.

Daryl.

No it's fine, I don't mind looking ridiculous.

You can have those braces. He hasn't worn them for about ten years.

I could've said that myself y'know.

No it's okay.

No have them.

Maybe she doesn't want them.

traffic slid from their bickering and went back upstairs to change again.

It was James who drove her home with the old sewing machine found on their street. He carried it up to her flat with a box of thread and bobbins then sat there patiently testing it while she made him coffee. James like all the others with so much facial hair you didn't really know what his mouth was saying when he spoke desultorily of going to Chronic on New Year's Eve.

Why aren't you playing? What's their problem?

I don't know traffic, they use a rotating roster.

But you and Slip were residents.

They did say last time that I played too hard.

But it's a techno party. And you can play all the way through the spectrum. And Transfix the other week was brilliant!

Well I don't know traffic, I don't really like where they're going anyway.

What about your party?

We're about to sign a contract believe it or not. James put his foot down. It works. Let me show you all the stitches.

He would ring three nights later saying they had a ticket to Chronic for her as well but right now James was his usual hurried closed self. Standing as soon as the machine was set up, waving away her thanks and offers of beer. Standing there in the room hands in pockets closed against her chatter about the party, saying Don't get too excited we haven't signed yet. traffic puzzled almost offended by his diffidence. He was so small. Still so withdrawn after all these years. But James was alone, that was the problem, James without the Professor or a joint or both couldn't function socially. traffic had a tiny bag of pot left, she offered him a joint but he was already crossing the room. She threw something at him she'd been longing to say for years. You ever think about stopping your job completely and just concentrating on music? I can't do that, I've got a mortgage. Is it worth it? He stiffened and turned away. traffic preferred Mr Hyde. Calling him that when she let him out, him turning on the stairwell looking at her shrewdly. I know who you look like now. Who? Oliver Twisted. traffic held forth two cupped hands. Please sir, I want some more.

He wakes at 4 am when the alcohol wears off. Churning stomach hot skin. Work in a few hours, too late for a sleeping pill. Dreading it as always, two hundred people laid off last week. When will he too join the thousands of unemployed? Doing parties instead not exactly an option, the venue the fucking venue after all these months letting them down right at the last minute. He showers, makes coffee and climbs the stairs to the room full of music and equipment. Rolls a cigarette. Turns on the computer, goes on line. 4 am, dead of night, no sound but the machinery and his own breathing. Years ago when the deaths were that much more frequent this was the time his friends would most often choose for departure. He checks his email and opens the ad for Chronic.

He works swiftly using techniques learnt from a renegade employee met in the Adelaide office. Leapfrogging in minutes passwords and security arriving quite quickly at the Chronic mailing list. Then returns to the advertisement and sits and looks and thinks for a while. He goes through his graphics files but there is nothing alive enough so like a crab he walks his chair sideways to the filing cabinet of old photos. There are three drawers of these photos still not properly sorted. For almost an hour he journeys back through the jokes and artwork and little acts of subversion of the whole family's past, lingering, remembering, ultimately rejecting most of the images as too recondite or celebratory. Coming finally to the General of the WUS Army.

Grinning now James scans the photo then begins to merge it with the Chronic advertisement. Blots out the cadet altogether, stretches the General's mouth, paints in some of that hideous visceral purple making him even more horrific. From the mouth James drags a word balloon featuring the London DJ's name writ large and beneath the General's boots pastes a row of little aliens in dunce caps, each marked with the names of the local DJs including Slip. Jim would love this. There is wallpaper done in an idle moment months ago which will work as the background, sixty-odd motifs per A4 of Matilda the kangaroo pulling from her cunt a jubilee Queen Elizabeth. This detail visible only to those intrepid enough to hold a magnifying glass to the image. James clicks on Save. It's finished, it's beautiful.

Light outside now, birds. Heat rising with the cicadas in the park. James writes the message MORONIC in the subject line and pauses on Send. Christ have I gone too far again, wake up Daryl I need to bounce this off someone. But if he were one of the hundreds of people to receive the doctored advertisement he would surely appreciate it. So would Jim and Fred and traffic and the rest of them. But how often is he told he has a sick sense of humour even by his best friends though in their mouths it's a compliment. Carnivale was never supposed to be an assembly line of perfect smiles, people are so afraid of ugliness which is the mask that truth wears half the time. Will they know it's him and does he care? Though only an expert will be able to trace its source its mindset is obvious. He has nothing more to lose from the bookers and promoters and did he ever have anything anyway? He clicks on Send.

The first venue was closed down after noise complaints from the luxury apartments next door and turned into a supermarket.

The second venue was closed down after noise complaints from the luxury apartments next door and turned into luxury apartments.

The third venue was turned into a twenty-four hour gaming lounge.

The fourth venue ripped out the DJ booth and replaced it with a large tv/video screen.

The fifth venue was full of promises but halfway through renovations the owner owing money all over town did a runner.

The sixth venue was turned into an Irish pub.

The seventh venue was turned into a backpackers' hostel.

The eighth venue put their hire fee up to two thousand dollars.

The ninth venue lost their licence after an overdose on the premises.

The tenth venue ripped out their DJ booth and installed thirty poker machines.

The eleventh venue ripped out their DJ booth and installed thirty poker machines.

The twelfth venue said We only deal with inhouse promoters.

The thirteenth venue said No we don't do parties anymore.

The fourteenth venue said We're concentrating on house music.

The fifteenth venue said We don't do parties but you can put on a weekly event. Wednesday nights are free.

The sixteenth venue said Yes. (Yes! Yes!) Meetings were had, methods agreed upon, the contract was drawn up and faxed through. They waited and rang and waited and rang and still no reply. The Professor rang again and reached the manager.

I just wanted to check everything was OK.

Well I received the contract, yes.

It's the adjusted one, all your clauses are in there.

You're doing a sex party aren't you.

No, it's a sexy party, but not a sex party, it's

No.

It's a dance party with shows and

No.

Nobody wants her tonight. It's not the first time. Dancing towards girls dancing away from disinterest, moving discontent between two rooms the music never good enough. Two roaming photographers shooting the dancers at close range on the floor, another middle-aged straight man hanging around inspecting. She hasn't got much on her but they can do her for twenty bucks worth now if they want. Looks like a narc, traffic nudges the Professor. Don't be silly, he's just a librarian from Canberra. traffic stops in the corner to share a joint with Stash and Bella, tries to dance, sits back down alone on the couch. A man in leathers comes over, puts his arm around her. Thirsty? I'll get it. He disappears into the scrum at the bar and traffic waits. Thank god for friendly poofters. Gary comes over. Have you got any pills? Not for me, for my best friend's mother. Is she sick is she. Yeh, bit of an emergency actually. Well actually I don't. traffic is lying. But I'll keep an eye out for First Aid and send Nursie over as soon as I see her. Gary leaves satisfied.

I've seen you perform, the man in leathers says on delivery. *Great* shows. That one at the party with the hotel room? Sexy! Thank you. traffic smiles, he moves up closer. And the one with all the words, in the catsuits, I couldn't believe how many were up there. That wasn't me actually. I always wondered where she put them all. Up her arse. He grins eyebrows raised, traffic finishes off. With a lot of class. That's unusual for a girl isn't it. We've got bums too. A very nice one if I don't say so myself, d'you like things up yours as well? His hand on her leg. traffic's trying to move away he keeps moving after her, saying how much he loved the puppet show too, you've got a gorgeous body. traffic's up and dancing.

He dances after her. Into the big room where the music's too hard back to the small room where the music's too soft, coming up behind her rubbing her arse, traffic ignoring him yet every time she turns around he's staring smiling moving towards her. Is he the narc then, is that the attraction? traffic finds Gary, takes him into the toilets. Nurse from First Aid said it's time for your medication. What are they called? Big reds. Are they any good? traffic tried one a week ago and didn't feel much but then again never feels much anymore anyway even though her tolerance has dropped, the half point of crystal she did before coming out went straight to her neck like a clamp put her right on the edge. Is it lack of feeling or just one long bad feeling, she is a robot, knows the big reds are more like wallabies but lies to Gary. I don't know, I'm just delivering. She comes back out to find the man in leathers waiting, dances over to Jimi. Help me Jimi, this guy won't leave me alone. Jimi holds her spins her dances all around her the man still hovering, Jimi pulls traffic toward him. They start to kiss, get lost inside each other's mouths. Wow! Jimi comes up for air and grabs her crotch. You're a dirty bitch. She grabs his back. Grrr! But the man in the leathers has come even closer like it's his own private show. Turn around and walk away, traffic says to him. Hey? he starts to put his arm around her. Jimi steps in. Listen mate, you're not wanted here. The man moves away.

So that's how it is. It doesn't matter what she says, having revealed her body on a stage she belongs to the man in leathers, his toy his confessional. You can tell a whole story and they see nothing but sex and have to conquer it. traffic is public property. Spotlight on the dancefloor, a video camera approaching. traffic shakes her head, Jimi holds up two crossed fingers but the camera keeps coming closer and closer following them blinding them. traffic turns on the cameraman and Jimi has to pull her away, calm her down.

traffic goes to the toilet, waits in the inch of water for the cubicles to empty. The blonde from almost two years ago, one of the first people traffic went home with after Billy, appears with her girlfriend. A door opens and traffic goes in. Can we join you? Sound of snorting on one side of their cubicle, fucking on the other. traffic sells them her last point and they start mixing up on the paper dispenser while traffic pisses. Hey you know Luke? Who? No. Yeh you do, works with a friend of yours in housing, had a fling with Jimi. Oh OK, what about him? He got committed this morning, totally flipped out. traffic looks at the floor, she can never remember the blonde's name though they have greeted one another across the dancefloor many times since. Can you tourni me traffic? traffic pincers her upper arm between thumb and fingers, the blonde going into a welt that wasn't there before. It's disgusting, she is tempted, she's disgusted that she is tempted. The girlfriend already talking up a storm. Hey traffic, I wanted to talk to you about a project. A group of us wanna get a party together on a friend's property up the Hawkesbury. Me, Skunk, the Chronic guys, Playschool, we're gonna apply for funding. Well why not? Dance parties are mainstream now. You know Xenogenesis made fifty thousand? We want to put alternative culture at the forefront, we wanna get the queers back out there, we've gotta unite. We're gonna get international DJs too, like this John Steele. We want you to get involved. We're gonna make money!

traffic leaves the toilet, goes over to Violet and her girlfriend. They've got no money, the cold water's been turned off again. Violet drinks from traffic's bottle. What are you *like*, traffic. You've gone boy crazy! It was Jimi, you know Jimi. If you go off with a boy I'll dump you. *Dump me!* Oh you know what I mean. Men are pathetic, says the girlfriend. Let alone the genitals. She pretends to gag. traffic can never remember her name either. Spotlight coming towards them again, traffic ducks till the cameraman's gone. Who the fuck is he anyway? He's making a documentary for some British TV station. Where are the release forms? You're really paranoid tonight aren't you girlie?

Sore back sore knee sore with the world. Sitting on the edge of the stage head between her knees, stretching. The music so harsh it hurts her ears, shrill banging monochromatic techno. Where's Slip, why is she on last, if Slip were playing now traffic could at least get lost in music. If not playing her presence would be a comfort. Slip where are you. Where's the Professor Jimi Stash and Bella, where's the man with the rooster tattoo, where are her friends. A hand on her back, up and down the spine, she sees the familiar leathers through the chink of her armpit. Sits frozen, helpless, leave me alone. Sees Bella through the dancers, help me Bella. Bella catches her eye and is quickly beside her, lifts the man's hand away. That wasn't invited. I was just being affectionate. He places it back on traffic. Bella in corsetry, big, imposing, places herself between traffic and the man in leathers. I said *That wasn't invited.*

traffic sits up at last. Stash on the other side of her now, arm around her, watching the dancefloor with disdain. This party sucks, *way* too straight. We're going home, wanna lift?

Gary by the door shaking his head, thumbs down.

Home through neon streets, stop for the papers, fight down an alley, boy smashing his fist on Stash's car bonnet. traffic drags herself up the three flights of stairs pulls off her boots lies on the bed reading every little detail. Alone with newspapers and the one working tv channel yesterday's lentils the only food, traffic draws the curtains and waits with dread for daylight taking the pollution of the world through her eyes and into her brain. Draws a bath scrubs herself raw, forces herself to eat the rank lentils then climbs between the sheets. This is her last smoke her last dose of G this is her last chance to sleep.

Spinning horizontal light as newsprint headlines tattooed across her eyelids her body lead heavy stays on the bed a roadkill. Aboriginal death in custody Riot in detention centre More refugees Teenage suicide. Gay men tortured in prison Lesbians executed Woman stoned to death for adultery Prisons overflowing. CEO aquitted of fraud More prisons to be built Politician denies rorts Terrorists threaten the entire free world Suspects incarcerated. Free world free world free world free. What's the free world anyway, all this week's mail either bills or advertisements, the bank offering her a credit card when she can barely afford to keep the lights on. The world's a marketplace and traffic a commodity, used up washed up tracked up fucked up, nothing to buy and nothing to sell.

She wakes in a wet patch axe in the guts, staggers to the bathroom throws up turns to shit, turns again to throw up turns again to shit. Washes herself shaking then back to the bed soaked and stinking, it's piss my own piss. She didn't measure the G properly the lentils were off, she stumbles to the bathroom for a towel, lays it on the bed, glances at the clock then through the curtain. Five o'clock, still, the room her entire body full of heat. Overcast timeless sky, is it night or day?

For so long now I seem to have been a drink on a tray. Order my cocktails. Look at my body. Buy my drugs. Come to my party.

None of it was mine. Nobody owns anything. Bought sold given taken, everything passes. The journey of a fifty dollar note from the mint to the flame of a reckless gesture years later. Falling leaves, falling years.

Dropped for attachment, the anchor through darkness.

Was it record seizures that had dried up the heroin supply, were they really record seizures? Or was it the suppliers provoking a price war? Like oil sheikhs or pharmaceutical giants with their captive markets the drug barons held everybody to ransom. Drugs were business. The price of a gram of heroin had tripled but there was more cocaine in Sydney and better and cheaper than ever before. traffic remembered TV footage of the Minister for Justice destroying the purported five hundred kilogram haul. Neil paid his taxes, Neil had contacts.

The most successful businesspeople were aggressive bargainers, disciplined, ruthless, astute in their deals. Neil was an aggressive bargainer though his habit ate into his discipline and acuity. He was an erratic, risk-taking entrepreneur, ruined and buoyed up by excess. traffic was never more than a corner shop, a peasant with a small stall at the markets prone to the vagaries of the season without the head for business nor the heart for so much stress. Her first day up and out of her sick bed, her first social security cheque, walking down the street wallet full of money to pay overdue bills, turning the corner and there was Neil like a wish before her. Hi darling! Hi. They hugged, stood back and looked at each other. Long time no see. I've been a bit under the weather. They moved to a slice of shade against a shop window, sweating she was sweating the heat unbearable blocked head yawning this constant exhaustion. Neil shaking his head at the mention of Luke. Luke had held a knife to Neil's throat for a point of crystal the week before he finally went in. This whole fucking town's gone crazy on the stuff, they just don't know when to stop, unlike you girlfriend. I'm no angel, traffic sees the easy solution. OK then, in the car . . . gee they're out early. She followed his gaze down to Taylor Square, two cops in overalls with sniffer dogs. It was the peak of party season, the streets full of naive tourists and locals on holiday, the cops had a captive market. Neil laughed. It's enough to drive a man to drink! traffic seeing the time on Neil's watch felt a pull in the opposite direction yes no yes no yesnoyes. Tell you what Neil, I'll go and pay my bills then give you a ring.

She went down to the bank but the branch had been closed. She went over to the post office and found it had moved. Ran down to the new one in the shopping mall, stopping to withdraw money from an ATM, time was running out. In the queue playing with fate watching the clock. If I'm not next in line by five to I'm going outside to ring Neil. The line moved forward then she was at the counter relieved of most of her cash, cleansed purified totally virtuous. Quick down the road to the real estate shit! Doors closed, staff still moving around inside. traffic knocked waved pleaded did a little dance for them hands together in prayer. But the doors stayed locked. She crossed the road to telephones, lost coins in the first the second broken too, lost her last coins in the third. Now she had energy now she had a purpose, around the corner and up the road she bought some gum to get more change then raced further up to the next telephone booth. Neil's phone was turned off.

The sun pressed its angry red finger onto her head. Oh it's so good you're not doing drugs it's so good you're clean so good you've dried out. Clean, dry, what a load of crap. Why is it good. What's the point. Why am I alive.

Now everybody wanted to be a DJ. Electronica had moved into history. David Morales was piped into supermarkets, Fatboy Slim was on mobile ring tones, Moby sold sports goods. The media applied faces to sounds, the nameless magic of dance music acquired an ego. Overseas artists flew out of Sydney tens of thousands of dollars richer. Megaclubs came like travelling circuses, Trade Manumission Home Heaven. Venues hiked up their hire fees, Chronic along with so many others going for bigger and better going broke in the process. There had only been one performance night in the last year, small oneoff parties were rare. Clubs were safer, the entertainment understood in advance.

Friday night at Pandora's Box had been a disaster. Another new venue with the DJ booth tucked so far from the dancefloor you could hardly see your crowd let alone hear the levels properly. There was actually a sign on the wall near the turntables saying NO DANCING WITH SHIRTS OFF. Cool clean intelligent lighting, girls coming up to the DJ box requesting Ultra Nate and Tori Amos, girls everywhere not a man in sight though the club advertised no gender restrictions. One of the promoters came over and asked for something more friendly, Slip trying to mix in the next track and respond at the same time lost the beats and the promoter walked away shaking her head. Slip was filling in for D Coy, Chrissy doing the second set spent most of the night near the DJ box, going down to the floor every so often to check the sound for Slip. A catfight broke out near the bar. Alcohol had to be the worst drug for dancing, Slip played on to her imaginary chemical brothers and sisters. She had always had a good rapport with Chrissy and D Coy and other dyke DJs, they were solid and friendly and mostly supportive. Chrissy had played an amazing set at Pimp and D Coy at Chronic more than once but they made their living most of the time playing to limited briefs at gigs like these. It left Slip cold.

On Sunday afternoon she compared her latest liver function test with all the previous. Well in the red and rising steadily. She packed her records and CDs and took a cab into town, the driver a big Greek talking about the Sydney he'd known. It was a novelty to find a cab without a driver's cage. You've got no protection, Slip leant forward.

Aren't you scared? No darlin I got these instead, they're compulsory now. Stupid idiots, I been driving thirty years never had a problem. Slip leant back from the microphone and camera taped inside the windshield. You gonna be famous now, they're filming you, don't you wanna be famous?

She played her last set at the Royal to an almost empty room. The pokies were in place now and the regulars had fled. She had a leather party, Xenogenesis II, a possible gig in three months and that was all. Work tomorrow and not enough sleep never enough sleep. Where were they meeting on Sundays now there was no gay pub without poker machines or a video screen? She thought of them all in the cab back home to Bondi. She missed them, she missed traffic, she missed Mr Hyde.

Half asleep on arrival at the hospital, forms filled out, waiting in the white room. Then dressed in a gown and laid on a bed adjacent to a huge tattooed Maori, prison tears down his cheek, huge academic tome on Himmler in his hands. Waiting, dozing, hunger widening, idle chatter with the Maori, the nurse eventually coming around to explain the procedure. A vein opened in the wrist for a sedative, then a local anaesthetic, then the long fat biopsy needle. Then four hours recovery time. Curtains drawn around the Maori, movement, a moan, curtains parted again and the gastroenterologist and his nurse were by her side. But there was no vein opened in the wrist, there was no sedative. Just the thick sting of local anaesthetic then the needle puncturing her liver, into her ribs and up her side the electric shock of pain coming to rest on her neck like a metal claw. Couldn't move couldn't breathe metal claw tightening, the nurse came back fifteen minutes later with a shot of pethidine. A disappointing stone, so mild as to be barely perceptible. An hour later she was allowed to lie on her side.

When the ward had filled with people waiting for procedures Slip and the Maori were moved into another ward and given sandwiches.
   Good book?
   Yeh, he was a sick puppy. You going back to work this afternoon?
   No not really.
   I've got the whole day off.
   It's a good way to spend it isn't it. Getting your liver punctured and lying around hospital reading about psychopaths.
   Yeh we got the right idea.

Can I walk the dog? he asked the gastroenterologist when they were discharged. Play with the kids 'n' that? Slip bid him goodbye and walked down Victoria Street, she was fine, it was nothing. Then black behind the eyes, cold sweat, made it to the bus stop. Waited and waited through the three o'clock changeover, eventually catching a cab home.

Holmes dreams of traffic. She is back at the warehouse, he sees her from behind standing naked on a plinth as he comes in the front door. Arms horizontal one leg cocked as though ready for crucifixion. Sleek, chunky with some sort of halo, she looks like a boy painted by Caravaggio. There are two people at her feet, Holmes shifts to see their faces. Sailor and Jimi intense, enraptured. Holmes is aware of quick flicking movements and traffic's exhilaration. More, give it to me, more more! But Holmes is uneasy. He walks past the table round to Sailor and Jimi and the front view of traffic. She is smiling beatifically and covered in hypodermics, the halo is a helmet of them. Clusters sticking in the crook of each arm in the divet where collarbone kinks below throat on her thighs between her fingers. Sailor and Jimi aiming for her torso now, throwing the loaded syringes like darts while traffic sings and sighs with the strike of each target. Her liver sprouts attack. Holmes grabs Sailor and Jimi and takes them into the kitchen. They are aghast as is traffic because he is *making a scene*. He lectures If you think it's OK to stick needles into her like that you can leave my fucken house. But he's wrong, it's not their fault it's nobody's, nobody can do anything. He wakes traumatised.

All day every day people came to him for help. Another new arrival in Sydney expecting immediate accommodation. The electrician too sick to work evicted for a second time by a developer. The Koori boy just accommodated waking to racist graffiti on his door. The mother of two, one positive as well, with no complaint he could rectify mainly here for someone to talk to. Then there were the increasing crystal casualties with nowhere else to go. He listened to them all holding the dream of traffic like a pebble in his pocket. For days it pressed against him. Bella said she had been pretty messed up at the last Chronic party, Gary said Neil said she wasn't using at all. Without Luke the workload had increased and Holmes stayed back later, in rare minutes alone drawing up weekly budgets to see if he could afford combination therapies. His viral load up his t cells down, his spirit more determined than ever. He was alive again he was living and wanting more than the rudimentary groceries rent and fuel. He wanted regular acupuncture, goat's cheese not cheddar, maybe even the theatre now and then, he wanted the occasional night on the dancefloor and disco biscuits to accompany him there. He couldn't bring himself to pick up the phone and dial traffic's number. The advice he gave to clients was meant for her as well. Don't stress take care. Be positive. He was counselling himself. He sat on the floor to arrange the day in the bottom drawer of the filing cabinet. When he looked out the window again it was dark.

He was aware for the first time how much they had both changed. Softened, worn, opened in different directions. It was Slip he had been looking at from the street but he hadn't recognised her, hadn't even recognised this window as the one he had leant from every morning to touch the sun in his first year back in Sydney. Suddenly they were having dinner alone together for the first time since Slip had moved here two years earlier. The city was like that. Busy busy you were always too busy. You saw your best friends on the altered dimension of a dancefloor or around its construction during bump in, ran into them on the street, at openings, in cafes. It was hard to catch up. It was shocking to Holmes to think they no longer knew one another.

Living together down the coast, Slip in the kitchen cooking for his birthday while he watched television in the room adjacent, their conversation passing between the open doorway. Those wide mismatched double doors that made the house into an agora waiting for people though there hadn't been many visitors. Across the evening news came her clear lilting voice like the cat's body slinking past. She was so dilatory. Motionless at the bench yet when Holmes passed on his way to the fridge he saw over her shoulder the hands trimming meat. They were moving so fast it was impossible to see what they were doing, she seemed to have twenty-five fingers but when he stopped to watch more closely the role of each became clear. Two pushing back the fold of flesh, two adjacent with the thumb delineating fat while the knife in the other hand excised it. The movement in rapid variation repeated all along the leg which was then bound with herbs like an offering. The whole procedure was over in minutes. She had been talking to him all the while probably about music but Holmes had been too absorbed in the choreography of her hands to take it in.

He didn't see her cook tonight. The food had been brought home from the restaurant already prepared along with a bottle of red wine. She was handsome in the patchwork jeans he had passed onto her with the flat, he would have thought her self-assured but after two hours in her company the paraphernalia of traits attached to her by others gradually came unstuck. He could see why they read timidity as aloofness, the way she stiffened when approached by strangers with compliments, her understated dancing, moving around the edge of the floor waiting to go on. But she wasn't stern, just . . . preoccupied. They drank a toast to Holmes's birthday. Slip gave him a tape and Holmes gave Slip half a tray of valium. Impossible now to get any sort of muscle relaxant or sleeping pill prescribed, especially if you were hep C positive so Slip when in pain syphoned whatever was available from her HIV boyfriends. Two weeks after the biopsy she could still feel the metal claw.

What did she gain? Technical knowledge, figures on a page, no great recommendation, telling Holmes nonetheless he may as well get a biopsy and find out his hep genotype. Holmes said nothing. Slip like everyone submitted to the constant testing because it was just about the only thing to do. Testing your liver function, viral load, t cells, reminding you they weren't necessarily an indication. He couldn't be bothered, his liver function tests were fine, he couldn't be bothered to investigate the hep C further, the HIV already took up too much of his time. He pulled his sleeve up and showed her the massive purple bruise inside his elbow from the latest blood tests.

Fuuuuck. Why'd it do that?

Platelets. I don't know Slip, you're working too hard.

We all are. I'm getting old.

We all are.

I found a good doctor though, she's into alternative therapies. I'm saving up for herbs again. I miss the escarpment you know.

She refilled their glasses and they drank a toast to their livers. Holmes turned on the heater and edged closer to the bars as they filled with orange light. Felt guilty again about not ringing traffic, she could have come over tonight as well, she was frozen in his mind needing him. He couldn't get warm. A bath, there was a bath here. traffic and Billy used to travel all the way to Bondi from the warehouse to sit in it together. Holmes turned on the taps as Slip left the flat to put the bottles out.

The cold night air shocked her face. Slowly and quietly Slip had become drunk. She placed the bottles in the recycling bin and floated down to the corner. From the east the distant sounds of surf or wind breathing through the she-oaks. Three tall forest she-oaks blotting the streetlights like a castle, the wind the surf the wind the surf. Into the next street finding the lavender bush in the dark she leant over the wall clipped three branches and took them back to the flat for Holmes to float in the hot water. He talked to her figure behind him in the doorway.

I saw that friend of yours from Xenogenesis the other day.

Which one?

Tall guy with glasses.

I can't remember.

He came up and gave you a hug before you went down to the courtyard to do the second set.

Oh him. We'd only met once.

But he seemed like an old friend.

He just interviewed me on the radio.

But he asked after you and everything, Holmes grabbed the side of the bath to turn and look her full in the face. We were talking about you for ages. He seemed so *genuine*.

Probably is in his way.

Holmes looked away, devastated. Her mouth cracked a smile.

You're a sentimental bloke aren't you.

He could hear her in the kitchen from below the waterline, warped long knocks and thuds. A tap turned on right beside his ear. He rose out of the water then went under again. He was soft, too soft, he was sentimental. Into the bath his limbs would separate from his body and float away, he would melt into the bath flesh faded to translucency the bubbles would subside the water chill, he would wake in the morning and find himself like that. The bath a still prism containing his

325

rearranged form like a Cubist painting, in the top corner a window of dark blue sky gridded by scaffolding.

She missed the escarpment she missed her garden, her cats the compost heap the empty beaches. She missed the long walks in the forest beneath the cliff or alongside the sea uninterrupted by other humans. The food wasn't as close up here, she wasn't even allowed windowboxes in this building and there was nowhere inside with enough sun for herbs. Staying home shifting pots all day wasn't an option. The dinner Slip had cooked for Holmes's birthday down the coast would have been impossible in the city. He had reminded her of it as they ate. Beef wrapped around rosemary from the garden, potatoes from Holmes's supermarket shopping, the first field mushrooms of the season found growing beneath pines near the beach and greens from the garden. His birthday cake was inspired by special cooking chocolate her mother had given her. From an old book bought second-hand at markets in Florence ten years before she found the blueprint of a recipe then improvised the final result according to other ingredients at the back of the cupboard. Cooking all day, cooking for pleasure not for money, cooking that had no fixed menu.

On her stomach waiting for the masseur, face nestled into the cavity. Quiet footsteps then the blanket was lifted and her body revealed. The stranger's hands explored her flesh finding the tender spots prodding and pressing till traffic groaned and finally surrendered. Heat, pain, pummelling and rubbing the knots to pulp, her mind receding then a second man arrived. He picked her up and arranged her gently like a special doll then *crack* a warm flood released down her spine to her toes, crack again and a cool flood followed. Four more cracks and traffic light-headed was laid back down on the bench. A third person arrived. As the hairs of steel slid into her back her neck and her knee the tears poured down through the cavity into her upturned palms. She hardly heard the acupuncturist leave the room. Weightless she wafted over her body, a map of damage, needles marking the ruined metropolises.

She slept away the darkness. Missing midnight waking at dawn sometimes but there was nothing beyond the bed to entice her so traffic slept again till morning sun had ripened in the room. Too many bedclothes red glare of the heater disappearing in daylight, her swollen brain carried like a burden to the bathroom compressed again beneath cool water. Then the long hot showers sloughing off dead skin every single window wide open. All through March's rainy days alone in the room or running to the shops returning with food splitting the thin plastic bags.

She cooked herself luxurious breakfasts and ate them reading the juggling book at the small table. Then washed the dishes, turned on the midday dance music show and lay a blanket on the grey floorboards. Exercises, stretching, knee exercises, abdominals. Yoga sometimes, lengthening her muscles over the weeks back to their natural pliability, working towards the splits. Then she went to the sewing machine and piece by piece over the weeks repaired her linen, shirts, skirt, jeans, then she began sewing by hand everything that couldn't be done by the machine.

The special events were fortnightly deposits of sickness benefits, phone calls to friends, an invitation from Slip to eat Thai and the afternoon Bliss finally returned her calls informing her of the place to buy juggling clubs. Overwhelmed by the choice of clubs or balls that lit up when thrown, traffic bought both. Butts were smoked and pulses eaten for days after the purchase, bills unpaid till the windfall of the next cheque. The juggling was a reward for all those inane chores, a celebration when the music from the speakers and her hyperactive hands synchronised perfect as a movie. Rhythm, said Bliss. That's what juggling's all about, rhythm, a kind of dancing. Once Jimi gave her a bush bud and the veer of her mind was clear and startling as the red arc of balls in the air. On crystal she could have gone through a small bag in a night, now a few puffs was all it took to bend her world. Sick of the sight of herself and starved of entertainment she whitened her face then overlaid new features, scrubbed out the mistakes, tried again exaggerating the assymetry and brightening the colours, then raided her wardrobe for dressups creating a new companion in the mirror. This all took at least two if not three hours. Transformed she turned up the music picked up the clubs and continued, one eye on the clubs in the air the other on the path before her, a third on herself viewed from afar.

Juggling at home could be dangerous. She smashed two lightbulbs before finding a rudimentary shade in the street and fixing it over the globe. Her hands now addicted picked up any and every object and made them airborne. Shoes jars of Vegemite rolled-up socks apples eggs and her small milk pot, the different efforts each required learnt by every muscle in her body. She began to feel the world through mass and weight. As she grew more ambitious and increased the balls in her throw, moving to clubs halfway through, the ceiling itself could be an impediment. So she walked down to a sheltered private corner of Beare Park and threw facing the sinking sun. One day she woke with a stinging cheek went to the bathroom mirror and pulled out a shard of lightglobe with tweezers.

Sundays were sad. The lack of a genial pub to go and sit in was felt more keenly each week. A place not just in which to meet good friends but a place in which to watch the passing parade some of whom would inevitably turn out to be known to you. Violet, for instance, whose new number traffic didn't have. Or Gary or the man with the rooster tattoo. She missed them all. The cravings never stopped yet the day that Shifty came over with some crystal traffic's excitement before the shot wasn't matched by the high after it. Just the pleasure of the feel of steel then giddiness, a hilarious four hours with Shifty followed by three more of cleaning and anxiety. Then the comedown. It took her three days to recover. She felt like the loneliest person in the world.

traffic and Jimi went to Bondi to watch Gary perform. He said to be there at midday so they got up early packed food and drink and caught the bus down to the beach, stopping by Slip's flat to wheedle her out of bed. A brass band from Tonga was playing when they arrived at the pavilion. They paid their fifteen dollar entrance fee then arranged their cloth in the last sliver of shade to the blare of post-colonial kitsch. Next up were Cook Island drummers seducing the audience to dance near the stage, the grass auditorium gradually filling with adults children and more performers.

It was cold in the shade so they moved forward, close enough to see the faces of the performers and sat there exposed, traffic stripping down to a singlet Jimi soon shirtless. D'you reckon it's OK to have a smoke here? Sure, smell that, someone else is. In the distance by the back entrance a group of uniformed police watching the crowd, arms crossed. Jimi lit a pipe, passed it to traffic, traffic puffed then elbowed Slip, Slip puffed, elbowed traffic back. traffic elbowed Slip, Slip elbowed traffic. Sunlight speared their eyeballs from the mirror waistcoat worn by the singer of a Warlpiri rock band now taking the stage. Beanpole in black stovepipes wild hair and big sunglasses. Hey! he yelled to the people picking their way back to their rugs. You yeh you! You betta not stop dancin! Come back here! The drummer counted the band in and thirty minutes of raw blistering desert punk screamed over Bondi. They had no idea, absolutely no idea what they had come down here for apart from Gary and lay back now astonished and laughing. Women and children the most persistent dancers, singer like a snake whipping across the stage and Stash there now his white replica dancing vigorously on the grass before them, Bella a sunflower in wide yellow hat and lowcut fifties swimsuit moving slowly over to traffic and Jimi. Then Stash gave up and slumped down drenched, the last and most beautiful dancer a woman thrice the width of the lead singer travelling at his speed a mirror to his music.

They moved back when loin-clothed dancers from the Central Desert took the grass in front of the stage, half the men in wraparounds against the afternoon sun legs pistoning from the tops of thighs, kids from the audience imitating as they swivelled hissed and pounded the grass to dust. The didge player nestled his instrument in the cave of an overturned plastic chair for amplification and the peal of clapper sticks spun and bounced around the walls of the pavilion. traffic in a break found a cold tap and drenched her head then all the exposed skin that Bella's sunscreen had arrived too late to save. Skin tight all the way down to her hands, heart beating she returned to the rug when the Torres Strait Islanders came on. They knew Gary's body, knew his style from all those hot shirtless nights on the dancefloor but in feathers face paint and the extra height of a headdress, weaving and stomping aiming his spear, he was no longer Gary but a hunter, a warrior. Like the Green Woman's sashay which obliterated Turkish Jim's quiet shuffle or the deepsea creature's bobbing that had nothing to do with James or the disjointed court jester inhabited on occasion by traffic.

So all day they feasted. Men women and fa'afafine from Samoa, dancers from Rotorua, Polynesian rappers from the western suburbs, until dusk when after the last show drunk with sun and song and dance they went down to the sea peeled off their clothes and ran into the freezing surf.

It was the Samoans that finally decided Jimi. The Samoans' black tattoos neat and heavy as transfers, the huge extravagant Torres Strait headdresses, the Guro mask he worked beneath five days a week and his first savings in years. Two rooms back from the noisy street stretched on his stomach face to the wall, this the second sitting, Jimi drifted as the needle cluster scored his skin. Drifted into and beyond the pain of the mask completing on his back, saw all his friends dressed in his ideas. Bee's hair piled up in vertical curls coloured burnt orange or Holmes's pressed straight, shoulder length, dyed in exact alternating stripes of purple and fluorescent yellow, his goatie dyed as well. Stash with his thin pale face could carry something big and round. Dye his hair a fresh blue black sculpt it out and up and weave in strips of coloured foil. Shock treatment. He imagined a bowl, a thick black bowl created from the hair she would have if she let it grow, perched on the crown of Shifty's head, sprayed stiff and silver perhaps filled with medical implements, the sides and back of her head to be shaved and a fine bright red wig attached above the earline so the bowl was real hair and the hair itself fake. The other boys would have to wear his wigs except for Gary on whom Jimi would model a giant rocker quiff. The Green Woman how he longed to style the Green Woman, turn her gothic, a dark shimmering emerald pulled high off her forehead like an Elizabethan. And traffic, what could he do with traffic who had come to him more than anyone and submitted to any and every idea. traffic had no money now and for months had worn the shaved head of an ascetic. Dazed and euphoric, Jimi left the tattoo shop with that smooth globe in his imagination waiting for adornment.

Back out on the street padded against the wind by leather cotton and a layer of gauze, the heat from his back flooding his body, Jimi walked on air to the Indian takeaway for a lassi. Took a phone call and moved to a wide doorway off the main drag to better hear his brother. Four o'clock in the afternoon, clear chilled sky. A boy walked past eye contact the boy kept walking. Jimi's brother in his ear. She's making my life a fucken misery. Well maybe you have to split up then. That's easy for you to say we've got three kids remember. It's not *easy* for me to say Stefan. The boy was back, stepping into the doorway staring hand on crotch. Surfie type, broad shoulders sun-bleached hair, Jimi's number-one lust object. I think she needs help, I really do! Well have you suggested that to her? She goes mental at me *anything* I say. The surfie was actually getting his cock out, pulling on it slowly. Sydney boys! Jimi talking sober advice through a wide grin and endorphin high, checking the street phew it was empty turning back to watch the show not two metres from his face. I don't know, maybe you all need a holiday. The boy was moving out of the doorway still wanking, Jimi swallowed. Listen Stefan, why don't I call you on the landline when I get home? He followed the boy around the corner up the alley and into 32.

He shouldn't have been fucking with a fresh tattoo he shouldn't have even been in a sex on premises but the elation of the moment carried him in. His body robust from the gym, prednisone and constant feeding felt firm around him like a new suit. He payed and went into the lounge cock heavy in his pants, checked out the porno. Another Californian blond begging his master Daddy gonna fuck my little pussy oh yes Daddy *please*. 32 like nearly every other place in town coloured by the dialling days when dependence on viagra or caverject had developed. Once he and Luke had shot up some crystal, gone out to 32 couldn't get it up, gone home and shot caverject into their cocks, gone back to 32 the erections so intense they were hurting, gone back home for more crystal to calm their cocks, gone back to 32 and fucked themselves stupid for the next six hours. Jimi put his jacket in a locker and got a coke, the lounge area repainted, black again how interesting. The place was quite empty, surfie boy nowhere to be seen. He went upstairs up the back of the suckatorium, only one guy there and not the surfie. Cock wilting Jimi went down into the maze passed a couple of occupied cubicles, one with three preppies the other with two older leathermen. He passed the first sling room then the second, both empty except for a young fat guy hanging around but Jimi kept walking past the theme rooms till he reached the prison cell. It was him it was the surfie boy closing the door somebody waiting on the steel frame bed. Jimi approached, the surfie looked at him blankly and disappeared into the cell. Well that was a waste of time then and fucken money, it hadn't even occurred to him to come here till the surfie had appeared, he hadn't even been horny. He went up the road to the pub.

Two hours later Jimi was walking home down Forbes Street eating a kebab, aware of someone metres behind him, turning to check. No not a threat, just some guy he'd seen at the pub. Then again. Jimi tensed ready to punch or run as the man caught up. Hi. Hi. Hard to tell what he looked like out of the streetlights, Jimi kept walking head down. The man stayed abreast. Wanna come for a drink? Nah mate, I'm going home. I mean at my place, I live just down here. Honestly, I'm exhausted. I was watching you at the pub, you were in a total daze. I've just been tattooed for three hours. Oh. So . . . yair . . . The man stopped in the doorway of a small apartment block, watched a man and woman walk past, looked back at Jimi. Maybe some other time, I like you y'know, I'd like you to do me over. Jimi hesitated, felt a twinge. The man spoke quietly. I've got a playroom.

Jimi followed him up two flights of stairs into his apartment. Domination wasn't Jimi's usual trip yet the endorphins had left him feeling calm and powerful. Can I get you a drink? No, just present yourself. He followed the man into a sparse room, very little lighting, a St Andrew's cross behind the door. The man took his jacket off followed by his shirt, took off his chaps and jeans and placed himself at Jimi's feet in slave position. About the same height as Jimi, fortyish, a hungry boot licker. After a while, Jimi bade him stand up against the cross. The man's jaw shoulder and a full round pec its haze of hair catching the light. Jimi put his hand on it, squeezed and stroked unbuttoning his fly. Both hands on him now, the right pec with an edge smooth and shiny like vinyl or patent leather. Why would he only wax on one side? Mmm, when he circled tighter around the man's nipples, so faint that Jimi could hardly hear him. He leant to the man's mouth. The ropes are over there. Jimi selected two long ones from the low hand rail. How are your shoulders? Fine. OK, spread 'em. With a charge of cruel empathetic lust Jimi probed a knee between the man's thigh and the man spread his legs, Jimi pushing up against his balls the man's hot breath on his face. Cock throbbing Jimi criss-crossed the rope over the man's leg looping it into the hooks each side of the beam. He tied off at the ankle, then the other leg then each arm above his head finishing off around the shoulders. He stood back and admired this vision of the stranger spread-eagled waiting for his touch. Pecs tits breasts Jimi loved them, one in each hand

and that strange sleekness of the right one, his fingers exploring the texture further down to the ribs where a clump of sinew and knots rose beneath the skin, up his arm and around to his back where the thinly corded sticky flesh was finally read by Jimi's fingertips as burn scarring. He put his hand on the back of the man's neck, scarring there too, took the man's cock in his other hand and drew their mouths together.

For a minute Jimi became literal, conditioned and hesitant, his hand moved away. No please it's nice, nobody ever wants to touch me. Jimi looked at the man's face thinking the side in darkness was probably scarred as well. He touched it lightly, the burns began just below his jawline. Aren't they really sensitive? Not really, they're old, just my lower back. So Jimi set out again one hand on the unburnt hip the other moving across the landscape of damage. From the smooth planes of chest and stomach his fingers delicate and quiet as ants discovered again that clump of sinew and knots over the ribs, moved into a delta rose on a ridge that wound like a road all the way round the man's back stopping just short of the spine. Across the corded scapula melted plastic clay riverbed, then down further where the canyons deepened, Jimi stepping back questioning him with his eyes, gently gently touching the mess of lower back, sharp intake of breath and Jimi's hands came to rest once again on the man's pecs.

He was afraid to whip him on the right side at first but the burns began on the very edge of his pec and the whip was small. Jimi whirled it over his chest the man urging him on, back and forth harder closer, shot at the left nipple then the right, harder both again this was what drove the man crazy his nipples. Aiming for them over and over cock dribbling he never topped anyone not like this, till his hand grew tired and he dropped the whip, soothed the burning pecs with his palms cock pressing against the man's moaning body. Then he picked up the clamps placed them on the man's nipples, untied his arms and legs cuffed his hands together behind his back. Hooked a finger in the chain stepped back and pulled on the clamps, the other hand wanking himself. He watched the man's eyes begin to glaze pushed his knee up into the balls pulling the clamps harder and harder till with a loud groan the man ejaculated all down Jimi's thigh. On your knees and lick it off, said Jimi. Every last drop.

A guy comes to me with a spark

I fan the spark until it becomes a flame

I feed the flame until it becomes a fire

Then I feed the fire until it becomes a roaring blaze.

That's what I have to do.

Spark . . .

Flame . . .

Fire . . . !!!

Once upon a time, not so long ago nor so very far away, some twisted faeries decided to have a party for all the creatures of the underworld. Spring was coming, there were no birthdays death days queer feast days religious feast days public holidays departures arrivals or special events of any kind and they decided to celebrate. Their local watering hole had been poisoned so they gathered at Turkish Jim's eyrie to discuss arrangements.

Feast your eyes on my pornaromic view, said Turkish Jim. We can have first course here.

My worker's cottage would be perfect for a deviant main course, said Fred the troll. It's dark and cramped and there's furry mildew all over the bathroom walls.

We'll host dessert, said the Professor. We'll paint the house up like a nightmare and vamp up the sound system. Make it a refuge where goblins, ogres and freaky paedavestites can dance the night away.
Starved so long of carnal festivities the twisted faeries began to flap their wings with excitement, their tummies rumbled, they licked their lips.

What should we call our party? asked Mr Hyde.

Fast, said the Professor.

Why?

Well . . . because . . . time's running out.

Hooray! they cried, and flew home to begin preparations.

There was no specific dress code for *Fast* but arrival in a vehicle and strict punctuality was mandatory. Anybody who arrived on drag queen time would miss out.

The circus was in town but she couldn't afford to go. traffic had no VCR so she took the videos over to Jimi's along with her juggling book. Every single circus video she could find went into Jimi's VCR, traffic rewinding the juggling scenes over and over. His 1920s building, sparse living room with its high ceilings, large cushions in place of a couch and stereo tucked in the far corner, was perfect for traffic. She stretched out smooth and confident, OK watch this. She lifted a knee, Jimi on the edge of his seat but the balls stayed up in their spinning circle even with the knee insinuated inside it and Jimi whooped. traffic wound down by deftly placing the balls one by one in her pockets. I've gotta show you these ones now. She pulled out the luminescent balls which when static appeared duller than the others. I thought you were going to use clubs. I am, I just wanna show you these first, can you switch the main light off? traffic got three in the air, dipped her head catching a ball on the back of her neck, dropping the other two repeating the trick until successful. For over an hour the firefly spin mesmerised Jimi, each attempt at each trick an improvement. The same thing happened every time traffic brought a new video and her balls and clubs over. After a fortnight or so of this, tired and dizzy, his flatmate protesting after catching traffic in the kitchen juggling fresh eggs, Jimi offered to lend traffic his VCR. traffic realising once she was home alone that although unable to do every featured trick there was little more she could glean from the videos at this stage. Taking the balls over to Jimi had accelerated her progress, the impetus an audience.

Passing the two dollar shop she found wheels of bright pegs on special. She bought four packets and home alone attached them to the back of her upper arms, her skin ideal for the sprung pincers, lifting from muscle easily, not like Billy's which had been so full of collagen. She juggled a while, the pegs flipping off gradually. Juggled again trying to flick them off with a sharp backwards jab until her arms were too sore to continue. She went to the mirror and eyes watering attached the pegs in a close row around her jaw. Her face framed with pain. Then keeping still as possible, trying to deny the tilt of her head, jerking it upwards pegs flying through the loops of balls. The patterns of Jimi's dilapidated ceiling stayed in her mind as she fell asleep. Over them the balls in their continuous sideways figure of eight, the symbol of infinity.

They began in the afternoon with their hair, green diagonal lines across traffic's bleached top, Jimi's pulled upright in three points each veering off at a different angle. Forty minutes later, rinsed and ready, traffic sealed her eyebrows with soap, whited her face out and on her forehead painted two high black eyebrows the left continuing vertical to her hairline. Next were the starry eyes of a clown in red, a small red nose, red septum bar and curved green triangles on each cheek. Jimi vying for the mirror, the two of them like cards swapping places. As Jimi inserted spikes into his eyebrows and septum, traffic slowly and carefully enhanced the stars over the clown's eyes with jewels. Last of all, twisting her glory to something sinister, she painted a black horizontal line across her lips then small vertical stitches giving her the sewn mouth of a scarecrow. Then Jimi secured his long leather laplap and laced traffic into her leggings and jerkin over voluminous white shirt.

After so long in hibernation the dressups for *Fast* were extravagant. Shifty arrived as Mal Practice in a suit and white doctor's coat, round glasses with thick black rims, thick black eyebrows high on her powdered forehead. She had been with Mel the acupuncturist two months now, a shy polite long-limbed blonde, glamorous in a long latex dress, who complimented the evil clown on her strong even walk and shied away from her face. They parked Esmerelda and stepped from sunset into the bottom of the tower, re-emerging at Turkish Jim's place thirteen storeys up. Corridors of red plastic strips hung from the ceiling to shoulder height so all that was visible were legs and torsos, faces appearing briefly as people breached the plastic. Here against the wall was Bee on the couch with Holmes in cowboy attire, his belt buckle saying The South Will Rise, Bee catching sight of the evil clown and winking with her late sixites eyes. The clown winked back then stepped into the next corridor and was face to face with the Professor who shrieked in fright then hid behind a mask of Marlene Dietrich held on a stick in his hand. She took some chips and a glass of punch from Dietrich's tray, lifted the plastic strips again. Stash and Bella talking to three leathermen she knew vaguely from the pub, at the end of the corridor a twenty-four inch television showing a sped-up version of Cindy Crawford's exercise classes interspersed with porn, and all around them the slashing buzz guitar of a CD by Mr Hyde. The fourth corridor was haunted by dusk. The clown struggled to open the sliding glass doors. Sudden wind, the harbour, red sky over the city and behind her the empty corridor populating as the last guests arrived. Soon there were thirty-odd people crammed into the one bedroom flat and the clown overwhelmed stayed on the balcony as the dancing got going. She wanted to walk out into the last sunlight, down the soft air currents across the water to the verdant darkness of Bradleys Head. Then Slip in a tall chef's hat and butcher's apron on which she had painted in crude red the words Deep Fried. I've got your music. Fantastic, thank you. I've got two tracks actually, I found another one with a similar rhythm, the juggling beat I call it. OK then, I suppose I'm committed. Of course you are. The chef glanced back through the doorway. Quick, there's a show on.

Nice musak was drifting through the speakers, the red plastic strips were lifted then Turkish Jim's new boyfriend William hung a sign over the kitchen doorway. LIPOSUCTION CLINIC. Jim in a long white coat brought out an effigy and sat it on a chair below the sign. Weedy little body, perfectly caricatured oversized head lolling like a giant watermelon behind its giant glasses. It was the Prime Minister. The heckling began almost immediately. Shoosh, Jim admonished. He's having his treatment. As snippets of the Prime Minister's speeches began to lace the soundtrack Jim took a length of clear plastic tubing, attached one end to the Prime Minister's ear the other to a perspex vat on the table adjacent. Other sounds were creeping into the soundtrack now, the speeches distorted, the national anthem the United States national anthem, a woman saying Oh John! and as Jim began to pump, the sounds of sludge and groaning machinery. William held the head in place while Turkish Jim pumped a thick translucent yellowy red matter slowly from it down the tube and into the vat. *We* decide who enters this country *we* decide who enters this country *we* decidiediediedie enters this cunt enters this cunt, the glasses falling to the floor long black and grey tendrils of eyebrow poking bravely through the Prime Minister's skin as he warped and wrinkled and the vat filled with pus, we will not tolerate illegal illegal, his speech crescendoing to a high rapid babel not toleratenotolerate till the head shrank to the size of a human's then slumped forward over the little body.

Eeuugh, Mel approached the effigy afterwards, touched the eyebrows admiringly. What'd you make these out of? Fred's pubic hair. Turkish Jim motioned politely to the vat. Would you like a glass? No thanks I'm vegan. Oh it's all vegetable, I can assure you. The chef stopped to inspect it. Is that the acid punch?

Then they were outside piling into their vehicles, Jimi removing parking tickets from each windscreen and tearing them up. How ridiculous! Don't they know who we *are*? The cavalcade drove slowly up the hill from Elizabeth Bay headed by a decommissioned ambulance driven down from Newcastle by a friend of Fred's. The Cross getting crowded with Saturday-nighters, streetlights coming on. On Macleay Street where the ambulance had stopped at the lights, Holmes in Mal Practice's car second from the front spied the Professor out the window amongst the crowd near El Alamein fountain. All along the cavalcade windows opened, heads jutted. The Professor dressed as a gangster in pinstripes and spats was training a cap gun on a boy in track pants. Drop the cocaine! he shouted and shot the boy as he dropped a large zip-lock bag of white powder. A crowd gathering as the Professor made off with the white powder, one distraught lady rushing over to the boy on the ground red spreading across his stomach. The lights changed but the ambulance remained stationary and the street behind them filled with car horns. The Professor was ambushed by another gangster in flares and gold jewellery who shot him and grabbed the bag of white powder. Turkish Jim that's who it was, heading for their car now water pistol cocked a righteous bystander in hot pursuit. Christ! Mal gunned the motor. The cop station's right *there*. The evil clown opened the door and Jim launched himself across the crowded back seat as Fred jumped out of the ambulance in a white coat printed with DRUG SQUAD and bundled the shot gangster and boy inside. And as the cavalcade took off down Darlinghurst Road they saw two sleepy constables come up the steps from their station behind the fountain and into the bedlam.

Who was the boy?
James.

It was not.

It was.

He was too young.

He shaved.

My god. Jim?

The evil clown is right. It was James.

Drug-dealing little fiend. Hey Jim . . .

Yes clown?

Rack up will you?

She was fake, she was faking it. Skating the surface, fooled by the veneer. The possibilities of white powder engrossed her as they drove slowly towards Surry Hills, Jimi's hand on her thigh his face in her neck, everybody pissing themselves everywhere the mnemonics, the Royal the Oxford the leather shop Oxford Street. But as the magic continued to unfold around her, a drag show to Nina Hagen by William at Fred's place, lushly decorated, the kitchen table covered in food, as they continued on foot through the dark blue streets of Surry Hills to the house of the Professor and Mr Hyde, its interior painted entirely with speed stripes that narrowed in the far corners, Slip's music beckoning, as she took in the amount of work everybody put into one day and night of play, their passion, their labour, as she and Jimi posed for Bee's camera against one of the zooming walls, the evil clown lost sight of it. In the corner with Jimi, her pulse began to accelerate with pure fear.

I can't do it Jimi.

Yes you can.

I can't, I've had some acid punch.

Hours ago, one cup.

I haven't done a show for nearly two years Jimi, my heart's going mental.

All the better, you'll be fresh.

It's this house, it's manic! I can't see straight!

Nobody can, that's the idea. High ceilings baby, you can try and get four up.

I can't measure up to the liposuction clinic and Nina Hagen.

It's only a competition if you want it to be.

I can't Jimi I can't.

He took her by the shoulders and hissed at her face. If you don't do your thing, I'll smudge your make-up. He led her into the bathroom. traffic took off her jerkin and shirt, put the jerkin back on then offered her arms to Jimi. Jimi carefully placed two dozen red and green pegs on the extremities of each, then another dozen along her jaw. Good to see you've got a bit of fat there now girlfriend. The clown winked. He put the last peg in place and stood back to check. It's an Aztec clown! And we know what happened to *them*.

She found a dark spot in the shadows over the turntables over which to focus on the balls and placed herself in the corner where the speed stripes converged. The chef put on the first track and the rhythm began to beckon. James adjusted the lighting and the last arrivals were greeted by the evil clown juggling with lights, pegs flying off her arms and face, a bright shape of madness and energy over the vortex.

Dawn sky like a religious postcard. Low cumulus, no waves, the water was clear. On her way to *Fast* the evening before, Slip had passed the beach when it was covered with people lured out by the heat. It re-emerged from night scraped clean and pockmarked by gull prints as though pounded by a thousand tiny nocturnal dancers. They drove on around the headlands, traffic burrowing into her bag for cleansing wipes, removing the clown, passing a wipe to Mal Practice, reaching over and placing a jewel in the centre of Slip's forehead.

Slip was the last to go in, shedding her clothes on the rocks by the pool. Diving in, smoke and grime and music of last night lifting from her body to the air over the water. Down to the bottom skating hillocks of rock and purple anemones, weeds swishing, the pale warped legs of girls entering and exiting in churns of fine bubbles. Alone in the pool now heading for a wall. She surfaced and dived again and swimming like a frog below the waterline, limbs gulping and straightening, was traffic ahead, her body turning upright against the end of the pool. Slip was heading for her belly touching it as she surfaced kissing her too late to care about the surprise on traffic's face. Who opened her mouth anyway and moved into the kiss, into Slip.

By late morning the temperature had almost reached thirty. Out the back window low cloud was coming across the harbour. Strange to feel herself properly inside the flat now though she had been here before, but the rooms and furniture had seemed to need Slip's cue to unveil themselves fully. traffic noticed for the first time the detail of books and clothes, notes for last night's set on the floor by the bed. And even when Slip went to the kitchen the sense of her nakedness, her blood heat, stayed with traffic as though she was still inside her feeling her pulse. Slip standing over her now with water, tall, gawky. I'm too tall for you traffic look, she lay back down on the bed. traffic held her cigarette hand aloft and leant against Slip's body, mouth to mouth her pubic bone pressed Slip's belly. She wriggled down and touching ankles with her toes put the cigarette in the ashtray over Slip's shoulder, pulled Slip towards her tasting the salt of armpit, then lower toe to toe then sliding her feet into the arches of Slip's, mouth on nipple.

345

They went back to the beach around midday when white mist covered Ben Buckler entirely, wisps floating down into Bondi Bay. They sat together watching white tropical fog seep over sand and ocean like dry ice. The first sight of Bondi Beach on a hot day under a strange sky had brought hundreds of people out to stand on the grass and sand. In the thick pale silence they looked out to sea. It disappeared.

After breakfast Bee went into the darkroom. She had dozens of rolls of film processed now, the good images marked off on the proofsheets. She inserted the first roll, projected, placed the paper. Stood over the chemical stench waiting for revelation. Shot one. Four ambulant poker machines coming through the Cross the morning after Hotel Quickie, a couple of astonished street people to one side. Shot two. Dressups revealed, James and the Professor fitting cardboard on the roofrack, the Green Woman to one side pulling the lever of her machine and traffic standing before the fourth desperately digging into her pockets. Shot three. Fred outside the sex shop bent over, Slip aiming the giant dildo at his arse. Shot four. James on the edge of the frame holding up CONFERENCE IN PROGRESS, the Professor beside him back to the camera bare-legged, trenchcoat open, Shifty's surprised downward stare. Shot five. Sunrise over William Street.

Then there were the show shots, every single one a gem. Still simple shows perfect for capture, she had shown Stash the settings on the camera so that even the suits were there. A photo of her own show! traffic and Holmes's like a still from a Fassbinder film, bottles fringing the stage and the set so intimate as though the lights when they were dimmed had sucked in the walls. Rose light mostly, and purples and blues. There were three rolls each of Panic and Scum, only one of Pimp. The tension that night with Shifty returned like a bitter taste, all the things she had missed because of that long painful tension. Next surfaced a compensation. The photos of Turkish Jim's show at *Fast* were brilliantly grotesque, Jim's fastidious concern, the lolling head, Mal Practice examining the aftermath. A series hung in Parliament House would be good. Heart sinking, Bee pegged alongside them the show at El Alamein fountain. Nothing more than a blur in the distance. She was too far back in the cavalcade and of course had no warning, one minute they were there the next they were gone. The best moments were often those that eluded the camera, the best photos often the unplanned. Slip at the decks in chef's hat and apron. The court jester at Scum the court jester at the leather party then finally the evil clown at *Fast*, what a difference in the look even if the clothes were the same. The court jester and Billy in the bandana bustle, how she missed Billy.

That taste again, bitter bitter she had been so bitter. Like a toxic sediment it had accumulated over the years of working for money over fulfilment, of trying to fit the world into her own private ideal.

Full of remorse and nostalgia Bee stopped for a break, splashed cool water onto her eyes then half an hour later re-entered the darkroom. Took down the photographs that had dried, took them out to the main room laid them on the long wooden table then went back in and began printing again. Half a roll of the evil clown at *Fast*, there were at least five good shots here. traffic had almost perfected the makeup and her juggling poses were crisp as sculpture. Pegged and still, waiting for everybody's attention. The blurs of pegs and balls in the air, the clown in their midst perfectly straight, palms and face raised. One leg cocked at a ninety degree angle or bent back behind her like a puppet, the masterstrokes of backhand catches and a couple of hooks beneath her raised knee, the glowing ball on the back of her neck. And always the balls joined by slow exposure into circles of fire so she wasn't so much throwing and catching as pulling a continuous string. Nobody had expected this much of traffic.

For three days solid Bee conjured up memories. Long finicky dressups, recovering from Chronic, the Royal recoveries, the Professor's birthday. traffic backstage after the puppet show at Heresy, wide-eyed, bleeding, Bella backstage after the same show at Bliss's performance night more than a year later, this version not as good as the first. On the fourth day Bee printed the rolls of cityscapes shot to and from work at Utopia, the dusks the dawns the summer middays, the brick pits at St Peters, railway lines, King Street. She printed till the air was so thick with imagery and chemicals and the past that she could no longer breathe and had to retreat to the main room exhausted. Fresh night air, indigo sky, on the sink a plate stained orange, so Holmes had come home with Indian takeaway and gone back out again. Bee took a cucumber from the fridge, sliced it, and lay down in her bedroom with the cool discs on her eyes. A Victorian lady swooning in the darkness.

She went over to James's place before work with all her new records. He took her up to the attic room of equipment and showed her his latest acquisitions. Another programme for drums and percussion, new sequencer, new CD burner and something else he carried over from the corner.

What's that?

What do you think?

Well it looks like a guitar.

Cos it *is* a guitar.

I didn't know you played.

I don't. He put it down in front of her. Go on.

She unclipped the case and opened it. A Fender, second-hand, plectrums and spare strings in the pocket. She took out the instrument and cradled it in her lap, ran her hand down the neck. The soft polished wood and weight against her body brought back the days of instrumental music. She began to tune it.

It's beautiful.

Is it a good one?

No idea but it feels good. I played bass you know. And I haven't played in *years*.

They're not that different. He took a cloth off a box in a corner, revealing an amplifier, and brought a lead over to plug into the guitar. Come on, play me something.

She tried a minor scale. Amazing, her fingers remembered. The strings like blades in her fingertips softened by years of dials and buttons. She had picked up guitars whenever possible at band practice but it was only the bass whose intervals had stayed with her. Frets closer here, a tighter more delicate fingering. James fiddled with the amplifier and the notes wobbled out across the room. She played the scale again, up both octaves and further this time, all the way up the neck then jumping back down thirds and fifths. Play a chord. She struck an A. Yair, harder, slash it, play another one. Go down one, you know? She struck a G, then A again, tentatively at first then harder and stronger, sliding in and out of them so even mistakes sounded right. She bent closer to the neck to hear the puck of her fingertips beneath the electrified wall of sound coming at her from the other side of the room. Saw out of the corner of her eye James lay a pedal at her feet. She plugged it in fed her head through the strap and stood up. Paced around from the amplifier to the pedal then alone with the guitar, sticking to just three or four chords feeling for rhythm stepping around different voicings and on and off the pedal, finding the sounds they liked and going over and over them till her fingers were stinging so badly she could play no more. He passed her a joint.

I'll do you a deal. You play some guitar for me, I've got a vague idea of what I want, it doesn't have to be perfect, in fact the more warped the better.

But you can get any guitar sound out of your computer, and better.

Yeh but it's not quite the same. I want something just that little bit more raw, I'm just looking for another sound. I'll show you how this stuff works. You can come and use it whenever you want. When are you leaving?

A month, six weeks. Slip unplugged the guitar and plucked a string, whining a finger all the way up the neck. You wouldn't believe it but I got offered a residency at the new Pawn. I like it down there, it's got a good vibe.

So you'll be up here to play anyway.

As long as they want me I'll keep coming. Hey I've got a new double CD of sound effects here. It's got all these different footsteps. High heels on paving, armies marching, tramping through mud. It's insane, you have to hear it.

At *Fast*, Slip first up. Cool towards James at first though his eagerness to please had been evident from the minute he had rung her weeks before. Surprise us, was the brief. There are no rules. Apart from Mr Hyde there was no audience either at the beginning. Nobody in the house but her and Mr Hyde making last-minute changes to props, opening the door and checking the street to see if the guests were approaching. Dancing alone to her music in the speed striped room a ball in a flashing pinball machine, Slip pushing buttons flicking him around.

Hard to say exactly what had changed here. The warehouse she left had been fraught and cold, now it opened up to her again. It was late morning, gentle and dim, a time so often given to sleep back then. It was her first year living here and she was freshly awake, moving through the space vacated by others, enjoying the solitude. By the time traffic left the warehouse two hours later the sun lay in orange blocks all along the floor.

Bee took traffic into her old bedroom. The partitions had been raised and painted magenta, the entire room kitted out as a dungeon.

It looks fantastic! traffic went over to the shelves to examine the implements. You must've been working your arse off.

Yes but for me, for my *soul*. I make more money now because nobody's getting a cut so I don't have to do as many sessions as at Distopia. I think of you sometimes when I'm here with clients.

Really?

Yep, traffic's naughty ghost whispering in my ear.

What are these? traffic picked up a perspex cube attached to a fine steel cable with a small crocodile clip on its end.

Card holders.

Yow, they're vicious.

They're good to hang off balls. I woke up today with that image of those pegs flying in my mind. It looked so good. I'd like to see you do it with

Needles. Exactly. Not near the elbows obviously. These are cute. She fixed a couple of miniature clothes pegs to her wrist. What's the ghost saying?

Oh you know her, More more!

traffic held out her arm. Bee took more of the miniature pegs from their box and began to attach them up traffic's arm. Further up where the forearm muscle swelled Bee moved to regular clothes pegs, placing them as close together as possible. Last of all on the deltoid she attached two bulldog clips. traffic gritted her teeth. Then Bee lifted traffic's T-shirt and attached a card holder behind the barbells on each nipple. Oooh mistress you're *hurting* me, seriously! Do you promise to be good from now on? Um . . . No. Ow! But thank you for the punishment. Bee released the card holders, released the bulldog clips and with a sweep of her hand removed the pegs making traffic bellow. She rubbed her arm. I think you need to be punished too. I think I do. Select your instrument. Bee bit her smile and brought over a cane, sanded back and lacquered to perfection, then bent over and wiggled her arse. traffic delivered twelve strokes the final six building to vicious then hugged Bee from behind. I'm really sorry for all the shit that went down.

At the long wooden table Bee gave her an envelope containing prints of her shows and parties. traffic overwhelmed held it in her lap like a cat for comfort while Bee gave her the brief for Cabaret Crisis. The venue where Playschool was held, a Thursday night, performances to run from 7 till 10. Then everybody had to be out, the makeshift dressing rooms in the back toilets to disappear entirely and make way for the club crowd. Bee had persuaded the manager it would be worthwhile, only one bar person needed for three hours and extra revenue when the club would normally not even be open. traffic had two months to think up a show.

So many epiphanies. From the puppet show to the backhanders of the evil clown, sweat draining makeup into the collar of her shirt. Gust of applause, needles through skin, dancers swirling beneath the tin skeletons, the beautiful briefly empty room of Pimp before the arrival of partygoers. Slip feeding that manic laughter through the mix while she juggled, right up close to her anticipating her moves from the other side of the room. She had all that pink satin and the striped fabric from Turkish Jim, she had all that time.

Friday night, upstairs in the new Royal cocktail bar. Holmes was three months into a drug regime similar to one Jimi had been on for two years before him. I got my own pill tray now, he announced. I feel like a real grownup. Jimi had started another combination when his viral load rose and so far had no problems. He stood over Fred and Holmes at the corner table, swivelling to the music as he talked. This one's gonna work for me, I know it. I don't have that toxic feeling anymore. Holmes's worst pill was Videx. One every morning as soon as he woke, no food for half an hour afterwards then clenching, butterflies, bolt to the toilet. Fred's latest side effects were cramps in his arm and kidney stones, the pills made him hyperactive, his lips peeled constantly. He said he felt like a chemical factory. It was his third regime and he didn't want to change again, he had almost died seven years ago and was too afraid to stop altogether.

I've got one more possibility. They're only available on trial. And not for six months. So I'm sticking to what I'm on for the time being.

D'you know anyone else who's been on the same ones?

Yes, Fred smirked.

Well how are they handling them?

Actually, they're dead.

Holmes and Jimi cracked up.

A man in black jeans and T-shirt was behind Jimi, tapping him on the shoulder. No dancing. Pardon? You can't dance up here. I'm not dancing, I'm just . . . *gyrating*. Who are you anyway? I'm the manager. I don't mean to hassle you, but we'll lose our licence. Well I used to work here and people danced all the time. Yeh but the police are cracking down and we don't have an entertainment licence. You're kidding, you used to. No we didn't, we just used to get away with it.

Holmes was the first to leave, stopping to buy the weekend papers. A hot night and people were out on the streets, ten cops with sniffer dogs stationed at every point around Taylor Square. A tall boy and girl stopped to talk to him, young, alternative looking. Hey, is there anything on tonight? Um, I don't know. Just, like, a groovy bar or something. We just want to hang out. Holmes was stumped, he pointed to the Royal, watching the cops all the while. Bit pooncey said the boy. We can't afford the drinks. Isn't there like a leather bar or something? Well yair, but they won't let women in. God, what's happened to Sydney? There used to be so many freaks on the streets. The three of them stood and watched the passing parade. Holmes was embarrassed, three years ago he would have taken them for a drink somewhere. Now all he wanted was to go home to bed. In the time it took him to chat to the poof and dyke from Melbourne a dozen people were stopped. Seven of them were searched. Three were taken away.

NO dancing.
NO smoking.
NO drugs.
NO open-toed shoes.
NO nudity.
NO bodily fluids.
NO penetration.

Drinking.
Gambling.

It was better like this, she was able to think. Better to have time than to have money. While her hands laid out the pattern from Turkish Jim and cut and pinned, her mind had no other distractions. There was no one to serve, no customer to entertain, no stock to watch. There was nothing to empty or wipe or refill, nobody to sell to. All the world passed unfettered through her mind as she worked.

She fed the fabric beneath the foot of the sewing machine. All those hours she used to spend working in the midst of everybody else's recreation, working so often altered by substances to keep up with the mood of the room, working to pay for more than she needed. She would need a job when the sickness benefits ran out. There was Josh's eighth birthday at the end of the year, she imagined missing it again as she had every other. Or going empty-handed, she didn't want to do that. Better to give him something else, something incorporeal, something of herself by herself. Those were the best presents anyway, the unexpected, the personal and homemade. Like *Fast* or Slip's latest tape or the copy of Litany playing while she unpicked mistakes. She strained as she repinned to hear the words of the prayers buried inside the music, thought about Slip, her hands and mouth. The cool journey of tongue tasting salt. Checked the fitting in the mirror. Jim was right, the pattern was simple, it was coming together.

She thought about Bee asking her to perform, all her little victories all her little failures. She thought about Roger saying gay was now main-stream and Fred saying women were pretty much equal. She thought about all those glib cosmological predictions, that one day soon there would be no wars, no racism no sexism no homophobia. That the apocalypse would come with massive earthquakes and tidal waves, that there would be a nuclear holocaust, no coastline as we know it, no forests rivers, no Antarctica. That one day soon there would be no religion, that there would be a spiritual renaissance. That soon there would be no books, that everybody would own a PC.

But people were like that. Egos. Measured everything against their own lifetime. Forgot about the insects and the stars, the shifting sands beneath their feet, forgot the intransigence of doctrine. Forgot most of all the significance of the ephemeral gesture, repeated, reinvented. Everlasting.

Sydney. Hectic. Unplanned, unpredictable. The long, hot, late summer days. Twisted streets densely parked, overhung with paperbarks. Sudden birdsong, sudden rainfall, sudden views across vacant lots and down sudden hills. You never knew what was around the corner.

With traffic's help she packed all the fragile music equipment into Esmerelda and left an hour before the removalists. Stayed in second gear through the city, pausing at the lights where heat pushed through the windows like stuffing. Past the park towards the airport, into third then into fourth, music streaming from the stereo on a four lane potholed highway shimmering in the sun.

She observed the cats. The dark one appeared at the sound of her in the garden, rolling onto his back beckoning affection. Following her inside for more, pushing his face against her cupped hand. The light one tolerated a scratch behind the ears then stalked away to preen himself on the highest point of the verandah. He was a hunter. Doves skinks shoelaces mice leaves his own tail. At night he stayed outside the longest escaped whenever possible or curled alone at the foot of the bed. He ate little. The dark one demanded and announced the completion of his meals ostentatiously, insinuating himself beneath the covers to sleep against her belly. The light one who was born with a lung infection could be heard purring only with your ear pressed to his neck. The dark one was stertorous at the touch of a human. Holmes had put his purr on the answer machine saying it was like a Ducati. When the silent light one was suddenly on her lap stretching his paws to her collarbone placing his head under her chin, she let the kettle boil over to accommodate him longer. The cats bit and licked one another with equanimity.

Now after years away and a different human it was the light one who ate first while the dark one crouched beneath the table reticent. So Slip took him to another corner of the room and placed him before food with endearments and caresses. He ranged around the house in the early hours nosing every crevice for exit. It was disturbing.

They were never named, names were labels. They were just the cats. They were animals, they changed.

For the first week Bee was stunned. She functioned like an efficient machine, scanning the real estate section in the papers and every agent within walking distance, making phone calls. Cabaret Crisis was postponed. Arrangements were made with Stash and Bella to seek a large terrace house together, two bedrooms, another room as a workspace, a fourth as a dungeon. Everybody was invited over to help themselves to all the items that weren't worth moving.

In the second week Bee became inconsolable, Holmes too cursing that by barely three weeks he had missed the opportunity to move back into Bondi. There were tears in the morning, tears at night. Nothing would ever replace the warehouse. They were losing not just a limb but a heart and soul as well. The third week brought anger against the developers. But they were powerless, disposessed. It was a death.

In the fourth week with time off from work they began to mourn properly, extending their walks to potential accommodation, saying goodbye to all their old haunts. Sydney was a lost world from the past, an unattainable jewel, seductive, ellusive, full of people who had somewhere to live. During the last days a yellow-black pall moved over the sky as bushfires began all around the city. They woke with the burn of smoke in their throats, soot drifting through the rooms into their packing. Drove to the beach in the evening and cooled off in water sealed with ash, cigarette tip of sun burning a dirty sky. The world was ending.

Did they see the city from Mount Steele in Moore Park as night fell? Most would be heading home in their cars eyes on the road while misty black crept up the mass of trees, hardening into the city silhouette beneath a chemical sky. Or the lone cabbage tree palm towering over Surry Hills from a backyard off Crown Street, its thin line and topknot sneaking into so many vistas of the suburb. The grimy end of Newtown tucked inside the fork of King and Enmore like a dirty secret, the shabby buildings they found with relief even in the renovated sections of Oxford Street, the lanes of Surry Hills cluttered with vegetation and rubbish. Lurid shops forgotten windows small warehouses shonky terraces bad modern buildings and the occasional good one all crammed up against one another in no particular order. The cars like crustaceans down every street, every alley.

Then there were all the uninhabited buildings, beautiful in their neglect, enticing as ballgowns worn for an evening then discarded. The Hub in Newtown, the huge Foster Street warehouse, Griffiths Teas, the Graphic Arts Club, the old dancehall at the beginning of King Street for years a junk shop and empty ever since, warehouses along Botany Road and more in Alexandria and more in Ultimo. Locked up by money bureaucracy and politics. Nowhere to live, nowhere to party. Please open up. Give us accommodation. Let us party, let us in.

Lulu's paid more than the Tunnel of Love but the stakes were that much higher. She had to create more shows more often, more outfits and more wigs. She had to remove all her piercings apart from her navel one, she had to make a choice between getting a new tattoo or losing her job.

The girls at Lulu's were more classy. Two including Bliss were trained acrobats, three trained dancers, three had tit jobs, none had habits apart from Chloe on a low dose of methadone. Her also the youngest at twenty-three, nearly all of them fantastic to watch. traffic in the first weeks felt insecure. All her earnings went straight back into props, costumes and make-up. Bliss was still her foremost teacher, Bliss gave her lessons on the pole twice a week before the club opened. Gave her a show at a small party called Cake Cave five weeks away after Genie pulled out. Bliss had perfected a series of routines built around a fifties bombshell complete with vintage costumes and music. But Natasha was the revelation. Tall, dark and graceful as a panther, clear perspex shoes that seemed to be her own feet, effortless backbends and splits and long auburn hair that spun around her. Natasha on special occasions did a hula hoop routine that brought the house down.

So traffic dug into her truest essence, greatest attributes and resources. Heat, libido, a compact and flexible grace, exotic makeup and costumes from her own hands and the advice of Turkish Jim, and the endless well of music from her lover. She called herself Ava, she slowed everything down, her moves, expressions and her music. Stillness, energy, stillness and energy.

She could dream while up here slowly stripping. When her body began to move of its own accord no longer needing instruction, her mind rose clear and roamed through possibilities as it did on a dancefloor. Of all the other things there were to learn, trapeze, stilts, hula hoops, five ball juggling tricks and all the outfits in which to frame herself a constantly changing picture.

She practised juggling with squash balls, devising a show where they would emerge from her mouth cunt and arse at the end of her strip

362

then be juggled offstage. An extension of the pingpong ball routine, a fine and unique hat trick. But penetration was against the law and Lulu's abided by the law. She put the idea away for later.

Another message from Roger that night. Hey, I know this sounds like a wank but can you wear a dress? Maybe a hat? Not a hat hat just something to cover your hair? Just that Dad's going to be here and you know what he's like . . . And like I said, you really don't have to do this if you don't want to. We can get a professional.

She knew her brother didn't trust her.

In the afternoon Slip walked around the headlands and back up the beach to the hotel. All along the soot-stained shoreline muttonbird corpses thrown up by the warming seas bereft of krill. Beach closed again, the sky lowering over white-peaked waves till joined they would push the sun over the escarpment. The blues began to fall around her like pages torn from a book as she crossed the oval inside her shadow then stopped in the cool of pines to put her sandals back on. Galahs pecking the grass behind her. She lost the music then turned a corner and found it, lost it then was walking straight into it down the main street.

The blues! Walking in rhythm, those twelve bars wrapping around her again like an old scarf buried at the back of a cupboard through irrelevant seasons. She had learnt then lost them to stories whose ends were beginnings and whose centres were everywhere, the resolution broken on every second phrase. Still that clear trajectory lay beneath so that even before when the sequence blocked by buildings had come to her in no particular order she was walking along the anchor points ready for the wandering solo to fall on her once more.

The band moved into the next tune sweating, sun sheering from the paving to their shining faces and instruments. Slip walked through the beer garden to the bottle shop and at the counter realised she had no idea what traffic drank. She stood at the fridges while the salesmen chatted behind her. We want to open up something a bit trendy down here y'know. Tap that niche market?

Back in stress city, woken by jackhammers. Quick breakfast then over to Chippendale to buy make-up, then to Lulu's for a show. A takeaway eaten while watching the other girls then another show then home and straight to her work table.

She was more drawn to the ancient religions whose spirits and beings contained contradiction. The rainbow serpent, Horus, Set, Pan or Lilith before the Zoroastrian way of thought divided the world into good and evil and cast them down with the latter. Quetzalcóatl inspired the headdress which was made to last beyond the show for Cake Cave, the long green feathers sewn then glued into place, the chin strap made from scraps of strong silk. A simple white mask from the magic shop was painted with the features of the evil clown and two metres of translucent synthetic which fell beautifully was cut and sewn into four simple pieces. The entire costume and show workshopped with a boom box beneath a floodlight on the oval near Slip's house, one hot night down the coast when there was nobody else around. The needle-bound cloths needed some work, the headdress perhaps a wider band. She was almost there. They gathered up props and costumes and Slip took traffic's hand as they walked home. What a vision. I wish I had a camera.

She could hear it from down here sometimes, she imagined she could hear the city beckoning. Waking alone early Friday to the sound of birds and cicadas. 3 am, hot night, full moon emerging from clouds to trick the animals. Slip lay there disoriented in the white liquid air loud with birds and insects, imagining the beat and flicker of the city till the clouds moved over again revealing silence and darkness.

She went back up to Sydney the next day, straight over to the house by Moore Park, upstairs to the attic of Mr Hyde and into music. He played the track they had been working on. It began with footsteps, hollow, sonorous, like steady breathing, then the footsteps moved outside into heavy tramping. Put the foghorn on a loop, they had a bass line. On into dark pumping beats with dub guitar wafting through, then the washes of chords ripple of bass and they were out on the floor, it was music, they were dancing. Then the instrumentation fell away and it was nothing but a beat and murmuring, voices like wind rising and falling in rthythm, one new sample towards the end, James watching her. Recognise that? Hang on, I think so . . . He rewound. It's from that interview. I didn't realise you recorded it. I record everything. Slip gave him her cassette. You have to remember my mixer's pretty primitive. So they listened to another version of the same track.

Sparse, moody, smoking around them. Colourless wasn't the word, with the old-fashioned artistry of a black and white photographer she had stripped it all back to a desolate beauty. It was all light and shade, a trail along wide horizons and burning skies then sudden tunnels, bass line like a python weaving beneath the canopy of percussion. Music so spacious you could stretch right out inside it and still not reach the furthest extremities.

James's beard was now fully grown back, he looked older. He ran his tongue down the lip of paper, inserted a filter.
Have you heard of droplifting?
No.
You take your CDs into a music store and put them into a rack without anyone seeing. Then the customers come along and if you're lucky they buy it. It's called droplifting.

What about barcodes and stuff?

Shop computers are always fucking up. They'd find out eventually but initially they'd just write it down.

So your stuff gets out there even if you don't make any money.

Which isn't such a departure from the norm for us anyway.

Maybe we'll get a contract and get our stuff out even further.

Maybe we will.

I need your voice now for traffic's soundtrack. And the Professor if he's around.

What is it again? What do we have to say?

Oh you know. Have you paid the phone bill it's on automatic debit well speak to the bank can you pick up the kids. Stuff like that.

Story of my life.

Basically. Minus the kids.

We're the kids.

traffic let her in. Kissed her on the mouth holding her body away. Slip ran her fingers down the fine ridges beneath traffic's shirt. What's this? It's my first birthday present to you. She stood passive, arms by her side inviting inspection. Slip unbuttoned her shirt. Twenty-four needles in two vertical lines from breast to pubis, each with a scroll of paper inserted in the hollow of the plastic ends. traffic lay on the bed while Slip gloved up then one by one from the top extracted needles from skin then scrolls from needles. She unravelled each prayer and laid it on the table in order, speaking it to a giggling, heavy-lidded traffic. When all the needles were extracted she washed traffic down with calendula.

traffic fed her, bathed her, then laid a blanket on the floor and Slip in child's pose gave her back to traffic. With fingertips traffic traced the f holes, put on gloves, swabbed Slip down. Pinching skin, watching the rise and fall of Slip's lungs, the rise again. Fang of needle through flesh, hot steel, snakebite. Sting after sting of metallic heat. An easy run then another landmine of nerve endings, Slip's feet drumming the

367

floor. traffic placed her hands over the completed f holes, her cheek against Slip's. The neck piercings with a larger gauge made her groan, she was rushing by then, sweat trickling from armpits. The last four were difficult, two either side of the divet of cocyx where the skin full of collagen kept escaping traffic's fingertips and the needles went in deeper, Slip squealing. Subsiding at last exhausted as traffic looped four strings from neck to arse and came around to her head and held it. Sorry, they're a bit crooked. That's alright. It's folk art. Eventually Slip rose and traffic stood her with her back to the mirror, holding another before her. So Slip saw she was an instrument, a cello, a double bass, and leant into traffic who pressed against her, face in her neck arms reaching around to pluck the strings.

Later she turned her around again. Much later when the ice was wearing off and light was seeping into the sky she turned her onto her back, gave her the amyl, one hand inside the other on her belly feeling the movement of her hand through flesh. Slowly then she took out her hand and after she had inhaled began to turn her fingers inside her arse, burrowed and turned and opened and burrowed. By the time she was past her second sphincter she could hardly speak, eyes rolling back breathing long and slow, looking at her through slits, whispering. Then she went completely still, shuddered, and in one sudden move-ment pushed her body onto her hand.

O Lord, of Thy heavenly bounties deprive me not.

O Lord, deliver me from eternal torment.

O Lord, forgive me if I have sinned in my mind or my thought, whether in word or deed.

O Lord, free me from all ignorance and heedlessness, from pettiness of the soul and stony insensibility.

O Lord, deliver me from every temptation.

O Lord, enlighten my heart which evil desires have darkened.

O Lord, as a man I have sinned, have Thou mercy on me, as the God full of compassion, seeing the feebleness of my soul.

O Lord, send down Thy grace to help me, that I may glorify Thy holy name.

O Lord Jesus Christ, write me down in the book of life, and grant unto me a blessed end.

O Lord My God, even if I have done nothing good before Thee, help me, in Thy grace, to make a good beginning.

O Lord, sprinkle into my heart the dew of Thy grace.

O Lord of heaven and earth, remember me, Thy sinful servant, cold of heart and impure, in Thy kingdom. Amen.

O Lord, receive me in my penitence.

O Lord, forsake me not.

O Lord, lead me not into misfortune.

O Lord, quicken in me good thought.

O Lord, give me tears of repentance and remembrance of death, and contrition.

O Lord, make me solicitous of confessing my sins.

O Lord, give me humility, charity and obedience.

O Lord, give me tolerance, magnanimity and gentleness.

O Lord, implant in me the root of all good – Thy fear in my heart.

O Lord, vouchsafe that I may love Thee from all my soul and mind and in everything do Thy will.

O Lord, shelter me from evil persons, from demons and passions, and from any other unbecoming thing.

O Lord, Thou knowest that Thou doest as Thou willest, let then Thy will be done in me, sinner, for blessed art Thou unto the ages. Amen.

traffic waited for the red and yellow blotches to dry on her wide white tie, then dialled Jimi's number and wrote as she spoke Tomato Sauce with an arrow pointing to the yellow, Mustard with an arrow pointing to the red.

What about eleven? I'm on at two. That'll give us a couple of hours.

Have you got the roo?

Yeh and I found a couple of sheep too.

Is there room for them up there? You think your head's big enough?

Well maybe just one then.

What's the green like?

Lucerne darling. It's perfect for this show and Cake Cave as well.

I've decided to use superglue, you don't want your fences falling down.

No of course not.

She poured rice into the third fake remote control and rang Slip's number, stitching the vinyl together with the phone in the crook of her neck.

I'm only using three balls cos I can't throw that high in there. It's more about the overall effect

of chaos

than tricks. Yeh that's right chaos.

Hang on a sec, I thought you were doing this show outside. And isn't it supposed to be . . . *serene?*

No, that's at Bliss's party. The children's clown performs indoors. What time are you coming in?

As soon as I get up. But I get up earlier here so I'll see you when you're getting up. Listen I can make phone calls with one hand and operate the stereo and TV and all that with the other. God I hope I don't get the real remotes mixed up with the fake ones.

You can't. *I've* got the fake ones. Why don't you come in earlier? I've got about forty needles to prep.

So I *do* throw them to you? This is turning into quite an operation.

No I mean into town. You can't get them mixed up if you only have the real remotes and I've got the fake ones somewhere on the counter. At Cake Cave I'm only using clubs. I painted them, you should see them.

I'm confused now.
I'm nervous. Why don't you come in tonight?
That might be better eh. It might sort out my confusion.
I could check all your body parts are working.
I could get rid of some of your nervous energy.

He had come downstairs for a break to watch Aphex Twin videos with a joint on the couch by the window. Tired and hungry after a four hour session ears still hot from the headphones, he waited smoking for the Professor to bring home pizza. Holmes was coming over later then they would go to Cake Cave. James wanted them all to join forces and put on a party called Shameless. A knock at the door, he must have left without his key. James went over and opened it to find two uniformed police officers standing there. The male one spoke first.

Hey mate, you reckon you can close the window next time you have a smoke?

Sorry. He scrambled behind him to find an ashtray, shutting the door inadvertently. They pounded on it. James began to shake, he opened the door again. Sorry about that. The female cop had her pad out.

Name?

Pardon?

Name and date of birth please. How do you spell that? Can I see some ID please? What nationality are you? Is this your residence? Are you an Australian citizen? She took down his details then looked at him blankly. We'd like to come in.

Why?

We'd like to have a look around. How much do you have?

Just a little bag.

OK, can we come in please?

Do you have a search warrant?

The female cop looked bored. Chubby baby face, narrow eyes. She exchanged a glance with her colleague, looked back at James.

How much do you have?

Look I can show you if you like, just the rest of a twenty dollar bag. Can you wait here?

He left the door and went upstairs. He had just done a shop for both himself and Fred, he had two ounces stashed at the back of a crate of records. He was trembling. His uncle had been shot in Chile. Ears stretching all the way back downstairs what was to stop them walking in. He was being irrational, this wasn't a police state, he couldn't stop trembling. His mother wailing, phone to her ear. The drip of his blood in a Brisbane lockup. He got a little drug bag and transferred some heads from the ounce bag into it, sealed it, took it back down the stairs. He would most likely lose his job if he got charged. He was shaking as he handed it over, Fred's excuse came out of his mouth.

Look I've got AIDS. It helps my appetite. I'll shut the window in future.

The male cop looked embarrassed, the female took the bag, wrote something on her pad.

We're going to have to take you down to the station.

They must have been on foot patrol. They rang base and waited in James's doorway while he fetched his wallet. Holmes and the Professor rounding the corner with dinner to see four police officers and a paddy wagon outside the house, James being ushered inside.

They needed two hours to get ready, the first to do traffic's make-up, mark the piercing sites and lay out the needles, the second for the piercing itself and the fixing of the headdress and mask. Ben was back performing for the first time since Scum with a new boyfriend Paul, and Slip and traffic paused in their preparations to watch the show. Paul was taken on stage by another master and tied to a pole, his entire face and body powdered white. Whistles from the crowd when Ben, a Tom of Finland in chaps and cap, strode on stage hand on his cock. Paul strained at the ropes, strained his muscles watching Ben with imploring eyes, dark pools in his pallid face. Ben coming closer running his hands over Paul's body stepping back beginning to wank. Soon white fluid began to issue forth, a coil of judgement tightening in some pockets of the audience, most of them bellowing with glee, Ben spraying Paul from every direction with luminous milk, Paul ecstatic twisting and turning in the shower, Ben turning to give the front row a quick spray turning back and shooting more all down Paul's body until he was empty and came to untie Paul and carry him offstage.

Slip and traffic ducked back into the dressing room, a two metre square windowless office. Her makeup completed, traffic undressed. The needles tied one to the other with fine string were laid out on trays and Slip gloved up. Ben and Paul rushed in laughing. Great show guys! Did you like it? Ben began to undo the tube that ran beneath his cock and balls through a cock ring up inside his arse, squatting slightly then to remove the empty condom from his colon as Slip swabbed traffic's shoulders and arms and began to insert the needles, point downwards in alternating sites along the ridge of her arms. Everybody treading on everybody's toes. Woops, sorry. Ouch! Was that a hurty one? No I'm so nervous I can't feel the needles but something's poking in my arse. Sorry, that was me. Christ that milk stinks, is there a shower here? As if. How much did you have up there? About half a litre. You pig! Is it the excitement Ben or is it viagra? Aaww you know all my show tricks. Ben began to swivel and bark, cock slapping his hipbones. Bliss's head appeared in the doorway. Settle petal, the orgy's *later*. Don't make her laugh I'm putting them in crooked! Did you know the manager's taking a cut of the door? Twenty percent? That's a bit rich. *And* we paid a hire fee. Bliss looked furious, blew a kiss to traffic. Sorry, timing, break a leg luv. Both arms pierced from shoulder to forearm, Slip took the first piece of fabric and placed each loop around the green strung plastic needletips so the fabric hung down traffic's back like a cloak. Wow, look at you, can't wait to see your show. The second fabric that covered her to the waist was looped over the red strung needles, the tags of each string brought forward to hang either side of her throat. OK baby, the green's the back fabric, the red's the front. Mmm. Slip bent down and began to swab traffic's lower back for the strip of fabric that was half her skirt. Beginning to drift? Yair, but I'm buzzing. Good. Alright chicky babes, we're going out there. Ben turned at the door. I don't think I've ever seen you perform, what are you doing? You'll see.

She was still as a plinth till the crowd around her grew subdued, those in front sitting on the ground. Her body coated in translucent shimmering red, the green hair and feather headress hinging her face powdered red with gold lips and eyelids and the mask of the evil clown on the back of her head. The clubs painted in geometric green and red designs slowly rose from the folds of the fabric which draped like wings from her outstretched arms over the narrow split skirt. She waited then released the clubs into the air took her first small step and at that moment struck a chord. She calmly walked the length of each moment that stretched to infinity. There was the pain behind her smile, her body so still and the whirl of clubs at the end of her arms. A triple throw and in the extra split second a hand reached for the green string and pulled out the zipper of needles holding the back fabric. The clubs back down to regular singles as the fabric floated to the ground, her turning so gradually you hardly noticed. Crunch of needles beneath her soles and Bee with her camera on the edge of her vision shuffling for the best angle. Another triple throw and the red string was released, trickle of warm blood now moving down her breasts and she paused the clubs momentarily, flexing them at the ends of her arms like Balinese nails. She had completed a one hundred and eighty degree turn and now faced the other side of the audience, the chord still playing. She was there, inside herself, among people, hidden. An animal, a sculpture, a principle axis. The clubs went up again and blood began to flow from her arms, with the third triple throw she released the string of needles that ran across her lower back so all that she wore was a long piece of sheer fabric hanging from her waist. She slowly completed the revolution, releasing the final string, naked juggling and bleeding.

A full twelve minutes had been needed to face at one point every member of the audience in the round so for some she was beatific in the beginning, shimmering, golden, and for others a malevolent force. For some she ended serene and triumphant while the last thing others saw was bad and negative. She caught the clubs one by one, let her arms fall to her sides and slowly turned her head to a profile.

She woke still crestfallen at the absence of the boys the night before. Slip went out for coffee and croissants then climbed back into bed with a tray. Don't stress, you're exhausted, you're doing two shows in one weekend after a full week's work. traffic forcing herself to eat. Slip began to cut up a peach. I had a funny dream last night. Oh yair? The war was on, I mean it came here. Sounds hilarious. It was chemical warfare and after the bomb had been dropped the only survivors were the military and the fetishists. What do you mean? I don't know, all these soldiers were coming up from the bunkers followed by the fetishists in their heels and gas masks . . .

They went over to Jimi's and traffic got a decorated flat-top, Jimi insisting he come to the party as well. You can't go to a gig without your stylist darling. Then into a cab to Woollahra, sneaking into the house and up to Roger and Katherine's bedroom to finish her make-up.

Jimi and Slip went downstairs to stash the props and prepare for the show, Jimi waylaid by a child when he was sidling out of the living room. Did that hurt? the child pointed to Jimi's facial piercings. A little bit. The child stared then smiled and walked away pinching his eyebrows and septum thoughtfully. Slip in the kitchen was negotiating with Katherine over the appliances. Are you using the oven or the microwave? Not right now, why? Can I set the timers on them? Oh . . . well sure, can I ask why? Just for the show. What are you guys cooking *up*? You're making me nervous! Jimi passed a young English woman on the stairs, probably one of the children's nannies. Oh wow, you've got both eyebrows done and your nose. Did it hurt? A little bit. One of my girlfriends had her navel done but she let it grow over and I heard about a bloke who got his ear done up here and it became totally infected, it blew up so big you couldn't even see the earring! Jimi continued back up the stairs. Roger approached Slip on her way out of the ktichen. Hey um, she's not going to do anything too full-on is she. No of course not, it's just fun. Cos they're just kids and you know . . . It's okay Roger, she's just doing a clown show.

The clown was invisible. First an upside-down green boot and striped sock, then two hands. Then a paddock of hair just above the kitchen counter, moving up and down. She stood suddenly, kangaroo wobbling on the crown of her head, the evil clown of *Fast* transposed into a children's with a wide red mouth. Sshh! I'm not supposed to be here! She flicked some switches in the kitchen then tiptoed out from the counter in her bright pink plus-fours, satin striped shirt and stained tie. The nanny was in the laundry and the clown had crept down from her room where she was supposed to be doing her homework. She tiptoed past the grinning children and into the living room, high exaggerated steps like a bird. Snooped in every corner of the room, found one ball beneath a cushion, another hidden in the pot plant, the third emerging from her pockets like a bird once the others were up and spinning. She entertained them for a while with the balls, their eyes crawling over her taking in every detail. An audience of children so immediate and sensitive she knew from the look on a girl's face that one of her braces had come adrift. Caught their frank disappointment when a ball was dropped and blew it up into a comic tragedy. Juggling right in front of them now, smile stretching to her ears, flecks of her audience visible. Three faeries, one wizard, one cowboy and two soldiers in camo gear, Joshua wide-eyed in his jaguar suit, one swagman a girl the loudest laugher. The red smirking faces of her father and brother and Katherine, Slip and Jimi quiet in the background, some of the children still inspecting Slip and Jimi. One by one the balls slipped back into her pockets and she picked up a fake remote control from the counter. The clown wasn't supposed to be watching television. The television came on. Two remotes in the air and the channels changed then 101 Dalmations on video barged onto the screen. The stereo came on with the third remote, zoomed up and down the tuner before settling onto a CD. From then on it was mayhem. Playstation came on the television, the oven alarm went off followed by the ping of the microwave then the telephone rang right next to traffic's father's ear. Are you in bed yet? said the Professor's warped voice. Clean your teeth. Can you pick up the kids? I'm busy, Holmes's voice now, I'm busy I'm busy. The clown valiantly juggling three remotes, a set of keys, a ball, all the children shrieking and wriggling. Roger's mobile rang followed by Katherine's followed by traffic's father's. Look darling I have to work late, did you pay the cleaning lady? All three scrambled to take the bogus calls as the clown in a spare split second placed a fake mobile phone against her ear with a look of horror while the voices continued. You'll be late for school have you done your homework? Your father's *tired* clean up your room clean up your room. Leaning back over the counter, overwhelmed by voices, then lying back on the counter defeated in the rain of remote controls.

Slip went over to the stereo, took out the soundtrack and slid in its place a CD of light trippy dance music. Then to traffic by the bathroom door. That was a nice touch with the keys. I hadn't planned that, they were just there, they fucken hurt though look at this. Oh my poor baby. The jaguar ran over to traffic as she collected her things. Thank you traffic. Happy birthday Josh. He stood watching her. You dropped one. I know, wasn't that sad. But you were really funny. He hugged her hips then began to jump up and down. You look really funny. Her father came down the hall. Well! he took her by the hands. I don't think they know what hit them! The swagman interrupted, corks bobbing along the rim of his old akubra. Are you a boy or girl? traffic bent down and whispered in the swagman's ear. Both. The wizard arrived with his father, held a big piece of paper aloft. Can I have your autograph? traffic's father shaking his head and laughing in the background. The kangaroo! The hair!

Slip went out to collect the props, stooping to one of the remotes in the doorway when the children came squealing over her like a flock of lorikeets. One of the faeries stayed out in the garden looking miserable then bent over the roses and vomited. Her mother brought her inside rolling her eyes at Slip on the way past. Too much cake. The first soldier's father passed Jimi in the kitchen and grimaced. God, you're brave, did that hurt? Jimi shook his head in horror. It absolutely killed, there was blood everywhere. God, I don't know why you do it. The swagman was adding another rip to his shirt, touching up his makeup with earth from the pot plant when the jaguar came growling over. He said he was both Joshua. He isn't. He is! But she's a she! She's my aunt! Joshua held his hands in front of his chest. I've seen these! Looking around then seeing Slip, biting his lip.

Now the children were in the living room, some dancing some

379

running all of them shouting. The cowboy and the first soldier began to fight, the second soldier struggling in the embrace of a faerie. Roger watched the pandemonium. Oh dear, the sugar's kicking in. The mother of the sick faerie approached traffic. How would I go about booking the clown? Katherine pulled the fighting soldier's father over. This is Dave. Her father to one side watching traffic quizzically, the mother taking her faerie off to the bathroom, Katherine rushing away to break up the cowboy and the sailor. Dave rocked back and forth back and forth on the balls of his feet, hands behind his back. So you're Roger's sister. And what do you do?

The big bang.

The ultimate hero of low frequency

the divine intergalactical bass-drum

connecting the tribes of our solar systems.

If we could communicate from our tiny piece of solar driftwood to another galaxy, what would we say?

We can send out pictures, symbols, chemical formulas, or language.

The magic of music is a sign of consciousness that could be understood on far-flung worlds millions of light years from our horizon.

Music is an interstellar language from a highly insignificant planet, one of nine in our system, which sails through time and space, till the next one.

The next

Inevitable

Big

Bang.

keep going . . . . . . keep creating. Have fun, keep going . . . keep creating. Have fun, keep going .
creating. Have fun, keep going . . . . . . keep creating. Have fun, keep going . . . keep creating. Ha
keep going . . . keep creating. Have fun, keep going . . . . . . keep creating. Have fun, keep going .
creating. Have fun, keep going . . . keep creating. Have fun, keep going . . . . . . keep creating. Ha
keep going . . . keep creating. Have fun, keep going . . . keep creating. Have fun, keep going . . .
creating. Have fun, keep going . . . keep creating. Have fun, keep going . . . keep creating. Have f
going . . . . . . keep creating. Have fun, keep going . . . keep creating. Have fun, keep going . . . ke
ng. Have fun, keep going . . . . . . keep creating. Have fun, keep going . . . keep creating. Have fu
going . . . keep creating. Have fun, keep going . . . . . . keep creating. Have fun, keep going . . . ke
ng. Have fun, keep going . . . keep creating. Have fun, keep going . . . . . . keep creating. Have fu
going . . . keep creating. Have fun, keep going . . . keep creating. Have fun, keep going . . . . . . ke
ng. Have fun, keep going . . . keep creating. Have fun, keep going . . . keep creating. Have fun, k
ng . . . keep creating. Have fun, keep going . . . keep creating. Have fun, keep going . . . . . . keep
ng. Have fun, keep going . . . keep creating. Have fun, keep going . . . keep creating. Have fun, k
ng . . . . . . keep creating. Have fun, keep going . . . keep creating. Have fun, keep going . . . keep
ng. Have fun, keep going . . . . . . keep creating. Have fun, keep going . . . keep creating. Have f
going . . . keep creating. Have fun, keep going . . . . . . keep creating. Have fun, keep going . . . k
ng. Have fun, keep going . . . keep creating. Have fun, keep going . . . . . . keep creating. Have f
going . . . keep creating. Have fun, keep going . . . keep creating. Have fun, keep going . . . . . . ke
ng. Have fun, keep going . . . keep creating. Have fun, keep going . . . keep creating. Have fun, k
ng . . . keep creating. Have fun, keep going . . . keep creating. Have fun, keep going . . . . . . keep
ng. Have fun, keep going . . . keep creating. Have fun, keep going . . . keep creating. Have fun, k
ng . . . . . . keep creating. Have fun, keep going . . . keep creating. Have fun, keep going . . . keep
ng. Have fun, keep going . . . . . . keep creating. Have fun, keep going . . . keep creating. Have f
going . . . keep creating. Have fun, keep going . . . . . . keep creating. Have fun, keep going . . . k
ng. Have fun, keep going . . . keep creating. Have fun, keep going . . . . . . keep creating. Have f
going . . . keep creating. Have fun, keep going . . . keep creating. Have fun, keep going . . . . . . k
ng. Have fun, keep going . . . keep creating. Have fun, keep going . . . keep creating. Have fun, k
ng . . . . . . keep creating. Have fun, keep going . . . keep creating. Have fun, keep going . . . keep
ng. Have fun, keep going . . . . . . keep creating. Have fun, keep going . . . keep creating. Have f
going . . . keep creating. Have fun, keep going . . . . . . keep creating. Have fun, keep going . . . k
ng. Have fun, keep going . . . keep creating. Have fun, keep going . . . . . . keep creating. Have f
going . . . keep creating. Have fun, keep going . . . keep creating. Have fun, keep going . . . . . . k
ng. Have fun, keep going . . . keep creating. Have fun, keep going . . . keep creating. Have fun, k
ng . . . keep creating. Have fun, keep going . . . keep creating. Have fun, keep going . . . . . . keep
ng. Have fun, keep going . . . keep creating. Have fun, keep going . . . keep creating. Have fun, k
ng . . . keep creating. Have fun, keep going . . . keep creating. Have fun, keep going . . . . . . keep
ng. Have fun, keep going . . . keep creating. Have fun, keep going . . . keep creating. Have fun, k
. . . keep creating. Have fun, keep going . . . keep creating. Have fun, keep going . . . keep creat
un, keep going . . . keep creating. Have fun, keep going . . . . . . keep creating. Have fun, keep go
p creating. Have fun, keep going   keep creating. Have fun, keep going   keep creating. Ha

Have fun, keep going ...... keep creating. Have fun, keep going ... keep creating. Have fun, keep going ... keep creating. Have fun, keep going ...... keep creating. Have fun, keep going ... keep creating. Have fun, keep going ... keep creating. Have fun, keep going ...... keep creating. Have fun, keep going ... keep creating. Have fun, keep going ... keep creating. Have fun, keep going ... keep creating. Have fun, keep going ... keep creating. Have fun, keep going ...... keep creating. Have fun, keep going ... keep creating. Have fun, keep going ... keep creating. Have fun, keep going ...... keep creating. Have fun, keep going ... keep creating. Have fun, keep going ... keep creating. Have fun, keep going ... keep creating. Have fun, keep going ... keep creating. Have fun, keep going ...... keep creating. Have fun, keep going ... keep creating. Have fun, keep going ... keep creating. Have fun, keep going ...... keep creating. Have fun, keep going ... keep creating. Have fun, keep going ... keep creating. Have fun, keep going ... keep creating. Have fun, keep going ... keep creating. Have fun, keep going ...... keep creating. Have fun, keep going ... keep creating. Have fun, keep going ...... keep creating. Have fun, keep going ... keep creating. Have fun, keep going ... keep creating. Have fun, keep going ... keep creating. Have fun, keep going ...... keep creating. Have fun, keep going ... keep creating. Have fun, keep going ... keep creating. Have fun, keep going ...... keep creating. Have fun, keep going ... keep creating. Have fun, keep going ... keep creating. Have fun, keep going ... keep creating. Have fun, keep going ... keep creating. Have fun, keep going ...... keep creating. Have fun, keep going ... keep creating. Have fun, keep going ...... keep creating. Have fun, keep going ... keep creating. Have fun, keep going ... keep creating. Have fun, keep going ... keep creating. Have fun, keep going ...... keep creating. Have fun, keep going ... keep creating. Have fun, keep going ... keep creating. Have fun, keep going ... keep creating. Have fun, keep going ... keep creating. Have fun, keep going ...... keep creating. Have fun, keep going ... keep creating. Have fun, keep going ... keep creating. Have fun, keep going ...... keep creating. Have fun, keep going ... keep creating. Have fun, keep going ...... keep creating. Have fun, keep going ... keep creating. Have fun, keep going ... keep creating. Have fun, keep going ... keep creating. Have fun, keep going ... keep creating. Have fun, keep going ...... keep creating. Have fun, keep going ... keep creating. Have fun, keep going ... keep creating. Have fun, keep going ...... keep creating. Have fun, keep going ... keep creating. Have fun, keep going ... keep creating. Have fun, keep going ... keep creating. Have fun, keep going ... keep creating. Have fun, keep going ...... keep creating. Have fun, keep going ... keep creating.

With love and thanks:

AñA Wojak, Bill Morley, John Doe, Julie Callaghan, Kate Oliver, Lance Cunynghame, Lanny K (to whom I am also indebted for the title), Miss Yetti, Oberon, Peter Schouten, Raven, Rhys Cumpstone, Robert Lake, Steven Lee, 2 Hard, Waded, etc. etc. etc.

Acknowledgements

p. 1 Lyrics from the work *Turkish Bazar* performed by Emmanuel Top, published by Emmanuel Top Editions: ©Emmanuel Top Editions

p. 23 Lyrics from the work *The Healer* performed by Hardsequencer. Original source unknown.

p. 29 Lyrics from the work *Mean Machine* performed by the Last Poets, written by Alafia Pudim and Nilija and published by Douglas Music Corp. have been reproduced courtesy of Festival Music Publishing Australia.

p. 43 Lyrics from the work *The Rings of Saturn* performed by Underground Resistance. Original Source unknown.

p. 59 Lyrics from the work Flash performed by Green Velvet, written by Curtis Alan Jones and published by Cajual Music have been reproduced with the kind permission of Cajual Music.

p. 96 UNKIND CUTS. Fantale Wrapper – trivia.

p. 168 Lyrics from the work *Who Wants to be a Millionaire*, written by Cole Porter (1953), parodied by Fiona McGregor.

p. 275 Lyrics from the work *The Next Phase* by D.A.V.E. the drummer and Lawrie Immersion performing as Kextex: ©Truelove Music. Printed with the kind permission of www.truelovemusic.com.

p. 285 Lyrics from the work *Old Rugged Cross* written by Rahsaan Roland Kirk and published by Rokir Music Corporation have been reproduced with kind permission: ©Rokir Music Corp.

p. 373 Prayers of St John Chrysostom (b. 347 d. 407) for every hour of the day and night.

p. 385 Lyrics from the work *Solar Driftwood* performed by Yello, written by Boris Blank and Dieter Meier have been reproduced with the kind permission of the authors and licensed courtesy of Warner Chappell Australia Pty Limited.

Born and bred in Sydney, Fiona McGregor has
lived there most of her life. This is her third book.